PRAISE FO

“A lit

—*The Daily Telegraph*

“Absolutely brilliant.”

—*The Daily Mail*

“Atticus Priest will be the star of many future novels.”

—*Richard Madeley*

“Nerve-shreddingly tense. Utterly addictive.”

— *MJ Arlidge*

“Dawson writes the kind of thrillers I love. Non-stop, grab-you-by-the-throat tales of doing the right thing no matter the odds. Simply excellent.”

—*Brett Battles*

“A terrific, fast-paced read. Mark Dawson knows how to tell a great story.”

—*Scott Mariani*

“Mark Dawson has all the skills. A great thriller writer on the top of his game.”

—*Steve Cavanagh*

MORE THAN 18,000
FIVE STAR AMAZON REVIEWS

"Fast paced and a wonderful read."

"Brilliantly written - Dawson's best yet."

"Totally hooked now."

"Unbelievable!"

"Made me fall in love with reading again."

"Cannot get enough of these books."

"Wow - what a read."

"Brilliant, brilliant, brilliant!"

ALL THE DEVILS ARE HERE

MARK DAWSON

ALL THE DEVILS ARE HERE

First published in 2024 by Unputdownable Limited

A CIP catalogue of record for this book is available from the British Library.

Paperback ISBN: 978-1-0687754-0-6

Typeset by Riverside Publishing Solutions Ltd (UK)

Printed and bound by CPI Group (UK), Ltd., Croydon, CR0 4YY.

ALSO BY MARK DAWSON

In The Atticus Priest Series

The House in the Woods
A Place to Bury Strangers
The Red Room

In The John Milton Series

The Cleaner
Saint Death
The Driver
Ghosts
The Sword of God
Salvation Row
Headhunters
The Ninth Step
The Jungle
Blackout
The Alamo
Redeemer
Sleepers
Twelve Days
Bright Lights
The Man Who Never Was
Killa City
Ronin

Never Let Me Down Again
Bulletproof
Uppercut
Bloodlands

In The Beatrix Rose Series

In Cold Blood
Blood Moon Rising
Blood and Roses
The Dragon and the Ghost
Tempest
Phoenix

In The Isabella Rose Series

The Angel
The Asset
The Agent
The Assassin
The Avenger
Pretty Face

In The Charlie Cooper Series

Sandstorm
The Chameleon
Blood Brothers

To Lucy

"Hell is empty and all the devils are here."

— *The Tempest*, Act 1, Scene 2

PROLOGUE

The Haunch of Venison proclaimed itself as the oldest pub in Salisbury, and, as Samantha Hargreaves looked around, she wouldn't have been at all surprised if that were true. The building was hundreds of years old and said to have been frequented by the masons who worked on the spire of the cathedral. It had heavy oak beams taken from old galleons, and the litany of reported ghost sightings did no harm in luring credulous tourists through the door; they were said to include a prostitute's madam who hated men, another woman in a white shawl endlessly searching for her murdered son, and a man in a brown shirt and braces who had watched the landlords and landladies as they slept in bed.

Sam turned to the others. The five of them were in the taproom at the back of the building, where there was only just enough space for four tables. They were packed tightly around the table nearest to the fire. Sam had first visited the Haunch on a night out when she had told her parents she was going to go to Connor's house after school. Both Sam and Connor had been just sixteen, but, with impressive whiskers for a teenager and with a fake driving licence he'd bought from a classified ad in *Viz*, Connor had persuaded the barman to sell them two half-pints of Summer Lightning. Christopher had been here, too, all of them at this same table, and Sam remembered him pointing out the old bread oven next to the fire and regaling her with the story of the mummified hand found inside it.

"Remember that?" she said now, pointing to the oven.

Connor looked over and grinned. "The hand?"

"The *what*?" Gaz said.

"You don't know about the hand?"

"*What* hand?"

"There used to be a hand in the oven."

"Bollocks," Nikki said.

"It's true," Connor said. "You know how it got there?"

Nikki shrugged.

"There was a game of whist, and one of the men was caught cheating. The man who caught him was a butcher, and he had his cleaver with him."

"Come *on*." Gaz laughed. "He had his cleaver with him? Just by chance?"

"Chopped it off," Sam went on, "and the cards the man was hiding fell out of his sleeve."

Gaz made a show of sniffing the air. "What's that?"

"I don't know, Gaz," Sam said. "What is it?"

"Smells like bullshit."

Sam gave a shrug and leaned back, unable to stop herself from joining in when the others started to laugh.

Gaz got up and went to the oven, leaning in and looking through the iron grate in the door. "Shit," he said. "There *is* a hand."

Nikki had been looking at her phone, and now she held it up. "It's not real," she said, jabbing a finger at the oven and then at the screen. "The real hand was stolen. That's a fake."

Gaz finished the dregs of his pint. "Only in bloody Salisbury. Who nicks a severed *hand*?"

Nikki gestured at the empty pint glasses on the table. "Another round?"

They all said yes, and Nikki went down to the bar to place the order. Sam was a little pissed and enjoying the buzz of the alcohol and the company of her friends. The five of them hadn't been out as a group for two months, and it was good to get back into the swing of things.

They'd been friends for years—all the way back to when they'd been kids at St. Osmund's together—and although Sam and Christopher had diverted to London for their ultimately unsuccessful attempt to break into the music industry, she'd always boarded the train at Waterloo knowing that not much would have changed when she got back home.

Tom had gone into the Army, but Nikki, Gaz and Connor had stayed, still going out together on Friday and Saturday nights. Things were different as they got older—Nikki and Gaz got married, Connor shacked up with Tracey Paulson and had a kid before their divorce—but they'd made sure to go out as often as they could to get pissed and catch up. Sam's inglorious retreat from London had been barely remarked upon, save the ribbing that she couldn't cut it in the big smoke, and the pub nights continued as if the interregnum had never happened.

That Sam's coming home to the city—with the benefit of her London contacts and the opportunities they'd bestowed upon her—had allowed her to build a business that had made them all rich had been a bonus.

Nikki came back up the stairs with five pints balanced on a tray. She made her way to the table and carefully lowered the tray so they could help themselves to the pints.

"The stairs aren't level," Nikki muttered as she sat down. "Almost tripped and spilled the lot."

"'The stairs aren't level,'" Connor said with a knowing grin. "You don't think it might be that you're already pissed?"

"I've only had two pints," Nikki protested.

"I believe you," Connor said. "Millions wouldn't."

Sam took her pint and sank half of it. She looked around the table at her friends: Nikki was wearing a garish new top she'd bought for a fortune from a place in Southampton, ignoring Sam's regular injunction that they didn't want to be too flashy with their cash for fear of attracting attention; Gaz was looking at something on his phone; Connor was eyeing the two girls who'd taken seats at the table to their left; Tom took his pint and, as Sam watched with concern, drained it in one long draught.

"I always think of Christopher when I come here," Gaz said.

Connor nodded. "Same."

"Do you remember that time when you dared him to jump off the bridge into the river?"

"That was Sam," Connor said. "And he thought he'd broken his leg?"

"It'll be two years soon," Gaz said.

"Hard to believe," Connor said.

"We should do something."

Nikki looked over at Gaz and gave a little shake of her head. Gaz noticed it and looked uncomfortable, he was oblivious most of the time, but even he realised he'd put his foot in it.

Connor was too drunk to realise, so Sam reached over and put her hand over his wrist and gave it a squeeze. "We all miss him," she said. "What happened—well, there's no need to go into it now. Better to remember him as he was before."

An uncomfortable silence descended over the table before Tom gestured to his empty glass. "I'm going to get a vodka."

"Sure?" Sam said. "I thought these were the last."

"Changed my mind."

"You're not messing around tonight."

He shrugged, banging the empty glass back down onto the table. "Is that a problem?"

"Course not."

"So? Why'd you say it?"

Tom had been off with Sam all evening, and his attitude had worsened with every drink he finished.

"Are you okay?" she asked him.

"Never better." Tom smiled, but it was bitter and held no humour. He stood. "I'm going for a piss."

His outburst had silenced the table, and the four of them watched as he went out into the corridor and turned left for the toilets.

Nikki turned to Gaz. "*Why'd* you have to bring him up?"

Gaz exhaled. "Sorry. Stupid."

"Better not to talk about it," Sam said.

"I know that, Sam. I just..."

"Didn't think," Sam finished for him.

Nikki bit her lip nervously. "He hasn't said anything, has he?"

"Not to me," Sam said.

Gaz shook his head. "Nor me."

"Or me," Connor said. "At least not tonight."

"What does that mean?" Sam said. "He *has* spoken to you?"

"Now and again. You know how he is about what happened."

"I know he's had wobbles," Sam said.

"'Wobbles'? Come on, Sam. It's worse than that. He's messed up."

"It was more than a *year* ago," she said, "and nothing's happened. *Nothing.* The police have given up. What's he got to worry about?"

"It's never been about something happening," Connor said, lowering his voice to a whisper. "It's *guilt*. He has nightmares."

"He's told you that?"

Connor nodded.

Sam reached up and massaged her temple. She knew Tom had found it difficult to deal with what had happened with Christopher, but she kept coming back to the same thing: it was more than a year ago, and nothing negative had ever come of it. The police had never come calling after the first routine interviews, Christopher's family—as frightening as they were—had no idea what had happened, and the five of them had been bonded together even more closely by it.

She'd made sure of it.

At least that was what she thought.

But she was still convinced: Christopher had got greedy and deserved what had happened. It'd been the right thing to do, and it had led to all the success that had followed.

Why couldn't Tom just accept that?

* * *

Things went downhill after that. Tom came back with five vodkas and continued to drink, his mood darkening. Sam suggested they go and get a kebab from Mani's, but Tom said he didn't want a kebab, so they settled for a burger from Chick-o-Land.

They took their take-aways to the Market Square and found a bench where they could sit down and eat. Sam sat down next to Tom and wondered if she should say something. The two of them had been close before she and Christopher had gone to London, and, out of the others, he was the one she held in the highest regard. He'd been bright and sparky before he joined the Army, sharper and more incisive than Gaz and Nikki, funnier than Christopher and less needy than Connor. Sam didn't consider any of them to be her equal, but she had the most time for him.

His Army career had changed him. He never spoke about what he'd seen in Iraq and Afghanistan, but he came back home with the humour and sense of fun smelted out of him. It had been Sam who had persuaded him to go and get help, but she didn't think it had done much; she certainly hadn't seen any improvement, and, if anything, things had deteriorated.

The night at the yard had made it ten times worse.

Sam took a bite from her burger and watched as a lad ambled across the square toward them. It was late—nearly midnight—and he was obviously drunk, stopping to put a hand down against a bin in an attempt to stay upright.

"Jesus," Nikki muttered. "Look at the state of him."

"He's just a kid," Sam said. "It's not like we weren't like that twenty years ago."

The lad bent double and threw up, vomit splattering onto the cobbles.

"I was never like *that*," Nikki said.

The young man wiped his mouth with the back of his sleeve and continued in their direction.

Tom stood up, a little unsteady on his feet. "Hey."

The man stopped and blinked. "What?"

"What you looking at?"

"Nothing. I—"

Tom took a step toward him. "You were staring at *me*."

"Just looking for a taxi." The man turned to Sam and the others. "Just looking for… a taxi."

Sam half-rose and put a hand on Tom's arm. "It's fine." She turned to the man. "You can get one from the rank opposite Pret. That way."

The man frowned and took a step to the side, but before setting off, he shook his head and gestured at Tom. "Dick."

Tom lunged at him, but Gaz was in the way and grabbed him before he could get close enough to launch a punch. Tom tried to shake him off, but Gaz held on tight as Nikki told the young lad to shut his mouth and piss off before he got himself beaten up. Tom struggled harder, he was bigger and stronger than Gaz, but he was raging drunk, and Gaz was able to drag him back as the man took Nikki's advice and staggered off.

Tom tried to break out of Gaz's grip again, but Gaz managed to get his arms around his torso and clasped his hands tight.

"Get off me," Tom grunted.

"Settle down."

Tom forced both arms up, and Gaz lost his grip. Tom turned and squared up to him. "Don't tell me what to do."

"Come on, Tom," Sam said. "Relax. There's no need for that."

"There you go again. 'Calm down, Tom.' 'Relax, Tom.' 'Take it easy, Tom.'"

"That's right. You need to—"

"Easy for you to say," he snarled at her. "You don't have what happened banging around in your head all the time, do you? Not like me. I mean, *Jesus*. Why'd you all bring that up again?"

Gaz winced. "Sorry, mate. I forgot—"

"Did you think it'd be a laugh? Is that it? A joke at my expense? Make me think of him?"

"Of course not."

"Yeah, you did," he said, nodding his agreement at his own suggestion. "That's *exactly* what it is. You all got together and thought it'd be hilarious to bring it up."

Sam drew nearer, close enough to smell the booze that was coming off him in waves. "Why would we do that?" she said, keeping her voice calm. "We all knew him, and none of us wanted it to happen like it did, but it was *his* fault—not yours. He was stealing from us. And he would've killed me. You stopped him."

Tom wasn't listening. "'Poor old pissed-up Tom. Let's bring him out, make him relive it all, have a laugh when he falls to pieces, point at him and joke when he makes a tit of himself, just like he always does.'"

"It's not like that," she said. "Gaz made a mistake, and he's sorry."

"I am," Gaz said. "It was stupid of me."

Tom swayed a little from side to side. They were all drunk, yet Tom—who could usually drink the most—was the worst of all of them. Sam wondered whether he'd been drinking before they came out. He'd always had a problem with booze—even back when they'd first started going to pubs as kids—and the Army had made it worse. He'd told them before that he'd gone so far as to go to AA meetings in an attempt to get it under control. But that—like everything else he'd tried—had had no effect.

"You want to know something?" he said. "Something you lot can have a chuckle about when you go out without me?"

"We don't go out without—"

"Yes, you do," he slurred. "Gaz told me. Last month. You went to the Chapel."

Gaz spread his arms. "Come on—it was just the once. You were in a bad spot. I didn't think you'd want to come."

"Whatever—I don't care." He reached down to use the back of the bench to support himself. "I've been seeing someone. I told her what you're like. I told her how you treat me. You want to know what she says? She says you take advantage of me. She says you ignore the way I feel because you know—deep down—that you should be feeling the same way, too. She says I'd be better off without you."

Sam's blood ran cold. "What did you say?"

"You heard."

"The way you feel? About what?"

"About what? What else is there? About *him*."

"What did you tell her?"

Tom started to talk, then stopped. It was as if what he'd just said had taken that long to permeate his drunkenness, and now that it had, he regretted it.

"Tom—*what did you tell her?*"

"Nothing."

"What have you *said*?"

"This and that." He wobbled again. "I suppose you'd rather I didn't say anything at all."

"Of course I'd prefer that," Sam snapped. "Jesus. Do you know how *stupid* this is?"

"Don't care," he said, his regret mutating into a flare of drunken anger. "Maybe that's what needs to happen. Maybe I'd be better to go to the police and tell *them* what I did. What *we* did. I've thought about it—I've thought about it a lot. I don't know how all of you can live with the guilt, but I can't."

Sam lowered her voice. "Stop talking like that. He was stealing from us. And he had his hands around my neck when you got there—don't you remember? He was going to rape me. You didn't have a choice."

Tom laughed: sudden, raucous, out of control. "You should listen to yourself. None of it would've happened if we hadn't done what you persuaded us to do." He turned to the others. "Remember what she said? 'No risk. Nothing bad will happen.'"

"Jesus, Tom. Shut *up*."

He snorted with laughter. "I'm going to the Chapel."

"No," Sam said. "That's not a good idea."

"Don't care."

He tried to step to the side, but Gaz mirrored him.

"Get out of the way."

Gaz held up his hands. "Calm down. You need to sober up, and then we need to talk."

"Get out of my way."

"He's drunk," Gaz said to the others. "Let's get him back to his place so he can sleep it off."

"I don't *want* to sleep it off. I want another drink. I'm going to the Chapel."

Sam put a hand on Tom's shoulder. "Come on."

"You're smashed," Connor said. "They won't let you in."

Tom shrugged Sam's hand aside and stepped to the left. Gaz blocked him again. Tom raised both hands and shoved Gaz in the chest. It was sudden and unexpected, and Gaz had been off balance, plus Tom was strong; he stumbled backwards, caught his heel against the kerb and fell. Nikki shrieked. Gaz had a temper, and he wasn't always able to keep it in check. He got to his feet, and, before Sam could tell him how stupid it was and how much better it would've been to put an arm around Tom and get him somewhere quiet, he clenched his hand into a fist and punched Tom in the face.

Tom's head cracked back, and blood splashed from his nose onto his lip and down onto his chin. He reached up with a hand and dabbed his fingertips into it; he grinned, showing blood across his teeth from a cut in his lip.

Gaz knew he'd made a mistake. "I'm sorry," he said, raising both hands in an attempt to pacify Tom before things could get any worse.

It didn't do any good.

Tom barged at him, flailing drunkenly. His knuckles grazed Gaz's cheek, and then he flung both arms around him, wrapping him in a clinch. They overbalanced and fell, Tom on top.

Nikki shrieked again.

A voice from somewhere off to the left shouted, "Hey!"

Gaz punched up, finding the point at the bottom of Tom's chin. Tom's eyes rolled into his head, and he went limp enough so that Gaz could push him off.

"*Hey!*" the voice called out again. "Police. That's enough."

But Gaz had lost his temper completely. He scrambled to hands and knees and then got to his feet, close enough to Tom to drive a kick into his ribs.

"Leave him," Nikki snapped as Gaz reached down for him.

Sam turned to see a uniformed officer. The man wrapped his arms around Gaz's shoulders and dragged him away.

"That's *enough*," the officer said.

Gaz tried to struggle free.

The officer tightened his grip. "You're under arrest, mate. You both are."

* * *

Salisbury's custody suite had been lost when the police station moved from the Wilton Road, meaning that Gaz and Tom would be driven all the way to Melksham. Sam got a taxi home and used the twenty-minute trip to think about what had happened, and what she would have to do next.

She felt exposed and vulnerable. She was terrified that Tom would say something he shouldn't. They all knew he'd been struggling with his mental health, but she'd been shocked by just how bad it'd been allowed to get. They were going to have to do something about it, but she knew that—for now at least—it was out of her hands. Tom *had* to keep his mouth shut, or everything was going to come tumbling down. The police would find out what they'd done to Christopher, and then they'd *all* be in the shit.

Maybe Tom would say nothing, and the police would let them out in the morning. What would they do after that? The situation couldn't be allowed to continue. Tom needed help, but before they could look into it, Sam needed to be sure that he wasn't going to say or do anything that'd make things worse than they already were.

He'd had the same amount of money as Nikki and Gaz and Connor, but he'd blown it all: drink, mostly, but he'd given *thousands* to the parasites and grifters who attached themselves to him. The list was endless: Rick from the Huntsman, who'd said he needed money for an operation to cut out a tumour that Sam knew didn't exist; the woman he'd met on Hinge who said she needed a deposit for a flat to get away from her abusive husband; the men and women he met at the pubs around town who knew he was a sucker for a good sob story and put out their hands for alms. Tom had emptied his account for the last woman he'd been seeing; she'd milked him for as much as she thought she could get away with and then ghosted him. It had got nasty a couple of times, and one bloke from the Pheasant and his mate had tried to threaten Tom into making a payout; he'd battered both of them and had been charged and convicted for assault as a result.

Sam had wondered whether it'd be better to hold onto his share of the money until he was better, but he'd said he didn't want it. He'd called it 'blood money', said it was poisoned, and told her to donate it to charity on his behalf. He said he was trying to make amends, but his mental health continued to get worse.

He'd lost his house and moved into temporary accommodation provided by Alabaré, the Christian charity that helped the homeless in the city, but she wondered now whether it'd be better to get him away from there and put him somewhere they could keep an eye on him. But where? Gaz was taking the truck over to Ireland to pick up the next shipment, and Nikki wouldn't want him in their house while she was alone. Sam had space at the yard, but it was too sensitive to bring him there with the delivery of the shipment and Freeman coming to buy it.

That just left Connor. Sam doubted he'd be all that pleased with the idea of babysitting Tom, but needs must, and he'd do what he was told if Sam explained how important it was. Connor liked to be useful and was always looking to Sam for praise. She could play on that if she had to, make him feel useful and valued, make him feel like he was doing something important for the benefit of the others. And make him feel, perhaps, that going along with her plan might bring them a step closer to the relationship he'd been aching for since they were in their teens.

Sam sat back, drew in a breath and then blew it out. She allowed herself a moment of anger—at herself, for not handling tonight better, and at Tom for his weakness—before dismissing it as a luxury she couldn't afford. There had been challenges over the last year as she set up the business, and there'd be others after she'd dealt with this one. And that was fine; she'd chosen a path that offered outsized returns in return for accepting risk. That was the bargain, and Sam—and the others—had accepted it. They trusted her to navigate the difficult moments, and they'd trust her with this, too.

She started to think of a strategy to get them out of the mess, and as the lights of the yard came into view, she had the bones of a plan.

PART 1

1

Lyndhurst was one of the largest towns in the New Forest, its chichi High Street busy with well-heeled shoppers and jammed with expensive cars. It was the only town Atticus Priest could think of that had a Ferrari dealership opposite a café and newsagent and funeral directors. And, perhaps most unusual of all, it was less than a minute away from the wide heathland where the forest ponies carried on with their business, oblivious to the cars that waited to drive around them.

Atticus drove carefully over the cattle grid at the edge of town and dabbed the brakes as a pony ambled slowly across the road in front of him. He glanced in the rear-view mirror and looked at Bandit. The dog was sitting up, staring at the animals.

"Fancy living here?" The dog turned at the sound of Atticus's voice, his tongue lolling out of the side of his mouth. "Well, don't get your hopes up. I can't afford it."

Lime Wood Hotel was five minutes down the road, and Atticus had been summoned there to meet a potential new client. The email from Frank Green had arrived yesterday afternoon, asking whether Atticus was available to take on what Green had described as a "very significant" piece of work. Atticus had clicked on the link beneath the email signature and found that Green owned a successful property development business. The most cursory of social media searches showed him flaunting his wealth: a red Lamborghini, different Rolexes on his wrist, pictures from five-star hotels in Monaco and Singapore and New York.

Atticus wasn't particularly busy, and a man of Green's means would be able to pay top rate. Atticus had been hoping to take Mack away to Paris for the weekend so she could forget about the custody battle with her ex-husband, and he knew it wouldn't be cheap. Her legal bills were eye-wateringly high, too, and Atticus had been helping with them as best he could. Perhaps he could charge Green enough to afford to take Mack away *and* pay off her lawyers.

The pony reached the other side of the road and trotted over to join the half-dozen others that had preceded it. The New Forest was famous for the thousands of ponies that were allowed to roam freely, and Atticus recalled family walks that would conclude with roasts at the pubs that dotted the area. He brought Bandit down here whenever he had the time; Mack had joined them last Sunday, their five-mile walk finishing with lunch at the Trusty Servant while the dog warmed himself in the sun. The next day, Atticus had texted her to suggest they should find a place in the Forest and half-jokingly sent over listings he'd seen on Rightmove. The houses were all on the market for millions and way out of their price bracket, but that wasn't the point; he'd sent the list to gauge her interest in the prospect of them moving in together. She'd replied with a series of emojis—rolling eyes, crying with laughter—that made it impossible for him to get a read; he'd have to bring it up in person if he wanted to judge whether it was something she might consider.

Frank Green was an interesting character, and to say that he had a chequered past would be to underplay it. Atticus had uncovered several threads, and once he'd started to pull on them, others had been revealed. Green had made his fortune with the development of luxury houses. His *modus operandi* was to buy plots of land, get planning permission and then build multi-million-pound houses, selling them on at ridiculous mark-ups. Atticus had found a profile in a national newspaper where it was said that he'd made his first million by the age of twenty-five, his tenth by the age of thirty and then five times that by the time he hit forty. He'd built a reputation as a local philanthropist, sponsoring students through college and engaging in other conspicuous acts of kindness, always reported on by the *Salisbury Journal*. There was a feature with him dressing up as Santa Claus and distributing a hundred turkey meals at Christmas. "I just like to give back," he reported with a teeth-grindingly fake selflessness.

But Green's carefully curated reputation had taken a hit this year, with the service of legal proceedings against him by one of the banks that funded his projects. The bank had hired expensive London litigators to investigate an anonymous tip-off that Green had, for many years, bribed local councillors to secure planning permission for the sites he bought for development. The allegation was that he picked up the sites at a discount after they'd been refused planning, with the certainty that he'd be able to change the decision once the purchase was complete. The practice enabled him to make enormous profits, but was, of course, entirely fraudulent. The allegation had been covered in depth by the *Guardian*, and Green and two councillors had subsequently been arrested and charged under the Bribery Act.

Atticus had replied to the email and asked what Green wanted him to do but had been rebuffed; Green wasn't prepared to discuss it over email, only face to face. Atticus imagined it had to be connected with the criminal case and was intrigued enough to agree to drive forty minutes to the hotel rather than insist that Green meet him in Salisbury.

2

Atticus turned off the road and followed the signs for Lime Wood. The drive was long, winding its way to where the hotel sat on the brow of a hill. It had once been a lodge that served royalty while they hunted in the Forest, but now an array of expensive cars were parked on the drive outside the entrance: a Porsche, a vast Range Rover with blacked-out windows, two Ferraris and a Lamborghini with the vanity plate FEG1.

Atticus brought his car to a stop, climbed out and watched with a wry smile as one of the bellhops approached. The man wore an expression of bemusement; Atticus's battered old Volvo was out of place.

"Good morning, sir. Are you staying with us?"

"No." Atticus went around to the boot and opened it. "I'm here to see one of your guests."

Bandit hopped down and immediately trotted over to the bellhop, who put down a hand for Bandit to sniff. "What's the name of the guest, sir? I'll see if I can find out where you need to go."

"Frank Green. He said he'd be in the scullery."

Atticus was about to ask whether he could bring Bandit inside when a man came out of the front doors, spied him and made his way over.

Atticus recognised him: it was Green.

He was frowning. "Mr. Priest?"

"Mr. Green."

"You're late."

"I don't think so. We said—"

"We said eight thirty, and it's nine. I've been waiting half an hour."

"We said nine."

"No—we said half *eight*."

Atticus was prone to absent-minded mistakes, but he'd checked the email from Green before leaving the office this morning and was sure that they'd agreed upon nine. But he could see that Green was the kind of man who liked an argument, and, given that Atticus suspected this would be easy work for a weighty fee, decided that discretion was the better part of valour.

"I'm very sorry, then. I must have misread your email."

"Never mind. You're here now."

Bandit finished with the bellhop and, keen to introduce himself to the second newcomer, bounded over to Green and leapt up at him. Green tried to fend him off, but too late; Bandit's front paws left muddy prints on his crisp white shirt.

Green stepped back, shooing Bandit away. "Bloody dog!"

"*Bandit*," Atticus said.

The dog trotted back.

Green looked down at his shirt, trying—without success—to brush the paw prints away. He glared at Bandit, then at

Atticus. "You need to keep that bloody animal under control. *Look* what he's done—this was clean on this morning."

"He's a little bit too enthusiastic for his own good sometimes."

"He's a *menace.*" It looked like Green was about to say something else, but perhaps realising that Atticus had put himself out by travelling here to see him, he held his tongue. "I'll get changed and meet you at the bar."

Green turned on his heel and went back inside.

Atticus crouched down and scrubbed Bandit's head. "Naughty dog."

He glanced up and saw that the bellhop was trying not to laugh.

Atticus went back to the car, opened the boot and waited for Bandit to hop inside. He took the dog's bowl and filled it with water from the plastic bottle he kept in the back. "Stay here," Atticus said as the dog settled down. "I won't be long, and then we can go for a walk in the forest."

3

The hotel had been impressively and extensively refurbished. A glass roof had been fitted to span the two wings, creating a covered courtyard with a bar at one end. The scullery was off to the right, where guests were enjoying late breakfasts. Atticus took a seat, and a waiter asked if he was going to be eating; Atticus said he wasn't and ordered a coffee. The man went through to the kitchen and came back with his drink just as Green reappeared, his dirty shirt replaced by a clean one. He spotted Atticus, crossed the courtyard and allowed the waiter to pull out his chair for him.

"I'll have one, too," he said, pointing a finger at Atticus's cup. He didn't seem particularly concerned about being polite, and the waiter—perhaps familiar with his brusqueness and inured to it—said he'd get one right away.

Atticus sipped his coffee, using the opportunity to look over the top of his cup and form an impression of his potential new client. Green had a seasoned, confident look. His hair was neatly styled, brushed back from his forehead, revealing a touch of grey. His eyes were a clear, piercing blue, set beneath brows that arched with a natural condescension. The corners of his mouth turned down ever so slightly in a permanently dismissive sneer.

"Thank you for coming."

"Not at all," Atticus replied. "How can I help you? Would this be something to do with your ex-wife?"

"How could you possibly know that?"

Atticus pointed to Green's left hand. "You recently stopped wearing a ring."

Green held up his hand as if to remind himself of it.

"Your skin is lighter where you would've worn it."

"Showing off?"

"I'd like you to be confident that you'll get your money's worth."

"That's an easy trick. I don't impress easily—you'll have to do better."

"I'll bear that in mind." He forced a smile. "Why don't we get started."

"Assuming I haven't decided you're *not* the right man for the job."

Atticus was about to say that he knew he *hadn't* decided that—there was nothing in his posture to suggest he was about to get up to leave, and he was still holding direct eye contact—but, for fear of being accused of showing off again, he stopped himself just in time. "I hope you haven't."

"Are there any other private investigators in Salisbury?"

"None that I'd recommend."

"So I don't have the luxury of choice, then, do I? Looks like I'm stuck with you." The waiter arrived with Green's coffee; he took it without acknowledgement or thanks. "How do we do this?"

"Tell me what you need, and I'll let you know if it's something I can help with."

"What about money?"

"Last of all."

"Fine. You were right—it *is* about my wife. I have a problem with her, and I need it taken care of."

Atticus reached into his bag for his digital recorder. He held it up. "Do you mind?" Green waved his hand with airy diffidence, and Atticus thumbed the device to record and set it down on the table. "Tell me how I can help."

"Can I count on your discretion?"

"Absolutely."

Green glanced to the side, and Atticus predicted he was about to be given a highly selective version of what had happened in the Green marriage.

"Alice and I are separated. We never had the happiest marriage, but things came to a head last year, and she moved out."

"How long were you married?"

"Fifteen years."

"And what happened?"

"She's a *psychopath*, Mr. Priest. I stuck around for as long as I could, but it got to the point where it was all too much."

"Was there anyone else?"

"Not on my side," Green said, glancing away just long enough for Atticus to read his lie.

Atticus let it pass. "On hers?"

"What do you think? I've started divorce proceedings, and I need evidence. We didn't have a pre-nup when we got married. I'd made a bit of dough by that time, and I felt like it was the right thing to do, but she said it was unromantic, and I stupidly went along with her. Worst decision I ever made, and I've made a few. She's trying to clean me out. She's got this whole sob story about how she needs financial support, but it's bullshit. She's not being honest."

"She has her own money?"

"Lots," he said. "And look—hats off to her. She's built her own business, and she's pulling in six figures, maybe even seven. You'd never guess that from her witness statement. It's sackcloth and ashes and woe is me."

"You want me to find out how much she's making so the judge can make a proper financial assessment."

"Exactly."

Atticus nodded. It wasn't an unusual request for someone in his line of work. It would be dull and intellectually prosaic, but Green was loaded and desperate: an excellent combination.

"I can help with that."

Green ran his finger around the rim of his coffee cup. "There's another thing. Bit delicate. The divorce has been difficult, right from the start, and it's got worse the longer it's gone on. The whole thing has put *darling* Alice's nose out of joint, and now she's punishing me for it. She promised to make my life a misery when she walked out, and she's *really* done that. She spread rumours about me in the village, and I caught her putting sugar in the petrol tank of my Portofino. Ruined it—she got done for criminal damage, but that's not the point. It's been one thing after another, and that's not even the worst of it."

"You're talking about being charged for bribery?"

"You've read the stories in the papers?"

"Not really," Atticus lied.

"You don't do any research before meeting potential new clients?"

"I prefer to let them tell me their stories themselves," he said, deciding to keep the extent of his knowledge to himself. He'd get a better read on Green that way.

Green shifted uncomfortably, and Atticus knew he was about to be given another slanted version of the truth. "You know my business?"

"Property development."

"Been doing it for years. Best houses you'll find around here. Good quality. None of the shortcuts you see with the big builders. We've won awards."

Atticus smiled and encouraged him to continue.

"I was contacted by the *Guardian* in March. They'd been told I'd bribed the planners for permission to build on a plot of land in Pitton I bought last year."

"Is that true?"

"Of *course* it's not. Do you know how stupid that would be?"

"And you told the newspaper that?"

"Like it did any good—they published anyway. My lawyers are involved now. I'll be bringing a claim for libel against them, and it's going to cost them thousands when I'm finished. *Hundreds* of thousands. But that's not what I want."

"You want to know where the story came from."

"I *know* where it came from. It came from her."

"You want proof."

He nodded.

"Why?"

"Why do you think? Because I'll sue her into oblivion."

Assuming the story *wasn't* correct, Atticus thought to himself, given that truth was a bulletproof defence to libel.

"You see what I mean about her?" Green tapped his finger against the side of his head. "She's mental. Got a screw loose, hasn't she?"

Atticus sipped his coffee. Green was as unpleasant as Atticus had feared he would be. But he was also rich, and the opportunity to double his hourly rate was reason enough to hold his nose.

"I think I can help you with all of that," he said.

4

Atticus took out his notebook and a pen and opened to a fresh page. He adjusted the recorder so it was closer to Green, then wrote his name and the date at the top of the page. "You'd better tell me about your wife, then. What's her name? Alice, wasn't it?"

"Yes."

"Alice Green?"

He nodded. "She hasn't changed it yet—at least not as far as I know. It'll be a hassle for her."

"Why?"

"She's in business as an *influencer*," he said, loading the word with sarcasm. "She started teaching people about the benefits of wild swimming. 'Cold-water immersion,' she'd say. It's what you'd call 'wellness.'" He said it with another disdainful sneer. "Want to know what *I'd* call it? A lot of new-age, hippy-dippy bullshit. The name's all over her branding. 'Wild Swimming with Alice Green.' She'd have to change everything—website, her videos, social media, the works."

"How does she make her money?"

"Sponsorship. She built the business up over the last five years, and she did well—making a few thousand a month, anyway—and because it was all online, it scaled easily." He leaned back and shook his head, and, for a moment, Atticus might almost have said he spoke in admiration. "Then she started doing these daily videos where she'd go down to the river or the beach and jump in—she'd spin this yarn about the difference it'd made to her life, how it had solved medical problems she didn't have, how it had fixed mental issues. Blah, blah, blah. There was one video where she said she had a client who'd been cured of cancer, all because he went for a morning swim in water cold enough to freeze his bollocks off. It's all rubbish, of course. Snake oil. But there are a lot of gullible people out there, and she hasn't had any problem building a brand. You'll see when you check her out—her Instagram has a million followers, and she's not far behind on TikTok."

"And companies are sponsoring her to talk about their products?"

He nodded. "She's done videos for vitamin companies, people making cold-water baths." He snorted disdainfully. "She's not fussy—if you offer her enough money, she'll pimp you to her followers, and it doesn't matter if it's a good fit or not." He was into his flow now, animated by his disdain and, Atticus thought, a little jealousy. "She's built a name for herself in online communities where people are looking for cures for their problems. Mental health issues. Physical illnesses. But here's the thing: she doesn't believe *any* of the stuff she's selling. It's all transactional—totally mercenary. She saw that there was an opportunity for someone to make a killing, and she reinvented herself to be the perfect person to do that. It's shameless."

"You almost look impressed," Atticus said.

"I admire *hustle*," he said, "and she has that. But she's a hypocrite. Tells people she has a strict vegan diet, but she doesn't. Total bullshit. Eats steak every week. Sells a detox program for a hundred quid, but she doesn't follow any of her own advice. Smokes and drinks even though she goes on and on about how bad they are for you. She doesn't believe in *any* of the stuff she says—she admitted to me she thought it was nonsense, but that was before we had trouble. Otherwise, I'd've recorded it and exposed her. She thinks the people who follow her are naïve fools. And you know what they say: 'a fool and his money are soon parted.'" He smiled. "Thing is, though, that's all going to come crashing down around her ears soon."

"How's that?"

He winked. "Keep an eye on her social media on Wednesday—you can watch along with everyone else." He grinned and then bit his lip, obviously keen to show off how he was going to exact his revenge and how clever he thought he'd been despite his stagey reluctance. "I can't say *exactly*, but let's just say we managed to get her to do something on camera that'll prove to everyone just what a hypocrite she is."

"I'll bear that in mind."

Green brushed out a crease in his shirt and stood. "So I take it you'll be happy to get started?"

Atticus said that he would. He explained how the retainer would work and that he'd need an amount up front, with the rest to be billed at an hourly rate with extra for disbursements. Green nodded his agreement before reaching into his pocket and taking out a thick wad of banknotes.

"How much do you need now?"

Atticus looked at the wad; he saw the red-and-purple of a fifty on top and guessed there were maybe twenty notes held by a platinum-coloured clip. He thought about the weekend in Paris and the legal bills Mack was struggling to pay. "A thousand."

Green didn't flinch, and Atticus wished he'd asked for more. Green removed the clip, revealing that all of the notes were fifties. He held them out. "Do I get a receipt?"

"Of course. Can I email it to you?"

Green said that'd be fine and recited his email address. Atticus took the money and put it in his pocket. He switched off the recorder, put it and his notebook back in his bag, and stood.

"Get started today," Green said. "She's sitting on her arse, thinking she's got one over on me. I can't be having that. Get me what I need, and I'll see you get a nice payday."

5

Connor Smith indicated left at the Huntsman Tavern and drove along Barnard Street until he saw the large modern building on the right-hand side of the road where Alabaré had some of its accommodation. It was a three-storey building, with enough windows to suggest at least six apartments on each floor. Tom had been given one of the flats two months ago, and, from what Connor had been told, he'd be allowed to stay there while he found somewhere permanent.

Connor pulled into a space adjacent to the building, took out his phone and texted Tom to say that he'd arrived. The windows on the ground-floor level were low, no more than a foot off the ground, and Connor was able to look through the dusty glass of the one closest to his car into the space beyond. The room looked bare, with hardly any furniture and nothing decorative to brighten the magnolia walls. Connor noticed a couple making their way along the pavement toward him and watched as they turned toward the front entrance. The man slouched, his clothing was stained from neglect, and an unkempt beard masked the lines of his jaw. The woman's eyes were dull, and her hands, with chipped nail polish, trembled as she clutched a cigarette.

Connor shivered. Places like this gave him the creeps. As far as he was concerned, addiction wasn't an illness or something that was too powerful to fight; it was just a question of *will*. He'd had plenty of dark times over the years, but he'd always pulled himself up by his bootstraps and sorted himself out. He liked a drink just as much as the next man, and, on those occasions when he'd had a bit too much, so what? You wouldn't find him blubbing to a room full of strangers about whatever it was in his childhood that made him think he was a special snowflake.

Pathetic.

Connor might've been the one out of the four of them who had the least time for Tom's problems, but Sam had asked him to get Tom away for a few days, and he'd said he would. He was probably the one with the closest relationship to Tom, and, like Sam explained, that was going to be important if what they planned to do was going to work. Tom was going to have to trust him. He was going to have to swallow the story they'd concocted and open up with the answers they needed.

Sam had buttered Connor up by making it abundantly clear that the next few days were going to be crucial, and what he was able to find out would have a bearing on *all* of their futures. It didn't really matter: Connor had never been able to say no to her and hadn't ever got over their month as a couple in the summer after they left school. Connor knew it was more than twenty years ago and that nothing had happened since, but he couldn't help thinking that if he kept at it, if he kept doing what she asked and being there when she needed him, then maybe—*maybe*—she'd realise what *he'd* realised years ago: that they were perfect together. Everything that happened in between—her relationship with Christopher and everything else—would be forgotten.

The front door opened, and Tom stepped outside with a rucksack over his shoulder. Connor raised his hand, and then, when Tom still didn't see him, he lowered the window.

"Over here, you dick."

Tom turned, shielded his eyes from the sun, and came over. "All right?"

"Are you ready?"

Tom nodded. "Think so."

"Got your stuff?"

He hefted his pack. "Three days?"

"Probably not even that long."

Tom pointed up at the sky. "What about the weather?"

Connor chuckled. "Not scared of a little rain, are you? Remember when we were kids? You took the piss out of me that time we went camping and the wind blew the tent down."

"What can I say? The older I get, the more I like my creature comforts."

Connor thought about the shitty little flats in the hostel but said nothing. He leaned over and opened the door. "Can't promise luxury, but it'll be a laugh."

"We need to stop for booze."

"Seriously? After the weekend?"

"What?"

"Not still hungover?"

He waved that away. "I'm right as rain. And we're *camping*. If you think I'm not going to drink when we're camping…"

"Sam's picking up supplies for us."

Tom opened the rear door and tossed his pack inside. He got in next to Connor, slammed the door and rested his arm on the sill. "Did you speak to her?"

"She's going to meet us."

"Is she..." The words drifted away.

"She's fine," he said. "Totally fine. Nothing to worry about."

Tom nodded with relief and pointed ahead. "Go on, then. We can pitch the tent and then open a can or two."

6

Mackenzie Jones went into the court building on Wilton Road with a feeling of dread in the pit of her stomach. It wasn't a lack of familiarity that made her nervous; she'd been to the court many times on police business over the years. It was that she was here today in her personal capacity and that the stakes were hugely significant. The court dealt with criminal and civil matters, and she was here for the latter; the case was displayed on the screen as Jones v. Jones, with the addition below that of 'In the Interests of Sebastian Jones and Daisy Jones, Minor Children.'

The custody hearing was due to take place in Court Two. Mack climbed the stairs to the first floor, saw her solicitor and went over to her. Kay Adams worked at Cadogan and Crane, a middling local firm that was about as much as Mack could afford on her salary, even with Atticus helping out. Kay was a bit of a plodder, especially when compared to Andy's high-powered London lawyers, but she was kind and honest, and Mack had come to rely upon her.

"Morning."

"Morning," Kay replied. "How are you?"

"Not great. Didn't sleep much last night."

"Understandable. You know what I'm going to say, though."

"Don't worry."

"Exactly—don't worry. They've completely overreached, and the judge will see that."

She smiled. "I wish I shared your confidence."

"It'll be fine—you'll see."

She followed Kay to the waiting area, and they both sat down on one of the utilitarian sofas. Mack opened her handbag, took out the little compact she kept there and opened the lid. She glanced at her reflection in the mirror: she looked about as tired as she felt, and no amount of make-up was going to disguise that. She'd gone to bed early last night in the anticipation that it might take longer than usual to drop off, but with her mind still racing at midnight, she had resorted to an antihistamine tablet that she washed down with a finger of whisky. The combination was guaranteed to put her under, but the quality of sleep was never as good as when it was natural. She'd woken up at five thirty, feeling worn out and hollow, the fatigue and anxiety written across her face. She'd knocked back two double espressos from Café Nero on the walk to court, but the hit of caffeine hadn't even touched the sides of her fatigue.

The last few months had been difficult. Mack's ex-husband, Andy, had petitioned for divorce, and knowing that their marriage was irretrievably broken, Mack had agreed. The procedure had been unpleasant but had moved along quickly given that they agreed about most things. Andy had stayed in the family home while Mack moved out into rented accommodation. They decided that the children would stay with him for now to maintain as much stability as possible, but Mack had made sure that she either took them to school or collected them at the end of the day, and that she spent each weekend with them.

She'd allowed herself to think they were behaving like mature and responsible adults, parents who put their kids first, and hoped they might be able to come to an agreement to share custody, but her optimism had been in vain. A letter from Andy's lawyers said he wanted sole custody on the basis that Mack was not a fit mother. Mack had read the accompanying petition with a sense of confusion that, as she read deeper into his reasoning, became disgust and then, finally, fear. Andy sought to demonstrate how Mack was more interested in her career than her kids, including an appendix in which he listed the hours she spent at work against the hours she spent with the children, including all the occasions she'd changed plans at the last minute because she'd been called in to deal with something that had happened. Reading the entries was like a punch to the gut; Mack knew that she'd often given the children the shitty end of the stick but didn't know how else she would be able to hold down her job without dedicating the time to it. And it wasn't as if it was *frivolous*; she was a very senior police officer, and, at least most of the time, she was only called out when something serious, with ramifications for the public, needed her attention.

But Andy ignored all of that. He continued by arguing that the children would be placed in an unstable and unsafe situation if she was allowed custody. Mack had already accepted that she'd cheated on Andy with Atticus, giving him that as simple grounds for divorce, but now he used it against her. He painted a picture of Atticus as a degenerate drug user who had been fired from the police. She'd long suspected that Andy had been responsible for the anonymous email alleging Atticus had been using drugs; the tip-off had led to formal proceedings being opened, with Atticus resigning before he could be fired. Andy went on to explain how Atticus lived in a room at the back of his office and how an environment like that was no place for children. He doubled down with a surreptitious photograph taken through the window of the door that opened onto the stairs leading down to the courtyard garden. Atticus's bedroom was in a typical mess, with his clothes strewn over the futon and empty fast-food packaging littering the floor. A saucer, precariously resting on the edge of a chair, held what looked very much like a half-smoked spliff.

The petition was clear: how could the court release children into the custody of a woman who had abandoned her husband in favour of a person who lived like *this*?

It was a series of low blows, one after another, and Mack was terrified that the court would take Andy's side.

Kay wasn't the first lawyer Mack had engaged. The first attempt had seen her spend the better part of a day explaining why Andy's points were all wrong. The partner dealing with the case was a woman of a similar age, and Mack couldn't help feeling that she looked at her with disapproval when Mack admitted that Andy's facts about her absences were correct. The woman had a framed picture of her perfect family on the desk behind her, and Mack suspected she'd made a comparison between their two lives and decided that Mack came up short as a mother. Atticus told her she was imagining things, but Mack didn't believe it, and, even if she had, would it even have mattered? Mack knew that her work-life balance was out of kilter, and all she wanted now was the opportunity to do better.

Kay nudged her. "Here they are."

Mack turned and watched as Andy entered the reception area with his entourage. There were three of them in his team: a barrister, a partner from the London firm and an assistant. Kay had heard of the firm and said they would've been *extremely* expensive. Mack had been surprised that Andy had been able to afford them. He was a computer programmer at a large local business, and she knew he wasn't making enough from that to be able to afford their fees. She'd mentioned it to Atticus, and he'd found out that Andy had set up a new IT business in Winchester and that he'd landed a very lucrative contract with the council. He'd evidently made enough money to afford a top-notch team with the express instructions to take her children away from her.

Mack wasn't quite so fortunate. She made just under sixty thousand a year as a DCI and had spent what was left of her savings on the rent for the house she'd moved into after the marriage had broken down. She'd been concerned she would have to act for herself, but on mentioning it to Atticus, he'd promised to help. Mack was still coming to terms with their relationship and didn't want to be in his debt, but, with typical stubbornness, he'd closed his ears to her protests and deposited ten thousand into her account. She knew him well enough to know that he was potentially a little lax when it came to financial propriety—she'd looked on aghast as he prepared his tax return in January—but there was nothing to suggest that he'd done anything improper to find the money.

She knew his business had been doing well in the aftermath of the two investigations that had received national attention, and that he'd been referring work to an agency in Andover because he was too busy to take everything on himself. She told him she didn't need his help, but it was a half-hearted protest, and he knew her well enough to know she didn't mean it.

Kay looked at her watch. "Are you ready?"

Mack nodded. "As ready as I'll ever be."

"Remember—we keep on an even keel, we don't react, we're reasonable, we don't lose our temper."

She nodded again.

"Because that's going to be important if we want to come out of this with something we can all be happy with."

"I know," Mack said. "I'm ready."

7

Atticus stopped off near Bramshaw on the way back to Salisbury so Bandit could have a proper run. The dog was beside himself with excitement, it was a new environment replete with dozens of new smells to investigate, and he barrelled away through the gorse and bracken at top speed until all Atticus could hear was the jangling of his name tag against the metal clip of his collar.

He took out his phone and checked the time, it was coming up to one, and Mack's hearing ought to be underway. He tapped the screen to bring up his most used numbers and held his finger over her picture, tempted to call, but eventually conquering the temptation. He'd promised to keep his distance until the proceedings had come to an end. Mack had explained how Andy was using him as an excuse for his attempt to gain custody of the children. Atticus had been furious about that: it was cruel and unnecessary, and he'd given serious thought to the idea of subjecting Andy to the sort of scrutiny he wouldn't enjoy. *Everyone* had secrets—Andy wouldn't be any different—and Atticus was very good at finding them. Maybe he'd unearth something embarrassing to even the odds a little.

But Mack had said no, and Atticus decided, for once, to listen. He'd satisfied his need to help by contributing to her legal fees.

Frank Green's money would help with that.

Atticus set off, following the path in the vague direction that Bandit had chosen. He allowed his thoughts to turn back to the meeting. Green was a deeply unpleasant man, and Atticus had no compunction at all about squeezing as much cash out of him as possible. The research he'd carried out before the meeting had suggested that Green would be odious, but, if anything, the reality was worse. He was vulgar and crass, and his venality was obvious, but it had been the underlying spite that Atticus had found most off-putting. Bad blood between feuding spouses was to be expected, but this had been bitterness bordering on hatred. He wouldn't normally have accepted the work, but the money was welcome and would be put to a good cause.

He pursed his lips and whistled, and, twenty seconds later, Bandit emerged from the bushes. He'd somehow managed to get soaking wet. He stood and shook himself dry, spraying droplets of cold water everywhere.

"Thank you."

The dog cocked his head to one side and wagged his tail.

Atticus reached down to scrub him behind the ears. "We need to get home. I've got work to do."

8

Atticus parked the car in the Cathedral Close, opened the boot and put Bandit on his lead. He set off back to the office, the dog tugging him along so as to more quickly get back to the biscuits he'd left in his bowl. Atticus turned onto New Street and stopped as he passed Thai Sarocha. Francine Patterson and Robbie Best were having lunch together at a table toward the back of the room, Mack had suggested the two of them might have hooked up after Francine had been tricked by Thomas Chandler, and it looked—from the way they were holding hands—that there was truth in the rumour. They were too occupied with one another to notice him, and with Bandit whining impatiently for his lunch, Atticus set off again.

He passed through the arch, checking his post as he did, and nodded to the jeweller who worked out of one of the offices at the back of the building. He climbed the back stairs, unlocked the door to the bedroom and let Bandit inside. The dog trotted over to his bowl, lowered his snout and started to eat.

Atticus and Bandit had been living in the second room of the office for months now, and Atticus wondered again whether he ought to suggest to Mack that they look for somewhere together. He was at her rented place two or three nights a week, but there was something about making the suggestion that brought him up short. He was hopelessly out of his depth when it came to understanding his feelings, and even worse when it came to the feelings of others about whom he cared. There was a pleasant ease to what he had with Mack, it was informal and loose and fun, and, although he wanted more, he was worried that if he tried to move things to the next level, he'd end up spooking her, which was what had happened the first time they had been together. The thing that bothered him was the possibility that *she* was waiting for *him* to make the suggestion, and by seemingly accepting the way things were, he was telling her that he *didn't* want more. It was an impossible situation, Mack was the person to whom Atticus would turn to help him navigate these kinds of tricky social issues, and given the context, he couldn't very well do that now. He was alone with a problem he was singularly ill-equipped to consider and petrified he would mess things up.

He went into the office, took a can of Diet Coke from the mini-fridge and popped the top. He'd bought an expensive sit-stand desk to help him fight the aching muscles he suffered from when he sat for too long. Now, he pressed the button to raise it, tapped a finger against the trackpad of his Mac to wake it, and waited for the three screens—the laptop's screen and two external monitors to the left and right—to switch on.

He connected the digital recorder to his MacBook and imported the recording of the meeting, dragging the file into an AI transcription app that would quickly produce a searchable text version. He opened a browser on his computer and navigated to YouTube. He typed in Alice Green's name. Several pages of videos were returned in the search results; the ones he wanted were posted by Real Wild Swimming and featured Alice's face beneath overlaid headlines in a bright red text that popped off the screen. The videos had been sorted in order of popularity, but all of the first page's results had been viewed more than a million times. The one at the top—'A Cold Swim a Day Keeps the Doctor Away'—had been watched more than fourteen million times. Atticus double-clicked, waited for the pre-roll advert to play, then sat back with his notebook and readied himself to take notes.

Alice Green was standing at the edge of a beach. The camera was facing her, with the sea in the background. She was wearing a swimsuit, and, over the top, a dryrobe monogrammed with RWS.

"I'm Alice Green," she said, beaming into the lens. "I'm here at my favourite beach at Studland Bay in Dorset. It's six in the morning—the sun's just come up, over there—and I'm about to go for my daily thirty-minute cold swim to help clear my mind of all the nonsense that comes with living a busy, modern life. I've been swimming like this—here at the beach, in rivers nearer home, in a barrel of water I keep in the garden—ever since the first COVID lockdown, and it wouldn't be an exaggeration to say that it's saved my life."

The video cut to a photograph of Alice when she was much younger: her eyes were rimmed with dark circles, suggesting sleepless nights; her complexion was pallid, lacking vitality; her hair fell in unkempt, straw-like strands; the set of her mouth and the downward tilt of her head suggested weariness, as if she was bearing a weight that was too much for her.

Alice spoke over the image: "This is what I *used* to look like. I was twenty-five in the picture, although you wouldn't be alone in thinking I must've been ten years older. I was leading what I thought was an exciting life in London. I worked in the modelling industry, booking models for photoshoots and going to different parties every night. The thing is, although I *thought* it should all have made me happy, it didn't. It was the opposite—I was depressed."

The video cut to another photograph of Alice. She looked even worse in this one: her dishevelled hair fell around her face and shoulders; her skin was pale and blotchy; one of her eyes was partially closed.

"This was my rock bottom. I used to be addicted to prescription drugs, and I was unable to find anything that could give me the tools I needed to get off them and stay clean. I'd tried everything—stays in rehab, talking therapies, medicine—and nothing worked long term. The whole thing was desperate, and my life looked as if it might as well be over—I decided that I couldn't take it anymore and that it'd be better for my friends and family if I wasn't here. I came to this beach meaning to walk out until the water was over my head and let the current take me away."

The video cut back to the beach. Alice had removed the dryrobe, and, if anything, her smile was even wider.

"Stepping into the water that day did something to me. It was almost *spiritual*—it gave me a jolt to my system that was like being electrocuted, and when I stepped out onto the beach again, things didn't seem as bad as when I went in. I did it the next day, and the day after that, and *everything* changed. It gave me what I needed to meet the challenges I'd been helpless to face, and, eventually, it helped me to stop the drugs, stop the drinking and lead a better, healthier, *happier* life. I've been trying to spread the word ever since. I've helped dozens of others with similar problems to me—people with depression, with addictions, with lack of energy and illness—and they've all been conquered with the regimen that I've developed."

A series of before and after photographs of men and women faded in and out. The people in the first set of photographs all had the same dead-eyed expressions, each suggesting the ailments that Alice had described; the photographs that replaced them showed the same people, but with wide smiles and eyes glittering with life.

"I'll show *you* how to bring the benefits of cold-water therapy into your own life if you subscribe to my mailing list. Click the link below, and I'll send you the first video in my free five-day introductory series to show you the amazing restorative power of cold water."

She smiled one more time for the camera, turned her back, and, after taking two steps away from the beach, dived beneath the water and swam out. She surfaced, turned back to the camera, and, with her arms spread wide, gave a loud whoop of exhilaration.

The video faded out, replaced by the same logo—the intertwined letters RWS—used to brand the channel.

Atticus shook his head. Alice was such a good saleswoman that it felt credible and exciting and was probably almost irresistible for those with the problems she said she could cure. He remembered what Frank had said: according to him, Alice didn't believe a word of what she was selling, but she'd seen how much money she stood to make from it and had inured herself to any pangs of conscience. She was brazen.

Atticus reached for the mouse and closed the video. He scrolled down and clicked the link that Alice had mentioned. He was taken to a webpage that was slickly branded: Real Wild Swimming ran across a strapline at the top of the page, with another video from Alice and then a series of testimonials, both videos and text. He scrolled down until he got to what was being sold. There was the opportunity to sign up for a free course, and below that were the paid offerings. None of them were cheap.

Atticus leaned back in his chair, steepled his fingers and chuckled. Frank and Alice deserved one another. Both fraudsters, both seemingly blind to the consequences of their actions. To find a single psychopath was unusual. To find two—*married* to one another—was bizarre.

He took out his phone and dialled the number for the Wiltshire Police Control Room.

"This is Sergeant Neil Blyford," Atticus said. "Oscar November nine-two-three-four from Bourne Hill in Salisbury. I need a PNC check, please."

"I can do that," the operator said. "Subject name, please."

"Alice Green. Forename: Alpha-Lima-India-Charlie-Echo. Surname: Golf-Romeo-Echo-Echo-November."

"Address?"

Atticus recited the address Frank had provided.

"Reason for the check?"

Detectives always needed a legitimate policing purpose for requesting the information, and Atticus had already prepared his line. "She's a suspect in an ongoing fraud inquiry."

"Hold the line, please."

Atticus listened as the man tapped out the details on his keyboard.

"Okay," he said. "Your subject has a record. One conviction for assault, five years ago, threatening a Mr. Frank Green with a knife. She got six months suspended for that. Investigated for battery several times—all against Mr. Green—plus criminal damage for..." He paused, perhaps scrolling the page. "For cutting up his clothes and putting sugar in the tank of a Ferrari Portofino."

"Anything else?"

"Historic convictions for fraud: identity theft, credit card fraud and obtaining a mortgage by deceit."

"When were those convictions?"

"Last one was fifteen years ago."

"Any time served?"

"Six months for the mortgage fraud."

"Current status?"

"No restrictions. Doesn't look like she's come across the radar since she was nicked for the assault."

Atticus finished his note and drew a line under it.

Alice came *exactly* as advertised.

"Anything else, Sergeant?"

Atticus thought for a moment, then nodded. "Yes—run a second check, please. Frank Green. Foxtrot-Romeo-Alpha-November-Kilo. Same surname and address as before."

Atticus heard the operator tapping out the details on his keyboard. "Okay—Frank Edward Green also has a record for assault."

"Details?"

"He got into a fight with the aforementioned Mrs. Green—lovely couple you've got there."

"What happened?"

"Drove the Ferrari over her foot."

"Anything else?"

"A couple of traffic violations—eighty in a seventy, forty-five in a thirty—plus a conviction for fraud. Suspended sentence for that."

"Anything current?"

"Yes," the operator said. "He's a person of interest in a bribery investigation being run by Salisbury Police. Suspected of paying backhanders to the local planning office."

Atticus thanked the operator and ended the call.

9

Mack pushed through the doors and took a lungful of air. The hearing had lasted for two hours and had been one of the most difficult things she had ever had to do. The judge, though, had been reasonable; after hearing testimony from both sides, and then the closing arguments from the lawyers, she'd said that she would retire to prepare her judgment.

Mack had been dreading her cross-examination, and it had been as awkward as she'd feared. The questioning had focused on her relationship with Atticus; she'd said that the two of them were not seeing each other and that she had no plans for them to get back together. Kay had said that the allegations of substance abuse made against Atticus represented Andy's best argument, and that they could cut the case down at the knees if she testified that the children would not come into contact with him. It had been a bitter pill for her to swallow, but she didn't know what else she could do. She'd told Atticus they had to be more discreet about their relationship and had expected him to protest; instead, though, he'd shown an empathy she would've said was beyond him. He told her that he understood, that he knew how important the kids were to her, and that he was prepared to do whatever it took to make her happy.

And so she'd lied in her witness statement, saying that the relationship was over, and had repeated the lie when she was prompted by Kay, and then defended it when Andy's barrister had expressed his scepticism. Andy had sat there with his arms folded, shaking his head as she spoke. Mack had watched the judge for a reaction but found her inscrutable. Atticus would have been able to analyse her body language, given her a clue as to what she might be thinking, but she couldn't rely upon him now. *She* thought it'd gone well, though, and Kay had congratulated her during their five-minute debrief once the case had been adjourned. But you never really knew how these things went, and that was more than reason enough for Mack to be concerned.

She looked up to see a young man she recognised making his way in her direction. His name was Simeon, she thought, and she'd nicked him several times after she transferred here from London, always for possession.

He saw her and smiled. "Afternoon."

She nodded to the doors to the court. "Not going in here, are you?"

He smiled and shook his head. "I told you—I'm going straight. I'm going to work."

"Where's that?"

"Braemar Lodge."

"The care home?"

He nodded. "Been there six weeks. I love it."

Mack knew that Simeon was a good lad who had fallen in with the wrong crowd, and had spent time trying to impress upon him the wisdom in finding a legitimate path before the weight of his convictions got too much and he found a judge in a bad mood who would send him down for serious time; she'd seen lads like him time and again, with options available before going inside and none at all, save a life of crime, when they got out.

"Well done," she said. "Keep your nose clean."

He winked. "Always."

She watched him continue down the road and was about to set off for Bourne Hill when she heard the doors open behind her.

She turned: it was Andy and his lawyers.

Bollocks.

He said something to his barrister and peeled away from the group, making his way across the pavement to where she was standing.

"Hello, Mack."

"Andy."

"It didn't have to be like that," he said.

"Like what?"

"Personal," he said. "But it's your fault it was. My offer was reasonable."

"Full custody is '*reasonable*'? What planet are you on? You're trying to stop me from seeing my kids."

"Controlling access," he corrected. "Because I don't want them near *him*."

"They won't be," she said. "I'm not seeing him."

"Come on, Mack. I know you better than that. And I don't believe you."

She shrugged. "Can't help you with that."

"You told me you wouldn't see him again before. Remember? You were lying then, and you're lying now."

"You're using it as an excuse. And you're using the kids to get back at me. None of that is fair." He started to respond, but she spoke over him. "I didn't do anything wrong. I tried to make our marriage work, and it didn't. We just came to the end of the road."

"Nothing wrong? You *cheated* on me."

She held up her hands in an effort to ward him off; his poisonous attitude was wearying. "Whatever, Andy. I've got to go to work—out of the way, please."

He stayed where he was for a moment, then snorted with derision. He stepped to the left so she could move away, and she did, her fingers trembling with anger at his attitude and her stupidity and the fear that she had just made things worse.

10

Francine Patterson pushed back from the desk, leaned back in her chair and scrubbed her eyes with the heels of her hands. It was three in the afternoon, the office was hot, and she hadn't had the best night's sleep. She was tired, and all she wanted to do was to find a quiet corner to curl up and nap. That wasn't going to be possible, though; she had a full workload and knew she was going to be here until seven or eight, and that was only if she was lucky. Having a quick dinner with Robbie had been an indulgence that she probably couldn't afford, and now she was going to have to work twice as hard to catch up.

She got up, went to the window and opened it. The heating was broken, with the radiators always on, and, with the temperature outside rising as summer established itself, the building had quickly become stuffy. She heard the rush of traffic on the ring road and the finches and wrens singing cheerfully in the branches of the trees at the edge of the Greencroft. She looked out over the park, watching as two women pushed prams and talked, and a dog ran circles around its owner. The breeze was pleasant; Francine breathed in the fresh air, opened the window as wide as it would go, and went back to her desk.

She'd volunteered to take on the majority of the work for the preparation of the trial of Thomas Chandler and Eddie Thorpe. Mack had taken her for a drink and told her that she wouldn't expect her to be involved, given what had happened between her and Chandler, but Francine had said she wasn't going to use that as an excuse to shirk her responsibilities. Mack had pushed back, reiterating that it wasn't necessary for her to take on the work, and that, if their roles were reversed, she wouldn't want anything to do with it. Francine thanked her for her concern, told her she really *was* okay and that she preferred to do it. And that was true, Francine had been embarrassed to have been so comprehensively tricked by Chandler into having a relationship with him, but, after speaking to Robbie, she'd decided the best way to address the embarrassment was to meet it head-on. And as she'd said to Mack, no one else in the station was as motivated as she was to make sure the case was watertight. Mack had accepted her request and never mentioned it again.

There was a lot to do. Two months had passed since Chandler and Thorpe had been charged. The police had arrived at a local farm to attend to a report of burglary, and, instead of that, had found a trove of videos that evidenced the sexual abuse that had been perpetrated over the course of many years by a group of local men. Chandler had been a victim of the men and had, together with his stepfather—Thorpe—been using the videos to frighten guilty participants before murdering them. Chandler had been arrested after attacking the leader of the conspiracy, and Thorpe had handed himself in and confessed shortly thereafter.

The Crown Prosecution Service had assigned a lawyer to get the documents into shape. Mack and Francine had gone to Trowbridge for the Initial Case Review, and the lawyer—an impressive young woman named Fiona around the same age as Francine—had run through the steps that they would need to undertake to be ready for the Crown Court. Fiona had provided ongoing legal advice on the additional evidence they needed to strengthen the case, and now they were working together on disclosing everything to the defence. All relevant information needed to be shared, including anything that might hurt the prosecution; there had been none of that so far; and Fiona had said that she was as confident about the prospect of success as she could be.

There was another reason why Francine didn't want to hand the case to anyone else. The investigation had been a big deal, and she knew that being involved with the trial presented her with an opportunity to polish her reputation. She'd feared that what had happened to her would blot her copybook, but Mack had assured her that it wouldn't and, as if to prove it, had put her up for promotion to detective sergeant. That was the second reason for her tiredness; the National Investigator's Exam—a theoretical test that assessed her knowledge of the law, evidence handling, and procedural justice—needed to be passed before she went before the Promotions Board. She'd been working late on the trial preparation and then going home to study until the small hours.

There was a knock on the door. She spun in the chair and saw Robbie peering in through the glass. She beckoned him in.

He had two coffees in his hands. "Afternoon," he said.

"Hey."

"You all right?"

"Struggling to keep my eyes open."

"Thought you might say that." He held up the coffees. "This'll help."

He handed her one of the cups, then, after a quick glance outside to make sure they weren't observed, he leaned down and kissed her. She kissed him back and felt a small surge of relief and gratitude wash over her. She had wondered whether what had happened between them had been simply her reaction to her experience with Chandler, she knew Robbie liked her, but she had worried that she'd turned to him for comfort and support, and that, once things calmed down, she'd conclude that a workplace romance would be a bad idea.

To her surprise, she hadn't concluded that at all; if anything, she'd found she had feelings for him. He was older and more senior than her—a detective inspector to her detective constable—and his experience and steady calm had been reassuring as she came to terms with what had happened. He was kind and thoughtful, and she found that spending time with him had been the best way for her to distract herself.

Days had become weeks and then a month, and their relationship had grown beyond a rebound or a fling into something that might, perhaps, have an element of permanence about it. They had talked about whether it was something they should be open about; Robbie said that he didn't have a problem with the others in the station knowing, but Francine—still chafing at her colleagues knowing more about her private life than she would've liked—told him she wanted to keep it quiet, for now at least. He did a good job at hiding his disappointment, but said he was happy with her preference and respected it. They tried to act as normally as they could when they were at work but spent more and more time together when they were off the clock. Francine couldn't really imagine being without him now.

He leaned against the wall. "How's it going?"

"Slowly. Putting the disclosure bundle together. The CPS want it by the end of the day."

"On track?"

She nodded. "Think so." She gestured to the papers on the desk. "I'll tell you what, though—going through it all brings it back. And how *nuts* the whole thing was."

He sipped his coffee. "I know." He pointed down at the table. "How much more have you got to do?"

"I've got to put the witness statements together, and I haven't checked the transcripts of the interviews yet. I need to have another look at the communication logs, too." She waved a hand. "It's probably another four or five hours."

"Come to mine when you're done?"

"I've still got to revise for the NIE."

"I'll help. I'll have dinner waiting for you, too."

She had intended to go home, but, thinking that it might be nice to have a little company—and it didn't hurt that Robbie was also an excellent cook—was reason enough for her to change her mind.

"Okay," she said. "I'll be there as soon as I'm done."

He glanced out into the office through the window in the door once more, then leaned down and kissed her again. "I'll do steaks," he said. "Maybe I'll open that nice bottle we got at the weekend." He was about to go and then stopped. "I nearly forgot. You know Saturday..."

"Your birthday."

"I thought we could go away for the night. Somewhere different. Up for it?"

She couldn't very well say no, and, anyway, it was a nice idea. "Sounds good. What do you have in mind?"

"There are these log cabins in the New Forest, near Sandy Balls."

"And you know how I *love* Sandy Balls," she said with a wink.

"See—I remembered? It's all pretty simple, but I thought it'd be nice to wake up in the middle of nowhere. Coffee on the terrace while we listen to the birds."

"Sounds great. It's your birthday, though. I should book, not you."

"You're busy. Leave it to me."

He squeezed her shoulder and then left her to her work. She punched holes in the statement she'd been reviewing, added it to the binder with the others, and moved on to the next. The coffee and the chat with Robbie had helped, but she needed to motivate herself for the hours of work that still needed to be done.

11

Connor drove south, taking them past the hospital, through Odstock and then into the countryside. He followed Nunton Drove until they reached the sign—Samantha Hargreaves Equestrian—and slowed. A track headed off to the east toward the extensive fields that the business used as paddocks, but Connor turned sharp right and drove on to the yard.

Connor was familiar with the yard and its history. It had been in Sam's family for generations, first as a smallholding before her father made the decision to specialise in horses. Sam lived in the farmhouse, a short walk to the west of the yard.

Connor drove into the yard and parked up. The set-up was impressive: the yard was formed on three sides by old barns that had been renovated and turned into stables. There was a horse walker behind the westernmost stable and, next to that, a solarium. There was a tack room, a large hay barn, a sixty-by-twenty manège and an indoor arena of similar proportions. It hadn't always been like this, though. The place had been in trouble when Sam had taken it over. Her father had built a successful livery business, but, as age caught up with him and his dementia worsened, he had lost control, and things started to spiral. Sam had been in London, dealing with the end of her relationship with Christopher, and had been looking for an escape. The yard still looked like a lost cause, but it offered something she could lose herself in.

She'd run things as they'd always been run for the first year before Christopher had come up with an unusual plan—a *radical* plan—that would really turn things around. Sam had seen the potential at once, and, knowing they'd need help, they had taken it to the others. She'd asked Connor whether he'd like to be involved, and with his life heading nowhere, he'd agreed. Christopher had asked Nikki and Gaz, and Connor had asked Tom, and they'd all agreed, too. The last year had been wild. Christopher's betrayal had been terrible, but, by and large, Connor hadn't regretted his decision. It had certainly brought in a lot more money than he would've been able to make if he had continued to follow his career as a handyman.

Most of the stables were occupied, and two of the horses whinnied loudly as both men got out of the car.

Sam came out from one of the stables. "Afternoon."

Connor watched warily as Tom turned to face her. "Sam."

Samantha smiled at him. "You all right?"

"I'm good."

Sam reached Tom, put her arms around him and pulled him into a hug. "I'm sorry about the other night. It was stupid and insensitive of me. I should've thought, and I didn't."

"I'm sorry, too," Tom said. "I had too much to drink. I let it get on top of me."

Sam released him, her hands resting on his shoulders. "Forget it."

"What about Gaz?"

"I spoke to him—he's fine. Water under the bridge."

"But I hit him."

"He's fine."

"I feel like a clown."

"Like you said—it was the drink. Really—just forget it. I have and so has Gaz." She clapped her hand against the top of Tom's arm. "Ready to work?"

"Which field is it?"

Sam pointed to the east. "You know the one south of Clearbury Ring?"

"Yes," he said.

"That one."

"It's big."

"There's a lot to do. It's going to keep you out of mischief for the rest of the week."

Tom looked around. "How are we getting out there?"

Sam nodded over to the vintage Massey Ferguson parked on the other side of the yard. "Take the tractor."

The three of them walked over to the vehicle. A trailer had already been hitched, and the material and equipment they were going to need had been loaded into the back. There were over a hundred two-metre-long mortice posts designed to hold two or three rails. Next to them was the heavy iron rammer they'd use to drive them into the ground.

Tom looked at the rammer. "Seriously? By hand?"

"The telehandler's broken down," Sam said, using the story that they'd prepared earlier. Standard practice would have been to use the telehandler's forks to push the posts into the ground, but that would have made the job much easier—and quicker—

than they wanted. They needed Tom out of the way for as long as they could get away with.

"A *hundred* posts, by hand?"

"It'll be fun," Connor said. "We get a sweat on in the day and get pissed in the tent at night."

"Speaking of which," Sam said.

She pointed into the empty stable next to the tractor, then led the way inside. There was a large tent, with flysheet and groundsheet, two sleeping bags, a portable stove and cooking gear, and three heavy-duty Tesco carrier bags that were full of canned goods and the other things they'd need. Two dozen cans of Stella Artois were stacked alongside, cellophane-wrapped into two packs.

Tom pointed down at the alcohol. "That's tonight sorted. What about tomorrow?"

Connor made a show of rolling his eyes.

"I'll bring supplies when you need them," Sam said. "There's a shortwave radio in the pack."

"Phones don't work?"

"No signal," she said.

"It's not a big deal," Connor said, hoping to head off any objection that Tom might have made. "It'll be nice to get away from everything for a day or two."

He needn't have worried. "I don't mind that at all," Tom said. "You're right—it'll be nice."

Sam reached into her pocket and fished out a bunch of keys. "This is for the tractor. You've got rain coming in tonight but at least it'll soften up the ground for the new posts. You'll want to have the tent up quick or you're going to get soaked."

12

Atticus took out his phone and opened the notes he'd taken at the meeting with Frank Green. He'd given Alice's address on Bishop's Walk, the road on the eastern edge of the Close.

He walked up New Street, turned on to the High Street and passed beneath the cathedral gate. He went by the hut that accommodated the guards who checked the vehicles going inside, and raised a hand in greeting, and the guard—a man called Alan whom Atticus had helped when his daughter ran away six months earlier—called over a greeting. He reached the lawn and turned left, heading toward the Deanery, a row of terraced houses that lined the road that led to the Cathedral School. It was an outwardly modest enclave where the last property to reach the market had sold for one and a half million pounds.

He looked up at the cathedral spire, high above, and found his thoughts turning back to how David Campbell, the clerk of works, had been pushed to his death and then the investigation that had culminated in the discovery of what had been going on at Hawthorne Manor. The conspiracy they had unearthed was long-lived and, in the time that it had been alive, had spread its malign influence throughout the city and the countryside beyond. The conspirators had been dealt with—they were either dead or in custody, waiting for trial—but others had been pulled into its orbit. There were the customers, now either dealing with their own legal problems or, Atticus guessed, living with the terror that they would soon receive an unannounced visit from the detectives investigating the case. There were the victims, too; the resolution of the case had brought closure for grieving families and justice for those dead and alive. And there was the family who had taken the law into their own hands when the police had failed them: Thomas Chandler and his stepfather, Eddie Thorpe, both waiting to be tried for murder; and Zöe Chandler, Eddie's stepdaughter and Thomas's sister, still at large after Atticus had let her go.

Atticus had interrogated himself as to the decision he'd made about her. He'd let her go and hadn't tried to find her. The truth was simple: he had sympathy for her and what she had done. She and her brother had been abused by Harry Summers and the others and had taken it upon themselves to dispense justice.

They were vigilantes.

Atticus would normally have had no time for extrajudicial punishment, but his view had been coloured by seeing what could happen when the criminal justice system failed. Alf Burns had evaded the consequences of his actions for so long and had inflicted untold suffering on young men and women for as long as he stayed under the surface and away from police attention. Summers and the others had acted with the same impunity, insulated by huge wealth and the network of connections that Atticus *knew* went deeper than what had been exposed so far.

And so, given all that, and given the abuse that Zöe and Thomas's vigilantism had prevented, was it really his place to see that she was arrested?

He hadn't mentioned any of it to Mack. He hadn't even told her that he'd been at the farm, that he'd called in the fake burglary and then crept away when the uniform arrived. She would've told him it wasn't his place to make those kinds of judgements, and that it would have been better to leave it to the police and the courts.

And maybe she would have been right.

Maybe.

Atticus had wrestled with what he had done and was no nearer to satisfying himself either way.

13

Alice Green's house was part of the Deanery. Her view of the cathedral couldn't have been more spectacular, the expansive lawn where Atticus exercised Bandit was just over the stone wall on the other side of the road, and the cathedral was fifty yards beyond that. The terrace was old, and Alice's house had mellow cream walls covered with wisteria, dormer casement windows and a striking front door with a fanlight and pediment. Atticus opened his mapping app, switched to the satellite view and then zoomed in as far as he could; the house looked to have a small garden courtyard to the rear, and then, on the other side of the boundary, was open space used by Bishop Wordsworth school.

Frank Green had said she'd bought here after moving out of the family home. The financial settlement attendant upon the divorce had yet to be decided, meaning that she'd found the funds from her own income. Frank had said she was doing well with her business, and it looked as if he was right. This was one of the most desirable addresses in Wiltshire, if not all of the country.

Atticus ambled down Bishop's Walk to the gates of the school and then retraced his steps, slowing as he reached Alice's address. He took out his phone and, as surreptitiously as he could, recorded video of the property as he slowly made his way past it. A pair of narrow sash windows were partially obscured by the flowers in the small front garden—tall hollyhocks and deciduous shrubs—but he was still able to see inside to what looked like a sitting room. The front door was painted a lustrous green, and a sign fitted beneath the pediment bore the house's name. A small window looked as if it belonged to a downstairs bathroom, and then followed a garage with inset windows that were too high to see through. A passageway led to the back of the terrace with another garage immediately to the left. Atticus stopped by the passageway, pretending to tie a shoelace so he could see if he could work out where it went. It was hard to be sure, but it looked as if it might offer access to the courtyard the satellite view showed at the rear.

Atticus stood, turned and made his way to the cathedral lawn. There were plenty of empty benches, and he found one and sat down. It was a pleasant day, with warmth in the late spring sunshine. A group of boys from Bishops were sat around one of the other benches on North Walk, and a tour guide encouraged a group of tourists to stop so she could introduce them to the cathedral, the flag she used to identify herself fluttering above her head.

He opened a browser on his phone and navigated to Alice Green's website. He copied the email address from her contact page, opened Gmail, found the fake account he'd set up for precisely this kind of purpose and clicked to begin a new message. He pasted Alice's email, typed *Women's Health*

Interview as the subject, and then tapped in the body of the message and dictated what he wanted to say. He changed a few words here and there and, by the time he was finished, was happy he had it right. He read it through one more time and pressed send. The email disappeared with the usual whoosh, and Atticus put the phone away and stood.

He had fixed his hook with just the right kind of bait, and now it was a question of waiting to see whether Alice would take it.

14

They loaded the trailer with the rest of their gear, and Connor drove them out into the fields. He sat in the cab with the radio on loud while Tom bounced around in the trailer with the posts. The field that Sam had chosen was half a mile east of the yard and was to be used when horses needed to be put out for extended periods. Connor had worked at the yard since Sam took it over, and still didn't really get on with the animals. They were large and unpredictable and liable to kick or bite without warning, she might have an affinity with them, but it wasn't something that he shared.

Not that it mattered, of course.

They offered the perfect cover for what the business was *really* about.

They followed Nunton Drove and then turned through a gap in the fence onto the track that led out to the field. It passed through two large arable fields, the fast-growing crop marked by the perpendicular tramlines that the farmer followed whenever he needed to bring the tractor out. There was a large, wooded tract to the left, and then they came upon the first of the fields they used for the horses. It was long and thin, a twenty-acre parcel that encompassed the northern part of Clearbury Ring. The field that needed work was to the south, fifty acres that was too steeply sloped to be used for crops. The boundary was marked by hundreds of metres of post-and-rail fencing from when the land had been used to graze sheep. The fencing hadn't been maintained for years, and great stretches of it had rotted away. It would've been a big job even if they had used the telehandler; there wouldn't be any problem in stretching things out to keep Tom in the field for several days. They could stretch it out for a week if that was what they needed.

Connor looked over at Clearbury Ring. It was a hill fort, thousands of years old, the location having been chosen for its all-round defendability. The views over the countryside were spectacular: rolling hills and fields stretching into the distance, speckled occasionally with clusters of dark green woodland and the neat patchwork of farmland. The chalk hill rose above the flat, its lower slopes steep and partly covered in grass and wildflowers. The summit was encircled by the remnants of the ancient earthworks, now softened by time into a series of low, grassy banks and ditches. The defences traced an oval shape around the top of the hill. Connor had been up there as a boy, cycling from the family home in Bishopstone and pretending to be an Iron Age warrior watching for approaching invaders.

Tom got down and opened the gate to the field. Connor drove through, the trailer scraping against the post as he turned the wheel. He drove on until the trailer was all the way through and then stopped and turned off the engine. He opened the cab, hopped down and looked up into the evening sky: inky clouds were gathering on the horizon, the beginnings of the storm that had been forecast.

"I reckon we've got an hour, maybe less. It's going to be wet."

Tom pointed to the trailer. "We can leave the posts in there and unload tomorrow."

"Agreed. No one's nicking them, and we need to get the tent up."

He turned, looking for the best place to set up camp.

Tom pointed to the copse at the bottom of the slope to the north. "Over there. Get underneath the trees."

Connor agreed. They unloaded their tent and the rest of their gear and provisions, then trekked across the field to the start of the trees. Two or three dozen yew grew in the wood, some of them obviously very old. Time had bent them into weird shapes, their branches reaching out overhead like elongated fingers. Many of them had been hollowed out, and as the breeze picked up a little, they both heard the creaking as the branches rubbed against one another.

They cleared an area of rocks and debris and laid out the tent, ensuring the entrance faced away from the prevailing winds. Connor stretched out the base while Tom secured the corners with heavy-duty stakes, then assembled the flexible poles and threaded them through the tent's fabric channels to create the skeleton. Connor snapped the poles into the tent's base, lifting the fabric into its full shape. Tom hammered the stakes firmly into the ground, adding guy lines, while Connor attached the fly sheet for weather protection and adjusted the tent flaps.

Tom said he'd go back and get the cases of beer. Connor took the opportunity to gather firewood and had already arranged a nice stack by the time Tom returned.

"Looks good," he said.

Tom put the beer down on the ground and tore the cellophane wrapper so he could take a couple out. He tossed one over and popped the lid on the other. Connor opened his and raised it for a toast.

"To old friends," he said.

Tom touched his can to Connor's. "Old friends."

Thunder rumbled overhead, and moments later, the heavens opened.

15

Atticus was out with Bandit for his late walk when the rain started to fall. He'd only intended to take the dog to the cathedral, but he'd been lost in thought, and before he realised what he was doing, he was on the stone bridge that carried St. Nicholas's Road over the Avon. His second surprise, upon looking up at the sky, was that deep black clouds had blown across the city, and, with a rumble of distant thunder, the first thick drops of rain splashed down onto his upturned face. He'd come out without a proper coat and was going to get soaked unless he was able to find shelter. It would take too long to get back to the office, so he hurried onto Ayleswade Road and cut through the alleyway at the back of the Greyfisher. The pub's car park was full; the chalkboard sign for an important football match suggested the reason why it was so busy.

Thunder boomed again, much closer this time, and the rain fell more heavily. Atticus jogged the rest of the way, Bandit tagging along behind him. He hadn't been in the pub before and didn't know what the policy was when it came to dogs, but at least he'd be dry while he worked it out. He passed beneath the porch and went inside, Bandit helpfully shaking himself—and sending droplets of water flying everywhere—just as he crossed the threshold. He looked around: the bar was busy with people watching the lead-up to the match, and, to his relief, he saw that two of them had dogs with them.

He led the way to the bar and ordered a beer. "It's okay to have him in here with me?" he said, nodding down to the unimpressed dog.

The barman looked over the counter. "Absolutely," he said, nodding to a glass jar of dog biscuits. "Can I give him one?"

Atticus said that he could; Bandit sat obediently with his head cocked to one side as the barman fished out a treat and flicked it down to him. The dog caught it deftly, swallowed it and stared up in hopeful anticipation of another.

Atticus felt his phone buzzing in his pocket. He took it out and saw a number he didn't recognise.

"Hello? Who's this?"

"Alice Green."

Atticus pressed his card against the reader to pay for his beer. "Mrs. Green," he said. "Thanks for calling."

"Is it a good time to speak?"

"Fine," he said.

"Bit noisy."

"I'm just watching the football," he said. "Hold on—I'll go somewhere quieter." He collected his drink and led Bandit to the far side of the pub where several tables had been left empty. "There—that ought to be a little better."

"I got your email. You're a journalist?"

He put the beer on the table and sat down. "That's right."

"For *Women's Health*?"

Atticus had thought about that and didn't want to give her an answer that could be easily checked. "I'm freelance."

He hoped she wouldn't ask for examples of his previous work; he would've said that he wrote under a pen name if she did, but, to his relief, she didn't.

"And you're interested in writing something about what I do?"

"Wild swimming—that's right."

"Are you writing this on spec?"

"No. It's been commissioned. The magazine's got a feature on Wim Hof, and they want additional context—ideally something on people who can talk authoritatively about it in this country."

Atticus had thought carefully about how to make the approach and had decided that flattery was as likely to be successful as anything. His analysis of Alice's online content told him she was likely to respond to having her ego stroked, and suggesting that he saw her as an authority was a good way to start. And associating her with Wim Hof—the charismatic Dutchman credited with popularising wild swimming and cold-water therapy—would amplify that. Alice was evidently a savvy businesswoman, and Atticus knew she'd be happy to have her name listed next to his in an article in a magazine catering to thousands of people in her ideal niche. She'd see money, and, if what Frank Green had said was true, she'd find that hard to resist.

"When are they going to press?"

"Next month's issue."

"So when do you need to give them your content?"

"That's the thing," he said apologetically. "By the end of this week."

There was a pause, and, for a moment, Atticus wondered whether she was going to take the bait.

He needn't have worried. "I'm sure I can find the time for a chat. What are you thinking—something over Zoom?"

"I was hoping I might be able to come and see you in Salisbury, actually. They want online content to go with the piece. Maybe we could do the interview, and then—if you were up for it—I could get some video of you in the water."

"I'm sure we could work something out. When can you get here?"

"Tomorrow."

"I can do that."

"What time?"

"Let's meet in the Cosy Club on New Street at midday. We can do the interview over lunch."

"Perfect."

"And you could get a hotel overnight and then get some footage in the water on Wednesday. I can get my assistant to send you some suggestions if that'd be helpful."

"Yes, please. You have my email."

"I'll get her to send something across."

"Thank you," Atticus said. "That's wonderful. I'll see you for lunch tomorrow."

16

The rain had started two hours earlier and hadn't shown any signs of letting up. If anything, it had started to fall even more heavily. Thunder rumbled over the fields, and lightning forked across the sky. They'd chosen their campsite well, though, and the canopy of leaves overhead provided enough shelter so they didn't have to retreat to the tent. They'd built a fire and lit it, and the flames provided warmth even as the temperature dropped. Sam had provided them with a metal tripod and a frying pan, and Connor had cooked them beans and sausages, the food washed down with beer.

Connor had waited until Tom was four cans in and showing the first signs of being gently pissed before edging the conversation around just like Sam had told him.

"I was thinking..." he said.

"You want to be careful about that," Tom said.

"About what happened at the Haunch."

A flicker of regret passed across Tom's face. "You heard what I said. I'd had too much to drink—one of you buggers should've made me stop."

"I know. You're right. We should."

Tom looked over at him with concern. "I thought Sam was okay with it?"

"She is."

"Has she said anything to you about it?"

"Nothing more than she said to you," Connor lied. "She's fine. You saw what she was like tonight. You said sorry; she said sorry—it's all forgotten about."

Tom gazed into the flames. "Yeah."

Connor watched him carefully. "Do you remember what you said?"

"Not much of it."

"You said you were feeling bad about what happened. You know—with Christopher."

Tom turned away to look into the darkness between the trunks of the trees, the fire reflecting against his face. "I think about it all the time."

"Why?"

"Seriously? You *know* why—because of what I did. And what we all did afterwards. Don't you feel bad, too?"

"It wasn't as if he didn't have it coming," Connor said. "He betrayed us. He was going to steal from us. I mean, come *on*—who does that to their *friends*?"

"I know. That's true, but what we did was..." He shook his head, unable to finish the sentence. "The *pigs*. I still hear what they sounded like when..." He looked down. "I don't know how you can just forget about it like nothing ever happened."

"I'm not saying that. I *do* think about it, and when I do, I remind myself what a lowlife he turned out to be and what would've happened. You said it yourself—he would've killed Sam if you hadn't stopped him."

"Maybe."

"Not maybe—*definitely*. He was strangling her."

"But if I hadn't hit him so hard..."

"Come *on*," Connor said. "Be serious. *Everything* would've come out then, and we would've been well and truly up shit creek. What would we have done? Spoken to him? Told him off? No. We would never have been able to keep it together, and the police would've found out. We would only just have started the prison sentences we would've been given." He shook his head. "It was his fault what happened. He gave us no choice. It was him or us. And I'd do the same if it happened again."

Tom looked away again. Connor could see that there was going to be no way of getting through to him tonight. And he reminded himself, they hadn't brought Tom up here to change his mind. That ship had sailed long ago, and what was done was done. They needed to understand how he felt about Christopher more clearly and, in particular, investigate what his state of mind meant for the rest of them. They needed to find out what he might have said. He'd made some frightening suggestions about what he might do—he'd mentioned the police—and they needed to know whether that had *really* been the beer talking or whether they were realistic threats that needed to be addressed.

But it could wait. Connor was cold and tired and knew it'd be better to get some sleep so that he could come at it afresh in the morning.

Tom held up his empty can, crumpled it in his fist and tossed it onto the fire. "You want another?"

"Not tonight. I'm knackered." He stood and stretched, then went over to his sleeping bag and unrolled it. "You should get some sleep, too. We're going to be working hard tomorrow."

"I'll have one more and then call it quits."

Connor took off his jumper and jeans, unzipped the sleeping bag and slid inside. "Night, then."

"Night," Tom replied.

17

Atticus would normally have kept working until ten or eleven, but he wasn't feeling it tonight. Frank and Alice Green were both deeply unsympathetic individuals, and he found it difficult to muster up the enthusiasm to unearth dirt on the latter for the benefit of the former. They were perfect for each other, and it struck him as a shame that they were drifting apart; there was an algebraic logic to their marriage, as if each's unpleasantness might balance out the other's, two negatives making a positive. He told himself he'd made satisfactory progress with Alice and that there would be no harm in putting it aside for now and picking it up again in the morning.

The rain had continued to fall, with regular booms of thunder and veins of lightning that spread over the city. He needed something to distract him, he would have played online chess, but his experience with Jack_of_Hearts—and how the Chandlers had toyed with him—had soured him to it, at least for the moment, and he'd searched around for something else.

He took his laptop from his desk in the office and brought it into the bedroom. He popped the lid from the top of a beer, sat down on the futon with his laptop on his lap, and opened a website he knew would present him with a captcha before it allowed him to log in. It was of the standard sort: a street scene divided into a grid of nine squares with the requirement that the user select all of the squares featuring a vehicle; in this case, a bus.

Atticus screen grabbed the captcha and then set himself a three-minute timer during which time he'd try to identify the location of the shot. It was an interesting theoretical challenge that he'd started to look into after geolocating a still from a video in the Hawthorne Manor investigation. He'd managed to locate a building in Brussels that time but wanted to improve his technique with the aid of the additional tools he'd subsequently discovered. The investigative journalism website Bellingcat, in particular, had developed open-source tools they used in their work, and Atticus had found one of them—the Open Street Map Search Tool—particularly useful.

He got started. The piled-up snow on the side of the road and a shop sign written in French, with other signs in English, suggested he might be in a French-speaking part of Canada; Montreal, perhaps. He used that as his starting point, then went through the picture and identified unique objects that might have been tagged in the tool: a tree, a four-way junction, a four-storey building with distinctive windows. He set the tool to look for those items within fifty metres of each other and then skimmed through the images that were presented in the search results, finding the precise location—Crescent Street in Montreal—with fifteen seconds left on the timer.

He found another captcha, ready to attempt an even faster identification, when he heard a light tapping against the window of the door. He got to his feet—Bandit grumbling that his comfort had been disturbed—and moved the curtains aside.

Mack was on the outside landing.

He opened the door. "I didn't think you were coming over. You were worried about the kids?"

"No one saw me. Can I come in?" She winced, plucking at her sodden shirt. "I'm drenched."

"Sorry," he said. "Of course."

He stepped aside, and she came in, pausing to kiss him before he reached around and closed the door. She really *was* soaked.

"Forgot my umbrella," she said. "I'm all over the place at the moment."

"You're freezing," he said. "You need a shower. You should've gone to your place and called me—I could've come over to you."

"I told you—I'm not thinking straight. I came here on autopilot."

"Are you sure you're okay?"

"Not really. I don't want to be alone tonight."

Atticus's place didn't have much in the way of facilities. The kitchen—although it would be misleading to describe it as that—was accommodated in a small alcove beneath the stairs that led up to the second floor. The bathroom was at the other end of the landing and offered only a toilet and sink. There wasn't any space for a shower, and a bath was completely out of the question. Atticus had been making do with the facilities at the gym, only latterly taking advantage of the more generously equipped bathroom at Mack's rented house.

"Have you got a towel?" she said.

"Of course. But your clothes are soaked."

"I left a pair of pyjamas here. Don't you remember?"

"You did," he said, although he had forgotten. "But I don't know where they are…"

"In the drawer," she said, shooing him out of the way. "Find me a towel—a clean one would be nice—and I'll get them."

"Have you eaten?"

"No," she said.

"I'm out of everything. And it's too late for Deliveroo."

"Forget it. Beer?"

"I always have beer."

"Anything stronger?"

"Vodka, I think."

"Vodka and beer, then. All the important nutritional bases covered."

Atticus suddenly remembered why she was as distracted as she was: the custody hearing had been scheduled for today.

"Shit," he said. "I forgot. How did it go at court?"

"Let me get dry."

"Sorry," he stammered, self-consciously anxious that Mack's day hadn't been the first thing he thought about when it ought to have been. "Of course. I'll get the drinks."

"And the towel?"

"I'll get that first."

18

Connor pretended to be asleep, waiting as Tom finished his beer. He drank the second can and then a third before climbing the slope behind the tent and relieving himself. He came back to the tent, unzipping his bag and getting inside. Connor waited until Tom was snoring and then carefully opened his own bag and crawled out. He got to his hands and knees and went over to where they'd left their packs. Connor glanced over at Tom, comforting himself that he was asleep, and then very carefully unzipped the main compartment of his rucksack. The noise of the zip was loud; Connor froze as Tom muttered something, then waited a moment before opening the compartment all the way. He reached inside and searched for Tom's phone. It wasn't in the main compartment, so he zipped it back up and tried the pouch at the front. He found it, pressed up against a packet of cigarettes. He pocketed it, then closed the pouch and made sure the bags were as he'd found them.

He tried to switch the phone on, but the screen was dead.

Out of charge.

Connor grabbed his own phone, then opened the door to the tent and set off, picking a path around the edge of the waterlogged field until he was a hundred yards away. He looked back to the campsite, the faint glow of the embers flickering against the dark canopy of the trees, and waited a moment to be sure that Tom hadn't noticed him getting up and leaving. He didn't think so—Tom had been happily drunk when he finally lay down. He could just have told him he'd gone for a piss if he did notice Connor wasn't there, but Sam had told him again and again that he needed to be careful, so he was.

He opened his phone, found Sam's number and called it.

She picked up on the third ring.

"It's me," Connor said.

"Anything?"

"Not yet."

"How is he?"

"Asleep."

"Drunk?"

"Reasonably."

"And? Did you talk?"

"A little. It's like you thought—he's struggling. I told him we didn't have any choice about what we did. I don't think he believes that. He's struggling with the guilt. *Really* struggling."

Sam muttered something that Connor couldn't catch.

"I am going to need more supplies," he said. "I'd forgotten how well he can hold his beer. We've finished a dozen cans between us."

"You've still got more, though?"

"Same again, but that won't be enough. The way he's putting them away, we'll be through them by lunch."

"I'll come tomorrow morning. What do you need?"

"Beer," Connor said. "And maybe a couple of bottles of spirits. He likes Grouse, doesn't he?"

"He likes *everything*."

"Grouse will do, then. Better bring some Nurofen, too."

"I'll be there after I've brought the horses in. Probably around nine."

"Fine."

"What about his phone?"

"I got it. Can't unlock it, though—it's out of charge. Have you got a power bank?"

"Yes—somewhere. I'll charge it up and bring it in the morning. What about unlocking it?"

"Fingerprint. Should be able to do it when he's asleep."

"Be *bloody* careful. You can't let him realise what you're up to."

"I know that, Sam."

"We need to know who he's been talking to. We need her name, we need to know what he's said, and if he's said as much as I think he has, we need to know how to find her. You've got to do it, Connor. It's up to you. We won't be able to get him out like this again. He might be a drunk, but he's not an idiot. He'll see right through it."

Sam was agitated. Connor knew she saw herself as the brains of the operation and, although they'd all have to concede she was right about that, she did occasionally talk to them as if they were children. Connor knew what was at stake and knew how important these few days with Tom were likely to be. He didn't need to be reminded of it every five minutes.

Connor gazed out over the dark landscape. "What about the delivery? Have you spoken to Gaz?"

"He got off the ferry an hour ago. He's picking up the horse first thing tomorrow."

"And the meet?"

"Nothing's changed. You don't need to worry about it."

"A little worry isn't a bad thing. We've got a lot of balls in the air at the moment."

"And it's all under control. Deal with Tom and leave the rest to me. Anything else?"

"Got any spliff? A couple of bags'd be nice. And some Rizlas. I might see if that helps him relax."

"I've got plenty," she said. "I'll bring it in the morning."

They rang off, and Connor shivered. He had come out of the tent without his jacket, and there was a damp cool in the air. With the screech of an owl sounding out from somewhere in the woods, he trudged back to the tent.

Tomorrow was going to be an important day.

19

The beers were in the fridge, but the vodka was in the cupboard above the sink on the landing. Atticus took it down with two glasses, glancing at the bathroom door and seeing Mack's blurred silhouette in the frosted glass. He hurried, not wanting her to come out and see him and think he'd been spying on her. He went back into the bedroom and looked around, noticing the mess that he'd allowed to gather since the last time she had been here—discarded clothes, a cheese-smeared pizza box from Nole—and tidied as much of it away as possible. He picked up the laptop and put it away, rearranged Bandit's bed and, while he was at it, poured a scoop of biscuits into his bowl.

"I'm an idiot," he said to the dog.

The dog trotted over to the bowl, ignoring Atticus as he lowered his snout and started to eat.

"She's had a difficult day, and I haven't even texted her once to ask how she was."

Atticus heard the bathroom door open and close. Mack came back in her pyjamas with her hair wrapped in the towel.

"I'm sorry I didn't ask about how it went," Atticus said. "I've had new work come in, and I lost myself in it."

"It's fine," she said, taking the bottle of vodka, undoing the cap and pouring out two large measures into the glasses as Atticus held them. They sat down on the edge of Atticus's futon, and Mack set the bottle on the floor between them.

"So?" Atticus handed her one of the drinks.

She put the glass to her lips and downed the measure—at least a double—in one gulp. "I don't know."

"But your lawyer must've given you an idea?"

"She said it went as well as could've been hoped. But she's bound to say that, isn't she?"

"Maybe."

"That wasn't what's upset me, though. I spoke to Andy afterwards."

"Oh."

"He followed me outside."

"And?"

"He's angry with me. I mean—*still.* I thought he might've moved on, after the divorce, but he hasn't. It's like I told you. All this, what he's doing with the kids—he's not doing it for *them*, or because he thinks they'd be better with him. He's doing this to get back at *me*. They're just caught up in the middle. Collateral damage."

Atticus didn't know what to say. He found it difficult to know how to react in moments like this, when someone—especially someone he cared about, like Mack—shared her feelings. It was a facet of his condition, and, although he was better at managing it now than he used to be, it was still a challenge. Mack knew and had made it obvious time and again that she understood him and didn't take his reactions personally. Atticus had never had anyone like that in his life before, and it was one of the reasons why she was so important to him.

"What can I do to help?"

She shook her head firmly. "Nothing."

"There must be something. Let me look into him. I'll find something you can use. Everyone has—"

"No," she said. "We spoke about this. We—"

"Everyone has secrets, Mack. Come on. You're fighting him with one hand tied behind your back."

"No."

"He's using us as a reason," he argued. "*Me*, I mean. He's using the fact I was forced out of the police—after *he* grassed me up for the drugs, I hasten to add—and it's not fair. None of it is fair."

"I don't want you to get involved," she said, reaching for the vodka and pouring herself another measure. "I know what he's doing, but I'm not going to go down to his level. The court will see through it for what it is. That's what my lawyer said. And I don't want the future of the kids to be determined by which parent said the most unpleasant thing about the other."

She was firm, and, while Atticus didn't agree with her, he didn't want to get into a fight about it.

She stared at him. "Atticus?"

He held up his hands. "I know—it's your decision. I won't get involved."

"Because you *promised* me, didn't you?"

"I know. I did."

"Good."

"But I just want to help. I—"

"I know you do," she cut across him. "And there is something." She sipped at the second glass of vodka. "You know I'm reluctant to ask, but I don't have anyone else to go to. My solicitor billed me for the work on the hearing."

"How much?"

"Five thousand."

That was more than he'd expected. "I'm obviously in the wrong job."

"I know it's a lot."

"I didn't mean it like that. It's fine. Not a problem."

"Are you sure?"

"Of *course* I'm sure. Money's good at the moment. Never been busier, have I? And I just took on a new client today."

"Really?"

"You know Frank Green?"

"Frank Green as in the developer?"

"The same."

"As in the developer we're investigating for bribery?"

He sipped his vodka. "Don't worry—I'm not fishing for information."

"I wasn't worried about that. I was thinking more about what happened with Ralph Mallender."

"Oh—*that*." Atticus had acted for Mallender during his trial for the murder of his family and had produced the evidence that led to the overturning of the case that Mack had put together. It had been the start of Atticus's success, but it had caused her trouble at work. "It's not anything about that. He's going through a messy divorce with his wife. He wants me to find dirt on her."

"Sounds grubby."

"Very. The pair of them are awful. I looked into them both, and they deserve one another. He might be the most arrogant man I've ever met, and she looks like a fraudster who's been taking advantage of vulnerable people online. But he *is* rich, and he didn't question paying me a very generous retainer. More than you're being charged, anyway. I'll transfer the money tonight."

That wasn't all strictly true—the money Green had paid on account would only dent the legal fee—but it didn't matter, he didn't want Mack to think she was asking too much of him, and he'd be able to find the money from his savings.

"Thank you," she said, finishing the second glass of vodka and putting it on the floor next to the futon. She rested her palm against the side of his face. "I don't know what I'd do without you."

"No reason to find out," he said as she turned his face to her and kissed him, the taste of the alcohol still fresh on her lips.

PART 2

20

Sam touched her heels against the gelding's sides and settled into the familiar up-and-down rhythm as the animal picked up a brisk trot. She guided it around the manège, following the path that had been worn into the rubber chippings by the dozens of horses who had used it since it had last been harrowed. The horse's name was Bran—short for Brannigan—and it was an Irish sport horse that she'd been hoping would have been a good fit for Carly Smith, a local woman who was just getting back into riding after having a baby. Carly was looking for a dependable mount who'd be good for hacking and the occasional event. Bran was eight years old, and the breeder had sold him on the basis that he had an easy-going temperament, yet, in the half an hour that Sam had spent with him this morning, she would've said 'easy-going' was not an adjective she would have chosen. 'Overly sensitive' described him better, although she might also have chosen 'opinionated' and 'difficult.'

She slid her outside leg back for the canter transition; the motion was smooth, but, as they reached the end of the manège and started to turn, the sound of a car door being slammed caused the horse to spook. He dropped a shoulder and spun, and, for a moment, Sam thought she was going to be thrown. She put her weight straight down through her stirrups as she sat up and grabbed the neck strap, and after going sideways, Bran came to a stop.

Sam settled back down in the saddle and shook her head. 'Flighty' might be an appropriate adjective, too. 'Challenging,' perhaps. Maybe even 'dangerous.' She swung her leg over Bran's back and slid down, landing on the loose rubber chippings. She took the reins and led the horse through the gate and back to the yard.

Nikki was sitting in her car, her legs extended out of the open door while she scrolled through her phone and listened to the radio.

"Thanks," Sam said.

"What for?"

"Slamming the door—you spooked him. I nearly came off."

"I thought you said he was supposed to be dependable."

"That was what I was told."

"So?"

"He's not," she said, slapping her palm against Bran's sweaty neck. "He's got potential, but not for a beginner. A little feistier than I thought he was going to be. A little stiff on the left rein, and I think he might be a little too spooky to hack."

"But you've got a buyer lined up?"

She nodded. "New mum just getting back into it. But he isn't right for her. He's too much horse."

"So?"

She shrugged. "I know Isabella Wright was looking for a new horse to event with—maybe she'd be up for a ride to see what she thinks. He's certainly got the scope for that."

Sam led the horse back to the stable, waited until he was inside and then shut the door. She'd filled a fresh net with hay and hung it on the wall, and now the horse reached over for it, tugged out a mouthful and started to munch.

She took off her helmet, loosened her back protector, and looked around the yard. She had taken the business on from her father when it had been on its arse. Her friends in London had looked at her as if she'd sprouted a second head when she told them she was going home to take over, but she hadn't been deterred. London wasn't for her. Her on-off relationship with Christopher had just taken one of its regular downward swings, and she needed to get away. And doing something completely different was attractive.

She'd introduced some new ideas to the business and brought it back into profit. Her father had been a superb trainer, but he'd been slow to adapt to new ways of doing things and had looked on helplessly as the yard had been sucked deeper and deeper into the vortex of debt. Sam had pulled it out and steadied the ship and then realised that the regular trips to and from Ireland to buy horses could be used to do something else, to facilitate another income stream that would make even the most opportunistic forecasts of what might have been possible with the yard look like chicken feed.

Christopher had stayed behind in London. He had fallen in with a bad crowd and had started a little import business of his own. He was buying kilogram bags of coke and then selling them to the lawyers and accountants who came to Camden to party, middle-class professionals who thought they'd be cool if they drank in the right pubs and hung out with the right people. Christopher had always told her how he thought they were pathetic, but he was happy enough to relieve them of their money in exchange for one of his little paper triangles with a gram of gear tucked inside. He'd told his father and brother about what he was doing, and they—already operating a number of criminal enterprises in Salisbury—had told him they wanted to get involved, but that they'd want to do it at scale.

Sam had been frightened by what they were proposing, but the rewards on offer were irresistible.

The others knew they'd never have managed to achieve a fraction of the success they'd seen over the last year without her leadership. Tom would've said that, too, once, but his squeamishness about what had happened to Christopher had been the final nudge she'd needed to decide that maybe it was time to start to think about herself.

Sam turned to Nikki. "Have you heard from Gaz?"

"He called half an hour ago," she said. "He's got the horse. He'll be at the pickup in a couple of hours."

"I'll be happier when he's back here," she said.

"He knows what he's doing," Nikki said, instinctively defensive when it came to her idiot husband. "Relax."

Nikki was right—Sam *did* worry, and maybe too much—but that was what made her good at doing what she did. She sweated over every detail, considered every risk and every alternative to mitigate those risks. There were a hundred things that could go wrong, and any one of them would lead to consequences that she had no interest in investigating beyond the theoretical. She applied the same care and attention to her own plans for what would come next.

"Text him," she said. "We need a pretext… tell him I'm worried about the horse. Get him to call me just before his stop. I want to have a chat before the meet."

Nikki looked ready to tell Sam not to worry, but a quick look at her face—and the flinty way she held her eye—persuaded her not to bother. "What about Tom and Connor?"

"I'm going to go over to the field now. Maybe we get some luck and Connor's persuaded him to talk."

"And if he has? What if it's bad?"

"We'll deal with that when we have to," she said. "Text Gaz and leave the rest to me."

Sam turned her back on her and walked over to where she'd parked the quad bike. There was a lot riding on what happened today, and it would make a difference to her mood to have some positive news. Maybe Connor could provide that, but she wasn't hopeful. Tom had said some disturbing things in the square on Saturday night. Sam didn't know how they'd be able to find a way back to where they'd been before in a way that would allow her to forget.

21

Connor woke up with the dawn, opening his eyes to the bloom of light against the roof of the tent and the sound of cheerful birdsong: wrens and finches in the trees, and a skylark trilling somewhere overhead. He could hear Tom's snoring as he unzipped his sleeping bag and crawled over to the mouth of the tent, unzipping the door. It was a beautiful morning, with bright sunlight lending a lustrousness to the landscape that hadn't been there under the dark clouds yesterday. The hill descended into the field, and then the ground rose up again, a gentle slope climbing to a distant ridge to the south. The area in between was a patchwork of arable land, with the occasional parcel dedicated to sheep and cattle. The boundaries were marked by fences, hedgerows and muddy brown tracks. He looked up into the powder-blue sky and saw the skylark he'd heard earlier; above it, a red kite wheeled around in graceful circles, borne aloft by the warm air.

He went to the clearing where they'd been drinking last night and relieved himself against the trunk of a tree. The fire had gone out hours ago, so he cleared away the ash and built another, lighting a handful of kindling and, when that had taken, adding a lattice of small twigs and sticks. He left the fire to establish itself, found the carrier bag that had held the beer, and filled it with the empties that were strewn around the fire. They'd chugged their way through fifteen cans. He didn't think he'd had more than five, so Tom had been putting them away twice as quickly.

The fire was nicely underway now, and hot enough for Connor to add larger pieces of wood. He set an old, blackened pot over the fire, supported by stones he placed in a circle, and poured in water from one of their bottles. As the water in the pot started to bubble, he sliced a few pieces of bread and speared them on a stick, toasting them just close enough to the fire to catch its warmth without charring. He poured ground coffee beans into a small filter and let the boiling water percolate through, filling two tin cups with rich, fragrant brew.

With the coffee gently steaming, Connor turned his attention to breakfast. He opened the cool box, collected strips of bacon and laid them on the cast-iron frying pan. He positioned the pan over the fire, and the fat began sizzling almost immediately, the aroma mixing with the smell of the coffee. The bacon curled at the edges as it cooked; Connor used a fork to flip the strips, ensuring they crisped evenly on both sides. He moved the bacon to the side of the pan and cracked two eggs into the centre. The eggs bubbled and hissed, their edges frizzling into a crispy lace. The yolks began to set, and he tilted the pan, letting the bacon grease slide under the eggs, adding flavour and preventing them from sticking. Connor divided the meal onto two plates and left them at the side of the fire to keep warm.

He went back to the tent.

"Rise and shine, you lazy bastard."

Tom rolled over again and groaned.

Connor looked down and saw that Tom had opened his eyes.

"Morning, beautiful."

Tom reached up with both hands and massaged his temple. "What time is it?"

"Eight. You okay?"

Tom groaned again. "Been better. Might've had a little too much last night."

"You *were* knocking them back."

"So were you," he protested.

"True," he said, deciding not to announce the disparity in their respective consumption. "But I've always been able to hold my beer."

"Piss off."

"What?" Connor gestured to the carrier bag. "The evidence speaks for itself."

Tom didn't have the energy to dispute the suggestion.

Connor took the bottle of water from his bag and tossed it over. "Finish that. Sam's bringing supplies in a bit—I asked her to get some ibuprofen."

Tom unscrewed the cap and slugged down several mouthfuls of water. "This'll help," he said. "Fresh air, too. I'll be all right."

"Glad to hear it. We've got a lot to do today."

"Do we get breakfast first?"

"It's waiting outside."

22

Connor took the radio from his pack, tuned it to Salisbury Radio and rested it on the overhanging branch of the oak that sheltered the camp. The DJ played an inoffensive selection of eighties and nineties pop, and they settled into a companionable silence as they set about their meals. There was something about eating food cooked over a fire, the smoke, perhaps, or something else that lent the eggs and bacon extra taste that couldn't be found at home.

Tom perked up as he ate, mopping up the grease and the remainder of the egg with his toast before putting the plate down and finishing his coffee.

"Have you seen my phone?"

Connor had been expecting the question and shook his head guilelessly. "No. Why?"

"Can't find it."

"Did you have it last night?"

"I *thought* I did."

"I didn't see you with it."

His forehead crumpled into a frown. "Might've left it in my room when I came out."

"Do you need it?"

He shrugged. "Probably not."

Connor decided to chance his arm. "What about this bird you were telling us about?"

"What about her?"

"Does she know where you are?"

"Course," he said.

There was something about the terseness of his reply that made Connor wonder if he wasn't holding something back.

"Wouldn't have mattered even if you did have it," Connor said. "There's no reception out here."

"Yeah—you said." He poured himself another mug of coffee. "What about you, then?"

"Meaning?"

He winked. "You and Sam?"

"Nothing going on there," Connor said.

"Her choice or yours?"

"Both," he said, annoyed with being put on the defensive. He shifted uncomfortably. "It was never really on the cards."

Tom took a bite of his toast. "You know what me and Gaz used to say—after she came back from London?" He stabbed the half-finished piece of bread in the air to punctuate the sentence. "We had a bet with Nikki that the two of you would end up together."

Connor felt the blood rising in his cheeks. He knew he'd end up getting angry if Tom insisted on talking about Sam and him. The truth of it was that he still hadn't dealt with his disappointment that the two of them had split up in the first place, even though it had been years and years ago. Connor had been obsessed with her when they were at school and had hoped that their youthful tryst would have grown to be as important for her as it was for him. They'd been together for a few weeks, but, while he would've done anything for her, she hadn't felt the same way. She'd broken his heart when she told him she was going to live in London and that she thought it best to bring their relationship to an end. He'd found out later that she'd been cheating on him with Christopher and that the two of them had made their relationship official soon after.

Connor had had other relationships, but he couldn't help comparing the women to her, and they always came up short. He'd been engaged to one of them—a woman named Melissa—and, after he'd broken it off, she'd told him he needed to see a shrink to deal with his baggage. Connor didn't have any time for that kind of nonsense, but, as he drifted from meaningless relationship to meaningless relationship, he found himself wondering about what Melissa had said and thinking maybe—perhaps—it wasn't such a bad idea after all.

"I don't know where you lot get all that from," he said. "You act like I'm obsessed with her."

"Come on, mate. It's obvious. The way you *look* at her sometimes." He widened his eyes, leaned forward and mimicked him. "'What's that, Sam? You want me to put my hand in the fire? Which hand? *Both* hands? *Absolutely* I'll do that, Sam.'"

"I've had more women since we split up than you and Gaz have had put together."

"Never had a serious relationship with any of them, though, did you?"

Connor was growing more and more angry and had to work hard to hide it. It was because he felt vulnerable about

Sam, and because Tom—of *all* people—was making him squirm. Tom had always been the one the others made fun of, and the thought that he and Nikki and Gaz—and *Sam*, for all he knew—were laughing at *him* was unbearable.

He finished his coffee, tossed the dregs to the side and stood. "Whatever," he said. "We need to get to work."

Tom leaned back, smiling smugly. "Changing the subject?"

"That's right," he said sarcastically, "because I can't bear the thought that you're all talking behind my back. Finish up and clean the plates. I'll get to work unloading the gear, and we can get started. I'll see you over there."

23

Connor led the way to the stretch of fencing that needed the most urgent repairs. The field was in the shape of a triangle, with the longest side to the south bulging inwards thanks to how the neighbouring arable field cut into it. Sam had said that the farmer had installed the fencing thirty years ago, and that the posts had been exposed to the elements ever since. The wood had rotted, with some of the posts so weak that they'd already collapsed. Others were loose and wouldn't need much in the way of a shove and a yank to pull out of the ground. The worst run was the stretch that ran from the wooded area on the slope of the hill down to the halfway point of the eastern side of the triangle; it was a stretch of two hundred and fifty metres, and thirty posts needed to be replaced, and all of the rails.

"We'll start here," Connor said, pointing to the run.

Tom raised his eyebrows. "*All* of it?"

Connor nodded. "That's just the first bit." He turned and pointed to the stretch of fencing that marked the western boundary. "There are ten-metre stretches all the way down there that we need to sort out, too."

Tom went to one of the posts, wrapped both hands around it and gave it a hefty yank. The wood was splintered down at the bottom, and the post broke apart and split.

"Give me the shovel."

Connor tossed it over and watched as Tom set to work. He pushed the blade into the earth, drove it down with the sole of his boot and scooped out the earth. The ground was still soft from the weeks of rain, and it didn't take long for Tom to dig out enough so that he was able to get to the buried portion of the post. He crouched down, grabbed it with both hands and hauled it out.

"There," he said, tossing it behind him. He gestured over to the tractor. "Go bring the new ones over. This might not take as long as I thought."

"This isn't all of it," Connor reminded him.

Tom nodded. "How long do you think?"

"Got to be two or three days. Doesn't matter if we take all week—as long as we're done by Monday when the horses need to be in here, that'll be fine."

"Don't think that'll be a problem. Go on—bring the tractor over. We'll get the old posts out first, and then we'll put the new ones in."

Connor checked the tractor's keys were in his pocket and, feeling the sharp edges against his leg, crossed the field to where they had parked the vehicle.

* * *

Connor reached the tractor, clambered up, then unlocked and opened the door. He slid into the cab, started the engine and pressed down on the accelerator. The tractor bounced over the ruts as he turned the wheel and set off to where Tom was working on the second post. He watched as Tom dug down with the shovel, discarded the loose earth over his shoulder, and then, the shovel set aside, wrestled the post left and right and back and forward until he was able to draw it all the way out of the ground.

Connor was halfway there when, with the benefit of his raised position in the cab, he saw Sam approaching along the track. She was on her quad bike, the distinctive red and black paint job visible against the brown mud and the green hedges. Connor steered over to the gate so he could intercept her before she was too far into the field.

"Morning," she said.

"Morning."

"How is he?"

"He had a bit of a hangover, but it hasn't stopped him getting to work."

"We need to—"

"I know, and I will—but it's not something you can just force. I know we laugh about him, but he's no fool. If I make it too obvious, he'll see right through me, and then where will we be?"

Sam nodded in concession. "I know. It's just… well, the whole thing's making me nervous. Does she know where he is?"

"He said he told her."

"What if she panics when he doesn't return her calls?"

"She'll think there's no signal."

"Maybe."

"There's something else," he said. "I asked about her this morning, and he looked uncomfortable. As if… I don't know. As if maybe what he's said to us isn't completely true."

"He's *not* with someone?"

He shrugged. "Don't know."

"We need to be sure. You need to get into his phone."

"Got the power bank?"

She took a bag from the pannier. "In here."

"I'll get it charging now and have a go when he's asleep tonight."

Sam nodded, then glanced up and over Connor's head. "He's coming over."

Connor turned and saw Tom making his way across the field. Sam held up her arm in greeting.

Connor turned back to her. "Did you get the rest of the stuff I wanted?"

"Booze, fags, some sandwiches from the farm shop and some other stuff I thought you'd both like. In the bag."

Connor cocked an eyebrow. "And?"

Sam smiled. "Got that too."

She reached into her pocket and took out a clear plastic bag containing a decent amount of a dark green fibrous material, together with a packet of Rizlas. She handed both over.

"From Freeman?"

"Yes," she said. "And plenty more where that came from."

Tom was just ten feet away now. "Morning."

Sam shielded her eyes from the sun. "How's the head?"

Tom nodded at Connor. "Has he been gossiping again?"

"He said you were both at the beers last night."

"Might have been a few."

Sam nodded down at the bag of supplies. "There are some pills in there somewhere."

Connor held up the bag of weed. "Sam brought this, too."

Tom grinned. "You beauty."

"Want me to roll one now?"

"Later," he said. "I want to crack on and get the first run of posts in."

"That's what I like to see," she said. "A little industry. I'd better get back to the yard. We've got a horse coming in, and I want to make sure the paddock's ready for her. There was ragwort that needed to be dug out. Shout if you need anything else."

Sam made her way back to the quad bike. They watched as she started the engine and bounced her way over the field to the gate.

Tom took a step toward the bag of supplies. "Pills?"

"Thought you were okay?"

"Wouldn't mind dulling it down a little."

"I'll bring them over. Want to wash them down with a brew?"

"Go on, then. Bring it over when it's ready—I'll drive the tractor over and get started."

Connor tossed the keys. Tom hauled himself into the cab and drove back to the fence.

Connor crossed the field to the tent, opened the flap and ducked inside. He put the supplies down, opened his bag and took out Tom's phone. He found the power bank, connected it to the phone and held down the power button. He saw the bright white Apple logo on the screen and waited for the screensaver to replace it. The picture Tom had chosen was of a woman Connor hadn't seen before. She was a little older than him—early to mid-forties, he thought—and good-looking. The mystery woman?

He tapped the screen and a caption appeared, suggesting that the phone was looking for a fingerprint to unlock it. He left it connected to the power bank and put both items in his bag, hiding them beneath a poncho and zipping it closed.

Connor scrubbed a hand over his scalp. The solution Sam had proposed to solve their problem was radical, and Connor didn't have everything he needed to get on board with it yet. He'd talk to Tom again when they were drinking tonight. It was funny: he *hoped* he'd be unsuccessful and find nothing, but he'd already heard enough to know that was probably a forlorn hope. Tom was a friend, and they'd all shared a lot together over the years, but, out of the five of them, he was the least suited to the business they'd chosen. And now, given the consequences that would befall them all if what *really* went on at the yard were ever to come to light, Tom's weakness had become an issue.

Connor might hope they were wrong about that, but he knew it was unlikely. It had fallen to him to find the evidence that would damn his friend.

24

Atticus had to be careful. The Cosy Club was just down the road from his office, and the last thing he wanted was for Alice to see him coming out of the door on his way to meet her. He waited until midday, made sure Bandit's bowls were full of food and water, and then descended the steps to the courtyard.

He was worried Alice might recognise him. He'd been interviewed on the television on several occasions in the aftermath of the Ralph Mallender case, and there had been a piece in the *Journal* that had featured a slightly cheesy photograph of him looking thoughtfully into the middle distance. Mack had mocked him for that, and with good reason, but his discomfort became more practical now as he allowed himself to be persuaded that Alice might have seen it. He mulled it over, eventually reassuring himself that it was unlikely and that he could reduce the odds with a few simple precautions. He left his favourite leather jacket on the hook on the back of the door and picked out the suit that he'd bought from Regent, the tailor on New Street, for his sister's wedding. Atticus had been a little heavier then, and the suit trousers were a little looser, but the waistband could be cinched in and then secured with a belt. He chose a plain white shirt rather than one of his preferred band T-shirts, then put on his off-white Adidas and a New York Yankees cap. He went through the passage to the street and checked his reflection in the window of the bridal shop as he went by; it wasn't much of a disguise, but on the basis that he suspected he was being a little self-aggrandising in expecting that she'd recognise him, it'd do.

The Cosy Club was less than thirty seconds away. It had taken the first two floors in an arts college that had been a bank before that and had a large open-plan bar area with leather sofas, an outdoor terrace at the back, and two dining areas: an atmospheric wood-panelled space on the ground floor with another lighter space on the floor above. Atticus had brought some of his first clients here before the office was presentable enough to host them, and occasionally stopped in to have the fruit pancakes and a coffee for breakfast.

Alice's personal assistant had emailed him with details for the interview. She explained that Alice would be at a table on the first floor at twelve, and that she was looking forward to the meeting. She had also suggested a hotel—the Red Lion—if Atticus was still looking for somewhere to stay overnight before concluding the interview tomorrow.

Atticus kept his head down as he walked through the restaurant to the flight of stairs at the back of the downstairs dining area. He saw several members of staff who might recognise him but put his phone to his ear and pretended to take a call, and they all took the hint and let him be. He climbed the stairs to the mezzanine.

The space was more open, with skylights in the ceiling and large chandeliers hanging over the open atrium. Alice Green was sitting at one of the tables. She had a laptop open, and her attention was focused on the screen; Atticus was able to assess her before she noticed he was there. She had a slender figure and long, brown hair that fell over her shoulders in natural waves. Her complexion was fair, and she was wearing light make-up that highlighted her natural features. She was wearing round glasses with a thin frame and was dressed casually, with a long-sleeved, horizontally striped shirt in white and black. The shirt was tucked into a pair of denim dungarees. She was sitting side-on, and as Atticus climbed the final step, he saw that her right leg was crossed over her left, the cuffs of the dungarees rolled up to reveal a pair of classic, low-top Converse. There was a small, black leather crossbody bag on the table, and the lid of her open laptop was decorated with stickers and decals with the same Real Wild Swimming logo she used across her social channels. There was an empty coffee cup next to the laptop.

"Good afternoon," Atticus said.

Alice looked up. "Ryan?"

He smiled and then made a show of noticing the empty cup. "I'm not late, am I?"

"No. I got here early. Had work to do."

She turned the laptop so Atticus could see that she was editing a video; her camera had been set up on the bank of a river and then angled down so that it showed her floating in the water.

"Where's that?"

"The Avon," she said. "There's a nice spot near Fordingbridge." She frowned. "Where's your gear?"

"Gear?"

"You said you wanted photos and videos."

"Oh, my cameras—I left them at the hotel."

"Sarah suggested somewhere?"

"The Red Lion. It's lovely—just the job." He took off his jacket and hooked it across the back of one of the empty chairs, then gestured at the empty cup. "Can I get you another?"

"Only if you're having one."

"Gasping."

She asked for a flat white. Atticus said he would be back in a minute and went back down the steps to the ground floor. He ordered two flat whites from the server behind the bar and waited as he ground the beans. Alice wasn't what he had imagined. Atticus knew she was younger than her husband, but she must have been a good twenty years his junior. He guessed she was in her early to mid-thirties, managing a cool image with a nod to vintage fashion that suggested money had been invested.

"Here you are," the server said, indicating the two coffees on the bar.

Atticus thanked him and took the coffees back upstairs. Alice saw him, closed the lid of the laptop and slid it into her bag. "How do you want to do this?"

He took his digital recorder from his bag, held it up so she could see it and then set it down on the table between them. "I thought we could just have a chat," he said. "I've got a few things I want to cover, but it'll be better if we get to them naturally. Is that all right?"

"Of course. Go ahead."

He reached down to the recorder, switched it on and then took his notebook from his bag and turned to the list of questions he'd prepared earlier.

"First one," he said. "How did you first find out about cold-water therapy? Was it because of Wim Hof?"

She shook her head. "God, no. I was doing it before he became famous." She leaned back in her chair. "Finding it was the best thing that ever happened to me."

Atticus watched her as she launched into an answer that was evidently pre-prepared. She spoke of an awakening that was almost spiritual, a communion with nature that kindled a passion in her that had helped her deal with problems that had been afflicting her for years. But it was all an act, and although reading people in a social context was not his forte, Atticus was not fooled by the show she was putting on. There was no spontaneity, and she was giving off plenty of cues that made it obvious it was a performance she'd given before: her eyes focused on a spot behind Atticus's shoulder rather than flicking around naturally as she accessed different parts of her memory, her voice was monotone as she remembered her answers rather than delivering them with natural inflection, there was no hesitation and no filler, and there was limited hand movement, again suggesting recitation. Atticus confirmed his suspicion by asking his first question in a slightly different way, and her answer was slavishly repetitious.

She spoke about the history of cold-water therapy, about how naked Tibetan monks sat in the snow, wrapped themselves in damp blankets and then dried them out with the power of their minds as they raised their body temperatures. She explained how she could only still her thoughts by being in cold water. She spoke about how breathing exercises and cold-water immersion could bring even better results when they were combined. She enjoyed talking about herself and was too self-absorbed to notice that Atticus was having to work to maintain a façade of interest. He checked his watch when they reached the end of the first hour and then again as they passed ninety minutes.

"So," he said when she paused for breath, "can I assume this is a profitable business for you?"

She held his eye and smiled, as if that was a foolish question. "I can't complain, but it should be obvious it's not about that."

"Really?"

"I don't do it for the money. I do it because I like to make a difference—"

He cut across her. "But you're making enough for you to be full time?"

She frowned. "Well, yes. But, like I say, it's not about that for me."

"Got to pay the bills, though?"

"Obviously," she said, her irritation even more obvious.

"And *how* do you make your money?"

"Sorry?"

"Your income—I was wondering what the main sources are."

"I thought you wanted to talk about wild swimming."

Atticus watched her carefully. He knew what buttons he needed to press: she was smart enough to see the disconnect between the altruistic motivation she claimed and her million-pound house. Her touchy-feely clientele might consider her mercenary if they knew how much she was making. But she was insecure, too, and he could see she wanted Atticus to approve of her as a businesswoman. It was a difficult line for her to walk, but Atticus was confident he could get her to talk about the money as a way of demonstrating how good she was at what she did. He'd acknowledge her selflessness—ignoring that he'd seen through it within the first few minutes—and then get her to talk about what he *really* wanted.

"That'll be the focus of the piece," he assured her, "but my editor is also interested in how people are able to support themselves financially while, at the same time, helping to make a difference in people's lives. Obviously, I can see you've made a tremendous success out of your teaching, and I think it's something that should be celebrated."

The drop of admiration was all that she needed. She shifted, pretending to find the direction of the interview embarrassing, but he could see she was ready to be praised. "Income sources, then?" She paused, then ticked them off on her fingers. "I have a series of courses."

"Online?"

She nodded. "Students can take them at their own pace."

"What are you teaching?"

"From the basics to more advanced techniques. From the things you need to get started as a wild swimmer, to the effects cold water has on the body, and then all the way to breath-work and guided meditation. It's a holistic package—very good reviews from students who've taken them. I can get some for you if it'd help."

"Sounds like something my girlfriend would like to try."

"It's all on my website," she said, with an alacrity that smacked of avarice. "Tell her to have a look."

"What other sources of income? You sponsor products on your socials."

"I have affiliate deals with a few carefully selected brands. And I have a rule when I endorse something: I won't do it unless I use it myself and I'm happy to vouch for the results."

He noted that down. "Profitable?"

"Yes, but I can't talk about specific numbers—it's confidential."

"Absolutely. Anything else?"

"Public speaking at conferences. One-on-one coaching every now and again, but I've stopped doing that quite so much now."

"Investments?"

Her eyebrows kinked up. "Investments?"

"I'm assuming you have a portfolio of investment products where you grow your money."

"We're going *way* off-piste there. And this is beginning to feel more like an interview you'd have for a financial magazine. I want to make it clear one more time—what I do *isn't* about the money. Okay? It never has been. I get more of a thrill seeing the effect that the things I'm teaching have on people's lives than what's in my bank account."

Atticus could see it from a mile off: another rehearsed line. He could tell from the way that she forced out the smile that it was an act, and that she'd most likely concocted the line precisely because she was concerned that people would see her motivation for what it was.

Atticus was nothing if not rational, and everything that he'd heard from Alice suggested that she was selling snake oil and knew it. He'd met some people over the course of his career who'd persuaded themselves that there was truth in their lies; he could see, very clearly, that Alice was not one of them. She had her spiel down pat and deployed it to protect her reputation and her ability to make money, but she didn't believe a word of it. A career as a huckster wasn't necessarily a crime—and it was hardly the gotcha that her ex-husband had asked him to find—but it spoke to her character.

He had got as far as he was going to get without attracting suspicion about his real motive for speaking to her. "No," he said. "You've made that very clear, and I'll be sure that the article focuses more on the therapeutic side of what you do than anything else."

"Good." She smiled, all trace of any previous suspicion banished. "Anything else for today?"

"I think that'll do. I've got what I need."

She leaned back and shrugged. "Okay. I might have a think about what I've said, and if I come up with anything else that might be interesting, I can tell you tomorrow."

Atticus had almost forgotten about the second meeting. "Where do you want to meet?"

"Come to the office. It's brand new—I bought it last month. It used to be a hair salon. It's an old building, right next to the cathedral gate. Really beautiful—lots of history."

She reached into her bag and took out a card. Atticus looked down and read out the address.

"That's the studio," she said. "I've just had a new immersion tank installed. Come over in the morning. Shall we say nine?"

"Perfect."

"We can do some shots with me in the tank."

"Sounds like that'll be *just* what I'm after," he said.

25

Sam took off her boots, slotted them into the rack in the boot room and went through into the kitchen. It'd been a long day, and she was filthy from being out with the horses and tired after an early start and then hours of hard work. Nala—a horse she'd been hoping to sell to a novice eventer in the Midlands—had lost a shoe, and Bertie—a retired racehorse being lined up to be a schoolmaster at a riding school—had an abscess that was going to require a visit from the vet so it could be drained and poulticed.

But it was more than that. She was anxious, with Gaz on the way back with a new delivery. Every trip across the Irish Sea came with a little jolt of apprehension despite the risks being minimised as much as possible, and she lived with the nagging fear that the police would descend upon them as soon as the lorry turned up. And on top of all of *that*, there was what was happening in the field with Connor and Tom and whether Connor would be able to find out what they needed without spooking Tom in the process.

There were a lot of balls in the air, and Sam was the only one capable of keeping them there.

She needed a coffee to perk herself up. She filled the kettle and put it on the Aga to boil, then decided that a little whisky wouldn't go amiss, either. She opened the larder, collected the coffee and her half-empty bottle of Glenfiddich, and, rather than wait, poured herself a finger's worth and sipped it as she took the glass into her study.

She went to the record player and absent-mindedly flipped through the stack of vinyl. She shuffled through albums from the Stones and the Beatles, through more modern cuts from Billie Eilish and Olivia Rodrigo, her fingers resting on the edge of the *Up the Bracket* from The Libertines. She drew it out of the pile, slid the record from the sleeve and put it on the platter. She started the player, lowered the stylus and waited as the bassline from the band's best-known song buzzed through the static.

She hadn't listened to it for months because it brought back memories of her life in London that she would—mostly—prefer to forget. At the time, she'd thought she was having a blast, but now, with the benefit of experience and the clarity of thought that had brought, she saw it differently: it had been a nightmare.

Her childhood had been difficult. Her mother and father had divorced when she was seven. She and her siblings went to live with their mum, but life had quickly become even more complicated. Her mother's new partner, Bryan, was an addict, and as he introduced her to harder and harder drugs, she took less and less interest in her children. She ignored the frequent beatings that Bryan handed out to the kids for seemingly insignificant infractions, preferring to lose herself in weekend-long benders with her children left to fend for themselves. Sam was the oldest and had taken on the responsibility for looking out for her siblings; she cooked for them, made sure they had clean clothes so they wouldn't bring undue attention upon themselves at school, and shepherded them out of the way whenever Bryan returned in one of his increasingly frequent black moods.

Sam ran away three times, and, when the school became concerned about her stunted progress—and the bruises on her arms and legs that were revealed when she changed for games—social services became involved. The children were taken from the house, and Sam's father was awarded sole custody, moving all of them into the farmhouse at the yard.

Sam found stability with her father and did better at school, passing her eleven-plus and taking a place at the local grammar. She started riding and demonstrated enormous ability. There had been talk of her becoming a jockey, but she broke her arm after a fall, and the accident knocked her confidence so much that she didn't get back on a horse until a year later, and by that time, the opportunity had gone. The girl described by her instructor as being 'so good she could ride Badminton on a shire horse' had missed her chance.

She passed her A-levels but, rather than continue her education at university, moved to London with Christopher and found work with a scout for an A&R firm. Her father had been disappointed, he said he was happy to support her decision not to work for a degree, but, in the absence of that, he'd hoped she might be persuaded to come and work for him. Her decision to draw a line under her old life had caused a rift that had only been healed when he was there for her when her life exploded ten years later, he made the offer again and, this time, she accepted.

Until it all went wrong, London certainly had been interesting. She and Christopher were a couple, and they threw themselves wholeheartedly into the hedonistic lifestyle. He played guitar in a band with just enough talent to arouse the interest of the industry, but not enough to lead to a deal. Her job allowed her to blag tickets to industry events, gigs, awards shows and the never-ending round of nights out that started in the Good Mixer or the Dublin Castle or the Hawley Arms and ended up in all-night house parties, finishing with what she came to see as shameful taxi rides back home as normal Londoners roused and set about their days.

Christopher was drawn to self-destruction like a moth to a flame, and she watched with increasing concern as he disappeared for days at a time with his bandmates. They cultivated local infamy for their dissolute lifestyle, and Sam was left with faded drunken memories of the two of them staggering, the worse for wear, out of pubs and bars and clubs. Her father accused Christopher of leading Sam astray and blamed him for introducing her to the harder drugs that had eventually dumped her at rock bottom. But that was sexist, she now knew, a patriarchal stereotype of the bad-boy musician despoiling his once-pure girlfriend. It was a lazy trope and untrue; Sam had no interest in claiming credit, especially not after Christopher's overdose; but it had been *she* who'd introduced *him* to crack and then heroin.

She'd found him after his overdose and, knowing that she was heading in the same direction, had used that as the motivation to check them both into rehab. Her father's offer to come back and help him on the yard had come at the perfect time, and her revived love of horses had been what she had used to get clean and then *stay* clean.

Christopher had stayed behind in London and made the acquaintance of the son of Irish gangsters who were looking for buyers of the coke they were smuggling into the country from South America. Christopher and Sam remained friends, so much so that it had been to her that he'd first confided his money-making idea and how importing the horses from Ireland offered *other* opportunities. Sam saw the potential at once and said she was on board. Christopher worked on the Irish and lined up his father as the onward buyer, Sam worked on the logistics, and everything would have been perfect if it weren't for him falling so spectacularly off the wagon and selling out their friendship for the sake of his greed.

The kettle whistled. She went back into the kitchen, removed it from the heat and then made herself a coffee. She was hungry, too, and, although she would have been happy to go to bed, she knew she still had work to do. Gaz was a couple of hours away, and she needed to feed the new horse before turning him out for the night. And she *still* wouldn't be done. The real work would begin then, and, if previous deliveries were anything to go by, she'd still be up in the early hours.

She opened the fridge and took out the plate of leftovers from last night's dinner. She put it in the microwave to heat up, added another tot of whisky to her coffee and then took the plate and her glass back into the study. 'Times for Heroes'—the Libertine's third single—was just starting, and she hadn't listened to it for years.

26

Tom got up and, a little unsteadily, went over to the pile of rotten posts and dragged another over to the fire. They'd built a generous pyre, and after siphoning off a little red diesel from the tractor to get things going, the flames had quickly taken hold. The temperature had dropped once the sun had dipped beneath the hills, but the heat of the blaze was considerable, and Connor wasn't cold. Tom tossed the post onto the pile and watched it hiss and spit as the moisture evaporated, the wood blackening and then taking light.

Tom pointed over to the tent. "Another beer?"

Connor held up his almost-empty can. "Go on, then." He held up the bag of weed. "Want a spliff to go with it?"

"Thought you'd never ask. Make it a fat one."

Connor took the Rizlas from his pocket, picked out two papers and sealed them together. He took the bag and carefully opened it, pulling away a chunk of weed between his thumb and forefinger and then spreading it out along the centre of the papers. He added a little more until there was a thick line, then rolled the papers to form a tube. He licked the edge and sealed it, took out his Zippo, thumbed a flame and held it so he could light the joint.

He drew down until the flame had taken, inhaling the smoke deep into his lungs and leaning back as his thoughts slowed down.

It'd been a long day, and the work had been demanding, but Connor found that he'd enjoyed himself more than he'd expected. The sense of unease he felt whenever he remembered why they'd brought Tom out here was never far from the surface, but the work had been enough to distract him, and as morning became lunchtime and then the afternoon, he was able to push it to the back of his mind and concentrate on the task in hand.

Tom worked like a demon. He'd always been the strongest of the five of them, and even though the abuse he'd inflicted upon his body had had an effect, he was still very capable. It had taken three hours to remove all of the old posts and rails, and they assembled a pile of them next to the tractor trailer. Most had been easy enough to extract once the earth had been loosened, but a couple had been stubborn, and Tom had forced them out by hand. The rails were easier, with both of them using claw hammers to prise out the rusted nails until the planks dropped to the ground. Tom had suggested they build the bonfire to get rid of the old wood, Connor had been thinking about how to broach the subjects they needed to discuss, and beers and food around a blazing fire might be just the right way to go about it.

Tom had been drinking all day. Connor had encouraged it, knowing that he'd stand a better chance of finding out what they needed if his tongue had been loosened. It hadn't been as easy as he had hoped it might be, he'd known that Tom was a big drinker, but the half-dozen cans didn't look as if they'd had any effect on him at all. He'd chugged one every half an hour, and save for an increased propensity to sing along with whatever was playing on the radio, nothing much had changed. Connor had been drinking, too, although he paced himself carefully so as not to get as drunk as he hoped Tom might become. Tom had finished his six-pack, while Connor still had two cans to go.

"Here."

Tom tossed over a Stella, and Connor caught it. "Swap," he said, holding out the joint.

Tom took it and put it to his lips. He sat down next to Connor and drew on the joint, the tip flaring a brighter red.

Tom popped the top of his beer, and Connor did the same. They touched the two cans together.

"Cheers," Tom said.

"Cheers."

Connor took a sip, watching over the top of the can as Tom chugged down half of the new can. "How are you feeling?"

Tom put the can down, turning it so that it dug into the soft earth. "Getting pissed. How about you?"

"Same." He took a second sip and put the can down. "Fun today, wasn't it? I enjoyed it."

"Me too. I'd forgotten how much I like working in the fresh air." He paused. "You think Sam might think about finding me something to do?"

"At the yard?" He made a show of considering it, knowing that there was no chance in hell that Sam would go along with the idea, but hardly able to tell Tom that. "Maybe. You should ask her—she'll be here again tomorrow."

"We've nearly finished the beer. She'll need to make another supply run."

Connor took a long draw on the joint and handed it back to Tom. "So," he said, trying to keep the anxious edge from his voice, "this woman you were telling me about last night?"

He frowned. "Did we talk about her?"

"You're not going to be coy *now*, are you?"

Tom leaned back, the light of the flames flickering across his face. "What did I say?"

"Not much."

He drew down on the joint, tilted his head and blew smoke. "Good."

"What's her name?"

He paused. "Alice."

"And when are we going to meet her?"

He paused and gazed into the fire. "I don't know."

"Why not?"

"We're going through a bit of a rough patch."

"Really? Why?"

He shrugged. "This and that. I drink too much. She's patient, but everyone has a limit—right?"

"True."

Connor felt sure that there was something Tom wasn't telling him but didn't know how to get at it.

"And," Tom went on, "I kind of want to keep the two parts of my life separate." He held up his left hand and then his right. "You lot on the one hand and her on the other."

"Ashamed of us?"

"Course not."

"I don't suppose it's a bad idea. Anything that makes it less likely she finds out about what we do at the yard's probably not a bad idea."

Tom's brow lowered into a frown. "Come on. You think I'm daft?"

"Why would I think that?"

"You don't *really* think I'd let her find out? Seriously?"

"I'm not saying that."

"Because I'm not getting her involved in *any* of that. That's the *last* thing I'd do—she'd run a mile."

Connor watched Tom's face and knew, from the sudden vehemence of his denial and the way he looked at him to register how he reacted, that he *had* told her. He took a breath. This was the moment he'd been dreading, but there was no way around it; it was the reason they'd brought Tom out here, and the question couldn't be dodged. It had to be asked.

He swallowed. "That night at the Haunch—"

"When I was off my tits," Tom interrupted defensively.

"I know you were," Connor said. "*We* know you were. It's just…"

"Just what?"

"You don't remember, do you?"

"Remember *what*?"

"You said you'd told her about what happened." He lowered his voice even though there was no one within a mile of them. "You know—with Christopher."

"No, I didn't."

"Mate—you *did*."

Tom bit his lip. "What did I say?"

"That you'd told her you'd done something bad. And you said she told you that you should think about going to the police to get it off your chest. You *really* don't remember?"

Tom couldn't hold Connor's eye, and Connor knew that what he was about to say would be a lie. "That was the beer talking."

"How much of it do you remember?"

"I had a blackout. I don't even remember arguing with Sam."

"What about the police?"

"I remember when I woke up in the cell." He took a long drag on the joint, staring at the glowing tip. "I know I've done some stupid things over the years, but come *on*—do you really think I'd do something as stupid as that? To tell her what we did? Tell *anyone*?"

"No," Connor said, forcing himself to laugh. "I don't. But you *have* done some stupid things. Do you remember when you ran naked down Fisherton Street after we got pissed in Wetherspoons?"

The anxiety on Tom's face dissolved into relief. "Jesus. How long ago was *that*?"

"Back when it was the Town House."

"Years, then," Tom said with a chuckle. "Nikki dared me."

"Or when you climbed down the outside of the Culver Street car park."

"That was after school."

"You were racing Gaz. First one to the bottom won ten quid."

It was heartbreaking. Connor knew his friend more than well enough to know when he was lying, and he was as sure as he could possibly be that he was lying now. He *had* told the woman about what had happened—either in detail or in general, it didn't really matter—and now Connor was going to have to tell Sam, and once he'd done that, things would pick up pace. Tom had made them all vulnerable, and he knew Sam well enough to know that she would be ruthless in making them safe again.

And that wouldn't be good for Tom or his woman, whoever she was.

27

Sam heard the sound of the lorry as it rumbled down the drive to the yard. She lifted the needle from the record, lowered it back onto its cradle and went outside.

The lights of the truck swung across the empty stables. The horses were all out in the fields now that the weather was warmer, so they would be able to get to work without disturbing them.

Gaz backed the truck up and stopped with enough space to lower the ramp at the side. He turned off the engine and jumped down.

"How was it?" Sam asked.

"Long."

She nodded to the truck. "Horse okay?"

"Had her moments. Kicked the shit out of the lorry when we were on the ferry, but she calmed down once we landed. Been all right since."

Sam went to the side of the truck, undid the two latches that secured the ramp, and then carefully lowered it to the ground. The interior of the vehicle was split into two separate bays, and the bay on the far side accommodated a grey mare. Sam reached down to unlatch the screen that divided the compartment and pulled it aside so the horse could be led down the ramp. It was a ten-year-old and was, once again, supposed to have a reliable and placid temperament. Sam led it to the nearest stable, opened the door and ushered it inside. She'd filled one of the nets, and the horse ambled over to it, quickly forgetting the indignities of the long journey and setting to work on the hay. Sam had decided that it would be one of the first horses to go into the new field; she'd give it time to acclimatise to its new surroundings before bringing it into the manège so she could judge it properly.

Gaz was inside the lorry. The floor was smeared with urine and excrement that the horse had trodden on, and he went and got a pressure washer and cleaned it out. Sam helped, taking down the empty hay net and then using a broom to sweep the foul mixture down the ramp, where Gaz sent it on its way with another carefully aimed blast from the hose. Sam cleared the area at the back of the compartment, then took the screwdriver from her pocket and used it to undo the four screws that secured the hidden panel. She used the tip of the screwdriver to prise it up, sliding her fingers between it and the floor and lifting it away.

The cavity beneath was reasonably large—a metre by a metre, and fifty centimetres deep—and had been carefully installed with a hermetic seal that kept the urine out and the smell from the cargo in. All of the available space was taken up by plastic-wrapped packages.

Gaz picked one up, turned to Sam and grinned. "This is the highlight of my month. Money!"

He tossed the package over, and Sam caught it. It was about the same weight as a bag of sugar, but the contents were worth *much* more. The wholesale price was thirty thousand for every kilogram, with a street price of sixty pounds per gram. Alexander Freeman would cut the cocaine with bulking agents before it was ready for retail, meaning that each kilogram bag would eventually be worth anywhere between seventy and ninety thousand.

Sam stood over Gaz and counted the bags; there were ten, exactly as many as she'd ordered. The consignment had cost Alexander Freeman three hundred thousand, but past performance suggested he'd clear four hundred in profit once all was said and done. The fee for importing the coke was fifty per cent of Freeman's profit, meaning Sam and the others would be looking at tens of thousands each if, as had been the case for the last few months, Tom's share went back into the pot.

Not this time, though.

Sam wasn't inclined to share any more.

"We need to get it out of the way," she said.

Gaz stood. "Better do it now."

Because why *should* she share? Christopher had offered her the opportunity, but making it work had been all her. She'd seen the opportunity when she'd come back home to help her father. He'd been buying horses from Irish dealers for years, and she'd realised that the vans—with horses inside—would be a reliable way of smuggling contraband over the border. The smell of their ordure would go some way to confuse sniffer dogs, and customs officials would be much less likely to require a search of a vehicle if that meant disturbing the animals inside. Christopher had loved the proposal. Sam had sold it to the others as an opportunity to get rich, and they'd all been enthusiastic in saying yes.

More than a year had passed, and they'd never had even the slightest inkling that they were suspected or that customs had any idea at all what they were doing.

Sam reached into the cavity and took out the second package, tossing it down to Gaz. They worked quickly, removing all of the packets and then closing up the false panel and screwing it back into place.

They took the bags to an empty stable and brushed aside the bed of straw that had been laid in readiness for the next inhabitant. Sam unlocked the padlock that secured the trapdoor that led down into the cellar. She opened the door, climbed down the stairs and fumbled across the wall for the light switch. She found it and had to blink her eyes against the sudden glare. Alexander Freeman had provided the cash to excavate the cellar when they realised they needed somewhere more secure and discreet to keep their product out of sight until he was ready to take it. The space wasn't large—Sam could stretch out both hands and touch the walls—but it was hard to find unless you knew it was there. It had a poured concrete floor and concrete walls, with double runs of metal shelving.

Gaz peered down. "Ready?"

"Go on."

He dropped down the first packet, and Sam slotted it onto an empty shelf. The next came down and then the next, the two of them continuing until the bags had all been stacked.

Sam climbed back up, switched off the light and let Gaz take care of securing and then hiding the trapdoor once more.

"Drink?" Sam asked him when the straw had been put back in place.

"Thought you'd never ask."

28

Connor waited until midnight before he thought about trying to get into Tom's phone. He lay in his sleeping bag and stared up at the roof of the tent until he was as sure as he could be that Tom was asleep. Connor knew he'd had a skinful and, remembering what Tom was like after a big session, was confident that he'd sleep through until the morning again. But what if he needed a piss? What if something disturbed him, and he woke up to see Connor with his phone in his hand? He'd have to tell him that he had found it—he could say it'd slipped beneath his sleeping bag—and hope that he'd be too dazed to see through the lie.

He went to his pack and took out the phone and the power bank. He took the phone, tapped the screen and stared at it. It was an old iPhone, not new enough to have Face ID and relying upon the old fingerprint scanner or a passcode to unlock it. He tapped the screen again and saw that the battery was now fully charged.

He was still nervous as he slowly unzipped his bag, crawled out and edged closer to Tom. He was on his side, his head resting on his bent left arm with his right hand reaching out across the groundsheet. His hand was palm down, with his fingers cupped into a loose fist. Connor looked at his left hand, but that was also palm down, with his cheek resting across half of it. It wasn't going to be easy, but he thought using the right ought to be easier than the left.

He reached down and, very gently, took Tom's right wrist and turned it so that his fist was perpendicular to the ground. He took Tom's index finger and started to straighten it when Tom snorted and jerked his hand away. Tom's eyes flicked open; Connor froze, turning his left hand to obscure the phone, scrambling for an excuse to explain why he had touched him, his thoughts frozen uselessly.

Tom's eyes stared, unfocused, and then closed. He drew in a deep breath and exhaled, lowering his head back onto his shoulder and stretching out his right arm once more. This time, though, his palm faced up, and his fingers were splayed. Connor moved quickly, waking the screen again and then holding the scanner against the pad of Tom's index finger.

He withdrew the phone and looked at the screen but saw it hadn't unlocked. He ground his teeth together, checked to make sure he was using the right part of the screen—he was sure he was—and tried again.

This time, the screen glowed as the phone unlocked.

Connor stood, stepped through the opening of the tent and went outside. He walked into the field, far enough away that he would have plenty of notice if Tom was to wake, and held up the phone. He'd had a similar model before, and his familiarity with it allowed him to navigate quickly to the settings. He found the controls for display and brightness, scrolled down to the auto-lock function and toggled it from 'after five minutes' to 'never.' The phone would remain unlocked, and he wouldn't have to go through this rigmarole again.

He opened the messages app and started to read.

29

Connor looked up into the inky black sky, knowing that the conversation he was about to have was going to move them another step—at least—along a path he'd hoped they wouldn't have to take. Sam had been unhappily confident that what came next was unavoidable but had allowed Connor to persuade her that it was worth getting Tom out here where they could talk. Connor didn't know what he'd hoped to achieve, perhaps Tom might have given him enough for him to persuade Sam they didn't have to do anything about the woman, but that had been wishful thinking. The messages he'd read on the phone had been eloquent about how much Tom had said, and how much trouble they were all in because of his indiscretion.

No turning back now.

They had no choice.

He took out his own phone and called Sam.

"Yes?"

"It's me," Connor said.

"Everything okay?"

"Not really."

"Did you speak to him?"

"A little—but it's not that. I got into his phone."

"And?"

"I know who she is and where she lives."

"How much has he said?"

"Looks like everything."

Sam muttered a curse, and then the line was silent.

Connor wondered if he had lost the signal. "Sam? You still there?"

"I'm here."

"There is *some* good news, though. Looks like they might have split up. It doesn't look like she wanted him to go to the police, but he made up his mind that he has to."

"Doesn't make any difference. She still knows."

"What are we going to do?"

"We talked about it—we all agreed. I'll get Gaz and Nikki to pay her a visit. What's her name?"

"Alice Green. She has a place in the Close. I'll send the details."

"Keep him in the field. How much longer do you think you'll need to finish?"

"I don't know," Connor said. "We had a productive day today. Got lots done. We could probably finish on Thursday if the rain stays off. Maybe Friday if I slow things down. How long do you think you'll need?"

"Aim for Friday. Thursday will be too soon. It's busy—Gaz got here with the delivery tonight, and I'm going to have to take care of that and then *this*."

"That was all okay, though? The delivery?"

"That was fine. Tom, though..." She cursed again. "*Jesus*. Why couldn't he have just kept his mouth shut?"

Connor pressed the phone to his ear and winced with discomfort at what they were proposing to do. "Are you sure, Sam? There's no other way?"

"We went around the houses on this for *hours*. If you have a better plan, I'm all ears."

He sucked on his teeth.

"Do you?"

"No," he admitted.

"No. So this is it—we don't have a choice. Send me her details, and I'll get them onto it."

He tapped through to the contacts app. "Sending it now."

There was a pause; then she reported that she'd received it. "Keep him in the field, and I'll let you know when it's done."

"What about him? Tom, I mean. What do we do about *him*?"

"I don't know," she said. "I'm going to need to think about that."

30

Atticus spent the rest of the day writing the report he would send to Frank Green. There wasn't much to say at the moment, but writing down his thoughts gave him a chance to think about the avenues he would need to consider when answering the questions about Alice's business and finances. Working on the report was depressing, given how unpleasant both the Greens appeared to be, but he consoled himself with how much money he could make and how helpful that would be for Mack.

He finished at four, and with the weather set fair for the rest of the day, he put the dog in the car and drove down to the beach at Hengistbury Head. They walked for an hour and then turned around and walked back. Atticus took off his shoes and socks and walked through the surf, throwing a ball into the waves so Bandit had to swim out to retrieve it. He was able to clear his mind of everything that had been bothering him, and, by the time he returned to the car and towelled the dog down, he was as relaxed as he could remember. He made a mental note to bring Mack down to the beach at the weekend; she needed the peace and quiet even more than he did.

* * *

Atticus got a take-out from Giggling Squid and ate it while finishing the final episode of *The Jinx*, the Netflix documentary he'd been watching. He finished it, reflecting upon how convenient it would be if all criminals were as inattentive as Bob Durst, and then undressed for bed. He took out his laptop and spent an hour identifying half a dozen captchas: a street in Rio, another in Denver, a building in Birmingham. He managed the last one in just over two minutes and was about to attempt another when Bandit got up and growled at the door.

"What is it, boy?"

Bandit glanced back at Atticus and then returned to his previous position, his posture rigid and his nose pointed at the door. It wasn't that he needed the toilet, he whined and pawed at Atticus's arm whenever he needed that, and, besides, he'd been out in the courtyard for fifteen minutes not long ago. Atticus got up, went to the door, pulled back the curtain and looked outside. The door opened out onto the platform that served both his rooms and next door, with a flight of stairs descending into the courtyard. It was dark down there, and Atticus wasn't able to see anything that might have explained what had agitated the dog. It could've been a fox, he thought. He'd seen them in the Close, scampering from bin to bin, and it wasn't too much of a stretch to think that one had found its way through the grounds of Sarum College and then over the wall.

Atticus might not have been able to see anything, but Bandit's agitation was not assuaged. He remained in the same position, head forward and tail extended backwards, hackles raised as he kept up the same angry growl.

"There's nothing there."

The dog growled louder.

"Fine," Atticus said. "Knock yourself out."

He unlocked the door, opened it, and watched as Bandit rushed out onto the platform. He turned right and then left, clattering down the stairs and arrowing straight for the alcove on the left-hand side of the courtyard, where the bins were kept. There was a motion-detecting security light on the wall of the jewellery workshop, and Bandit activated it, the light throwing out a sudden glare that picked out the tree in the middle of the courtyard and cast its shadow out across the cobbles. Bandit was frozen stock-still, snout aimed directly into the space where the bins were kept. The recess was deep, and Atticus wasn't able to see into it from his vantage point. Bandit didn't move, and, as Atticus realised with a sinking feeling that he was going to have to go down there and investigate, the dog started to bark.

Atticus muttered a curse under his breath, looked for his dressing gown and then cursed again as he remembered he'd taken it in to be dry-cleaned after he'd spilled half a can of tomato soup over it last week. He was wearing only his boxer shorts, but it was a warm night, and there was no one else around, and he couldn't be bothered to dress; he grabbed his phone for its flashlight, stepped out onto the platform in his bare feet and climbed down the stairs. He reached the bottom, and as he took a step toward the dog, he saw motion next to the large industrial bin that served the businesses around the courtyard.

He switched on the phone's torch and held it up.

"Hey!"

A man was standing with his back to the bin. The courtyard was gloomy, and Atticus's eyes hadn't adjusted to the glare of the floodlight. He only caught glimpses: unkempt dark curly hair, pale skin, eyes that were wide and urgent.

"Hey," Atticus repeated. "This is private property."

He held up his arm in an attempt to shield his eyes, and, as he did, the man edged around the wall and started for the passageway to the street. Atticus caught more detail as the man passed beneath the floodlight: he was dressed in a black hoodie and dark trousers, with both garments looking worn.

Bandit growled and looked as if he was going to give pursuit. Atticus reached down for his collar and held him in place as the man made his way through the passage to the door, passing through it and turning left onto New Street. Atticus would have given chase, but the prospect of pursuing him into the city while dressed in just his shorts did not fill him with enthusiasm.

Telling Bandit to sit and stay, he went to the street door and pulled it back. He was sure that he'd locked it again when he returned home, and since it had been late, he was reasonably confident that the occupants of the two other flats—his upstairs neighbour, Jacob, and the woman who'd moved into the adjacent flat—would already have been in bed. The door was intact, with no signs that it had been forced. He shone his torch on the lock itself, but any telltale scrapes or scratches from a pick or a wrench were lost amid the damage that had been inflicted through the clumsy use of keys over the years. He saw a dark patch on the wood beneath the cylinder and, already sure what it was, dabbed his fingers against it to check; they came away sticky, and, when he held them to his nose, he caught a distinctive smell.

Fish oil.

The trespasser had used it to lubricate the lock so it was easier to pick.

He wiped his fingers on his shorts, pulled the door closed and went back to the bins. One large industrial unit served all of the buildings around the courtyard, and its lid had been pushed all the way back. Atticus shone his torch inside, but it was impossible to see what the intruder might have been looking for. There was cardboard packaging from the jeweller's workshop, clear plastic sheaths used to protect the wedding dresses from the bridal shop beneath his office, bin bags full of cut hair from the salon. There was a dental practice on the opposite side of the courtyard, and Atticus settled on the most likely explanation: the intruder was a junkie who had found his way inside in the hope of finding drugs. It wouldn't have been the first time that had happened.

Atticus reached for the lid, closed it and was about to go back up to his room when he noticed two sheets of paper that had blown away from the bin, catching in the low shrubs in the middle of the courtyard. He knelt down, picked them up and shone the torch on them. He recognised his handwriting, and a page of notes he'd scribbled down during the investigation into the discovery of Alf Burns's body in Imber. Atticus would usually have been careful when disposing of anything from work, but this was a stream-of-consciousness dump of theories and suppositions that would have been inconsequential to anyone but him, and that had been enough to save it from the shredder. But the fact that it had been removed from the bin was enough to disabuse him of his first conclusion: the intruder most likely wasn't here for drugs or even for a random bin dip in the hope of finding something valuable.

He was here to look for information that came from *him*.

PART 3

31

Alice Green woke up and did the thing she always did first thing in the morning: reached over for her phone, woke it and navigated to the website that hosted her online courses. She smiled: another twenty Real Wild Swimming courses and eight Real Wild Meditations had been sold, bringing in a total of ten thousand pounds and change. It'd been a lot of work to build her reputation, prepare the material and then put together the marketing system that sold them, but now the work was done, she didn't have to do very much at all. This was the best example of that: her system was so finely calibrated, so expertly tuned, that it made money for her while she slept.

Frank had always made her feel second-best in their relationship. It was *his* success and *his* money, and when things started to go badly between them, he'd painted her as a parasite. He'd called her a succubus—as if *he* knew what that meant—someone who'd latched onto him as her meal ticket. She'd started her Real Wild businesses to insulate herself against that and to prove to him, and also to herself, that she could be a success on her own terms.

The first sales, and the promise they represented, had given her the guts to walk out of the marriage. Frank had reacted about as badly as she'd expected, and the rancour between them had increased as the lawyers tried to find a divorce settlement that would be acceptable to both. She was doing well, but he had resources that far outmatched hers, and his lawyers were the best that money could buy. The divorce was one-sided, but Alice had accepted the terms in the knowledge that she'd punish him in another way. She'd been given half a million, and that—and a hefty mortgage—was enough to buy the house in the Close.

She'd waited until the ink was dry on the settlement, and then she started to exact her revenge.

She opened her calendar and remembered that she had a second meeting with the journalist from yesterday. What was his name? She'd quite enjoyed the first meeting. There was something unusual about him—his manner was more awkward than she would've expected from someone who made a living speaking to people—but he seemed interested in her and the business, and there was no getting away from the fact that coverage in a popular magazine would do wonders for her exposure. She'd seen it happen before: the BBC had asked her to go on *South Today*, and, despite grumbling about the schlepp down to the studio in Southampton, she'd gone and done it and saw a flurry of enquiries in the days afterwards. She was good at using social media to find leads, but there was nothing wrong in opening other channels, too. A half-dozen sales on the back of the interview would be a decent return on the time spent, and besides, the journalist—Ryan or Ronan or whatever—had been easy on the eye, too. That didn't hurt.

She wasn't quite sure whether she was single, but the last messages to and from Tom suggested they'd reached the end of the road. He had issues, and Alice didn't have time to deal with them, especially when he made it obvious he was going to ignore her advice and do something that would be catastrophically bad for his future prospects. He was going to get arrested and charged, and she wasn't the sort of dutiful little woman who'd go back and forward to prison to see him for the next fifteen years.

She didn't care. She hadn't made any promises of monogamy, and, even if they *were* still together, what he didn't know wouldn't hurt him.

And Ryan *was* cute…

32

Gaz had only just bought the new Discovery and was still inordinately proud of it as he pulled away from the kerb outside the house on Bouverie Avenue. Sam had warned them about being careful with making flashy purchases, and, when they'd started out, Gaz and Nikki had been just as careful as all the others. But they'd been doing this for a while now, and there'd been no suggestion that the police or customs or *anyone* had any idea of what they were up to. The mess with Christopher had put the wind up them, but even that had passed without consequences.

And he'd always wanted a Disco…

Sam had been the one who reminded them to be discreet, but it had been *her* who'd been the first to splash out. The price of the horse she competed on—what had it been, forty thousand?—was *way* more than she would've been able to justify from the money made from the yard. That'd been the green light for Gaz, and he'd splurged on the car. It was funny, he thought: out of all of them, it was Tom who'd stuck to the advice for the longest, yet *he'd* been the one who'd done something that had them all fearful of being found out.

Nikki had her feet up on the dash.

"Come on, babes," Gaz said, pointing. "What did I say about that?"

She lowered them. "Sorry. Forgot." She glanced over at him. "Someone's feeling grouchy this morning."

"Are you surprised? I'm knackered."

"What time did you get into bed?"

"Two." He checked the clock on the dash. "I've had three hours' sleep."

She reached over and squeezed his knee. "Poor baby."

"Unlike *some* people I could mention. You were snoring, too."

"No, I *wasn't*."

He reached the Harnham Gyratory and stopped at the lights. "Cork and back. You know how many miles that is?"

"I know, babes. It's a lot."

"Three hundred and eighty-seven," he said. "Three hundred and eighty-seven miles *there* and three hundred and eighty-seven *back* in a horse box that stinks of piss with ten kilograms of coke hidden in the floor and a horse kicking seven shades of shit out of the walls whenever we stop." The lights went to green, and he pulled out. "Twelve hours there, spend the night in a shitty hotel, pick up the horse, drive to meet the Gallaghers—who were scarier than normal, by the way—then another twelve hours back. Twenty-four hours on the road in two days, and then, when all I want is a lie-in and a greasy breakfast, Sam has us both up at four in the bloody morning."

"She says this is important."

"I know she does," he said. "What do you think?"

"I think this'll turn out to be a waste of time, babes."

He nodded emphatically. "Me too."

"We see her; we make it *crystal* clear that she needs to forget everything that Tom's told her, make her realise what a stupid idea it'd be for her to open her mouth and start blabbing. We do that, we put the fear of God into her, then we go. That's it."

Gaz waved his hand dismissively. "It's all bollocks."

They reached the Exeter Street roundabout and took the second exit, heading into town.

Nikki took her balaclava out of her pocket. "Got yours?"

Gaz patted his pockets and feigned dismay. "*Shit*. Left it at home."

"Don't joke, babes."

He pulled the balaclava from his pocket and held it up.

Nikki picked at a loose thread on her balaclava. "So this woman goes out every morning to swim."

"Five Rivers won't be open yet."

"Not there. Wild swimming—in the countryside."

"In the river?"

Nikki nodded. "She has an online business. Teaches people about how cold water can fix all their problems."

"Seriously?"

"I know. It sounded nuts when Sam told me, too, but apparently people pay good money for it."

"Sucker born every minute."

"I know—*right?* So she records videos of herself in the river early every morning. Sam said we follow her and then have a word when she gets there. No one will see us, and it'll be more frightening when she realises she's in a swimsuit in the middle of nowhere on her own."

"All right," he said.

Gaz reached forward, switched on the entertainment system and navigated to Salisbury Radio, where the new Taylor Swift song was playing.

33

Alice took a quick shower, pulled on her swimming costume and dryrobe, grabbed a towel for her hair, and went downstairs. She made herself a coffee, pouring it into a flask to drink on the way, and went outside. It was a reasonable drive to Standlynch, and she wanted to be there before the early dog-walkers so she could film today's video without anyone else around. She had two products to pimp: a line of sustainable swimsuits from an ethical brand in Cornwall and a lotion infused with CBD that was marketed as a way to 'intensify' the experience of wild swimming. Alice knew the manufacturers of both products were full of shit but didn't care, they'd agreed to pay her five thousand each to be featured in one of her videos, and that was good enough for her. She'd be in the water for ten minutes, and that would be long enough to bank what her parents would've made in two months. Her dad had been sceptical about the business until she'd told him how much money she was making for such minimal effort; 'money for old rope' was what he'd said, and for once she couldn't disagree.

* * *

Alice drove through Downton, turning left just after the church for the five-minute drive to the spot on the river she'd chosen for the morning's swim. The countryside was open once she was out of the village, and, as dawn broke over the fields, the only other people she saw were a farmer ploughing the large field to the right and a cyclist struggling up the hill that would eventually lead down into Alderbury.

She reached the left-hand turn that would take her to the water. It was little more than a track, winding right and then left; she passed a holiday cottage and then a construction site where it looked like they were going to build another house, and then came to the old chapel. The building had been closed for seventy years and was reputed to be the resting place for many of Lord Nelson's relatives, erstwhile residents at the nearby Trafalgar Place. She continued, driving carefully until she reached the section of track that had been paved with concrete, finally coming to a stop at the side of the road next to the old mill.

She got out of the car, went around to the boot and took out her equipment. That was another thing about an online business like hers: you needed to be professional, but there was something to be said for the authenticity of a simple set-up. She shot all her videos on a simple Sony DSLR, setting it up on a tripod and recording her sound with a Zoom recorder she placed as near to the water's edge as she could. The resulting videos weren't flashy or impressive, but that didn't matter. Alice knew it was essential to build a connection between her and her audience, and flashy videos tended to add distance rather than closeness. That her videos were cheap and easy to make was a virtue.

She took the tripod and the recorder and walked the rest of the way to the river. The Avon split here: one stretch fed the mill pond, the water rushing beneath the building and out the other side; the second stretch rushed over a weir into a deep pool before the two merged again. A footpath crossed the weir and allowed access to the water meadows to the east of Charlton-All-Saints. Alice walked to the weir and found her usual position: a raised bank where she could set up the camera above a muddy crescent of beach that sloped down into the water. She opened the legs of the tripod and set it up, attaching the camera to the mount and switching it on, waiting for the shot to come into focus and then adjusting it a touch so that it included everything she wanted. She connected the microphone, wedged it against a rock at the edge of the bank, and, after checking that everything was good, took off the robe and stepped carefully into the water.

The mud slurped around her feet as she stepped out, the water reaching up to her knees and then to her waist. She continued into the deepest part of the pool, gasping as the cold reached up to her heart. She took another three steps until the water was too deep for her to stand, and then trod water as she turned to face back to the camera.

"Good morning," she said, remembering to raise her voice so it was audible over the steady rush of the water running over the weir. "I'm Alice Green from Real Wild Swimming, and I'm here this morning in my favourite pool near Downton in Wiltshire. It's five thirty, and I'm here alone—just me, the sound of the water and the birds in the trees. I read an article in the *Daily Mail* yesterday doubting whether wild swimming and cold-water immersion really is all it's cracked up to be, and I decided I'd spend this morning's video addressing some of the points raised and demonstrating that it was written by a hater who was just looking for clicks."

She'd been making these videos for long enough now that she could rattle them off with minimal preparation. The article in the *Mail* was still fresh in her head, and she had more than enough ammunition to refute the claims that had been made. She'd been hesitant in front of the camera when she'd started and had taken down some of her early videos on account of the fact that she stuttered, repeated herself, and generally looked embarrassed. But, because she'd recorded something every day for the last eighteen months, she'd grown into a much more confident and persuasive speaker. She'd been told it was one of her 'superpowers'; potential students felt a bond with her, thanks to her 'unflinching honesty.' She saw it in the comments, with people she'd never met writing about how amazing she was, how much she'd changed their lives, what a difference she'd made. She'd excitedly shown Frank, but he'd dismissed the messages as confirmation bias, just gullible marks telling themselves that the person they'd given their money to was as valuable as they believed. Frank had never *once* praised her for what she'd built; it was another reason why she was better off without him and why she was enjoying the ordeal she was putting him through now.

She finished the first part of the video and then moved straight on to talk about the swimsuit. She'd memorised the points that the manufacturer wanted her to cover—sustainability, ethical credentials, handmade in England, blah, blah, blah—and included them smoothly, ignoring the fact that the material was uncomfortable, that it was almost certainly put together in a Chinese sweatshop and didn't look like it would last for very long. She put all of those concerns aside and concentrated on the money that would be in her bank account by the end of the day.

She finished, kicked for the bank and clambered out. Her skin tingled in the cool air, and she felt the familiar buzz as endorphins were released. She put on her dryrobe, went over to the camera and reached for the button to end the recording. She looked down at the screen and saw, to her annoyance, that the recording had stopped.

The display flashed that the memory card was full.

She cursed under her breath.

She was going to have to record it again.

She checked her watch. At least she had plenty of time before she was due in the studio for the rest of the interview with the journalist. She had a collection of empty memory cards in the car. She'd go and grab one, record the video again and then the video for the ointment, then head straight back to Salisbury.

She hated having to repeat a task, but at least it'd be quick.

She left the camera and the microphone where they were and made her way back to the mill.

34

Alice made her way back along the track to the mill and got into the car. She had a small Tupperware box in the glove box that she used to keep her memory cards, and she opened it and took one out. She was warm in the dryrobe, and the prospect of getting back in the water—especially when she ought not to have had to—was annoying.

Think of the money, she reminded herself.

She'd take a moment for herself before going back in, though. She reached down for the flask of coffee that was wedged into the cupholder and took it, and her phone, outside. The sun was just peeking above the trees, and light filtered through leaves that rustled in the gentle breeze. Two mallards called from overhead, swinging around to line up with the mill pond and then descending steeply, carving furrows in the green-blue water as they splashed down. This was an idyllic spot, and, of all the places she had found to swim, probably her favourite. It was quiet, she was rarely observed, and it had a bucolic English charm—the river, the old mill, the oak tree that spread its canopy over the pool—that translated well in videos and was like catnip to those looking to emulate her lifestyle. She could come here and relax and, as she did, make money.

She unscrewed the top of the flask, filled the lid with coffee and took it over to the grassy bank that ran down to the millpond. She sat, taking a sip of the coffee before resting the cup on the ground and taking out her phone. She frowned; she'd missed a call from Sarah. It was unusual for her to call this early; she got up later before making her way to the studio to start work.

Alice opened the phone and saw that it wasn't one missed call, but three.

There were text messages, too, including one from Frank. There was no reason for *him* to be in touch, and it was with a tentative finger that she opened it. The message had no words, just the meme from the video for *Thriller* with Michael Jackson eating popcorn and a link to a page on Medium.

She tapped the link, waited for her browser to open and then saw the headline on the article:

WELLNESS INFLUENCER AGREES TO PROMOTE UNTESTED PRODUCT.

Alice immediately felt sick.

There was a clamminess in her palms and down her back, and her legs felt empty, as if they had been hollowed out. She scrolled down, saw a photograph of her—it looked like a still from a video with her studio in the background—and then, beneath that, bullet points that summarised the content of the article. She scanned quickly—'British influencer secretly filmed agreeing to promote harmful product', 'Guru Alice Green has over 1m followers', 'Green told product contained poison'—and then saw the ticker reporting the level of engagement.

The article had been posted only hours earlier, and there were already more than two thousand comments and five thousand likes.

Her head felt like it was going to explode.

She remembered: the guy who'd come in last week from a pharmaceutical startup, saying they had a miracle anti-anxiety drug that was going to do more for mental health than Wegovy had done for weight loss, offering her fifteen thousand to film an endorsement for her followers. She panicked again, trying to remember what he'd told her about the drug and what *she'd* said. He'd mentioned something about it being untested, but he'd been persuasive about their confidence that it'd work and that the side effects would be minimal, and, he'd argued, just *think* about the benefits that a drug like that could bring and the changes it could make to the lives of people who suffered from anxiety.

Alice hadn't cared about any of it.

It was the money…

She'd been unable to ignore the money.

What had she done?

She scrolled down to the comments, glanced at them—they were *all* hostile—and looked away, then closed the window and opened Facebook. She had dozens of notifications, many more than would have been normal, and, as she tapped to open them, she saw she'd been tagged in posts and comments and messages from students, a flood of negativity that polluted her page, her group and the comments on the video she'd posted from yesterday's swim. She swiped up to close the app, opened her mail and saw more than a hundred unopened messages, their subject lines mixing anger and gloating and confusion.

Bile raced up her gullet. She had the sudden certainty that everything she had worked toward, the life she had willed into existence through hours of hard graft and dedication, was at risk of being torn from her grasp.

She lowered her phone and, for a moment, was sure she was going to be sick.

She needed to speak to her lawyer. There must be something they could do to put a lid on this. Her mind whirled.

It was Frank.

He was behind this.

He'd tricked her, sent a fake rep to reel her in and had their meeting recorded?

This was his revenge for what she'd done to him.

There must be *something* that the lawyers could do to put a lid on this, to get the post taken down, *something*.

Her lawyer was usually in the office by eight.

There was no time to waste.

She had to get back to Salisbury.

Now.

Alice tossed the rest of her now-cold coffee onto the ground, went back to the car and took the bag with her clothes from the front seat. The track was still quiet in both directions, and she'd changed beneath her dryrobe enough times for it to be quick. When she was done, she put her wet costume into the empty bag and tossed it onto the passenger seat. She towelled off her hair, then removed her dryrobe and tossed it and the towel onto the floor in the back.

And then she heard the car.

35

Alice turned to watch as a large black Land Rover Discovery negotiated the left-hand turn after the chapel and continued down toward the mill. It looked as if there were two people in the car—the driver and a passenger—and she looked on as the Discovery turned and blocked the road. It looked as if the driver was going to execute a three-point turn, but they didn't. Alice's confusion quickly became annoyance as the passenger opened the door and stepped out.

Alice could tell from the slender frame that it was a woman, but her face was obscured by the balaclava she was wearing. The woman stared at her but didn't speak. Alice felt a knot of ice in her gut. She was alone, and the first dog walkers didn't usually get here for another thirty or forty minutes. Alice could feel the woman's eyes on her as she collected the coffee flask and put it into the car.

She hoped that the woman might take the hint that she was about to leave, but she didn't.

The woman—and the Land Rover—were unmoved, still in the same position and still blocking the track.

The driver turned off the engine and stepped out. He was male, around six feet tall and well built. He was wearing a balaclava, too.

"I know what this is," Alice said.

"Do you?" the woman said.

"It's obvious. And *pathetic.*"

"What is it?"

"You work for Frank."

"Frank?"

"He sent you to give me a scare. Well, you can tell him to piss off—I'm not scared of him, and I'm not scared of you."

The passenger turned to the driver. "Who's Frank?"

"Don't know," the driver replied.

The passenger took a step toward Alice. "Who's Frank?"

She'd tried to find the chutzpah to lend a little credibility to her defiance, but she didn't feel it, and it was obvious the man and the woman were not in the least bit daunted.

"Leave me alone," Alice said. "Come a step closer, and I'll scream."

"Fine," the passenger said. She turned to the driver. "Where did you say the nearest house was?"

"The holiday cottage," he said. "But there's no one there."

"Hear that? No one there. Scream all you like—no one's going to hear a thing."

"There's a dog walker at the weir," Alice said.

The passenger shook her head. "No, there isn't."

"I'm calling the police."

The man stepped toward her, a sudden movement that caught her by surprise. She tried to step back, but he was too fast. He reached down for her wrist and grasped it firmly, dragging her closer to him and then spinning her around so he could wrap his other arm around her. Fear washed over her, and she tried to scream, the exclamation quickly muffled as the man let go of her wrist to reach up and clamp his hand over her mouth.

Alice sank her teeth into the muscle between his thumb and forefinger. She tasted his blood in her mouth and heard his sharp yelp of pain. His grip loosened, and she managed to duck down so that she could slide out from beneath his crooked elbow.

The man looked down at his hand. Blood was welling in the indentations left by Alice's teeth. "Silly *bitch*."

Alice turned back to the track that led to the weir and ran.

She filled her lungs and sprinted as hard as she could, the sound of pursuit right behind her. She was barefoot, and sharp stones cut into her skin. She risked a glance back, stumbled over a rut in the track and landed face first in the muck. She tried to get up, but her feet slipped, and she fell again, finally regaining her balance just as the man reached her.

"Stay away from me," she said, backing away.

The man reached for her and grabbed her by the wrist.

"Get… off… me…"

She tried to wrench herself out of his grip, but he held on tight. He pulled her in close enough for her to knee him in the groin, he grunted in pain and let go, but the effort had overbalanced her, and she stumbled back, her heel catching in a rut. She lost her balance completely and fell, her head cracking against something hard at the side of the track. There was mud and water in her mouth and nostrils, but she was barely aware of it before the darkness raced up and swamped her.

36

Gaz stared down at the woman. She wasn't moving.

"*Babes,*" Nikki said.

"She *kneed* me—you saw, right? She kneed me in the *nuts.*"

"Shit," Nikki said.

"I know—she bit me." He held up his hand to show the blood in the cleft between his thumb and forefinger.

"Not that," Nikki said. She pointed down at the woman. "Look at her, babes—she's not moving."

Gaz knelt down next to her body and prodded her. "You can stop that now, you silly bitch. You think we're going to fall for that? You think we're *idiots*?"

She didn't move.

Nikki knelt down next to him. "Maybe she isn't messing around."

"She *is,*" Gaz said. He gave the woman another poke. "Come on—stop being daft and open your eyes."

Nikki bit her lip. "Are you sure?"

"I didn't touch her," Gaz said. "You saw—she tripped."

"Is she breathing?" Nikki said. "I don't think she's breathing."

Nikki bent over so she was closer to the woman's face. Her eyes were closed. She looked at her lips, then held her hand down over them in the hope that she might be able to feel her breath.

"Do her pulse," Gaz said.

Nikki rested her fingers on the side of her neck, turning her head a little so she could reach the artery. The woman's head had been resting on a large stone—a chunk of chalk—and the white of the rock was stained with brown earth and the bright red of blood.

Gaz swore and pointed down at the bloodied stone. "She must've hit it when she fell."

"Looks like it."

"Can you feel anything?"

Nikki held her fingers against the side of her neck, then moved them to a different position, then moved them again. "There's nothing." She moved her fingers again and again. "She's dead."

Gaz tore off his balaclava. "Bollocks."

Nikki bit her nail. "*Bollocks.*"

"What do we do?"

Nikki looked around: the river, the trees and bushes growing behind the banks, the empty mill house, the path that led to the weir and, in the other direction, to the derelict church. They were alone.

"It's still early," she said. "There's no one here—no witnesses, no one to see *any* of this. If we're smart, move fast, we'll be all right."

"But *what* do we do?"

Nikki paced. "We make it look like she drowned."

"Chuck her in?"

"Why not?"

Gaz pointed to the blood on the stone. He crouched, slipped a hand beneath the woman's neck and angled her head until they could see the blood oozing out of her scalp. The hair was already matted with it, and, although the flow was slowing, there was still a lot of it. "What's that going to look like?"

"I don't know, babes. Use your imagination—she bumped her head on a stone when she fell in, knocked herself out and drowned."

"What if they can tell the difference?"

Nikki bit down on her lip. "Yeah. You're right. Maybe we shouldn't do that." She bit harder. "What, then? We can't just *leave* her here."

"I know." Gaz gave a definitive nod. "We take her with us."

"We can't—"

"We can't leave her, and we can't throw her in, so we put her in the Disco and take her to the yard."

"And then?"

"What do you think? Like before."

"No," she said. "Not that."

"What, then? At least she'll be gone."

"Sam's going to be mad."

"Whatever," Gaz said. "She'll have to suck it up."

Nikki gestured to her car. "We leave everything else just as it is. It'll look like she came down here for a swim and had an accident or topped herself."

"And the body?"

"It's a *river*, babes." She stabbed a finger in the direction of the dark water. "They'll come down here and look for her, she won't be here, and they'll think she's been swept away. Look at it. The current's like that all the way to Downton, and then for who knows how much farther—all the way to Christchurch. They'll think she's ended up in the sea."

"Maybe," Gaz said.

"Definitely. Do you remember that thing last year, the woman who went missing? They didn't find her body for days. *Days*, and they were on the news saying they might *never* find it. It'll be like that."

Gaz reached down for the bloodied hunk of chalk, heaved it up and hurled it into the water. "All right—I don't know what choice we have. We need to get her out of the way. Help me."

They moved quickly: Nikki grabbed the woman's ankles, and Gaz grabbed her by the wrists. They hauled her up and carried her to the back of the car. Nikki opened the boot and glanced nervously at the sticky mess at the back of her head. Gaz spread out the travel blanket that he used to keep the compartment clean, and once he was happy, they heaved the body up and over the sill and deposited her inside.

Nikki pressed the button to close the boot and followed Gaz back to the river. She looked down at the spot where the stone had been, looking for blood or anything else that might reveal what had happened here. She couldn't see anything.

"What if we've left something?" Gaz said.

Nikki gestured down. "Can you see anything?"

"No, but—"

Nikki spoke over him. "We haven't, babes."

Gaz pointed down at the path. It was muddy in places, and they had left footprints. "What about those?"

"Dog walkers probably come down here all the time. They'll think it was one of them. We get rid of our shoes as soon as we get back to the yard."

"Clothes, too," he said. "We find an oil barrel, make a fire, burn the lot."

"Bollocks." She ran her hand over the top she was wearing. "I only just got this. Two hundred quid from Addict, babes."

"I'll buy you another one. Come on."

They walked back to the woman's car and glanced in at the bags strewn across the back seat. Nikki knew they were going to miss something. There would be something in the car that would cast doubt on the conclusion they hoped would be drawn. She wanted to stay, to think slowly and carefully and take proper care, but knew Gaz would say they couldn't, and he'd be right. They hadn't been seen by anyone yet, but, as the clock edged around to seven, the odds of an early-morning dog walker coming down to the river would increase. And if anyone saw them here, the game would definitely be up.

"We need to go," she said.

They went back to the car and got inside. Gaz started the engine and put the Discovery into gear, edged the nose around, reversed into the space between the front of the woman's car and the track that led around to the rear of the mill, and then, pointing the right way, drove carefully back up the track to the road.

37

Atticus lay in bed and listened to the sound of breathing: the deep in and out of Bandit, from his bed on the floor to the left of the futon, and Mack, shallower, from right alongside him. Mack had come around last night after he'd found the man going through the bin. She had crept up the rear stairs and knocked on the window; it felt like an illicit assignation, a forbidden teenage love, and he'd been surprised to see her. She'd been to the Pheasant with Robbie Best and Francine Patterson, but, after they had gone home, she'd carried on to the Wig and Quill for another by herself. It was not lost on Atticus that the pub was just down the street from his office, and that she'd been drifting in his direction again. She'd been tipsy and emotional and hadn't needed to tell him it was about her kids.

Atticus listened, his anger quietly stewing, and, when she fell into his arms and sobbed into his shoulder, he decided that his promise to stay out of things was unsustainable. Andy had already crossed him with the report to the police about his drug use, but he'd ignored his instinct to strike back then on account of making things more difficult for Mack. This, though, was something else. Mack loved her kids, and what Andy was trying to do was wrong; he was using them as a way to get revenge on Mack, and, with a budget that outstripped what she could manage—even with Atticus's help—there was a good chance he'd be successful. Mack had asked him to stay out of it, but he didn't think he could do that anymore.

Andy had secrets—*everyone* did—and maybe it was time for Atticus to dig them up.

He rubbed the sleep from his eyes and, careful not to wake Mack, reached for his phone. He opened Facebook and saw he'd been tagged in a post on the largest Salisbury community group. The poster said she'd just watched the BBC documentary on the Mallender killings and that she'd found Atticus's contributions interesting. There were a dozen comments beneath her post: most were positive, two suggested Atticus was a media whore who was looking for a TV career, while another posted a screen grab from his interview and compared it to a still of Benedict Cumberbatch in *Patrick Melrose* with the comment 'Separated at Birth?'

He scrolled down, skimming over posts about a missing kitten, the Salisbury Neighbourhood Development Plan, a meme lamenting the state of potholes on local roads, endless complaints about the new River Park in the Maltings, and a BBC period drama that was filming in the Close. He stopped when he saw a picture of Alice Green—a screenshot from her website—and a comment from a poster Atticus remembered as one of the more inveterate drama queens.

I always thought there was something untrustworthy about her.

Atticus clicked the link. It took him to an article on the *Daily Mail*'s website.

The headline grabbed his attention at once:

INFLUENCER PROMOTES FAKE MENTAL HEALTH SUPPLEMENTS.

Wellness guru Alice Green has been tricked into promoting fake supplements on the basis that they could help 'cure' people of mental health issues, including anxiety and addiction. Green was secretly filmed during a meeting where she was asked to promote the new tablets even though she had no experience of them and after she had been advised that they had not yet received medical clearance.

Atticus opened Google and searched for Alice's name. The first page, which had previously presented generally positive results that usually ended up depositing searchers at her website, had now been flooded with links to the article from the *Mail* and other newspapers and online sources. Atticus picked one from *Vice*, tapped to open it and scrolled through the story. It was a rehash of the *Mail*'s piece, but, this time, there was a video. Atticus lowered the volume, squinted until his eyes had focused and tapped play. The video looked as if it had been shot in the same way as Alice's morning swims. She was speaking to the camera, and, as Atticus watched, she announced that she'd recently been introduced to a new product that was reputed to be effective in reducing anxiety and depression. The video was obviously an advertisement, mixing pre-prepared information with supposedly candid reflections from Alice in an attempt to tailor the message to her followers.

"The ingredients are all natural and organic and have been through vigorous peer-reviewed trials to prove the formula delivers real results. Each sachet contains turmeric extract, prebiotic beta glucans, ashwagandha extract, saffron, soluble keratin, strychnine and vitamins K and D."

What?

Atticus scrubbed back through the footage and pressed play again.

"…saffron, soluble keratin, strychnine and vitamins K and D."

He stopped the video with Alice staring into the camera and smiling.

Strychnine?

Atticus shook his head in bemusement.

Surely Alice knew strychnine was a poison?

He rolled his eyes as he realised what must have happened. Frank Green had said he had other irons in the fire when it came to his campaign against her, and this must have been what he meant. She'd been tricked. He could see how it must've gone: she was offered a large sum of money to promote the product to her followers, except that the product didn't even exist, and, even if it *did*, she was lending her name to something that would be lethal to anyone who took it.

The consequences would be serious. The Advertising Standards Agency would probably be interested, her rivals would jump on it as a sign of her lack of ethics, and her followers would never trust her again.

Career ending?

Very possibly.

38

Sam was bringing in two of the horses when she saw Gaz's shiny new Discovery turning into the yard. She led the animals into their stables, made sure their hay nets were full, and, brushing muck from her gilet, walked over to where Gaz had parked. Nikki got out of the car and Sam could see, with a sickness in the pit of her stomach, that something was wrong.

What was it now? Why couldn't they do the simplest things without messing up?

"Problem," Nikki said.

"Not what I wanted to hear."

Gaz came over. "I'm sorry."

He couldn't hold her eye.

"Go on, then," Sam said. "Spit it out. What happened? Did you follow her?"

"Waited outside the Close for her," Nikki said, "like you told us, then followed."

"And?"

"She went to the river at Standlynch. We waited for her to come out of the water and went over to give her a fright."

"Didn't go to plan," Gaz said.

"What happened?"

"Probably easier if you have a look for yourself."

Gaz led the way around to the back of the Discovery, and after taking a deep breath that filled Sam with nauseous trepidation, he reached down and pressed the button to open the boot. The motors whirred as the door was raised.

Sam looked down to see the body of a woman.

"Oh my God."

"It was an accident," Gaz said. "She got into my face and bit me"—he held up his bloodied hand—"and then she tripped."

"She *tripped*?"

"Tripped and fell. She banged her head on a rock."

"She's dead," Nikki said.

"No shit." Sam wanted to scream. "So you brought her back here?"

"We didn't know what else to do."

"But you thought *I* would?"

"Where else were we going to go?" he said.

Nikki eyed her. "And it's not like this is the first time, is it?"

Sam felt a flash of anger and the urge to slap her; she clenched her fists and took a breath, knowing that losing control now was the last thing the situation needed.

Gaz gestured over to the back of the yard. "We use the pigs."

"Like before," Nikki said.

"No evidence," Gaz added. "We make her disappear."

"As simple as that?"

Gaz nodded, then clicked his fingers. "*Poof.* Gone."

"What about her car?" Sam clicked her own fingers. "You made that go *poof*, too?"

"We left it," Nikki said.

"Right." She sighed. "Of course you did."

"What *else* were we going to do?"

"We made it look like she'd drowned," Gaz said. "She comes out for a swim, she trips, falls into the water and bangs her head on a branch or a rock, and the river carries her away."

"The river runs fast down there," Nikki said. "She could've been carried miles downstream."

"Could be carried all the way out to sea."

They both nodded at her, as if willing her to accept the logic of what they'd decided to do. Sam wanted to tell them what she thought of them and their ideas but bit her tongue. Later. She needed to sort this out, and quickly. Her own plan was underway, and she couldn't let this derail her. The *last* thing she needed was to be worrying about the body in the back of Gaz's car.

"The pigs—right. They probably are the best way to do it. Drive around to the pen. They haven't been fed yet. We'd better do it now."

39

Atticus took out the business card that Alice Green had given him and checked the address. Her studio was on the High Street and only a short walk from his office. He gave Bandit a quick leg stretch in the courtyard before leaving him with his breakfast and making his way to the address in plenty of time for his appointment.

The building was next to the cathedral gate, with the offices of a local estate agency to the left. Atticus went up to the door and pressed the button with Alice's name next to it, then waited for the door to be unlocked.

Nothing happened.

He tried again, waited another twenty seconds, and still the door remained locked.

That was odd. He was sure he was here at the right time.

He stepped back into the street so that he could take in all of the building from top to bottom. It was three storeys tall, and its renovation had emphasised its architectural qualities: stucco ground floor, a projecting bay window above, ornamented roundels, bracketed and moulded cornicing. A large wooden model of a ram stood above the door with a plaque that announced the building had previously been used in the local wool trade. Atticus jumped at the sound of a horn and had to step back onto the pavement so that a delivery van could slide through the narrow gap, the driver eyeing him irritably as he went past.

He took out his phone and called the number for Alice's mobile.

It went to voicemail.

Atticus ended the call and was about to turn back and retrace his steps when the door opened. It was a young woman in her mid-twenties with tattoos and hair that had been dyed blue and pink.

"Hi," Atticus said. "I'm looking for Alice?"

"You're the journalist?"

"Ryan," he said. "I had an appointment this morning. I had it in my diary for now, but I'm wondering if there was a misunderstanding."

"It's in her diary too, but I'm afraid she's not here."

"Oh."

"I'm sorry. It's not like her at all. She's never late."

"I just tried her phone."

"Same—she's not answering."

"Do you think I could come in?"

She looked reluctant. Atticus could guess the reason why: she must've seen the avalanche of negative publicity about Alice's ill-advised video endorsement and the comments that had flooded her socials. She was probably concerned about how they were going to put out the flames, and, if they couldn't, what that would mean for her job.

Atticus decided to lean into it. "I've seen the controversy this morning. Alice has *obviously* been tricked—I'm sure she'd want to take the opportunity to rebut what's been said."

"It's *ridiculous*," the woman said. "And you're right—she's been taken advantage of. I mean, I set the meeting up, but I told her there was something off about the guy who came in to see her, and she said it was fine and..." She stopped, reluctant to say anything else.

"Look," Atticus said. "I'd rather wait than go back to London. I'm writing a positive piece about her, and I can give her a sympathetic platform to get her side of the story out."

"Yeah, I get that, and I'm sure it'd be great, but I'm not sure if now's the right time."

"I'll just wait quietly in a corner until she gets here. It'd be a shame for her to pass up the opportunity."

Atticus hoped that the woman would pick up on the suggestion that it would be *her* fault if Atticus left with the interview half-finished and the chance to refute the negativity lost. Judging from the classic signs of discomfort in her body language—shifting weight from foot to foot and touching her neck—the implication had been duly received.

"Maybe you *should* come in," she said. "I'm sure she'll be here soon, and she'd hate it for you to go without speaking to her again."

40

The yard was open to Nunton Drove to the east but enclosed by thick woods on the other three sides. The pigs were kept in a field to the northwest, reached by way of a muddy track that led through the trees. Sam walked to their pen with Nikki and Gaz following in the Discovery.

Sam's father had been casting around for ideas to save the business for years before she'd returned to take over. He'd tried sheep, buying a herd of a hundred Aberblacks and putting them into the west field. That hadn't worked—the price of wool had plummeted the day after the deal had been done and never recovered—so he sold them and tried pigs instead. He'd purchased a dozen big Tamworth sows and set about breeding them. That business had failed, too, and Sam had been set to slaughter them until they'd been useful in an unexpected way.

It was around the time of the situation with Christopher. Sam had been watching a true crime documentary about two brothers who'd been convicted of murdering two hunters whose bodies were never found. The case against them relied upon testimony from a witness who said the brothers had fed the bodies of the hunters to their hogs. Sam had a similar problem to deal with and had done her research. She found the story of a farmer who had been eaten by his pigs, with just his dentures left behind, and found websites about the mafia in Italy that suggested that victims were disposed of in the same way. It turned out that pigs would eat almost anything; they'd eat pork, too, including their own piglets, given half the chance.

The track climbed a shallow incline between two big oak trees and then bent around to the right, eventually reaching the post-and-rail fence that they'd erected to house the animals. A number of shelters had been installed along one side of the field, but they were all empty this morning. The pigs were out, rootling for food in the slop of the churned-up field.

"Morning, ladies," Sam said as she filled a bucket with pig food.

The animals were medium-sized, with the biggest full-grown sow weighing around six hundred pounds. They were a gingery-red colour and known for their voracious appetite. Sam shook the bucket so the pigs could hear the pellets rattling inside and waited for them to hustle over. They came up to the fence, snorting in anticipation, the biggest barging two others out of the way so she was closest to the bucket. Sam leaned over the rail and emptied the pellets out, scattering them into the muck so that all of the pigs could have some. They wouldn't even begin to satiate them, but it would get them interested in what would come next.

The Discovery drove between the trees and through the gate and came to a stop next to the fence. Gaz and Nikki got out.

Gaz looked like he was going to be sick. "I don't know if I can do this."

"You don't have to *do* anything," Sam said. She pointed to the pigs. "Just leave it to them."

"I can't be here when…" He stopped.

"When they get started?"

He nodded, then turned to the side and doubled over and vomited onto the grass.

"For God's sake," Sam muttered. "Pull yourself together."

Gaz held up a hand, still bent over as more vomit splashed down.

Sam looked over at Nikki. She, too, looked unwell. That the two of them were so hopeless was par for the course; they'd always been the weakest of the six. Sam had known she'd need others working with her if she was going to make a success of what she had in mind and hadn't been comfortable with asking any of her contacts in London. They were all fair-weather friends, and she hadn't known any of them as long as she'd known Gaz and Nikki and Connor and Tom and Christopher. They'd been a gang as kids and had stayed close as they moved into their teens and beyond.

Connor, at least, had initiative. Tom had always been big, and it could have been useful to have his brawn when they'd needed to intimidate anyone. Gaz was too stupid to realise that he was taking the biggest risk by going over to get the coke, but Sam knew he'd keep his mouth shut if he ever had his collar felt. Nikki was shrewd, and Sam had paid her special attention while she was making her arrangements. If anyone latched onto what she was planning, it'd be her.

She put her hands on her hips and waited for Gaz to spit the last of the phlegm from his mouth. "Better?"

He held up his hand again, retched, and when nothing more came out, he straightened up.

"*Babes*," Nikki said, resting a hand on his back.

"Jesus," Sam muttered.

Gaz looked up. His skin was clammy, and his cheeks were tinged with green. "You don't feel the same?"

"What difference would it make?" Sam said. "It wouldn't change anything. We'd still have to do it." She pointed to the back of the Discovery. "Get her out."

The pigs snorted hungrily now that they had found all of the pellets.

"Let's go," Sam said.

Gaz reached down for the woman's ankles, but, before he could lift her out, he swore and jumped back.

"What?"

"Shit!" Nikki said.

"What *is* it?"

"Shit, shit, *shit!*"

Sam went around the car. Gaz pointed down into the boot space, and before he could say anything else, Sam saw it for herself.

Alice Green's leg twitched.

And then she groaned.

"Bollocks," Sam muttered.

41

Atticus went through into the room at the back of the building and found himself in a large space that had been turned into a studio evidently used for the creation of content for Alice's business. One section was dominated by a ring light mounted on a tripod, casting a flattering and shadowless light that would be good for close-up shots. Two DSLR cameras had been mounted on tripods to offer multiple angles for filming, and the backdrop was a green screen that would allow for graphics to be added in post-production. The wall to the left was decorated with a neon version of the Real Wild Swimming logo, and the wall to the right held shelving lined with products from the brands with whom Alice had partnered: clothing brands, companies offering CBD oil and energy drinks and protein bars, brands with a focus on the environment and sustainability. A table was cluttered with hard drives and camera equipment. There were LED strips and smart bulbs to set the mood with customisable colour, and acoustic panelling to remove echo. The studio included audio equipment—microphones and soundboards—and, in a smaller room to the side, Atticus saw an edit suite with two large monitors and a Mac.

Alice's assistant gestured over to a sofa positioned on the wall to the left of the cameras. "Take a seat," she said. "Hopefully she'll be here soon."

"I didn't catch your name."

"Sarah," she said. "I'm Alice's PA."

"Nice to meet you."

"Ryan?"

"That's right."

They shook hands.

"Can I get you a drink?" Sarah asked. "Tea or coffee?"

"Coffee would be great."

Atticus sat down, looking at the desk as he made his way by it. He saw the same MacBook with the decals and stickers that Alice had been using before their first meeting. Sarah had left the room for the kitchen, and, as he heard the sound of the kettle being filled, Atticus reached forward to open the lid and tap the keyboard. The screen lit up, but he saw—to no surprise at all—that it was locked.

He heard Sarah coming back and sat down on the sofa, opened the folder with his social media apps and looked for anything Alice might have posted. He skimmed Facebook and then Instagram and, finally TikTok, seeing that she hadn't posted any updates since yesterday morning. The flood of negative comments had continued, but she'd made no attempt to address the fast-developing controversy.

"One coffee," Sarah said, placing a mug down on the table.

Atticus held up his phone. "It's not good, is it?"

"Awful."

"Would you have expected her to address any of it?"

"I don't know," she said. "We've never had anything like this before. I don't know what she'll be thinking."

"Posts on social channels she controls can be removed, though—right?"

"Yes."

"Weird that she wouldn't?"

"It is."

"She didn't strike me as someone who'd take something like this lying down."

"She isn't," she said, "but how do you handle something that's spreading as fast as this?"

"You'd probably make a statement."

"Saying what? They've tricked her into saying something really damaging. What's she going to say?"

"It's not really my area of expertise."

"But you're a journalist. You must have an idea?"

"You'd need a crisis-management specialist for that," he said.

"What you were saying, though—about her being quiet. It *is* strange."

"And she hasn't been in touch at all about this?"

"Not this morning."

"She's not normally late?"

"No—and never without telling me, and never when she has something in the diary like this." She took out her own phone and spent a moment tapping and swiping across the screen. "She's seeing you first, and then she was supposed to be posting content for Charlotte's Web."

"What's that?"

"They make CBD oil products to help with inflammation. Alice has a deal with them. They're sponsoring a video, and today was the day we agreed it'd be posted. She was going to go out and film it this morning. I think she was going to do a video for a swimsuit, too."

"Do you know where she would've gone?"

Sarah shook her head. "She doesn't always tell me. She wakes up and decides what she feels like. There are a couple of pools on the Avon she often goes to, though."

"I saw a video outside the old mill in Harnham."

"The town path gets too busy, even when it's early. And, between us, she's been warned off filming there."

"Why?"

"Private land."

"Where else would she go?"

"There are a couple of nice pools at Lacock—there's a deep one upstream of the rapids near the Abbey."

"Probably too far for her to go this morning," Atticus said.

Sarah nodded. "Same for the weir at Claverton or the lake at Holt. She might've gone to Fordingbridge. That's close enough. It's hard to say. She walked the Avon Valley Path all the way down to Christchurch in lockdown, and she has a list of quieter places she's been working through. It might well have been one of them."

Sarah directed her attention back to her phone, her finger swiping down the screen as—Atticus guessed—she scrolled through the comments under the video. Atticus didn't push for anything else; it was obvious that she was as in the dark about Alice's no-show as he was.

He was concerned. Alice hadn't struck him as being particularly sensitive, but it was difficult to predict how this kind of negativity would affect her. Would she hurt herself? He wasn't concerned enough yet to think about suggesting that Sarah contact the police, but he'd be more concerned the longer she was out of contact.

He wondered about telling Frank, but given he was almost certainly behind the story, he didn't want to give him the satisfaction.

42

Sam took a step forward until she was close enough to look right down on Alice's body. She was still lying in the foetal position, but her eyelids were flickering, and the fingers of her right hand were flexing open and closed.

Gaz stepped away from the back of the car. The colour had drained from his face.

Sam clenched her fists. "I thought you checked for a pulse?"

"We did," Nikki said.

"You couldn't even do *that* right."

"There *was* no pulse. I tried twice." She looked to Gaz for support. "Right?"

"Don't look at me, babes. *You* looked, not me."

"My God," Sam snapped.

"What do we do?" Nikki said fretfully. "We can't chuck her in the field with the pigs *now*, can we?"

Sam wondered whether they *could* still do that. The pigs were hungry, and it didn't look as if Alice would be able to do much to defend herself. But she didn't know enough about the animals to know whether they'd go for her unless she was dead, and, anyway, the prospect of condemning her to being eaten alive was a bit much, even for her.

She reached up and pressed the button to close the boot.

"What are you doing?" Gaz said.

"She doesn't know where she is," Sam said. "Right?"

"No."

"And she doesn't know what you look like?"

"No. We were wearing balaclavas the whole time."

"Sure?"

"We're not idi—"

"Yes, Gaz, you are. *Massive* idiots. But maybe this isn't as bad as it looks. She doesn't know where she is or who brought her here. We put her somewhere safe and keep an eye on her, and, in the meantime, I'll have a proper think about how risky it'd be to let her out. We've just given her the biggest fright she'll ever get. She won't want anything to do with Tom after that. That'll be the end of it."

Nikki shrugged, unconvinced. "I don't know. That sounds like trouble."

"There's only one other way of dealing with her."

She shook her head. "Not now."

"Got a better idea? You were happy enough to feed her to the pigs five minutes ago."

"I thought she was *dead* five minutes ago."

Gaz raised both hands. "What if she needs a doctor? If she's concussed?"

"Or maybe she has brain damage," Nikki added.

"We can't just take her to A&E," Gaz said.

"We'll deal with that if we have to," Sam said. "Look—you want to let the pigs do their thing? Be my guest. I'll be at the yard."

She turned and started off down the track.

"Fine," Nikki said. "Fine. You're right. We can't do that. So what *do* we do?"

Sam stopped and turned back. "We need to get her out of the way." She tried to think of somewhere safe where Alice could be stashed, and there was only one real answer. "Drive her back to the yard. We'll put her with the coke underneath the stable."

43

Sam went into the house and came out with the things they would need: a towel, a bunch of cable ties, a dish rag, and a roll of tape.

She held up the towel. "Blindfold her until she's in the cellar. We don't want her seeing where she is."

Gaz nodded.

She held up the dishrag and the tape. "Put the rag in her mouth and use the tape to hold it in place. I've cancelled the buyer I had coming over today, but that's not to say someone turns up and she starts screaming. And then use the cable ties on her wrists and ankles. Not too tight that you cut the circulation, but tight enough that she knows there's no point in trying to wriggle out."

"Is that necessary? She's not going anywhere."

That was true enough. The trapdoor had a bolt that would make sure it couldn't be opened from below, but Sam wasn't interested in taking chances.

"Just do it, Gaz."

"What about the coke?" Nikki asked.

"We can leave it there. It'll be fine."

"How long do you think she'll be here?"

"I don't know," she said. "Depends on what Connor gets out of Tom."

Sam had been thinking about that ever since it had become obvious that Alice wasn't as dead as the two of them had made out, and her answer was as much as she could say. If Connor *did* find out that Tom had told Alice what happened to Christopher, then Sam was going to have to make a very difficult decision. She clung to the hope that Tom had exaggerated the extent of his confession, and if Sam could be persuaded about that, perhaps they could let Alice go.

Perhaps.

But that would be taking a chance, and the consequences for them all if Alice went to the police and the police worked out what had happened—and could she be sure that Nikki and Gaz hadn't left anything incriminating at the river?—well, those consequences would be serious.

The safest thing to do would be to make the difficult choice: to make them both disappear.

And, in the meantime, she'd *definitely* speed up her own plans.

"Come on," she said, pointing to the back of the car. "Get her down there."

She stood to the side of the Discovery while Gaz and Nikki went to the back. Gaz blindfolded Alice with the towel, and then they reached in, one on each side, and dragged her out. She was more responsive than she had been before, and she tried to struggle as they each grabbed her beneath a shoulder and half-dragged, half-carried her to the stable door. Sam followed them, staying outside but close enough to watch as Nikki climbed down the ladder and then reached up to help support the woman's weight as Gaz lowered her through the trapdoor.

Sam took the opportunity to go back to the Discovery. She'd been irritated that Gaz had spent so much money on it, especially after she'd reminded him that showing off with flashy purchases was a bad idea. The only consolation was that it had been early in the morning when they'd taken Alice, and the chances of anyone seeing them were slim. She went around to the open rear door and looked into the cargo space. They'd need to get it professionally cleaned. She didn't know how much evidence would remain inside, but she'd seen enough in TV shows and documentaries to know that there'd be hair and skin particles and bloodstains that would give them away if the police were ever to investigate. A thorough clean would eliminate that risk as much as possible.

44

Atticus stayed for an hour and then gave up, telling Sarah to call him if Alice turned up. He went out into the street and decided he *did* need to speak to Frank Green. Alice missing the appointment was one thing—unprofessional, but hardly sinister—but the context lent it an edge that was making him increasingly nervous. The morning's exposé gave him more reasons to fear that something was very wrong. He knew there was too much rancour in the Greens' relationship for Frank to be concerned—and that Frank was behind the damaging posts—but Atticus wanted to report what had happened, nonetheless.

Atticus stopped at the office to attend to Bandit—giving him a quick walk around the cathedral and filling his bowls with food and water—and then went out again. Frank Green's Salisbury address was a new development on Salt Lane, hidden away behind the building where the old Salisbury Steam Laundry had been situated. Atticus took out his phone, looked up the address on Rightmove and found, to his surprise, that it had been listed for sale a week earlier. He scanned the particulars: it was a three-bedroom pied-à-terre, unusual for the city, and valued at one and a half million. He scanned through the details and noted that Green had purchased it only six months ago, paying just over a million. It wasn't difficult to work out what had happened: Green had bought the place following the end of his marriage to Alice, but, after she'd dropped him in the shit with the police, he'd found himself in urgent need of funds and had been left with no option but to sell, bumping up the price in the hope that he might be able to use the profits—plus any equity he had in it—to sort out his affairs.

Atticus put his phone away, returning the warm smiles of a couple who looked as if they were going to Tinga, the excellent Mexican restaurant down the street. He went through the arch beneath the sign for the laundry and found his way to the gate to the property. He pressed the intercom and waited for Green to answer.

"Yes?"

"It's Atticus Priest."

"Oh. Is everything all right? Have you found something?"

"I have, actually—do you think we could have a chat?"

"Will it take long?"

"Not long."

Frank didn't reply.

"You'll want to hear it," Atticus said.

"Come up."

It looked like the building had been used for industrial purposes and had only recently been converted. Atticus climbed the stairs to the door and waited for Green to open it.

He was wearing a suit and tie and looked as if he was about to go out.

"I'm catching a train in forty minutes. This'll have to be quick. Come in."

Atticus followed him into a large space given over to a combined sitting room and kitchen. It must have been forty feet across and was marked by a polished concrete floor and expensive-looking cabinetry and appliances. A huge television, seventy or eighty inches across, was fixed to the wall. Green had been watching the boxing from last night, two heavyweights circling each other, with the volume muted. The place had a sophisticated, minimalist design with high-end finishes and artwork that suggested wealth. The absence of child-friendly furnishings and the expensive gadgets—a top-of-the-line MacBook had been left on the sideboard—gave Atticus everything he needed to diagnose a bachelor lifestyle.

Atticus followed him to a large eight-person sofa. Green sat down but didn't invite Atticus to do the same.

"So?" he said. "What've you found?"

"Have you seen the story about Alice from this morning?"

He smirked. "The one where she's endorsing a product containing poison? Yes—I saw it."

"And that was you?"

"Do you mean was I responsible for it? Whatever makes you think that?"

"Because the timing would suggest it's connected to your dispute. And because you said what you were asking me to do was part of a wider campaign. 'Other irons in the fire'—I think that's what you said. You told me to watch her social media."

"She's only got herself to blame," he said, leaning back and folding his hands behind his head. It would have been difficult to look more self-satisfied. "What did you think of it?"

"I think it'll be incredibly damaging."

He smirked again. "Can you believe how *stupid* she is? It's greed—pure and simple. She took the money without even asking what it was she was going to be flogging. She deserves everything that's coming to her." He straightened up. "What about her finances? That's why you're here? Got something for me?"

"I've found bits and pieces."

"Go on, then."

"I'll let you have the report when I'm finished."

"And when will that be?"

"I need to write it up," he said.

"So write it up, give me what I asked for, and you're done—I'll give you the rest of the fee, plus a bonus on top for taking care of it so quickly."

"I have a couple of things I'd like to run by you first."

Green shrugged irritably. "You probably don't. It sounds like you're done, and I don't want to hang around. She's had too long taking free swings at me. I need her to start seeing the consequences of that."

"She will. But just humour me for a moment."

"Fine. What is it?"

"She booked me in for an appointment this morning. I went to her studio, and she wasn't there."

"So what? She forgot."

"Her assistant didn't think it'd be something that she would forget."

He paused and snorted derisively. "She has a lot on her mind." He stared at Atticus. "I hope *that's* not why you've come over here?"

"I'm concerned about her." Atticus held his eye. "I think you should contact the police and report her missing."

"*Me?*"

"You *are* her husband."

"*Please.* Estranged. And soon to be divorced."

"But until that happens, you're still her next of kin."

"Are you deaf? I don't want anything to do with her."

"I think she might've hurt herself. What you did will have had an impact on her mental health."

"Oh, bullshit." He waved a hand dismissively. "Come on. You don't know her like I do. It'll be embarrassing, and it'll be damaging to her business, but it'll bounce right off her. She's got a thick skin."

"Have you seen how much vitriol she's having to deal with?"

"Not enough." Green rolled his eyes. "Let me tell you something about my wife. You don't know her like I do. She's shameless. Completely *shameless*. She'll be upset about what happened, but it won't last. Eventually she'll tell herself it was a travesty, it was a trap, that it doesn't reflect badly on her or what she does."

"I've seen this kind of thing before, when I was in the police—I've seen how this can affect people."

"You think she's *killed* herself? I can tell you now, with one hundred percent certainty, that she hasn't. I know *exactly* what happened. She saw the story, she looked at her diary and saw she was supposed to be seeing you, and she bailed. She's licking her wounds somewhere and working out what to do next. I'll bet you anything you like she'll call you tomorrow to rearrange whatever it was you were going to be doing with her, and it'll be like nothing ever happened. She'll probably rope you in to help launder her reputation." He stood. "If you want to report it to the police, you should. Your choice. But I don't care either way. Now, if you don't mind, I'm going to have to hurry if I'm going to get my train. Find what I'm paying you to find and get it to me. What happened this morning was the start, but I'm not finished yet. I haven't even started. She's tried to ruin me. She had a bloody good go, but it's not going to be enough. I'm not going to make the same mistakes. I'll make *absolutely* sure I ruin her."

45

Nikki came out of the stable door with Gaz just behind her.

"Give me that," Sam said, pointing at Nikki's balaclava.

"Why?"

"Because I don't want her to see my face when I go down to check."

"You don't need to check. She's not going anywhere."

"Are you serious? After how badly you two screwed up this morning? Of course I need to check."

Nikki looked as if she was going to protest, but, after seeing the expression on Sam's face, she demurred, shaking her head and handing over the mask. Sam put it on, wrinkling her nose at the sensation of the rough fibres against her skin and the smell of Nikki's perfume, and adjusted it so that she could see where she was going.

She went into the stable, strode over to the trapdoor, turned around and climbed backwards down the ladder. She stepped off the final rung and looked around. Nikki and Gaz had actually done a decent job for once: Alice's wrists and ankles had been secured with cable ties, her hands behind her back so she couldn't reach up for the tape that held the balled-up rag in her mouth. Her eyes were wide with fear, and she tried to speak, but her words were rendered unintelligible by the gag. Sam looked at the packets of cocaine that were stacked on the shelves and concluded she'd been right: no need to move them.

Alice mumbled something again, her eyes blinking as she tried to focus. There was no reason for Sam to say anything, and she preferred to be silent in any case. She wasn't worried that Alice would recognise her voice, but she didn't want to leave her with anything that might give her a way to identify her later in the event that Sam decided they could let her leave. Sam made doubly sure that the tape was secure and, happy that it was, climbed the ladder again.

She lowered the trapdoor and fastened it with the padlock, then joined Gaz and Nikki outside.

She turned and pointed to the Discovery. "You'll need to get that professionally cleaned. There's that place on the Southampton Road."

"The car wash?" Gaz said.

"They do valets, too. Take it over there and get them to give it a good going over."

"But it's new," he complained. "The insides are spotless. They'll want to know why I'm bringing it in."

Sam bit her tongue; why was it that she had to think for everyone? She looked around the yard, saw a five-litre plastic jug of Restore-Lyte that she had been putting in Nala's water to help with her energy levels, picked it up and made her way to the car. Gaz followed, evidently unaware of what she was proposing until she undid the screw-on cap and sloshed the reddish liquid into the boot.

He swore. "What are you *doing*?"

"There," Sam said, putting the cap back onto the container.

"It stinks!"

It was true: the minerals in the electrolytes gave it a salty tang, and there was a cloying sweetness from the flavouring agents.

"Now you've got a reason to get it cleaned," she said. "Chop-chop. The longer you wait, the more that smell is going to seep into your lovely new upholstery."

46

The minibus arrived in Alderbury and pulled up at the junction of Southampton Road and Avon Drive. Josh Yates said goodbye to the driver, got off the bus and waited as it rumbled away. He'd been going to Trafalgar School in Downton for the last year, and getting in and out was more convoluted than had been the case for the six years he'd spent at primary school before that. He'd been at Alderbury and West Grimstead Primary, and it'd been a ten-minute walk from his house. Trafalgar was much too far for that, and, since his mum and stepdad couldn't be relied upon to drive him, they had arranged for a seat on the minibus instead. It didn't matter, and he looked forward to the journeys; the driver was friendly and listened to Radio One, and he knew a couple of the other kids who'd also been at primary school with him before going up to Trafalgar. He preferred the journey in the morning since it meant he would be away from the house and his worries until the afternoon; he was sometimes nervous on the journey back, not knowing what he would find when he got home.

His phone buzzed with an incoming message. He took it out and saw that it was from Paul, reminding him that they'd agreed to go down to the river for a swim. Josh had homework to do, but he'd tried to cultivate new friends in his new school, and Paul was one of the popular kids in the class. He'd tried to get into his good graces, and he didn't want to mess up by blowing him out. He texted back, saying he'd get his bike and meet him at the end of the farmer's track.

He hurried back to the house and, seeing the curtains closed, knew that his mum and stepdad would be sleeping off another hangover. He got his bike from the back garden and checked his watch; he'd get back at six and hope that the atmosphere was better than it had been when he returned yesterday.

In the meantime, he'd have some fun.

* * *

Josh cycled to the post office, turned right onto Castle Lane and then headed south. He reached the farm buildings and saw that Paul was waiting for him, and that he wasn't alone; Becca was there, too. Josh had been trying to get her attention for weeks. He'd told Paul that he liked her, but Paul had said she wouldn't be into him, and he should forget it.

But here she was.

"Hey," Josh said.

"Took your time," Paul said.

"The bus was late."

"Can't believe your parents make you get the *bus*," Becca said.

"It's because they're always pissed," Paul said.

Becca's parents drove her to school in their fancy new electric Audi, and Paul's dad dropped him off on his way to work in Ringwood every morning. Josh liked the bus, but Paul had been telling kids at school about *why* he had to take it. Josh always laughed along with the joke, doing his best to hide the embarrassment.

They set off. The track beyond the gate was private, and the farmer had yelled at them more than once, but they couldn't see anyone now and decided the shortcut was worth the risk. They lifted their bikes over the gate and rode on, bouncing over the pitted surface for a mile until they reached the second gate where the track met Witherington Road. Paul led the way, turning left and freewheeling down into the hollow. They picked up as much speed as they could to help them get up the hill that climbed out of the hollow on the other side. They cycled by the entrance to the huge house at Trafalgar Park and then reached the track that led down to the chapel and the mill and the weir.

There was a car parked next to the old mill. That wasn't unusual—dog walkers often came down here so they could use the weir to get across the river to the water meadows on the other side—but there was something about this one that caught Josh's attention for longer than usual. He skidded to a stop and looked inside; the car was a mess, with clothes strewn across the back seat and a pile of papers in the front. The driver's door was ajar; that was what he'd noticed. Maybe whoever had come down here had just forgotten to close it properly. It wasn't as if anyone was about to nick it.

"Come on," Paul shouted.

Josh pushed off again, cycling along the track to the weir. He loved coming down here. It was always quiet and peaceful, and there was a spot on the other side of the water where you could climb over the fence and get into the trees. Josh and Paul had built a den here last month, and it was still intact. Josh liked to go down there with a book and lose himself for an hour or two. It was a secret place, somewhere he could go and be certain that his parents would never find him. It was almost possible to forget about them and the chaos that invariably greeted him when he got home.

They rested their bikes against the fence and were going to cross the weir when Josh saw something off to the left. He stopped and looked: the river opened out into a wide pool, and there was a raised bank that overlooked the stony beach that led into the water.

A tripod had been set up on the bank with an expensive-looking camera fixed to it.

Paul saw it, too. "What's that?"

"A camera."

"Just left there?"

There was no one anywhere nearby, at least not that Josh could see.

"Maybe someone taking pictures of the river," Josh suggested.

"Where are they, then?"

Becca joined them. "Having a piss in the bushes?"

Josh nodded. The camera must've belonged to whoever had left their car by the mill. They couldn't be far away. They wouldn't have left expensive gear like that unattended.

They continued across the weir to the other side. Josh hopped the fence and ploughed through the undergrowth until he reached the den. They'd built it from fallen branches and leafy boughs, the shelter blending in with its surroundings, so it would've been hard to find if you didn't know it was there. The branches were arranged to form a framework, with foliage draped over it for camouflage and insulation. Josh wriggled inside, lying down on the soft layer of moss and leaves next to the circle of stones that they used as a fire pit. The others joined him.

"Nice," Becca said.

Paul reached into his pocket and took out a packet of cigarettes. "Want one?"

"*No*," Josh said.

Becca said she would. "Where'd you get them from?"

"My mum," Paul said.

"Won't she notice?"

"Took them a week ago. She thinks she lost them."

He took out a lighter and lit Becca's cigarette. He held the packet out for Josh. "Sure?"

"I'm alright," he said.

Paul lit a cigarette for himself, and the two of them sat there and smoked, both trying hard not to cough or to signal that it was anything other than cool and enjoyable. They were sitting close enough to one another that their legs touched, and Josh thought he saw them sharing a look. Josh wished he hadn't told Paul that he liked Becca. It would be just like Paul to try to get with her himself and ignore the way that Josh felt.

"I'm going to go for a swim," he said.

"I can't be bothered," Paul said.

Becca nodded. "Me neither."

Whatever.

He crawled out of the den and went back to the water. The tripod and camera were still there. He ignored them, taking off his uniform and folding it carefully over a branch from a tree near to the bank. He undressed to his underwear, hearing a giggle from the direction of the den. He ignored it—thinking about what they might be getting up to would just make him upset—and stepped back far enough to give himself a run-up. He ran, launching himself off the bank, bringing his knees up to his chest and making a tight ball as he slammed into the deepest part of the river. The cold hit him, a sudden shock that had him gasping for air the moment he broke the surface. He took a deep breath and flipped onto his back, spreading his arms and legs until he was like a starfish, floating on the surface and staring up at the dense canopy of branches overhead.

47

Nikki and Gaz left the car to be valeted and decided to have a pint while they waited in the pub on Tollgate Road. It was an old-fashioned boozer that locals joked had two names: the sign to the left of the entrance was for the Railway Inn, and the sign on the right was for the Dust Hole.

Gaz went to the bar to get a couple of pints while Nikki took a table at the back of the room. It was quiet, with darts on the TV, and just one other afternoon drinker sat with his pint and a newspaper at the bar. Nikki watched Gaz as he paid for the drinks and composed herself, working out how she was going to broach the subject they needed to discuss. She knew Gaz would do whatever she asked, but what she was about to propose was significant, and she wanted him to buy into it rather than go along with her because it was what he thought she wanted. They'd been a couple for ten years, and, although they'd had their ups and downs—like anyone else—Nikki knew their longevity was because they usually wanted the same thing. Sam had approached Nikki when she'd started thinking about going into business, and it had been Nikki who had persuaded Gaz that it was a good idea. She'd worked on him, laid out the benefits, ran him through the risks, and then they'd both balanced one against the other and had agreed it looked like something they could get behind. It was only right they did the same thing now, when everything was pointing to the fact that it was time to get out.

Gaz put the pints on the table and sat down. "What a day, babes."

She picked up her glass, touched it to Gaz's, and drank.

She put the glass down. "I've been thinking."

"Yeah?"

She nodded. "I've been thinking that maybe this whole thing has come to an end."

"The business?"

She nodded. "What happened with Tom..." She shook her head. "It should never have been allowed to get to where it's got."

"It shouldn't," he said.

"Sam said she had that under control—right?"

"Right."

"And it's pretty clear she didn't."

He nodded enthusiastically. "And then she blamed us for what happened this morning."

"She did."

"And that wasn't fair. What happened—"

"Was an accident," Nikki finished.

"She tripped," he said.

"She did. It wasn't your fault."

"Try telling Sam that," he said.

"*Exactly*. You know what she's like—never blames herself for *anything*—and this whole mess is because of what happened with Christopher and Tom and her. It had nothing to do with us."

"We weren't even there," he added.

"Not when it happened."

"Just after," he said. "With the…" He didn't finish the sentence.

She ran her finger around the rim of the pint glass. "And now, with what happened this morning…" She sighed, sipped the pint again and then returned it to the table. "I don't know, babes. I don't see any way out that involves Tom and Alice walking away, and I'm not sure I want anything to do with what will have to happen if they don't."

"You think Sam will…" He let the sentence drift again.

"You *know* she will. She did with Christopher, and *he* was a friend."

He nodded. "The pigs were her idea—that's what Tom said."

"I've been thinking about Christopher a lot recently," she said. "Remember what Sam said about him?"

"She said he was going to steal from us."

"She did. Are we really sure about that?"

Gaz frowned. "You're not?"

"Do I think he might've done something like that? Yeah—maybe. But no one else was there that night before Tom showed up. I know what she said happened, but we only have her word for it. And you know my feelings about how much we can trust her."

"You've told me enough times."

"And you *still* don't think she's got it in her to stab us in the back if she thinks it'd be best for her?"

"I don't know. I still find it hard to get my head around it. We've known her for years—since we were kids."

"And how much has she changed? She never used to be like she is now, did she? She went to London, and she was like a different person when she came back."

"True," he said.

"Machia... Machia..."

"Machiavellian," she said. "Exactly. *Devious.*"

"Why are you bringing it up now?"

"Because there's something else we need to talk about." She reached over the table and took both his hands in hers. "I think now might be the time."

He winced. "Really?"

"While we still can."

He exhaled loudly. "I *just* bought the car."

"And we can sell it. This mess with Alice and Tom and what he said or didn't say... I don't know, babes. I think it's the last straw. We've been lucky before—with Christopher, I mean—but there's only so many times you can get away with that sort of thing before your luck runs out. And what happened with him was bad. This would be *much* worse."

"I couldn't do it this morning," he said.

"No shame in that. I would've been the same. But we shouldn't fool ourselves—it's coming. Maybe for both of them."

"So what are you thinking?"

"I'm thinking Spain."

"There are worse places we could go."

"I was looking," she said. "Somewhere like Marbella. Wall-to-wall sunshine, all year round. Nice golf courses. You'd be able to play every day."

"I could be tempted by that."

"And cheap, too. We get a place there—nothing fancy—and we just enjoy ourselves. We lie low for a year or two, don't do anything stupid, nothing to attract attention. Work on our tans and play golf."

"Eat paella and drink sangria."

"Just chill," she said. "And then, when things have calmed down, and if we want, we look around and try somewhere else."

He frowned. "But we'd need money."

She leaned closer and lowered her voice. "Sam told me Freeman's coming to buy the gear on Saturday night. You know how much that'll be?"

"Six hundred."

She pointed her finger upwards. "Might be even more. I'm thinking we wait until he's gone, and then we go in and help ourselves to the cash."

"Just like that?"

"Sam'll be there on her own. Connor will be with Tom in the field, but, even if he's there, it won't matter. What did you do with the shooter?"

"It's in the shed."

"So we bring it with us, babes—what's she going to do when we point it at her?"

"Nothing," Gaz said.

"Exactly. *Nothing*."

48

Josh stayed in the water for fifteen minutes and then climbed out and lay on the grassy bank until the warmth from the sun had dried him off. It was time to go back home. His mum and stepdad wouldn't miss him, but he was hungry, and he hadn't thought to bring anything with him.

Paul and Becca made their way back to the weir.

"Look," Paul said. "It's still there."

Josh had expected the owner of the gear to pick it up, but no one had come. Becca made her way to where the tripod had been set up, and Josh and Paul joined her. A Sony camera was fitted to the mount of the tripod, and now that Josh was closer, he saw another device: a black box with a microphone that had been left at the edge of the bank.

"What's that?"

"It's a voice recorder," Becca said. "My dad's got one."

"Valuable?" Paul said.

"Two or three hundred."

Paul looked from the camera to the recorder. "What are they still doing here?"

"It's weird," Becca said.

"Do you think they've been forgotten?"

"That doesn't make sense," Josh said. "Not if they're expensive."

"Go on, then—you explain it."

He couldn't. "I don't know."

Becca pointed. "We should take them."

"We can't do that," Josh said.

"Why not?"

"Because they're not *ours*."

She spread her hands. "So? They've been forgotten. How long have we been here?"

"An hour," Paul said.

"I'm telling you," she said. "Someone's forgotten them. We should take them."

Josh shook his head. "That's theft."

"'*That's theft*'," Paul repeated, mocking him.

"It wouldn't be theft if we were going to give them back," Becca said.

Josh didn't like the way the conversation was going. "How can we do that? We don't know who they belong to."

"I'll take them to the police station after school tomorrow," Becca said. "They'll know what to do. There might even be a reward."

Paul nodded. "And if *we* don't take them, someone else will. And they might not be as honest as us."

Josh didn't believe either of them for a moment. He'd heard the rumours about Becca—that she'd shoplifted stuff before—and Paul had nicked his bike from outside Five Rivers after cutting through the lock with a saw he took from his dad's shed. Josh knew they were only saying what they'd said about handing them in because they wanted them all to be in on it together.

Paul went to the camera and detached it, then took the recorder.

"What about the tripod?" Becca said.

"Leave that," Paul said, slapping a hand against it so it toppled over into the undergrowth. "It's too big to get home."

Not valuable enough to make it worthwhile to take, Josh thought.

49

Atticus had been in the office all day. It was a mess, and he'd spent a couple of hours tidying it up. It was therapeutic, but his mind kept going back to Alice Green. Her assistant hadn't called, and after waiting until after lunch, Atticus had contacted her himself. There was no news. Alice hadn't been in touch, and Sarah was increasingly worried.

His tidying blitz ended at his desk. He swept papers with doodled notes into the bin, shuffled through a pile of bills—resolving, for the hundredth time, that he would pay them—and took three used coffee cups to the sink on the landing outside. He sat down at his keyboard and opened Google Maps in a window on the monitor to his right and Instagram on the monitor on his left. He opened a fresh Word document next to it and then started to scroll through Alice's Instagram reels, noting down the locations she had used for the videos if she'd added them.

He reviewed April, then March and then—impressed that Alice was still going out in winter—he did February, too. He repeated the task for TikTok, stopping when it was apparent she used the same videos on both platforms. He added in the suggested locations that Sarah had given him and others from the search results after Googling 'best wild swimming spots near Salisbury.'

He was left with a decent list: Lacock, Fordingbridge, Holt, Downton, Farleigh, and the weirs at Warleigh and Tellisford.

He turned to the map and plotted each location, then calculated the amount of time it would take to get to them and back again. Alice had told him that she liked to start recording around six in the morning, so he decided it was reasonable to remove any destination that was more than an hour away. On that basis, he was able to strike a line through Lacock, Warleigh, Tellisford, Farleigh and Holt.

He was left with Downton and Fordingbridge. Each was close enough to Salisbury for her to get up at five, drive to the river for six, prepare and record the morning's video, and then return home to edit and post it while still being able to reach the studio in time for the appointment with him at nine.

Atticus went back to the videos and still images on Instagram and, using a combination of Google's satellite imagery and Street View, geolocated both locations.

He swung around in his chair and looked over to where Bandit was snoozing on the sofa. "How do you feel about a bonus afternoon walk?"

The dog's ears pricked up when he heard that final word, and as Atticus nodded to add emphasis, he hopped down to the floor and trotted off to the bedroom, returning with his harness in his mouth.

* * *

Atticus had parked his car in the car park at the other side of the Cathedral Close and had to walk past Alice's studio on the High Street to get there. He slowed down, looking through the window for anything that might suggest that she was inside, but there was nothing. He stopped by the door, his finger hovering over the buzzer, but decided against pressing it; Sarah said she'd contact him if there was anything to report.

He opened the boot of the car, waited for Bandit to hop inside and then went around to the front. He got in, turned the ignition, and as he waited for the engine to settle down, took out his phone and slid it into the holder that was stuck to the window.

Downton and Fordingbridge were both on the road to Bournemouth; he'd visit the water meadows first and then continue south.

50

Josh, Paul and Becca cycled back into Alderbury. They heard the sound of the farmer's tractor in the field to the right of the track and decided it wasn't worth aggravating him by trespassing across his land, especially not when they had the camera and sound recorder with them. Instead, they followed the lane further to the north and then turned right, following Old Vicarage Lane and then Lights Lane into the village.

They stopped at the junction of Avon Drive. Becca had been carrying the camera on a strap around her neck, but now she removed it and held it out for Josh to take.

"What?" he said.

"Go on."

"*I* don't want it."

"Just look after it."

"Why me?"

"My mum and dad will check when I go in."

"Mine, too," Paul said before Josh could complain. "You know what they're like—they'll be all over me, and it's impossible to lie to my mum. Yours don't take any notice of you."

"That's not—"

"But that's what you said, isn't it? 'It's as if I'm not there.'"

"Yes," he started, "I know, but—"

Becca spoke over him. "So get them upstairs to your bedroom and hide them somewhere."

"In your cupboard," Paul suggested. "Cover them with a jumper or something."

Josh felt the argument slipping away from him. "I thought you were going to take them to the police?"

"We will," Becca said. "By the end of the week. Just keep them out of the way until then."

He'd been tricked. Becca and Paul had spoken in the den, and it was obvious now that they'd cooked up this plan between them. They'd have Josh stash the stolen goods until they'd worked out what to do with them. Josh thought he remembered hearing that Becca's older brother had been in trouble with the police before, and he wouldn't have been surprised if the idea was for them to speak to him and see if he could sell the things on their behalf.

Paul held out the recorder.

Josh knew he should say no, but he didn't have many friends, and he knew Paul would dump him if he thought he was chicken, and any chance he had of impressing Becca would go up in smoke. He tried to rationalise it: it was just a camera and a recorder. Maybe they *would* take them to the police, and, even if they didn't, what was the harm in holding on to them for a day or two? Who would know?

He took the devices.

"Just until the end of the week."

51

Atticus drove out of Salisbury, following the A338 to Downton. He'd taken Bandit for a walk on the water meadows before, but it had been a while, and his first attempt to find the right spot to park the car took him up a private road that ended with a house; he reversed and retraced his steps, continuing on for another hundred yards until he found the right turning. He followed the track around the corner of a collection of farm buildings and parked next to the five-bar gate that blocked the way into the meadows beyond. He went around to open the boot, and Bandit hopped down, cocked his head at Atticus and then, seemingly taking his silence for permission, slid through the kissing gate and sped away toward the water.

Atticus followed, looking around as he made his way to the track that ran along the side of the river. He had no reason to think that Alice was here—or even that she had been here earlier—but there was something about her disappearance that was giving him an unsettled feeling that he couldn't shake, and he wanted to at least feel as if he was doing *something* to find her.

Atticus looked around. Water meadows were common in the chalk valleys around the city, allowing for the flooding of large tracts of land to produce more grass for sheep and crops of hay for winter feed. Hatches and sluices had been built on the river that enabled the flow of water to be controlled; they would be raised when needed to 'drown' the meadows. The hatches on the Avon had almost all been removed long ago, but this winter had been particularly wet, and the meadows had flooded anyway.

Atticus picked a path around the remaining puddles until he found the spot he recognised from Alice's videos: the bank curved into the chalk, leaving a slower-moving pool of deeper water. The pool was clear and, as Atticus knelt down, icy cold to the touch.

The thought of swimming in it was not appealing, but, he conceded, each to his—or her—own.

Bandit ran in ever-decreasing circles and then sprang away again, sprinting for the old bridge that crossed the river ahead. Atticus let him go. There was no sign that Alice had been here, and it was unlikely he would be able to do any more by himself; it would require organised canvassing by the police, but that wasn't going to happen until someone said she was missing.

Atticus wondered again whether he should make the call himself.

52

Atticus walked back to the gate. Bandit was ahead of him, and as he reached the gate, the dog's hackles rose.

"What is it?"

Bandit started to growl, and then, before Atticus could reach down to attach his lead, he raced away.

"*Bandit!*"

Atticus pushed through the kissing gate and set off at a jog. Bandit had sprinted in the direction of the car, and when Atticus turned the corner, he could see the dog was standing in front of the passenger-side door.

Atticus drew closer and saw that someone was inside the car. Bandit was close to the door, snarling at the intruder.

Atticus hurried along the track until he was close enough to see inside. It was a man, dressed in a dark hoodie with a blond hair spilling out of the back of a baseball cap. He tried to reach for the handle so he could close the door, but Bandit lunged for his arm, and he pulled it back and raised his leg, jabbing his foot in an attempt to keep the dog at bay.

"I don't think you want to be in there," Atticus said.

The man shuffled further into the cabin. "Get that dog away from me!"

Atticus recognised him: it was the same man he'd interrupted going through the bin outside the office.

"I saw you the other day, didn't I? Going through my rubbish."

He glared at him but didn't reply.

"And now you're in my car. Do you want to tell me why?"

Bandit growled.

"Probably better if you answer the question." Atticus gestured down at the dog. "He's not very patient."

"I'm working for Alice Green," he said quickly.

Atticus couldn't help a wry smile. "I suppose I should've guessed."

"Guessed what?"

"She and her husband have *both* paid for investigators to dig up dirt on the other." He laughed. "They're as bad as each other."

"She's missing," the man said.

"I know. That's why I'm here."

"You don't know where she is?"

"I don't."

Bandit took a pace toward the car. "Please," the man said. "I'm scared of dogs."

Atticus felt like telling him he shouldn't go through the stuff of someone who owned one but could see that he really *was* scared.

"What's your name?"

"Jeremy Hardwicke."

"I'm Atticus."

"I know that," he said.

"Of course you do."

He pointed. "The dog—please."

"You're not going to run off? I think it might be useful for both of us if we compared notes."

"As long as he's under control."

Atticus clipped the lead onto Bandit's harness and gently pulled him back so that the man could climb out of the car. Atticus half-expected him to bolt, but he didn't. He stepped back so that there was extra space between him and Bandit but didn't look like he was ready to run.

"Thanks," he said.

"He's actually very friendly."

He raised an eyebrow doubtfully. "Not from where I'm standing."

Bandit, perhaps ready to correct the impression he'd given, cocked his head to the side and wagged his tail.

"Look," Atticus said. "He's saying sorry. Give him a stroke."

Hardwicke reached out and—very carefully—ran his fingers up and down across Bandit's head, between the ears. The dog lowered his head a little more so he could get to the back of his neck. Hardwicke obliged him and was rewarded with a more vigorous wag.

"See?" Atticus said.

He didn't seem completely won over but looked a little less frightened. "Where do you want to talk?"

"Where's your car?"

"Round the corner."

"Want to follow me back to Salisbury?"

He nodded. "Could do."

"I don't know about you," Atticus said, "but I've had a long day, and I could do with a pint."

"I could go for that."

"How about the Yew Tree in Odstock? Know it?"

"No," he said. "I'm not from Salisbury."

"It's not far," Atticus said. "Follow behind me. We'll be there in ten minutes."

53

Josh went into the back garden and rested his bike against the side of the house. He could see his mother in the kitchen and didn't want to walk into the house with the camera and the recorder in his hands. He went to the garden shed, pulled the slider to release the door and stepped inside. His mum had been a keen gardener before the drinking got out of control, and the shed contained everything she'd used to keep the garden looking good. There were tools hanging from brackets on the wall, and a lawnmower had been pushed up to the back. Seeing everything here, all neatly arranged, reminded him of what she'd been like before she'd met his stepdad. He looked out of the dusty pane of glass in the window at the garden; it had been pristine then, attended to with loving care and attention; but the last few months had seen it become untidy and unloved. Sort of like his mum, he thought gloomily.

Josh found a Tesco carrier bag that was being used to hold boxes of grass seed. He took out the boxes, put both items into the bag and then, rather than taking the bag inside, found a place at the back of the shed and put it down there.

He couldn't see any reason why anyone would come in here, let alone find the bag, and satisfied, he went outside and shut the door, as confident as he could be that they would still be there tomorrow. He'd speak to Paul about them at school and tell him—no, *insist*—that they do what they'd agreed and hand them in to the police.

54

The Yew Tree Inn was a traditional pub: black-and-white timbered with a thatched roof, nestled at the side of a narrow tree-lined lane that disappeared into the countryside. Atticus pulled in and parked, and as he opened the boot and put Bandit back on his lead, Hardwicke turned in and parked his Ford Focus next to him. Atticus examined the car while he waited for him to get out and concluded it was in an even worse state than his Volvo: there were rust spots and scratches on the wings and doors that hadn't been attended to, and the tyres were threadbare and beyond what any garage would have considered safe. The seats were tatty, and there was a crack in the rear windscreen that would, just by itself, have failed the MOT. The condition of the car, and the jeans he was wearing—a supermarket's value brand—made it difficult to avoid the conclusion that Hardwicke was struggling for money.

Hardwicke gestured to the pub. "Looks nice."

"So—Jeremy?"

Hardwicke shrugged. "Most people call me Jez or Jezza."

"You said you're not from Salisbury."

"No," he said. "I'm from Winchester. I've been coming back and forward since Alice instructed me."

"How long ago was that?"

"Ten days."

"And how long have you been looking at me?"

"Since Monday. I saw you outside Alice's house."

"Where were you?"

"I'd just come out from seeing her. I was on a bench outside."

"And thought I looked suspicious?"

"Not really." He smiled. "Recognised you from the telly."

"Is that so?"

He nodded. "I know this'll sound pathetic, but I'm a fan. I couldn't believe it when I saw it was you."

"That's very flattering," he said with the discomfort he always felt whenever he received attention.

"The Mallender case was amazing. The work you did on it... I could talk to you about that for hours."

Atticus wasn't about to do that, although it was nice—despite the awkwardness—to get a little recognition. He pointed to the gate to the beer garden. "Shall we get a table outside? I'll bring the dog. I'd rather not leave him in the car."

"You're sure he's friendly?"

Bandit was staring up at them, his tongue lolling out from the side of his mouth.

"Look at him," Atticus said. "He's as soft as they come. Wouldn't say boo to a goose."

"I'll take your word for it."

"He just doesn't like people going through our stuff."

"Duly noted. You get a table, and I'll get the drinks. What are you having?"

"I'll have a pint of Landlord."

He said he'd see him outside, then made his way through the door to the bar.

Atticus went into the beer garden. There were half a dozen empty wooden picnic tables, and he found one at the back with plenty of space between it and the nearest occupied table. He tied Bandit's lead to the leg of the table and sat down. There was a delicious irony in the afternoon's discovery that wasn't lost on him: both of the Greens were thoroughly unpleasant people, the similarity evidently extending to the way in which they'd chosen to solve their problems vis-à-vis the other. Atticus had always been uncomfortable in accepting work from one spouse against the other; that the Greens had *both* instructed third parties to search for compromising material said all that needed to be said about their respective characters.

Hardwicke came outside with two pints and two packets of crisps. He put them down on the table and sat down on the bench on the opposite side to where Bandit was sitting.

"Thank you," Atticus said.

Hardwicke took his pint and held it up. "Cheers."

"Cheers," Atticus said, touching glasses and drinking the first inch of his ale.

He put the glass down and eyed Hardwicke. He was younger than he'd first thought, perhaps late twenties or early thirties. He wore a black hoodie that showed signs of repeated washing. His jeans were definitely from an economy line, and his black trainers were scuffed from daily wear. His hair looked overdue a cut.

"What's your story?" Atticus asked.

"How'd you mean?"

"Investigations. How did you get into it?"

"Used to be a journalist. Didn't get on with it, so I decided I'd do something different. I saw you on the news and thought I might be able to do something similar. It seemed as good an option as any."

"I'm your inspiration, then?"

"Yes," he said. "But don't let it go to your head."

"Too late for that."

"Haven't been doing it long—first month."

"Busy?"

"Not really. Just getting the word out."

"Is this your first job, then?"

"*That* obvious?"

"Just a guess," Atticus said, realising Hardwicke might take that as a slight.

"Well, it is—you're right. But I'll be happy if they're all as interesting as this. The two of them…" Hardwicke paused and leaned in as if what he was about to say was so indiscreet he couldn't risk being overheard. "They're both so *awful*."

"I couldn't agree more."

"Do you know what I've been thinking? Have you read *The Twits*?"

"By Roald Dahl? A long time ago."

"That's them, isn't it? Mr. and Mrs. Twit?"

"I hadn't thought of them like that," he said, "but you're right. That's them to a tee."

Hardwicke raised his glass, and Atticus raised his, touching them together.

Hardwicke sipped his ale and put the glass back down. "What do you *do* when you're asked to work for someone you think is a horrible person?"

"You take the money, do the best job you can, and then, when you're done, you take a long shower afterwards."

"Did you do that with Mallender?"

Atticus winked. "No comment. Was it you who found out about Frank bribing the planners?"

"She told me she thought that's what he was doing, so I asked around. I used to cover the council for the *Chronicle*, and I still have good connections. Frank was working on a development at Sleepers Hill. One of the councillors had made himself unpopular, and someone he'd offended told me about all the gifts he was receiving that he hadn't declared: tickets to the races, trips to London to see West End shows, football in a box at Southampton. I knew it was Frank who'd been giving him those gifts, so it was just a question of finding the proof. I put the squeeze on the councillor and got him to confess to everything else. Frank bought a five-acre plot of farmland for two hundred thousand and got planning permission to put four-million-pound houses on it. The locals couldn't believe it—the farmer who sold it to Frank had tried to sell it as a building plot for ten years, and it'd always been turned down. Frank paid two of the councillors and got what he wanted."

"And you gave all of that to Alice?"

"And she went to the press." Hardwicke sipped his pint. "I know it's messed things up for Frank, but I don't care. I found out other stuff about him—he's bad news. He deserves everything he gets."

"I'll drink to that," Atticus said, raising his glass again.

Hardwicke took another sip, watching him over the rim of the glass. "Your turn. Where's Alice?"

"I have no idea. But she's *your* client. I was hoping you might know."

Hardwicke shook his head. "I don't."

"When did you see her last?"

"At her house on Monday," he said, "but that was before the online stuff. Frank's doing?"

"Yes," Atticus said. "He's very pleased with himself."

"Was that your work?"

"Not my style. He's been working on it for a while. He brought me in to dig up anything else he could use against her. The two of them are obsessed—they'll end up destroying each other, and then they'll be fighting over nothing."

"I read the stuff when it came out—the article and then all the reaction. It's bad for her, isn't it?"

"Very," he said.

"Career ending?"

"Probably," Atticus said. "How'd you think she'll take it?"

Hardwicke shrugged. "I don't know her well enough to say."

"I didn't get the impression she's a shrinking violet."

"She's not, but you never know. That was pretty brutal."

Bandit's ears pricked up as another dog trotted into the garden, its owner close behind.

"So you saw me outside the house," Atticus said, "and then you started to look into what I might be doing for him."

Hardwicke winced. "The bins... Sorry about that."

He waved the apology away. "I would've done the same—but I wouldn't have been caught. I'm not in the business of giving out advice, but I would've made sure there wasn't a dog in the house, and if there was, I would've waited until it was out of the way."

"I'd already reached that conclusion."

"And if you're going to break into a car, make sure the owner's definitely not about to come back."

"Also noted."

"Other than that—you've done good work. The planning stuff is dynamite."

"Thank you," Hardwicke said, smiling at his compliment.

"You didn't tell Alice who I was?"

"No," he said. "I was going to do that this morning, but... well, you know. She's not picking up." Hardwicke opened one of the packets of crisps. "Has it crossed your mind that Frank might be responsible for her disappearance?"

"It has," Atticus conceded. "But I don't think so."

"You know Frank's violent?"

"I know he's loud and aggressive, but it's all mouth and no trousers."

Hardwicke shook his head. "He didn't tell you about the time he put her in hospital?"

"He didn't."

"Broke her arm. They had a fight; he pushed her over; she put her arm out to stop herself and snapped the bone. She was going to call the police, but he persuaded her to give him another chance." Hardwicke took out his phone. "There was this, too."

He opened the gallery and selected a photograph, then turned the screen so Atticus could see it. The photograph showed two shotgun shells within a torn-open envelope, lying on a wooden table.

55

Atticus stared at the photograph. The deep red plastic of the shells contrasted with the dull, off-white envelope.

"What happened?"

"Alice got them in the post," Hardwicke said. "No note, no message—nothing."

"When?"

"A couple of weeks ago."

"How does she know it was Frank?"

"There's an element of assumption to it, but, come on… who else would it be? He told her he'd shoot her if she ever crossed him, and he has shotguns at a house they have in the country—he uses them to shoot clay pigeons. She knew it was a message from him. A threat."

He hadn't thought Frank was capable of violence, but he didn't know about the broken arm, and he didn't know about *this*.

"I think you need to go to the police," he said.

"I'd already decided to. I just wanted to see if you had anything that'd help me work out what had happened."

Atticus sucked on his bottom lip. "I still don't think he'd do anything to her," he said. "I didn't get that vibe from him, and the timing would be strange—he's already caused a ton of damage with the online stuff, and I don't see why he'd escalate things. But I can't say that for sure. I think we have to assume everything is possible until she's been found."

"And tell the police?"

"I don't think you have a choice. Does she have anyone else who'd report her missing?"

"There was an on-off boyfriend," Hardwicke said.

"Do you know who he is?"

"She never told me much about him, but I got the impression it was more off than on at the moment. You think he might be important?"

"The police will want to talk to him," he said, "assuming she's been declared missing. He'd be the first person they'd speak to."

"After Frank."

"After Frank," Atticus agreed. "Jilted lovers have an obvious motive."

"As do ex-husbands you've just grassed up to the police."

"True, but I still don't think it's likely."

"What about her assistant?"

"I saw her this morning and told her she should make a missing person report. She didn't seem all that keen, but I'll give her a call on the way back and see if she's done anything about it."

"For all we know, Alice might have turned up."

"Maybe."

Hardwicke finished his pint. "Do you think she's done something to herself?"

Atticus shrugged. "I don't know. I am concerned, though. I think the police need to be involved."

Hardwicke pointed to his empty glass. "Another?"

Atticus shook his head. "Better not. I need to get back."

"I'll go to the police in the morning if she hasn't turned up."

"Go to Bourne Hill," he said. "Ask for DCI Mack Jones or DI Robbie Best. They'll look after you."

Atticus paused, teasing at an idea that he'd had while they were talking and deciding that he might as well go with it and at least see what Hardwicke thought.

"There's one other thing," he said. "How busy are you?"

"Like I said—not busy at all. Not at all until I see Alice, and, even then, I've pretty much done everything I can do for her. Why?"

"I have something that needs doing, and I was thinking maybe I could hire you."

Hardwicke's eyebrows kinked up in interest. "What do you mean? Like a referral?"

"Not exactly," he said. "You'd be acting for me."

"Paid?"

"Of course. But discreetly."

"What do you have in mind?"

"You said you've got contacts at the council in Winchester?"

"Quite a few. What do you want to know?"

"There's a contractor I'm interested in. He's based here, in Salisbury, but he landed a very big IT contract with the council, and it kind of came out of the blue."

"You're thinking it might have been incentivised—like Frank?"

"That's exactly what I'm thinking."

"I could ask around. What's the name of the contractor?"

Atticus glanced away, quickly considering whether this was one of his better ideas or one that would get him into a world of trouble. He'd promised Mack that *he* wouldn't investigate Andy, but he hadn't promised that he wouldn't instruct someone else to do it. He knew it was semantics, but Mack was fighting for her kids with one hand tied behind her back, and Andy deserved to get a dose of his own medicine.

"His name is Andy Jones," he said. "I can send you the details later."

56

It was nearly midnight. Tom had drunk himself into another stupor and had fallen into a deep sleep over an hour ago. Connor sent Sam a message to say that Tom was out for the count and that now would be a good time if she wanted to catch up. She told him he needed to come over to the farm and asked whether he could do that safely. Connor checked that Tom was still asleep; he was sprawled out on top of his sleeping bag, snoring loudly and with not even the slightest suggestion that he would stir for hours. The pattern had been established: he drank all day, accelerated once they put their tools down and then passed out after dinner.

Another storm had rolled in as the sun went down, and rain was hammering onto the canvas and pouring down in rivulets that formed a curtain as they spilled down in front of the open entrance. Connor was confident enough that Tom wouldn't wake, and, putting on a waterproof, he left the tent and set off to the farm.

***

The rain began to fall more heavily, and, although Connor was able to shelter beneath the trees for at least some of the way, he was still soaked through by the time he reached the yard. The office door was open, and light spilled out from inside. Connor jogged the final few yards and ducked inside.

Sam was sitting at the desk in front of the computer she used for the business.

"Cats and dogs out there," Connor said.

"Got the horses in earlier. They won't want to be outside in this."

"I know the feeling," he said, gesturing down with both hands. His sodden clothes were dripping onto the floor.

"Poor love," she said, gently mocking him as she went over to the tumble dryer in the corner and took out a clean towel.

He took off his jacket, accepted the towel and mopped his face and hair dry. "What was so important that you wanted me to come over?"

"Take a seat."

He pulled out a chair from the other side of the desk and sat down. "So?"

"Something's happened. You need to know about it."

"Not good news?"

"No. I sent Nikki and Gaz to go and give Tom's woman a scare this morning."

He felt his stomach fall. "What've they done?"

"She went out early for a swim in the river, and they followed her. They waited until she got out and then had a word. Problem was, she wasn't as frightened as she ought to have been, and she had a go at them."

"'Had a go'?"

"There was a scuffle, and she fell over and banged her head on a rock. They thought she was dead."

He cursed.

"You'd think I might've learned by now, but apparently not. They brought her back here. Their *brilliant* idea was to feed her to the pigs, but they were about to get her out of the car when we found out that, rather than being dead, she was very much alive."

Connor put his head in his hands.

"I *know*," she said. "I feel the same."

"Where is she?"

"In the cellar. We won't be able to keep her there forever, but it'll give us some time to work out how much Tom's said and how likely she is to either say something herself or get him to say something."

"If she wasn't scared before—"

"—she'll be shitting herself now," Sam finished.

"She doesn't know who we are?"

"Gaz and Nikki said they were wearing balaclavas when they jumped her, and she wouldn't be able to say where she is now."

"This is a *mess*," he said. "Look at the context. Tom blurts out at the Haunch how upset he is and that he's told her; then he's taken up into the field for a week; *then* she has this happen to her while he's away. I was always worried about that. I told you. I said—"

"I know what you said," she said impatiently. "But we agreed it was the best option from a bad bunch."

Connor held up a finger. "Hold on. I went through some of the older messages on his phone tonight. They've been talking about a divorce she's going through with her ex-husband.

It sounds messy. She was telling him how she'd dumped her ex in the shit with the police and now she was expecting him to come after her in return. She mentioned his name. I'll be able to dig it—"

"Frank Green," Sam said, pointing at the screen. "He's a property developer. I've been doing my research. There was a story in the paper about him bribing councillors for planning permission. He buys land for peanuts, gets permission, builds a big house and flogs it for a huge profit."

Connor ran a hand through his wet hair. "So maybe there is a way out of this. We make her think this was something *he's* arranged."

Sam bit her lip, thinking, then nodded. "Nikki said she said something along those lines before it all went to shit. Something about had they been sent by Frank to give her a scare. It's probably not going to be too difficult to convince her."

"Do you think that'd work? She'd have to believe he'd have her *kidnapped*. That's not a messy divorce, Sam, that's..." He shrugged helplessly.

"I know—it sounds over the top, but Nikki said *she* brought it up. And I don't have another alternative. It's either that or..." She drew a finger across her throat. "Well—you know."

Connor was still unconvinced. "That doesn't solve our problem. We still don't know how much Tom's told her about what we did. The whole *idea* of this was to find out what she knows, whether he's said too much, and to scare her into never opening her mouth about it."

"That's true. Nothing's really changed. Everything depends on what Tom's said." She got up, went to the filing cabinet and took the bottle of whisky that sat there and two paper cups.

"Nikki and Gaz are breaking into her office tonight. I'd like to be sure she doesn't have anything that could be used against us."

"And if we can't be sure?"

"Then it gets added to the things we'll weigh up."

She unscrewed the bottle and poured out two measures, handing one of the cups to Connor.

"What a mess," he said.

She touched her cup to his. The two of them sat in silence for a moment, listening to the drumming of the rain on the roof.

PART 4

57

It was four thirty in the morning when Francine Patterson woke up. She'd been waking before her alarm for the last ten days, and it was getting to be beyond a joke. The usual pattern was for her to struggle more than usual to get to sleep, and then to wake at three or four. Robbie would be asleep beside her, and rather than wake him, she'd lie quietly in the darkness, listen to his breathing and allow her thoughts to wander to the concern that had woken her.

Her lack of sleep was irritating, but she knew the reason for it: the National Investigators' Examination. Robbie had said it wasn't easy, and she believed him; she was expected to have a comprehensive understanding of the law on police investigations and to be familiar with the processes and procedures for conducting investigations, including specific topics on best practices for interviewing, evidence gathering, case file preparation, and the management of suspects. Francine had struggled in school, and it had only been years later that her difficulties had been given a cause when she had finally been diagnosed with dyslexia. Everything made sense after that, but the memories of exasperated teachers, confused parents and unkind kids had left a scar. Robbie had told her she'd be fine, but she couldn't help doubting herself. The daunting curriculum had just made things worse.

She reached out a hand for the nightstand, careful not to move too much for fear that she would disturb Robbie, took her phone and touched the screen to check the time. It was ten past five now, and, with her usual alarm scheduled for half an hour later, there was no point in trying to get back to sleep. She held her breath and slowly swung her legs out from under the duvet, her toes probing for the furry novelty slippers that Robbie had bought for her birthday. She found them, slipped her feet inside, and got out of bed. Robbie grunted and grumbled and turned over, his breath deepening again as he drifted back into deep sleep.

Lucky bastard.

She took her phone, went into the bathroom, undressed and ran the shower. Robbie had left his clothes on the chair. She'd told him to put them in the washing bin, but he always forgot.

A few minutes later, feeling marginally more human, she turned off the shower, stepped out and dried herself off. She kept her work clothes in the wardrobe in the second bedroom, so she went through and dressed. Her phone buzzed with her alarm, but she silenced it before it could wake Robbie. She went downstairs, filled her travelling mug with fresh coffee and took it and her bag outside. It was a bright morning, and she turned toward the cathedral to see the spire scraping against a blue and cloudless sky. She wasn't due on shift for an hour, but she would be able to find a quiet room and revise until then. The test was a week away, and—whatever Robbie said—cramming was the only way she was going to feel good about getting through it.

58

Atticus had hoped for a lie-in, but Bandit had other plans; he jumped onto the mattress and licked Atticus's face until he was awake. Atticus reached across to where he had left his phone charging on the floor, unplugged it and, blinking the sleep from bleary eyes, checked the time: it was early.

"Bloody hell," he muttered to the dog. "Would it have killed you to give me another half an hour?"

Bandit leaned down to lick him again, his tail wagging ferociously.

"All right, all right—stop pestering me. I'm getting up."

He sat, swung his legs over the side of the mattress and stood. His clothes were strewn over the floor, and he collected them, checked they were clean enough to wear again, and put them on.

Bandit disappeared into the office and returned with his harness in his mouth.

"Just let me brush my teeth."

The dog cocked his head to the side and eyed him expectantly.

"Fine. I'll brush them afterwards."

* * *

Atticus turned and walked along North Walk until he was next to the northeast corner of the cathedral lawn. He took Bandit off his lead and watched as he raced away. The Close was busy: parents drove their children to the Cathedral School, their vehicles edging around one another in spaces designed for horses and carts rather than oversized SUVs. Grammar schoolboys ambled across the path in the direction of Bishops Wordsworth, and early-arriving tourists took the day's first photos of the cathedral.

He called Bandit back and waited as the dog bounded back to him, pausing to sniff the bronze statue of the Walking Madonna, perpetually frozen in her journey across the lawn. It was unusually chilly for the time of year, and Atticus's breath clouded in front of his face as Bandit cocked his leg to mark his scent around the statue's skirts.

He reached Choristers Square, nodded a greeting to the guard in his cabin and continued to the High Street Gate. He stopped; a marked police car was parked outside Alice Green's studio. There was no sign of any officers, but, as Atticus continued down the street, he could see that the door to the building was ajar. He drew alongside and saw that not only was it open, but it had also been forced. The wood around the lock was splintered. Atticus examined it and saw that it had been prised open with a crowbar.

He pushed the door open. He could hear voices inside, the words muffled. He was wondering about the good sense of going in when Bob Carver came out of the studio.

"Morning, Detective Constable."

Carver rolled his eyes. "What are you doing here?"

"I was just passing."

"Carry on, then."

"I saw the door had been forced."

"You don't have to worry yourself about it. It's all under control."

Atticus was tempted to tell him he doubted that, but, for once, was able to hold his tongue. Carver had never been one of his biggest fans when Atticus had been police, and his antipathy had increased as he built his practice as an investigator. There had been a couple of run-ins over the course of the last few months, and even though Carver had come to his aid in the aftermath of the investigation at the manor house, the prospect of a détente still seemed distant.

He gestured into the studio. "What's happened?"

"Didn't you hear me? Clear off." Carver nudged him to the door. "And take your mutt with you."

"I'm only asking because it might be relevant to something I've been working on."

"Here we go." Carver sighed and rolled his eyes.

"This building is used by Alice Green."

Carver's face moved from doubt to surprise to irritation. "How'd you know that?"

Atticus was about to answer, but, before he could say anything else, they were joined on the pavement by Pete Britten.

"Atticus," he said.

"Morning. I was just telling Bob I might be able to help."

"He knows who works in the building," Carver said.

"Alice Green," Atticus offered.

"You know her?"

"Her husband—well, her *ex*-husband—asked me to look into her. The two of them are fighting. They're about as bad as each other, from what I can make out. She wrecked his business, and now he's trying to wreck hers."

"And you think the husband might have broken in?"

"I doubt it—he wouldn't do it himself, but I wouldn't put it past him to pay someone. I wouldn't mind a quick look if that's all right."

Carver turned to Britten and shook his head. "No."

"Come on, Bob," Britten replied. "He's here now. What harm can it do if he just puts his head around the door?"

"Exactly," Atticus said. "I won't touch a thing—promise." He held out Bandit's lead. "Could you hold him for a moment, Bob?"

59

Atticus stepped around Carver and followed Britten along the corridor and into the studio.

"The street cleaner from the council called it in just after seven," Britten said. "He saw the door had been forced."

"Crowbar," Atticus said.

"That's what it looks like."

"Any CCTV?"

"Haven't seen anything inside," he said.

"There isn't any," Atticus said.

"You've been here before?"

"I was in here yesterday. I meant cameras on the street."

"Nothing decent."

The front of the building opposite had been cloaked with scaffolding for weeks, and Atticus suspected any cameras would be obscured.

"This'll just be an opportunistic thing," Britten said. "It'll be a junkie. Some pissed-up scrote kicks the door down, has a rummage. Maybe they find something, and maybe they don't.

They get disturbed or freaked out, whatever, and they run. You know what it's like—we get it all the time."

"Maybe," Atticus said, although he didn't accept that for a minute.

"What about the husband?"

"Horrible man. There was a story about Alice online yesterday that would've done a lot of damage to her business. He planted it. I was supposed to see Alice for a chat in the morning, and she didn't turn up. She has a woman who works here as her PA, and she didn't know where she was."

"She's gone missing?"

"Possibly. I told her husband that he ought to think about calling you to report it, but he wouldn't."

"And why's he hired you?"

"He's looking for dirt on her. I doubt he'd be so stupid as to come in here himself, but I'd still check him out. See if you can lift any prints and compare them with his. They'll be on file. He was arrested last year on suspicion of bribery."

They reached the door to the studio. It had been forced in the same way as the door to the street. Atticus knelt down so he could look at it more closely. A blunt object had been pressed into the space between the door and the frame and then wrenched back, splintering the wood and forcing the lock. He looked at the damage: the paint had been scoured away next to the jamb, with flecks on the carpet, and the bolt had torn through the wood, with splinters left sticking straight out.

"It wouldn't have taken long," Atticus said. "There's nothing to the door at all."

He stood and followed Britten inside.

"Just a quick look," Britten said. "And don't touch anything."

Atticus looked around the room, comparing it to what he remembered from yesterday. The place had been turned over and bore the unmistakeable signs of a hurried search: drawers hung open, their contents strewn across the floor in disarray; the two desks had been rifled through, leaving a chaotic jumble of files and folders; overturned chairs and an upended wastebasket added to the turmoil. A filing cabinet had been forced, the metal bent and buckled where a crowbar had been pressed in and yanked back.

"You said there's a PA who works here? Do you have her details?"

Atticus took out his phone, found the number and read it out so Britten could write it in his notebook.

"Where are the SOCOs?"

"Don't be daft," Britten said. "You know as well as I do how difficult it is to get them out for something mundane like this."

"I don't think this is mundane. I think Alice might be missing, and I think you'll want to be very sure that her husband doesn't have anything to do with it. You'll want to be sure you find prints if whoever broke in left any."

"I'll mention it, but don't hold your breath. Cuts have made a big difference to the service we get."

Atticus heard a bark from outside. "Better go. Will you let me know if you find anything?"

"Of course," Britten said.

60

Sam warmed up a microwave meal and took it, a fork, and a bottle of water, to the empty stable. She put on the balaclava that had been left on the hook where they hung the nosebags and cleared away the straw so she could get to the trapdoor. She undid the padlock, pulled the door up, latched it open and then, stuffing the fork and the water bottle in a pocket of her jacket, carefully made her way down the ladder, holding onto the rungs of the ladder with her right hand and balancing the plate in her left.

She switched on the light and looked down at Alice Green. She was more alert than she'd been the last time Sam saw her. Her eyes followed Sam as she came closer, bulging with fear. She'd been in the cellar for a day, and Sam couldn't even begin to imagine what she must be feeling.

"I've brought you some food," Sam said. "Are you going to be quiet?"

Alice nodded. Samantha reached down and pulled the tape away, then picked at the edge of the rag and tugged it out of her mouth.

"*Please*," Alice said. "You don't have to do this. Let me go."

"Can't do that. Not yet."

Sam took the plate and reached into her pocket for the fork.

"At least let me feed myself. My wrists are sore. The ties are cutting into my skin."

"They won't if you don't struggle." They'd followed the same routine for the previous meals, but Sam still felt the need to reiterate the ground rules. "I'll feed you, just like before. It won't do you any favours at all to make any noise. For one thing, you're miles away from anyone, and you'll just be wasting your breath. And, for the other, I'll take the food away, and you can go hungry. It's up to you—be good and get fed, or piss me off and go hungry."

"I didn't make a noise before, did I?"

"No."

"I won't this time, either."

"Good."

Sam picked up the plate and shuffled a little closer, resting on her haunches and winding the fork in the spaghetti until she had a decent amount. She held it up and waited for Alice to lean forward, slotting it into her open mouth.

She chewed and swallowed. "Is this about Frank?"

Sam loaded the fork for a second time. "Who's Frank?"

"My husband. Did he put you up to this?"

Sam held the fork to her mouth and waited for her to take the spaghetti; she didn't answer. Nikki had told her Alice had said something about her husband at the river, but this was the first time she'd mentioned it to Sam.

"I mean," Alice said, "it's *obvious*. He set me up with that shit online—I mean, that was brutal enough—and then he goes and does something like this. But I'll tell you what—you tell him he needs to back off. You tell him I've got more on him that'll make what's been put out so far look like *nothing*." She took the mouthful of spaghetti and chewed.

Sam didn't reply.

"How much is he paying you?" Alice said.

Sam loaded the fork again, but, this time, Alice turned her head away and rejected it.

"How much?" Alice said.

"Eat or don't eat—it's no skin off my nose."

"I'll double it."

Sam proffered the fork. "Want it or not?"

"I'll *triple* it. Please—I've got the money. I just want to get out of here. I want to go home."

"Fine," Sam said, taking the fork away.

Alice's eyes went wide. "No, no—I want it, please. I'm hungry."

Sam held it closer and then repeated the routine until the plate was empty. She unscrewed the bottle and held it out, gently tipping it so that Alice could drink.

"Do you have any headache pills?"

"I can bring you some," Sam said.

"My head," she said. "It's really sore. I hit my head when I fell. I'm worried it's a concussion."

"So try to relax. It'll pass."

"The pills?"

"I told you—I'll bring some."

"I need the bathroom again."

They'd given her a bucket yesterday, but Nikki and Gaz had been here then, and Samantha wasn't about to take the chance that Alice might try something while she was guarding her alone.

"You'll have to wait. I'll be back in a couple of hours."

"I can't *wait* a couple of hours. I need to go now."

Sam exhaled impatiently; it wasn't irritation with Alice—her request was reasonable. It was with Nikki and Gaz, who'd put them all in this situation with their ineptitude. She didn't get any pleasure from letting Alice soil herself—none of this was her fault, after all—but what choice did she have? She had *no* choice.

"I'm sorry." She took the gag, stuffed it back into Alice's mouth and took a fresh length of tape and secured it in place. She got to her feet. "I'll be back as soon as I can."

61

Atticus was looking over his list of places where Alice might have gone to swim when his phone buzzed in his trouser pocket. He took it out.

It was Frank Green.

"Hello?"

"I just had a call," Green said without preamble. "Alice's car has been found."

"What do you mean?"

"I mean it's been found—abandoned. Somewhere near Alderbury."

Atticus searched for a pen in the debris on his desk. "Right. Go on."

"It's been there overnight, apparently. A dog walker found it. Saw it yesterday and saw it again today. They said they might not have done anything except the door hadn't been shut properly, and the keys are still in the ignition. They thought it was strange."

"But it's Alice's car—why would they call you?"

"Because the insurance papers in the glovebox have my name and phone number on them. I'd forgotten—I bought the car for her before we split up, and she never gave it back."

"And you insured it?"

"That's right."

"Do you have the address where it was found?"

"There's an old mill at Standlynch. That's all they said."

"Got it. What are you going to do about it?"

"About the car?" Green said. "Nothing. I'm going to London for work. I don't have time."

"But you want *me* to have a look?"

"I'm paying you well enough. And, anyway, it might be useful. God knows what stuff you might find inside it. Go over there and have a nose around."

Atticus sucked on his teeth, taking a moment to master his distaste for his client. The man was a sociopath. He might have hated his ex-wife, but she was missing, her car had been abandoned, and he didn't seem to have a shred of concern or compassion.

"Okay?" Green pressed.

"Okay."

"Good. I need to go. I've got a train to—"

"There's one other thing," Atticus cut over him. "Her studio was broken into last night."

"Right. And?"

"And that wouldn't have anything to do with you, would it?"

"No. I'm paying good money for you to find ammunition I can use against her in court. I wouldn't be able to use anything that was nicked, would I?"

Atticus listened for variations in Green's voice—his tone, pitch, and the speed of speech—on the basis that nervousness often caused people to speak faster or with a higher pitch, and nerves might indicate a lie. But there was nothing.

Atticus took a breath. "Aren't you even a *little* concerned?"

"Why would I be?"

"She's missing, her office has been broken into, and now her car turns up like this."

"No. I *told* you—she's all over the place. There'll be a perfectly good reason for all of it."

"I have to ask—again—after what you did to her yesterday. Is she the sort to hurt herself?"

"That's a good one," he said with a bitter chuckle. "Not a chance. She loves herself too much. I was going to say I wouldn't wish her ill, but, you know, that'd be a lie. I don't care what happens to her either way. I thought I made it clear when we met, Mr. Priest—she's dead to me."

Atticus took a moment, self-aware enough that if he didn't, he was going to say something he might come to regret. "Let me put it in a way you'll understand a little easier. If it were to come out that she *has* done something like that, there'll be an inquest. The coroner will want to find out if there was anything that might've given her a motive to hurt herself. The court will *certainly* be made aware of the story, and I think there's an *excellent* chance that it finds out that the story came from you."

"But that's not a—"

"No, it's not a crime." Atticus spoke over him. "But a story like that—salacious and tragic—will *definitely* end up coming to the attention of a national newspaper." Atticus didn't need to tell Green that *he'd* make sure the story reached the right people; he hoped that much was implied. "You might not have committed a crime with what you did," he went on, "but people won't see it that way. The court of public opinion isn't bound by the same rules as a court of law, and the verdict will be brutal. So I'd just ask you to think carefully for a moment about whether you want that kind of publicity, and the consequences that'll follow—for you *and* your business. Because I can't speak for the people you work with, but, if it were me, I'd be thinking very carefully whether I wanted to be associated with someone like you."

There was another pause, and, when Green spoke again, his voice was taut with anger. "Have you finished?"

"I have."

"Good. Stop moralising and go and sort out the car. And make sure it doesn't delay your report. I was hoping you'd finished it."

"You'll have it tomorrow. Goodbye, Mr. Green."

Atticus had had just about enough of Green for one day. He ended the call before he could reply.

62

Atticus opened a map and found the spot where Alice's car had been found. The old mill was to the north of the water meadows in Downton that he had visited yesterday; the location was less than a mile upstream. It looked as if Atticus had been right in his assumption that Alice wouldn't have travelled far for her swim on Wednesday morning and only *just* wrong on where she might go. He switched the map to satellite view, then zoomed in as much as he could. There looked to be a couple of buildings on the track that led down to the water, but, other than those, there was very little there.

He picked up his phone again and called Mack.

"What's up?" she said.

"You know I said I've been working for the most unpleasant man in Salisbury?"

"To find dirt on the most unpleasant woman in Salisbury—yes, I remember."

"The Greens," Atticus said. "Alice and Frank. Thing is, it's taken a bit of a turn. I was supposed to meet Alice yesterday, but she stood me up. I was going past her office this morning, and it seems someone broke in overnight."

She groaned. "Atticus… do I *want* to know about this?"

"I mentioned it to Frank, and he really couldn't have shown less interest if he'd tried."

"So you're saying she's missing?"

"I wouldn't have said that until five minutes ago, but now I'm not sure. Her car was found down near the Avon. The insurance is still in Frank's name, and he got a call from the dog walker who found it. Frank isn't in any hurry to go down and collect it, so I'm going instead."

"Why would it've been left there?"

"She has an online business—I think the kids would describe her as a 'wellness influencer.' She's into wild swimming. Very likely she was doing that."

"An accident, then?"

"Maybe."

"You don't think Frank could be involved, do you?"

"I don't *think* so. My first impression of him is that he's arrogant, but not nearly devious enough to do something unpleasant to her at the same time as I'm looking into her. Apart from the risk that I'd notice, what would be the point?"

"Why are you telling me this?"

"Because I think this is going to be a missing persons enquiry. Alice hired a private investigator to look into Frank, and I met him yesterday. His name is Hardwicke, and I think he's planning on coming into the station this morning to report her missing. I just wanted you to have a heads up… and it was an excuse to hear your voice."

She exhaled. "Okay—and now you have. I'd better get back to it. It's busy here. Keep me posted."

"Can I see you tonight?"

"No," she said. "Better not."

"I'll bring dinner," he offered.

"You know what we agreed."

"I'll climb over the back fence. No one will see me."

"Not tonight. We need to wait until after custody has been sorted. It's too risky now."

63

Atticus drove out on the Southampton Road, came off at the Alderbury turning and continued along the increasingly narrow Witherington Road as it headed south toward Downton. He checked the map on his phone and saw that the coordinates to the place Frank had suggested directed him down a track on the final corner of the road as it became Barford Lane. The surface of the track was pitted and rough, and the trees on both sides provided a canopy overhead that reduced the late morning light to a soupy, dappled glow. Bandit was standing in the back of the car, his tail slapping against the bars of the cage that separated the boot from the cabin.

Atticus drove on slowly and carefully, avoiding the potholes as best he could, knowing that the suspension on the Volvo was old enough that a good whack might do irreparable damage. He passed the derelict chapel he'd seen on the map, followed the track to the right and reached the abandoned mill.

A Skoda Enyaq had been parked next to the building.

Atticus pulled over and parked next to it. He got out, went around to the boot of his car and opened the lid. Bandit jumped down, his tail beating back and forth as he waited for Atticus to give him permission to explore.

"Go on, then," he said.

The dog raced away.

Atticus looked around and tried to get a sense of the place. The sun shone through the gaps in the dense foliage that bordered the river. Birds chirruped, and a swan paddled through the still water of the mill pond. He could hear the hiss of the water as it passed through the mill and continued downstream on the other side. Atticus stepped up to the car and saw that the dog walker had been right: the driver's door was open. He reached for the handle, then stopped; much better to be cautious. He went back to his Volvo, took out a cardboard box of nitrile gloves he kept in the mess of debris on the back seat, removed a pair of gloves and put them on.

He went back to the car, grasped the handle at the very edge and pulled the door back. The keys had been left in the ignition, as Frank had said. There was a plastic carrier bag on the passenger seat, along with a mess of envelopes and papers that had been dumped on the seat. He reached down and opened it and saw a swimsuit inside. He ignored that for the moment, leaned into the cabin and looked into the back, where a towel and a dryrobe had been tossed onto the floor.

He went around to the front passenger-side door and opened it, then flicked quickly through the jumble of envelopes and papers: he found the insurance policy with Frank as the insured party; there were bills, some with red ink; there was a claim form from the High Court in London, a quick scan revealing that Alice was being sued for misrepresentation by a company who'd paid her to advertise their products, but who didn't feel they'd received value for money. Someone had written BOLLOCKS across the form in thick black ink.

He took out his phone and stared at the screen for a moment as he decided what to do. He'd been concerned before, but that concern had grown now, and, if Frank Green wasn't going to do the right thing and report his wife as missing, he was going to have to do it himself.

He dialled the station and asked to be put through to the duty sergeant.

64

Atticus decided to have a look down by the river while he waited for the police to arrive. He followed the track, Bandit leaping out of the undergrowth and trotting along beside him. The path ran between two stretches of the river: one that fed the mill and the other that followed its natural course. A wooden fence, worn by the elements, was snaggled with weeds and colourful wildflowers. Sunlight dappled through the leaves, creating patterns on the water, a shifting mosaic of light and shade. The flora that lined the bank was untamed: wild grasses reached upward, swaying in the breeze, while insects hummed busily.

He reached the spot where the Avon broke into two branches. Most of the water went through a weir, with the rest going to the mill. The water gathered in large pools both upstream and downstream of the weir, and Atticus could see how both would be perfect for swimming. The path went across the weir, and Atticus went out to the middle and then looked downstream, recognising the backdrop from several of Alice's videos. He identified the spot where she had filmed before and retraced his steps, following a small track until he was at the place where it would be easiest to enter the water. It was like a natural beach, a broad shoulder that gradually led out into the deeper water. The tract nearest to the river was muddy, but the grassy bank reared up on either side, providing an ideal location to set up so that the camera lens could be angled down to keep anyone swimming in shot.

Atticus knelt down, lowering his head so that he was able to examine the ground carefully for anything that might indicate that Alice had been here. The bank was a mixture of dirt and stones, with vegetation growing behind it. It had rained between now and Wednesday morning, and, as Atticus examined the ground inch by inch, he couldn't find anything of interest. He lowered himself to his chest and wriggled forward so that he could get right up close to the lip of the bank. It was composed of compacted soil and loose gravel, interspersed with patches of grass and wildflowers clinging to the slope. The soil at the very edge was dark and rich, becoming lighter and sandier as he backed away. Weathered roots from nearby trees jutted out, offering additional bulwarks against the water. He was looking for something to suggest Alice might have fallen: displaced soil with fresh gouges and scrapes; clumps of uprooted grass if she'd grabbed out for purchase; stones and pebbles, disturbed by the slip, scattered on the bed of the river below.

There was nothing.

He stood and brushed himself down and was thinking about following the riverbank downstream when Bandit popped out from between the sedge and cow parsley. He gave an excited woof, turning back and pointing his muzzle back into the undergrowth. Atticus went up to him, reached both arms into the undergrowth and moved it to the side.

There was something long and metallic on the ground.

It was a photographer's tripod: the legs were extended, with two sections visible.

Atticus reached for it, then stopped; better to let the police deal with it. He was too interested to completely leave it alone, though, so he compromised, moving the fronds aside so he could take a better look. The rubber feet at the ends of the legs nestled among the foliage, fragments of dirt and grass stuck to them. He examined the tripod until he reached the top. It had been fitted with an aluminium mount with an adjustable clamp, padded with non-slip rubber, designed to hold a camera.

The mount was empty.

65

Atticus heard an engine from the direction of the mill and made his way back along the track, reaching down and clipping the lead to Bandit's collar. A police car was just coming around the final bend in the track, Atticus waved a hand, and the car pulled up next to his and parked. Two uniformed constables—Ryan Yaxley and Elaine Coverdale—got out. Yaxley had joined the nick just after Atticus had left, and Coverdale was fresh out of college and paired up with Yaxley to learn the ropes.

Yaxley took out his notebook and pen as he led the way over to where Atticus and Bandit waited.

"Morning," Atticus said.

Yaxley nodded. "Morning."

Bandit, sensing an opportunity for attention, tugged hard on the lead until he was within range of the newcomers. Coverdale knelt down and allowed the dog to nuzzle her, scrubbing her fingers through the fur on his neck.

"We're here on a call," Yaxley said.

"I know—I called it in."

"Possible missing person?"

"She's definitely missing, but it might be worse—I don't think it's impossible you've got a death. Maybe a suicide."

Atticus told them about Alice and that she hadn't been seen since Tuesday after receiving the kind of negative publicity that could easily have given rise to suicidal ideation. He pointed to the Enyaq, said it was hers and explained how it had been reported as abandoned. He went on to describe how Frank had been made aware of it, how he'd told Atticus and how Atticus had come down to check it out.

Coverdale stood, Bandit rubbing himself against her legs. "And you think she might've gone in the water?"

"She's a wild swimmer. She swims in the Avon most days."

"In *there*?" Yaxley said, pointing to the mill pond. "It'd freeze your tits off."

"Never tried it?" Coverdale said.

"Course I haven't. Have you?"

"Me and the kids do the Christmas Day swim at Swanage every year. It never seems like the best idea when you're all waiting to go in, but then you do, and when you get out, you feel amazing."

"If you say so," he said. He turned back to Atticus. "So where would she have been swimming?"

He pointed. "There's a weir down there. There's deeper water on either side of it."

"And she went in on Wednesday?"

"There's a bag with a swimsuit on the front passenger seat, and a towel and a dryrobe in the back of the car."

"More than likely, then," Yaxley said.

"I found a tripod down there, as well. Looks like it was knocked into the bushes."

Coverdale gently nudged Bandit out of the way. “You’d better show us.”

“You go down with him,” Yaxley said to her. “I’ll secure the car. I’ll call the nick, too. Might be an idea to line up CID, just in case.”

66

Josh had been thinking about Becca all morning. He'd seen her quickly when he got off the bus as it arrived at school, but she got out of her dad's car and hurried inside before he could get over to her to say hello. Josh was in the top set for all his classes, and she wasn't; they had art together, and sometimes sat together, but that wasn't until the afternoon. He spent maths and then English daydreaming about her and looked for her at the morning break without any luck. He knew she'd be in the canteen for lunch, but Mrs. Thomas had asked him to stay behind to tell her how he was getting on at home, and it had been ten minutes before he had been able to persuade her that everything was okay, and she told him he could go.

He diverted to the toilets to check his reflection. He wasn't happy with how he looked, his acne was playing up, and the doctor had refused to give him anything for it on the grounds that it'd go away on its own. It wasn't *too* bad, though, and at least his hair looked good. He spritzed himself with deodorant and then hurried across the playground to the canteen.

He usually ate with Paul, but, as he came inside, he saw that Paul was sitting with Becca. The two of them had found a table at the back of the room; the other seats were taken, meaning there would be nowhere for Josh to sit if he wanted to join them. He remembered how sick he'd felt at the sight of the two of them at the river. Paul *knew* how much he liked Becca; why was he behaving like he didn't? Josh saw him reach across the table and touch his fingers against the back of her hand. She broke into a wide smile. Paul took his hand away, but the smile remained.

Josh felt even sicker.

He took a plate and waited impatiently as the chef ladled on fusilli and sauce, then grabbed a glass of apple juice and made his way across the canteen to their table.

"Hi."

Paul looked up and smiled; there was a glint of something else there, too, something that might have been gloating. "All right?"

"Mrs. Thomas kept me back. Couldn't you have saved me a seat?"

"Sorry. Forgot."

Becca was watching the conversation with an amused expression. Josh could tell: the two of them had been talking about him. What had Paul told her?

The table was long, with eight chairs on each side. Two of the others got up, leaving a space for Josh to sit. Paul and Becca were at the end of the table, and Josh was separated from them by two boys from year eight. Paul and Becca started their conversation again. Josh would have had to speak over the two other boys if he wanted to join in, and there was no way he had the confidence to do that. He did his best to hide his concern at the way events seemed to be heading, smiling along when Becca laughed at a comment Paul made about *Jujutsu Kaisen*, the manga that Paul and Josh both liked.

The two boys got up, and Josh was able to slide across into the chair next to Becca.

"You still like it?" Paul said.

"What?"

"*Jujutsu Kaisen*. I was telling Becca that you're *obsessed* with it."

Josh was confused. Paul liked it, too, or at least he'd said that he did. They'd taken Josh's collection to the den last week and read them together.

"Do you?" Becca asked him.

"Yeah," he replied, uncertain at what Paul had said to her.

"Isn't it all a bit childish? For kids, I mean?"

Josh made sure he smiled. "No. It's pretty grown-up."

"Come on," Paul said. "It isn't."

"You like it just as much as I do."

"No, I don't," he said. "It's okay, but you'd have to admit it's immature. I mean, seriously—it's all pretty *stupid*."

Josh could see what was going on and wanted the ground to open up and swallow him. It was too awkward for him to just get up and leave, so he suffered through an embarrassed silence and tried to finish his pasta as quickly as he could.

Paul lowered his voice. "I wanted to talk to you about the camera."

"Okay."

"Bring it in tomorrow? I'll take it to the police."

"It's all right," Josh said. "I can do it."

"I'm going into town at the weekend. It'll be easy for me to do it then."

"I'm going into town, too," Josh said, even though he wasn't.

"Don't be a *dick*," Paul said. "Bring it in—and the recorder. I'll take care of them."

Josh was in no mood to be bullied. He knew *exactly* what Paul would do: he'd sell them and then spend the money on the new Adidas trainers he'd been saving up to afford. Or maybe he'd spend it on Becca, take her to the Everyman for a film and then Wagamama for something to eat or CUPP for a seven-quid bubble tea they wouldn't normally be able to afford. Josh wasn't about to let him do that. He was going to do the right thing, what he should've done yesterday, rather than play along with them.

Becca reached out and laid her hand on top of his. "Come on," she said. "What if we didn't take them to the police?"

"That's not what we said."

"But why not? It's not like anyone knows we have them. We could sell them and then have some fun together—all three of us."

Josh had to work hard to stop from sighing, it was desperate, and now that he saw through them, it was *pathetic*.

"She's right," Paul said.

Josh shook his head. "They don't belong to us."

"Who cares. Finders keepers."

"No."

Paul turned to Becca and rolled his eyes, making no attempt to hide it. "Told you."

They stood and headed off into the playground together. Josh watched them go, and saw Paul reach down to take Becca's hand as they left the canteen.

They didn't even try to hide it.

Josh pushed his pasta around his plate. Paul didn't like Becca—not like *Josh* did—and now he was going to show him that he could have her just by clicking his fingers, when all of Josh's careful wooing had got him precisely nowhere. It was just more childish point scoring.

Josh looked down at his half-finished plate, then put his knife and fork down. He'd lost his appetite.

67

Atticus led the way to the weir and pointed to the pool downstream. "I've seen videos of her swimming in there."

Coverdale wrote in her notebook. "Where did you say the tripod was?"

"Down there," he said, pointing.

Coverdale knelt down, moved the cow parsley aside and scratched the side of her chin. "No camera?"

Atticus shook his head. "There was nothing attached to it—I had a quick look, but I couldn't see anything."

Coverdale went over to the bank. "What do you think? Accident or suicide?"

"Suicide by drowning is rare. It's difficult to do. I'm not saying you can rule it out, though, and she *was* probably aware of something yesterday morning that would've seemed pretty desperate."

"What's that?"

"She got some very negative press. Google her—it'll be the first thing you see. It's possible it would've affected her in a way where she *did* think about taking her own life. But would she drown herself?" He shrugged. "Don't think so."

Coverdale pointed to the gentle camber of the beach. "She wouldn't have slipped getting in there," she said. "Look at it—it's almost flat." She stood and shuffled back to where Alice would have been if she were setting up the tripod. "Or she was getting ready here," she said, her back to the water. She took a backwards step and then another, deliberately catching her heel on a knotty root that protruded through the soil. "She trips, falls backwards and hits her head on a rock—like that one down there. She's knocked out and drowns."

"The body?" Atticus said.

Coverdale pointed south. "Somewhere downstream."

"That's possible. The water's flowing quickly enough to take her away."

Coverdale puffed out her chest, seemingly pleased that Atticus had agreed with at least part of her putative explanation.

"There's something else you need to know," Atticus said. "Alice and her husband are in the middle of a very unpleasant, very messy divorce. She's revealed information about him that's got him in hot water with the police, and he was behind the story about her that ran yesterday. Like I said—he contacted me about the car being found down here."

Coverdale looked up from her notebook. "Why did he call you?"

"I've been working for him. His name's Frank Green. He hired me to dig up dirt on her."

"And it's relevant because...?"

"A few reasons." He held up his hand and ticked them off on his fingers, one by one. "One—Green broke Alice's arm recently, and I've seen evidence to suggest he's made threats of violence against her. Two—Green has the motive to want to hurt her. Three—Green probably knows she comes to places like this on her own when there are unlikely to be any witnesses. And four—Green showed absolutely no concern for her when I told him she was missing."

Yaxley joined them just as his radio came to life. "Hang on," he said, reaching down to turn it up.

"Bravo Alpha Two-One, this is Control. Over."

"Control, this is Bravo Alpha Two-One. Go ahead. Over."

"Bravo Alpha Two-One, be advised that the individual you are looking for, Alice Green, has been reported missing as of ten hundred hours this morning. The report was filed by her personal assistant. All units have been notified, and an OBS has been issued. Any questions or additional requests? Over."

"Copy that, Control. What about CID?"

"DCI Jones is on her way."

68

Josh got down from the bus and walked the rest of the way back to his house on Avon Drive. He got his bike and set off for the river, following the same path that they'd all taken yesterday. Paul had texted him to remind him to bring the camera and recorder to school tomorrow, and when Josh had ignored him, he'd suggested that the two of them could meet at his house. Josh replied to say that he was busy; Paul texted back at once, bringing up the camera again; and Josh ignored him.

The rest of the afternoon had been a torment. Becca was in his art class and had made sure to sit at the same table. She had pushed her chair right up against his, close enough that their legs brushed up against each other. She stroked his arm and laughed much too easily when he'd said something about his work that wasn't even meant to be funny. She made *such* a fuss of him that there could be no doubt that it was fake. Josh would've given his right arm to have that kind of attention from her before, but now he knew it was all wrong. He couldn't stop imagining the conversation that she must have had with Paul, with him telling her how much Josh liked her, and how easy it would be to manipulate him. It made Josh angry: with Paul, his so-called friend, for betraying him, and with her for treating him as if he were a love-sick idiot.

They'd both been waiting for him in the playground after school, but he'd taken the side door out and got onto the bus without either of them seeing him.

He picked up speed as he descended into the hollow on Witherington Road and got out of the saddle and worked the pedals hard to power up for the climb on the other side. It felt good to work out, and he was sweating when he finally reached the track that led down to the river.

He stopped.

A police car had been parked across the junction, blocking the way.

Josh came to a stop and dismounted. A uniformed policewoman was standing next to the car.

"What's going on?" Josh asked her.

"You can't go down there."

"Why? What's happened?"

"Never mind that, but we'll be here for the rest of the day—might be here tomorrow, too."

He felt a little twist of unease. "Is it something serious?"

"None of your business. You'd best be getting home."

Josh bit his lip. He felt frozen.

"Didn't you hear me? Where do you live?"

"Alderbury," he said.

"Off you go, then." She made a shooing gesture with her hands.

Josh pointed down the track, then blurted it out: "I was down there yesterday."

The officer raised an eyebrow. "Were you now? About what time?"

"Same time as now. After school."

"And did you see anything?"

He thought about the camera, and, although he knew he *ought* to say something, he found himself tongue-tied. They'd taken the things when they belonged to someone else.

That was *theft*.

"No," he said. "I don't think so."

"What does *that* mean? You either did or you didn't."

"I didn't. There was no one down there."

She took a notebook from her jacket, flipped it open and took out a pen. "What's your name, young man?"

"Joshua."

"Surname?"

"Yates."

"Joshua Yates." She noted it down. "And your address?"

He thought of the things they'd taken and was suddenly fearful that if he told her, an awful chain of events would ensue: the police would come to his house, they'd search it, they'd find the camera and recorder, and he would be prosecuted for theft, convicted and sent to prison.

He backed away.

"What's your address?"

"Why do you want it?"

"You're not in trouble, Joshua, but we might want to come and have a proper chat with you just to make sure that you didn't see anything."

He knew he had no choice and told her where he lived.

She noted it down and told him to be on his way; Josh didn't need telling twice. He turned the bike around and pedalled hard, convinced that he had said something or acted in such a way to make it obvious that he had something to hide. One thing was sure: he and Paul and Becca couldn't take the camera and recorder to the police station and hand them in without him getting in trouble for being economical with the truth just now. But they had to be returned. He had to get them away from the shed. He'd leave them somewhere and let whoever found them deal with them.

69

Sam had spent the day as normally as possible, but it was as much as she could manage to do it without screaming. There were no two ways about it: she was *hopelessly* distracted. Connor was in the field with Tom, and he had texted to say that he didn't know how much longer he could realistically keep him out there. Tom's girlfriend was in the cellar together with the coke she'd arranged to sell to Alexander Freeman on Saturday night. Alexander was Christopher's father, and if he'd been scary before, when they were kids, it was amplified now.

Those things would have been enough, but there was more: she'd made up her mind that she couldn't wait a moment longer to press the button on her escape plan and had been running through all the things that still needed to be done.

There was a lot.

Sorting out the money was the most pressing thing on her list.

It was seven in the evening when she went up to her bedroom and opened her wardrobe. The clothes inside were a mishmash, some pieces from her time in London and others that had been bought after she had come home. Party dresses and chunky Doc Martens fought for space with gilets and checked shirts and ankle-high yard boots. The clothes could have told her story: a rural girl going to London to follow her dreams, then returning home after discovering that the dreams were not what she wanted after all.

She reached inside and took out the shoeboxes that were stacked up at the back. There was a large one that had come with her riding boots; she put it on the floor, opened the lid and looked down on the bundles of banknotes that she'd hidden inside. There was a hundred thousand here, in cash, carefully skimmed off the top of the fee they'd been paid for the last couple of runs. The others trusted her to do the books so completely that none of them took any notice of the money coming in and the money coming out; it was easy for her to massage the figures and take a little extra for herself. That had been the case when she and Christopher had done it, and nothing had changed since apart from the fact that she was able to take *his* share, too.

Sam might have been frustrated with how recent events had started to careen out of control, but she was reassured by one thing: she still had the others in the palm of her hand.

Tom was the one about whom Sam felt the keenest sense of regret. She'd always liked him more than the others. Her affection had only curdled recently, with a series of unwise assignations and his propensity toward indiscretion when he was drunk. The argument at the Haunch had been the final straw, and she'd been trying to find a way to get him out in a way that rewarded him for what he'd done while insulating the others from the unwanted attention that would be brought were he to say or do the wrong thing. Her inability to find a way to achieve that—without a finality she was desperate to avoid—had been keeping her up at night, but she knew she wouldn't be able to do what she knew had to be done.

And then there was Connor. Innocent, pretty, *naïve* Connor. It was obvious he considered himself her equal, as indispensable to the operation as she was. She'd persuaded him that she listened to his suggestions above all others, but he was too insular to realise that she fed him the answers she wanted days before she asked the questions, so he thought he'd come up with the solutions himself. It was pitiful. She'd hooked him so deftly he didn't even know he was on her line; what was coming next would be easy for her but devastating for him.

Whatever.

Sam didn't care about him and never had.

He was a means to an end.

They all were.

She moved the money from the boxes to her rucksack and tidied up. She took out her phone, opened the Trainline app and booked a return to London tomorrow. She'd been making these trips for weeks, and there wouldn't be time for too many more. This one, and maybe another one after that, and that would be that.

She'd have enough money salted away to do what she had decided to do.

70

Josh's mum was asleep when he got back, and his stepdad was out. He made himself a plate of baked beans on toast for tea. He finished it, tidied up the mess in the kitchen, and then went up to his room to do his homework.

He wasn't able to concentrate and had to force himself to stay at his desk and get through his maths and then his French. He kept thinking about what he had seen at the river after school, his imagination started to run away with him, and he started to panic. What if they'd done something worse than just stealing the camera and the recorder? The officer hadn't told him what had happened, so he went online to see if he could find anything that might give him an idea. He tried the local groups on Facebook, then went to the homepage of the *Salisbury Journal.* There was nothing. Whatever had happened there hadn't been reported, at least not yet. It wasn't reassuring, Josh's imagination started to fill in the blanks, and the more he did that, the worse he felt.

He took out his phone and messaged Paul to say they needed to talk, but even though he could see the message had been read, Paul didn't reply. He was probably with Becca. They'd be laughing at him again, at how easily they'd manipulated him to go along with their idea and then, despite his reluctance, to hold on to the gear even though they all knew it was stolen.

Josh pushed his books aside, got up and went to the window. He looked at the shed and bit down on his lip until it hurt. He left his room, hurried down the stairs and went outside to the shed. The door was ajar. That was odd. He was sure he had put it back on the latch. He went inside, going to the spot where he had hidden the camera and the recorder.

His heart fell.

The bag wasn't there.

He heard the squeak of the door and turned to see his stepdad. "Looking for the camera?"

"Where is it?"

He had a bottle in his hand. "You didn't think to tell me about it?"

"Where *is* it?"

"Sold it," he said triumphantly.

"When?"

"This afternoon. Took it into town."

"You can't."

"You know what I *hate*?" he slurred, slipping into his grievances just as he always did. "You live here in the house I pay for, eating the food I provide, and you never contribute a penny. Not a *penny*. You could've got a job—I had a paper round when I was your age—but you wouldn't even do that. You won't contribute, you never even say thank you, and then you come back with an expensive camera and whatever that other thing was, and you hide them in the shed."

"Please—"

"Didn't know I was watching through the window, did you? And you did a piss-poor job of hiding them. So I took them into town and sold them. We can treat the money as your contribution to the bills this month."

Josh felt icy panic close around his heart. He'd known they should never have taken the gear, and now he couldn't even do the right thing by taking them to the police. His stepdad put the bottle to his mouth and took a swig before staggering away from the door and catching his balance. Josh hurried out of the shed, bypassed him and went back inside. He raced up the stairs and went into his room, shutting the door and resting against it as he waited for his heart to stop thundering.

"We'll talk about this tomorrow," his stepdad called up to him.

Josh went to his desk for his phone and saw that Paul had replied to his message.

>> *Can't talk. Remember to bring the stuff to school tomorrow.*

71

Atticus sent Mack a message suggesting they meet for dinner. Mack replied at once, saying she was probably going to be too busy with the Alice Green investigation. Atticus told her that he wanted to speak to her about what he thought had happened, and, when she didn't reply, that he didn't think Alice was in the water. Atticus saw that Mack was composing a response, and when it didn't arrive, he told her he would be in Nole at ten, that he'd have her favourite pizza waiting, he'd find a table upstairs where they wouldn't be seen, and that it was important that she remember to eat. That last reminder was an echo of what she regularly told *him*, and, knowing that she wouldn't want to give him the opportunity to accuse her of hypocrisy, he wasn't surprised when she sent back an exasperated emoji and a single word—yes—to signal her acceptance.

* * *

Nole was on the Market Square. It was the closest the city had to a trendy pizzeria and would probably be described as 'artisanal' if it were in Hackney or Dalston. Atticus ordered pizzas for them both: mushroom and ricotta for Mack and pepperoni and honey for him.

He knew she would be careful to avoid being seen with him in public, and that had been one of the reasons he had suggested here. There was a small area of seating upstairs that offered a reasonable degree of anonymity, and he negotiated the narrow flight of stairs to the first floor and sat down at the table by the window. He looked down onto the square and saw a couple stagger away from the Market Inn and a handful of youngsters practising skateboard tricks near the public toilets. He tore a slice of his pizza and started to work on it, wiping a strand of melted cheese from his cheek as he saw Mack crossing the square from the direction of Salt Lane. He sent her a text telling her he was waiting and held up a hand in greeting as she looked for him.

She climbed the stairs, took off her jacket and hung it from the back of the chair. She sat down and allowed her head to fall back against her shoulders. "What a day."

"Busy?"

"What do you think? We had a missing person enquiry in the morning, and now it looks more like an unexplained death."

He eyed her over his slice. "Is that what you think?"

"A car found next to the Avon belongs to a woman with a history of swimming in places where she shouldn't be swimming?"

"And that woman has just had some very bad news."

She tore a slice of pizza. "Yes," she said. "When you add that all together, it looks like an accident or a suicide."

Atticus winced apologetically.

"But you don't think so?"

"I'm not saying that it's impossible," he said. "But I think there's evidence to suggest it *might* be something else."

She took a hungry bite, chewed and swallowed and then washed it down with a mouthful of Coke. "Am I sure I really want you to tell me what you think?"

"I think you probably do."

"I'm only asking because it usually makes things more complicated."

He shrugged. "Can't help that. Just telling you what I think."

She took another bite. "Go on, then. Make my day even worse. What do you think happened?"

"There are some things that suggest you ought to keep an open mind." He held out a finger. "First thing: have you been told what was in the back of the car?"

"I've seen the inventory. What in particular?"

"The dryrobe."

"And?"

"Why would it be in the car if she went for a swim and never got out? Surely, it'd be on the bank so she could put it on when she was finished. She wears it when she goes down to the water, takes it off when she gets in. If something happened, it should still be there."

She pursed her lips dubiously. "Maybe she didn't wear it yesterday. It wasn't cold."

"The water was *very* cold. I checked that when I got back to the office—fourteen degrees. And why would she have brought the robe with her if she wasn't going to use it?"

"Because she keeps it in the car."

Atticus shook his head. "No. I'm sure she would've wanted it when she got out. She was wearing it in the video she posted.

And it's part of her branding. She sells them on her website for a ridiculous mark-up. If there's one thing I've found out about her today, it's that she doesn't leave money on the table."

"Not convinced, but go on."

He finished his slice and held up two fingers. "Second thing: what about the swimsuit in the plastic bag?"

"It was dry," she said.

"So?"

"So it was still in there from a swim she took the day before yesterday."

He shook his head. "She was wearing a red swimsuit in Tuesday's video. This one is blue."

"And?"

"And isn't it strange that the swimsuit she was probably wearing was in a bag in her car?"

"Hold on," Mack said. "We don't know she was wearing the blue one yesterday, do we? That could've been there for days. She might have worn that one at the weekend."

"It's possible," he conceded. "But that, plus the dryrobe…" He shrugged. "I think, when you take them together, it's more likely that she was wearing that swimsuit and she did wear the dryrobe, and that she finished her swim and went back to the car and got changed."

"The swimsuit was dry," Mack persisted. "Wouldn't it be damp?"

"I checked," he said. "It was a warm day yesterday, and the car would've been in direct sunlight for most of the afternoon. My best guess is that it would've been twenty-five degrees inside the cabin. The swimsuit is made from Lycra, and Lycra dries quickly in warm temperatures. I'd say three hours, or four hours as an absolute maximum. It definitely wouldn't have been damp today."

Mack rolled her eyes. "You've thought of everything."

"Apart from what happened to her. I can't work that out." He picked up another slice of pizza and took a bite.

"Anything else?"

He swallowed, held up three fingers and then spoke around his mouthful. "Third thing: where's the camera that would've been on the tripod?"

"I did wonder about that," Mack said.

"Two possibilities that I can see," Atticus said. "If she's been abducted, whoever abducted her took the camera."

"Maybe because they're on it?"

"Maybe," Atticus said.

"And the second possibility is that it's been nicked."

"Although is that likely? The only people who go down there are dog walkers. It's not Brixton. They'll mostly be elderly, middle class and law abiding. It's a bit of a stretch to see someone like that pinching a camera."

"Maybe they took it to hand it in," Mack said. "It's feasible someone saw it on Wednesday and then saw it again today. It'd be obvious that it'd been left. I can see someone thinking it'd be the neighbourly thing to do to keep it safe and then post it on Facebook."

"I checked that," Atticus said. "Nothing has been posted."

"Maybe something will come up when we start canvassing."

"When's that?"

"We already started," she said. "We'll be going up to Charlton-All-Saints tomorrow and going door-to-door."

"Do Alderbury, too."

"We will," she said.

They ate in silence for a moment.

"One thing about the suggestion she's been abducted," Mack said. "No sign of struggle. I had a good look—there's nothing. No blood—"

"That would've been ridiculously lucky," Atticus cut in.

"No signs of a struggle or a disturbance," Mack went on. "No drag marks. No personal items left behind. No scratches or damage to the car. No evidence that anyone else was involved."

"No broken or displaced vegetation," Atticus said. "No tyre or skid marks."

"No fingerprints," Mack said. "We checked the car. Pretty much just hers." Mack finished the slice and wiped her fingers on a napkin. "So we don't think she's in the water, and we don't think she's been abducted—what is it, then?"

"I'm not ruling out anything. She might be in her clothes. She might have changed and then fallen in. She might have willingly got into another car. All of those outcomes are possible."

"Which one is most likely?"

He breathed in and out. "If you made me guess? I think someone's got her."

PART 5

72

Josh left the house before anyone else was awake and walked into the village in time to catch the minibus. He'd found it difficult to get to sleep last night; his mother and stepfather had been drinking until past midnight and had played music loudly enough for the next-door neighbours to have banged on the wall. Josh had eventually stuffed tissue paper in his ears to deaden the sound and, with his mind still whirling with what his stepfather had done, had eventually fallen asleep.

Josh dumped his bag on the seat beside him and took out his phone with the intention of messaging Paul and Becca to tell them they had to talk, but saw he had a WhatsApp waiting for him. He opened the app and saw that it was from Paul, with Becca also copied into the conversation.

> *Have you seen this?*

Josh saw that Paul was composing another message and waited for it to arrive: it was a link to a page on the *Salisbury Journal*'s website.

He tapped it, waited for the page to load and then read:

The desperate sister of missing wild swimmer Alice Green said she would do anything to have her back, as police said they currently have no idea where she is.

Mrs. Green, 39, an online entrepreneur with premises on Salisbury High Street, has now been missing for two days, having vanished after swimming in the River Avon near Standlynch on Wednesday morning.

Green's sister, Teresa Herbert, told the BBC: "The family is incredibly worried. Alice is a strong swimmer, and the river isn't dangerous near where her car was found. We find it impossible to believe that she would have got into difficulties in the water."

Police divers with specialist equipment were seen searching the river downstream from where Green's car was found.

Mrs. Herbert appealed for public help. "The area by the river is popular with dog walkers, and I'd ask anyone who was down there on Wednesday to think if they saw anything strange or unusual and to get in touch with police."

Detective Chief Inspector Mackenzie Jones of Salisbury Police said that Green's car was found by a dog walker on Thursday morning. She said that it was too early to speculate on what might have happened, but that they believe a camera Green used to film her swims was missing. She stressed that if members of the public have any information about it—or anything else relating to the disappearance—they should get in touch with police.

Becca replied to Paul's message:

> *Shit. What are we going to do?*

Paul typed out a response:

> *We take the camera to the police and say we found it. We haven't done anything wrong.*

Josh put his head in his hands. *He'd* wanted to take the camera and recorder to the police as soon as they'd found them, but it was Paul and Becca who had persuaded him to wait. But it was *him* who'd been down to the weir yesterday afternoon, and it was *him* who'd told the policewoman that he hadn't seen anything.

And now his stepdad had sold the things they'd taken.

How was he going to put things right now?

He looked down at the screen again and saw that Paul was typing out a message.

> *Josh?*

He was in so much trouble.

> *You've got to take the stuff to the police.*

The bus slowed down as it reached the school, pulling into the playground and slowing to a halt. Josh put his phone into his bag and waited for the driver to open the door. He waited until the playground was empty and then bypassed the school entrance, walking back into Downton and the bus stop where he could get a bus to take him into Salisbury. The X3 rumbled by him, and he jogged the last fifty yards, reaching it just before the driver closed the doors.

He paid the fare, sat down in one of the empty seats at the back and took out his phone. He read the story for a second time and then found one of the local Facebook groups and saw that the woman's disappearance was already being discussed. People were speculating on what might have happened; some said the woman must have got into trouble in the water and drowned, others that she might have killed herself.

He watched, agog, as comments continued to be posted.

Twenty.

Thirty.

Fifty.

The suggestions grew more lurid. Someone said maybe she'd been abducted. Someone else said she'd heard the police thought she'd been murdered.

Josh was going to get into trouble for skipping school, but what choice did he have?

He knew he was doing the right thing.

73

Francine reached Bourne Hill and turned onto the path that led to the station. They'd been sharing a space with the council ever since the nick on Wilton Road had been closed, although there had been rumblings for the last few months that they would be getting a new building. The current arrangements were far from ideal, not least because the nearest custody suite was forty miles away in Melksham, which meant they had to park their vehicles in the public car park next to the building. Salisbury was a city with more than forty thousand people, and to impose an unsatisfactory arrangement on its police like this wasn't good enough. The new location was said to be out at High Post, and, although a purpose-built building would be an improvement, Francine would miss her morning walks.

She opened the door and made her way toward the back. Nadia Bellamy raised her hand in greeting and gestured that Francine should come over. Bellamy was the public enquiry officer who worked the morning shift on the reception desk.

"Good timing." Nadia gestured to the elderly couple sitting in the waiting area. "They want to talk to a detective."

"About?"

"Missing person."

"I'm not due on shift for another hour. Isn't there anyone else who can take it?"

"No one here."

"Lynas and Archer are on shift, aren't they?"

"Both got called out—there was a punch-up on Fisherton Street last night. Two squaddies got into it, and one of them ended up in hospital with a concussion and a broken arm."

There wasn't going to be any getting out of it; Francine's exam revision was going to have to wait. She thanked Nadia and made her way across to the waiting area.

"Morning," she said. "I'm Detective Constable Patterson. You're worried about a missing person?"

The woman glanced up with a look of such gratitude and relief that Francine forgot all about the exam. "It's our son," she said. "We don't know where he is."

"Probably on the lash," the man said.

"He's not," the woman retorted.

The man exhaled and shrugged. "I tried to tell her," he said to Francine. "I don't think it's anything, but she insisted."

"You'd better come through," Francine said, gesturing to the door behind the desk. "We can find a room in the back, and you can tell me all about it."

74

All of the interview suites were empty. Francine took the couple to the one nearest the door and invited them to sit.

"Can I get you something to drink?"

The man shook his head. "We're fine," he said, speaking for both of them. "I'm worried that we're already going to be wasting your time as it is."

The woman looked over at him with a mixture of unease and irritation; it was obvious the two of them had argued about coming in, that he was here under duress and that he was going to make her feel bad for insisting.

"I'm going to get myself a coffee," Francine said with a reassuring smile. "Are you sure I can't get something for you while I'm at the machine?"

"Coffee would be lovely," the woman said.

"Sir?"

"Go on, then," he said, conceding. "Two coffees. Thank you."

Francine went out into the corridor and made her way to the junction where the vending machine had been installed. She selected a cappuccino, waited as the drink was prepared and then ordered another two. The chances were good that the interview wouldn't come to anything, but she'd seen enough in the woman's face to know that she'd feel better in sharing her concerns. It was inconvenient, given how busy Francine was at the moment, but she wouldn't have felt comfortable sending her on her way without at least hearing her out. Mack had told Francine that one of her strengths as a detective was her human touch; it was one of the reasons she said she'd put her up for promotion, given the lack of empathy in an otherwise male-dominated department.

She took the coffees back to the interview room and put them down on the table. She sat, took out her notebook, and found a clean page. "All right then," she said. "As I said, I'm DC Patterson. You're worried about your son."

"He's gone missing," she said.

"I'm sorry to hear that." Francine noted down the time and date, then looked up with a smile. "Could I start with your names, please?"

"Harry Brennan."

"Eliza Brennan."

Francine noted the names down. "And your son?"

"Thomas Brennan—Tom."

Francine added the name and drew a line under it. "Tell me what's happened, and I'll see what we can do to help."

"Tom's been struggling of late," Eliza said.

"How's that?"

"Alcohol."

"He's always liked a drink," Harry said.

"There's liking a drink, and then there's being an alcoholic," Eliza corrected.

Harry folded his arms but didn't disagree.

"Tell me a bit about him."

"Tom joined the Army when he was eighteen," Eliza said. "Straight out of school. They sent him to Catterick for basic training, and then he did parachute training for his wings."

"2 Para," Harry said proudly.

"They deployed him to Iraq after that," Eliza said.

"When was this?"

"Two thousand and four," Harry said. "Operation Telic."

Francine noted it down. "Basra?"

"That's right."

"What regiment?"

"The Paras," he said with obvious pride. "First Battalion."

"You've come to the right person," she said. "I was a redcap before I joined here. I've done a tour in Basra."

Harry sat up a little straighter. "Really?"

"Helmand, too."

"He was in Helmand in 2008," he said.

She smiled. "I'd say it was a small world, but it's not unusual to meet ex-soldiers doing this job in Salisbury. If he joined up straight after school, that'd make him—what—forty?"

"Thirty-nine," Eliza said.

"Thirty-nine," she said, noting it down. "Sorry to interrupt. Tell me about him."

She cleared her throat. "He had a rough time of it. His patrol was ambushed in Sangin in 2010. Two of his mates were killed, and Tom barely got out. That was the start of his troubles. He went back out for another tour, but he was never the same. They sent him home in 2013 and diagnosed him with PTSD."

"He was honourably discharged," Harry said.

"When was this?"

"Twenty-fifteen."

Eliza took out a tissue and dabbed at her eyes.

Harry looked over at her, then reached out and rested his hand on top of hers.

"He came back and rented a flat in town," he said. "He tried to find a job, but nothing stuck. He worked in a warehouse, but he struggled with the noise and gave it up. He did nights as a security guard, but the isolation made things worse, and he started to struggle with insomnia. He worked in the Nisa on Rowbarrow, but he has mood swings, and he upset the customers. He worked as a delivery driver for Evri, but he couldn't handle the traffic and the schedule, so they let him go. It was one thing after another. He's tried—no one can say he hasn't—but it's too much."

Eliza blinked back tears.

"He ran out of money," Harry said, "and lost the flat. We offered to put him up, of course we did, but he's too proud, and he said he'd found somewhere else. We only found out later that he was living in his car and then, when that was repossessed, on the street. His PTSD got worse, he started drinking more to try to deal with it, and… well, it kept getting worse. He got into trouble with the police in the end."

"Burglary," Eliza said. "He was desperate. He couldn't afford to eat, and he didn't know what else to do."

"He got community service," Harry added. "I'm sure you'll have it all on file."

"I doubt it'll be relevant," Francine said. "Please—go on."

"We found him a place with Alabaré and he's been there ever since. We thought he was making progress. We put him in touch with Help for Heroes, and they sorted him out with a psychiatrist to help with the PTSD. He told us last week that he'd had a couple of interviews for jobs, and he was optimistic that they went well."

"And then?"

Eliza dabbed her eye with the tissue. "He's disappeared. He..."

She looked down into her lap, choking back a sob.

"He was supposed to come over for dinner on Wednesday." Harry took over. "He didn't turn up. We called him, but there was no reply. He didn't answer yesterday, either. We started to get worried, so I went to the flat to see him, and he wasn't there. The warden said he left on Monday afternoon and hasn't been back since. They're not supposed to do that—just go off."

"And it's out of character," Eliza said.

Francine had seen plenty of cases like this before; someone with a history of alcoholism or substance abuse going missing, most likely out of their minds somewhere, to leave their loved ones fretting. The chances were he'd be back again when he sobered up, but she could see how worried the two of them were, and she didn't want it to look like she was downplaying things or fobbing them off.

Eliza blinked wet eyes. "Can you help?"

"Of course," Francine said. "What does he look like?"

"I have a picture."

She opened her handbag, took out a photograph and laid it on the table.

"That's the most recent one we have," she said. "It was taken at his sister's birthday party last year."

"It's not the best picture," Harry said, his brows lowering into a frown. "He was drunk."

"He was struggling," Eliza corrected him sternly. "It was before he accepted he needed help."

Francine looked down at the photograph. Tom Brennan had a fair complexion and a neat, combed-back hairstyle that was a reddish-brown hue, with hints of grey indicating his age. His hairline was slightly receding, framing a broad forehead marked with natural lines. He had piercing blue eyes, set beneath straight and well-defined brows. He wore a modest, close-trimmed beard that accentuated his jawline. He was wearing a black suit that looked too small around his big shoulders, a crisp white shirt and a black tie with a stain just below the knot.

"That was one of my suits," Harry said. "He turned up looking like he'd been sleeping in a ditch."

Eliza glared over at her husband. "I told you—it was *before* he started looking after himself."

Francine laid a finger on the photograph. "Do you mind if I hold onto this for a day or two?"

Eliza looked hesitant, as if reluctant to leave the photograph.

"I'll get a copy made, and then you can have it back again."

She nodded. "Of course."

"I take it he's not married?"

"No," Eliza said. "He never found anyone."

"What about friends? Anyone from the Army?"

"He's got friends in the city from when he was at school," Eliza said. "There are five of them—they used to be thick as thieves, but I don't think they're as close these days."

"It'd help if you could let me have their details," Francine said. "I can have a chat with them to see whether they have any idea where he is."

"I'll get them for you."

"Do you need anything else?" Harry asked.

Francine had dealt with missing persons before and didn't need to look up the procedure. She'd gathered the details she needed—age, description, circumstances—and she had enough to make enquiries. "I think that'll do for now. Just write down the names and contact details of his friends, and I'll make enquiries. If necessary, I'll be able to look at his bank details and phone records to see if there's anything helpful there."

Harry shook his head. "I don't think he has a bank account."

"Not a problem. There are lots of avenues we can explore."

"When will you start?"

"I'll speak to an officer right away. It'll be today."

Eliza frowned. "Not you?"

"Not *necessarily* me," Francine said. "It'll probably be a uniformed officer to start with."

Eliza reached across the table and took Francine's wrist. "Can't *you* do it?"

Francine was taken aback once again by the woman's plaintiveness. She was desperate with worry. "I'll see what I can do," she said. "Leave your details, too, and I'll let you know as soon as we've found him."

She kept hold of Francine's wrist. "You think you will?"

"Find him?" She nodded and gave the most reassuring smile she could manage. "We will. I know it's easy to say, but try not to worry. He'll turn up." She stood. "I'll be in touch."

75

Francine walked the Brennans out and then took the empty plastic cups to the bin. She knew that she ought to give the file to uniform so that they could make initial enquiries. It was the right thing to do in terms of procedure, and it wasn't as if she had the luxury of time to indulge the Brennans, no matter how evident their distress. She had a busy caseload of her own to deal with, plus there was the not inconsiderable demand on her time that was the sergeant's exam. But even as she listed out the reasons why she *shouldn't* take the file, she knew that it would ultimately make no difference. Tom Brennan's struggles with PTSD sent her thoughts spinning back to her father and the torment that had afflicted him after he had left the Army.

Her dad, George, had been born in Sheffield with a penchant for adventure and a sense of duty that led him to the Army. He rose through the ranks and served with distinction during the Falklands War. He was involved in several key skirmishes, and one—on Mount Tumbledown—saw him earn the Military Medal. Francine had tried to get the story out of him, but he'd always demurred, saying, instead, that he had been given his medal for rescuing a cow that had fallen into a ditch.

She followed him into the Army and had been able to pull out the details herself: his platoon had gone up the slope of the mountain and had engaged the enemy at the summit. The Argentinians had been well protected by the terrain, and, with his platoon commander injured and under heavy fire, her father had run at the foxhole and lobbed a grenade inside.

But the war left scars, and Frank had returned home a changed man. He withdrew from the family, taking an allotment where he would spend hours alone wrestling with his memories. Night terrors robbed him of sleep; he relived the battle and struggled with survivor's guilt, grappling with the loss of the friends who didn't make it. He'd struggled to deal with it himself, but it had been too much for him. He had gone out for a walk one day, but never returned. Francine had found his body, hanging from a tree with their dog running frantically around his legs. There was a note of apology in his pocket.

"All right?"

Francine turned. It was Mack. "Sorry, boss. Million miles away."

"What's going on?"

"Just had a couple come in and report a missing person."

"Who?"

"Ex-soldier. Homeless for a while, ended up at Alabaré. Mum and dad haven't been able to get in touch with him. They went to the home—he hasn't been seen since Monday. They don't have any idea where he is."

"And you want to take it?"

She bit her lip. "I thought I would."

"You think it'll be a tricky one?"

She shrugged. "Probably not."

"How busy are you?"

"I'm not *un*-busy."

Francine trusted Mack more than anyone else at the nick. They had been out for drinks on many occasions, and, once, when Francine had been upset at the approaching anniversary of her father's death, she'd told Mack everything. She'd responded just as Francine had known she would, with sympathy and understanding. It had helped. The day had been difficult, but Mack had made sure to keep her as busy as possible in an attempt to keep her from dwelling on it.

"Take it if you want," Mack said, "but don't let it interfere with the exam. I don't want you to mess it up. If it gets too much, let me know, and I'll look at handing off some of your stuff to the others. Lynas has been moaning about how he wants to take on more work—I could let him have the dirty doctor."

Mack was referring to the locum GP who had taken his PC into a shop to have it fixed, only for the owner of the shop to find a cache of covert pictures of his female patients. His trial had been scheduled for the end of the month, and there was a lot of running around to be done with the CPS to make sure everything was ready.

"Thanks, boss. I appreciate it."

"I mean it, Franny—don't take on too much."

Mack had told her before it was one of her weaknesses, and Francine had grudgingly conceded she might have a point. "I won't," she said. "Promise."

76

Atticus had spent the morning with Bandit at the river. He knew he wouldn't be allowed to park near the mill, so he continued to Downton, leaving his car in the same space as when he had visited the water meadows before and then walking north so that he could follow the Avon upstream.

The river fragmented into numerous smaller tributaries as he walked, and finding a path became more difficult. They reached Trafalgar Fisheries, with the river forced to divert several times so enough water could be sent into the long stretches required for the farming of the trout. Atticus stayed on the left-hand bank so he could avoid the buildings on the opposite side that he knew would be connected to the farm. He was trespassing and wasn't confident he'd be able to persuade anyone who questioned him that he was working for the police. At least he knew he didn't have to take his time here, the water levels were regulated by way of weirs and gates, and he doubted that Alice's body—if she was in the water—would be able to get through unimpeded.

He carried on, passing the northern boundary of the fishery and picking up the natural flow of the river again. Bandit trotted ahead as Atticus paced the bank, eyes sweeping over the water with particular focus on the thick vegetation that spilled down into the shallows. He walked slowly, stopping frequently to spend more time examining areas that seemed promising. He was looking for anything that would suggest Alice Green had gone into the water: her body, obviously, but also items of clothing or things that otherwise ought not to have been there. He traced the edge of the water, noting the patterns in the mud and looking for rocks that might have been displaced.

But there was nothing.

He wasn't surprised.

He still didn't think that she *was* in the water, but, even if she was, a combination of factors could make it difficult for her body to be found. The current could have carried her downstream, perhaps even over a considerable distance; her body might have snagged on underwater debris—a branch or a rock—holding it beneath the water and hidden from view; or it might have sunk thanks to the weight of waterlogged clothing, with buoyancy only returning as decomposition progressed, the gases building up in the body and causing it to float. Atticus crouched down and dragged his fingers through the water, confirming it was cold. That could also be a factor; the colder the water, the slower the rate of decomposition would be.

He heard the sound of engines and stood, watching as one and then another rigid inflatable came around the bend of the river. The boats were red and black, large enough to accommodate four searchers in identical red jackets and black trousers, with outboard motors at the rear. The motors hummed steadily, breaking the quiet of the afternoon. One boat was on the left bank, and the other was on the right, the two moving downstream in tandem. The searchers worked methodically, using long poles to probe the reeds on the banks. The boat nearest to Atticus chugged past slowly. The teams would have been sent from both Wiltshire and Hampshire Search and Rescue, and he didn't recognise any of the men and women on either boat.

"Afternoon," Atticus said as the closest boat drew up alongside him. "Any luck?"

"Afternoon," the searcher in the prow said, studiously avoiding the question.

The boat chugged on, the hum of the motors breaking the quiet of the afternoon.

Atticus waited for the two of them to make their way around the bend before proceeding, even less confident he would find something after they had already looked but hoping that they might have missed something he wouldn't.

His phone rang.

He took it out of his pocket and looked at the screen, seeing—to his surprise—that Frank Green was calling.

"Hello," he said.

Green spoke without preamble. "They want to interview me!"

"Afternoon, Mr. Green," he said.

"Didn't you hear me? They want me to go in for an interview."

"Who does?"

"Who do you think—the bloody police!"

"That's not surprising. You're her husband."

"How many times? Ex-husband!"

"And you've made it obvious you don't have any time for her."

"Only to *you*. You haven't said anything, have you?"

Atticus looked over at Bandit and crossed his fingers. "Of course not. Anything between us is confidential."

"They've told me to come over this afternoon," he said. "You're *sure* you didn't know?"

"I didn't."

"How long is it going to take?"

"It depends how many questions they have for you."

"That's not helpful."

"It's the best I can do."

"Do I *have* to go?"

"No," Atticus said. "But I'm not sure I'd recommend ignoring them. Innocent people don't tend to do that."

"I *am* innocent. I have no idea where she's gone."

"Then there's no reason to be worried."

There was a pause, and Atticus wondered if Frank had ended the call.

"You used to work there, didn't you?" he said at last.

"I did."

"I want to see you before I go in."

It was an instruction rather than a question. Atticus decided that he'd had enough of being told what to do by someone like Green, and that perhaps it was time to bring their relationship to a close. However, that was something he'd rather do face to face.

"What time are you going in?"

"They want to see me at twelve."

Atticus looked at his watch: it was half ten. It would take him forty-five minutes to get back to the car from here, and then half an hour—if Salisbury traffic was kind—to get to the station. It ought to be possible.

"I'll meet you outside five minutes before."

Green said that'd be fine and, without any suggestion of thanking Atticus, ended the call.

Atticus looked down at Bandit. "You were right about him. What a dick."

The dog wagged his tail.

77

Sam stood up from her seat as the train rolled into Waterloo, and made her way along the carriage to the vestibule. She felt nervous despite the fact that she'd made this same trip once a month for most of the last year. She had five envelopes in her bag, and each one contained ten thousand pounds in cash. Fifty grand that would be impossible to explain if the police were to discover it.

And what about the others? If *they* found out she'd been skimming off the top for as long as they'd been running the business, there was no telling what they'd do, especially after what had happened to Christopher. She had always relied upon her command of the dynamic in the group: the shared history they all had, the assumption of loyalty, their gratitude for what she'd built for them, and their acknowledgement that none of them would have been able to do it alone. She'd used it like a magician, distracting them with sleight of hand so that their attention was elsewhere, knowing their weaknesses and vulnerabilities and taking advantage of them all as she ripped them off.

The train stopped. She waited for the doors to be unlocked, and as the light came on, she pressed the button and stepped down to the platform. She was aware of the other passengers around her, but the train was as quiet as it usually was at this hour, and she'd seen nothing to suggest that anything was out of place. She reached the gate, held her phone to the reader, and stepped through and onto the station concourse.

This was her first meeting of four this afternoon; after this, she'd get a taxi to Hyde Park for the meeting on the bench near the Serpentine Bridge, then another cab to the British Library and a third to Southwark Cathedral, opposite Borough Market. The meetings were quick and businesslike, and she didn't expect to be in the city for more than a couple of hours.

She always made sure to arrange the meetings on the same day to avoid unnecessary trips, and that was especially pertinent today. She'd put on the balaclava and checked the woman in the cellar before leaving, ensuring that there was enough food and water upstairs for one of the others to give her. The woman had begged Sam to let her go, the same as yesterday, but Sam hadn't responded. She still didn't know what they were going to do with her. She didn't think that she would be able to identify any of them, but that relied upon Gaz and Nikki's account of what had happened when they had abducted her, which was evidence of their utter incompetence if nothing else. If they were wrong—or if they were lying about wearing the masks when they took her—then they were *all* at risk.

And Sam didn't know if that was a risk she could accept when so much was at stake.

She needed to be ready to go.

She crossed the concourse and took the escalator to the mezzanine. There was a café up there opposite the board with the times of the departing and arriving trains. There was a table wedged into the space between the glass partition at the edge of the balcony and the body of the café that was tucked away and not overlooked. Sam had found it when she first came to London with the idea to start changing her money and had used it for this particular meeting ever since.

The man was waiting for her.

"Afternoon," he said.

"Okay?"

"I'm good. Shall we?"

They'd never exchanged pleasantries, and Sam wasn't interested in starting now. The whole point of crypto was to allow anonymity, and each of them knew the other only by their username on the platform: Sam was EmeraldShift, and the man on the other side of the table was SilverFox76.

He nodded down to her bag. "You got the cash?"

She reached inside and took out the envelope. "Ten grand, twenties and fifties."

She handed it over and the man thumbed through the notes. He nodded in satisfaction and pulled out his phone. Sam could see the Bitcoin wallet app open on the screen.

"All done."

Sam pulled out her own phone and refreshed her Bitcoin wallet. The balance updated to show the new amount: a touch shy of six hundred thousand.

"Thank you," she said.

The man stood. "Same time next week?"

"I'm not sure," Sam said. "Maybe."

"Email me. Happy to keep going if you've got more."

"I'll let you know."

He set off, turning the corner around the edge of the café and disappearing. Sam looked down and watched as he crossed the concourse, heading for the entrance to the underground. She exhaled. She'd spent hours working out a plan that would allow her to take her money with her when she made her move. She knew taking hard currency over the border was too risky to consider, she couldn't safely put it in her luggage, and her research had turned up plenty of horror stories of tourists arrested at customs with money hidden on their persons. Neither was an option, so she had gone down a different path.

Cryptocurrency looked promising. Cash-to-crypto exchanges allowed people to buy it with cash, and her research led her to set up an account with a platform known as LocalBitcoin. She'd found half a dozen sellers in London and had been using them to convert as much of her money as possible; she'd break the funds down into several thousand at a time, travelling to meet them and then making the trades. She'd been exchanging the cash every month, and now she had enough to know she could leave whenever she needed to. That the price of Bitcoin had skyrocketed during the process was a welcome bonus; it had seen her holding double in value.

She went around to the other side of the café and ordered an espresso to go. She looked at her watch, she needed to be at her next stop in thirty minutes, but the map on her phone said the streets were quiet, and she ought to be there in plenty of time.

She paid for the coffee and took a sip, arranging her bag—with the remaining envelopes hidden inside—on her shoulder, and made her way to the escalator and back down to the concourse.

78

Francine decided that the best place to start her search for Tom Brennan would be the hostel where he'd been living until his disappearance. Alabaré was a Christian charity set up to help the homeless, including veterans, like Tom, who had fallen upon hard times. It was based in the southwest, with premises in Devon and Somerset but with a focus on Wiltshire. The charity owned a large building on Barnard Street, and it was here that the Brennans had said their son had been staying. Francine walked from the station, enjoying the sun that shone down from a clear blue sky. She reached the front door and pressed the button for the intercom.

"Hello?"

Francine took out her warrant card and held it up to the camera. "DC Patterson from Bourne Hill. Can I have a word?"

"Of course. Hold on—I'll buzz you in."

She stepped back, waited for the door to be unlocked and then went inside.

The door led into a reception area with a small office off to one side.

A man came out. He was wearing a name badge on a multicoloured lanyard; Francine glanced down at it and saw that his name was Peter.

"Good morning," he said. "How can I help?"

"I'm looking for a man who had a room here."

"I can probably guess," he said. "Tom, right? Tom Brennan?"

"Yes—that's right."

"His parents came in yesterday. I didn't have all that much I could tell them."

"They said. He's been gone since Monday?"

"Yes."

"Did he speak to anyone before he left?"

"Not staff."

"Other residents?"

"I asked around after his folks came in—it's the same. He didn't say anything to anyone."

"Is that unusual?"

"For someone to leave? No, not really. A lot of our residents have complex problems, and it's not unusual for them to struggle now and again."

"Can you tell me a little about him?"

"Tom? He's a good guy. He's honest, and he's got a great sense of humour. He worked in the kitchen when he got here, and I know he's been having interviews with a couple of restaurants to see if he could find work."

"His parents said he had PTSD."

"Again—not unusual. We get a lot of veterans, and you'd struggle to find anyone who *hasn't* been dealing with that."

"Drink or drugs?"

"Drink."

"What about friends? Was he popular?"

"You'd work hard to find anyone with a bad word to say about him."

"And friends outside here?"

"I think he kept in touch with old school friends, but that's it. He's not a big talker."

"Do you think you could have another ask around for me—see if any of the others have any idea where he might have gone?"

"Happy to," he said. "Why? Are you worried?"

"It'd put his parents' minds at ease if they knew where he was."

"Absolutely. Happy to help."

Francine took out a card with her details and handed it over. "Call me if you find out anything you think might be helpful—doesn't matter how insignificant you think it might be. It'll help me build up a picture."

79

Frank Green was already at the station when Atticus arrived, pacing back and forth across the path.

"You're *late*," he said, his cheeks already turning the shade of puce that heralded another of his splenetic outbursts. "I needn't remind you that I'm paying for your time, and—"

Atticus held up a hand to stop him. "Actually, you're not. You paid me for a report on your ex-wife, and I've done that. Handholding you while you're interviewed by the police about her disappearance is not part of the retainer we agreed."

His mouth fell open. "Are you *serious*?"

"I am. That's what we agreed. I'm running a business. I'm sure you wouldn't expect a customer to take one of your houses without paying for it."

He muttered a curse—something about Atticus's parentage—and took out his wallet. He flipped it open and took out a thick wad of notes fastened by a silver metal clip. He removed the clip, licked his thumb and peeled off four fifties. "Here," he said, proffering the notes. "That enough?"

Atticus held up his hand to refuse the money. "I don't want your money."

"But you said—"

"The next five minutes is gratis. I'm doing this as a public service and because I think you need to hear some harsh truths."

"You *what*?"

"First of all," Atticus said, "you're a dick. You might be the biggest dick it has ever been my misfortune to have had as a client, and I've worked for two murderers." Frank looked ready to protest, but Atticus silenced him with an upturned palm. "Second of all, you need to take this seriously. I know you don't have anything to do with what's happened to your ex-wife. I'm a good judge of character, and I'm especially good at being able to tell when someone is telling the truth and when they're lying. You're a braggart with an unusually overinflated sense of his own value, and you're a blowhard—but you're also all mouth and no trousers. You're not nearly as sophisticated as you think, and you're certainly not a good enough liar to be able to pull the wool over my eyes."

"Have you finished?"

"Not at all," Atticus said. "I was about to tell you what you should do to be in and out as quickly as possible."

"You needn't think that—"

Atticus held up his palm again. "Here's the public service bit. I'm not telling you this because I don't think a day in the cells wouldn't be something you might actually benefit from—I'm telling you this because, as I said, I'm friends with some of the detectives in there, and they'll appreciate anything that limits the time they have to spend putting up with your bullshit. So here we go." Atticus held up a finger. "One—answer their questions honestly." He held up a second finger. "Two—don't give them any attitude, or you might find they decide they'll dump you in a cell and forget about you until the last minute they can hold you, just because they can." He held up a third finger. "Three—I'm going to have a word with the senior investigating officer and tell her that, in my opinion, you *might* be a dick, but you are not the kind of dick who's clever enough to make his wife disappear. That might mean you're in and out a little quicker than would otherwise have been the case."

Green's face was not so much puce now as a deep beetroot purple. He took a step toward Atticus and then squared up to him. Atticus could see that he had needled him to the point where he was close to an explosion of anger. His eyebrows were furrowed tightly together, his eyes were wide open with the pupils dilated, his nostrils were flared, and his lips were curled into a snarl. Atticus had a fresh insight of what life with him must have been like for Alice, and, not for the first time, understood why she'd brought their marriage to an end. She had plenty of her own faults—avarice and a lack of ethics chief among them—but she was not as noxious as Frank.

"I'll send you a copy of the report on your ex-wife tonight," Atticus said evenly. "Give some thought to my advice when you speak to the police—don't give them a reason to arrest you. They get twenty-four hours to question you, but they can ask for another three days if they think it's necessary. And I don't think you have the temperament for that."

"Wait," Green said. "Wait. Look—I'm sorry. I know, you're right, I lose my temper sometimes and say things I don't mean.

Please—I need you to help me with this. Let me pay you. I don't know how this works or what I should do, and you used to work there, so..."

He trailed off as he noticed Atticus reaching into the inside pocket of his jacket.

Atticus took out his phone, navigated to the contact he wanted and then sent it to Green's phone.

Green took out his own device. "What's that?"

"The number for a solicitor I know. She's not cheap, but I've always found you get what you pay for with things like this. I'd recommend you give her a call."

Atticus put his own phone back in his pocket and, without a word, turned and walked away.

He reached the Greencroft and sat down on one of the park benches. He could see Green, his phone pressed to his ear and his free hand pointing and gesticulating as he spoke to whoever was on the other end of the line. Atticus had given him the number of Laura Crawford, a solicitor who had just opened an office near to the railway station. She might not thank him for introducing her to someone as difficult as Green, but she'd told him she was looking to get her feet under her as she got started; at least Green would be good for whatever she charged him.

Atticus allowed himself a smile of satisfaction. He'd been brutal with Green, but it wasn't as if he didn't deserve it, and, Atticus had to admit, it felt *good.*

80

Mack walked Frank Green to the exit. Robbie had handled the interview, but, after Atticus's warning that he might be tricky, Mack had sat in to offer support. She had been glad that she had, Green had complained about how he'd been treated, and Robbie would benefit from having her there to back up his version of events if he followed through with his threats.

"Thank you for coming in, Mr. Green," she said.

"And thank *you* for wasting my time. Completely ridiculous. I didn't say it in there, but you *do* know I'm good friends with the chief constable, don't you?"

"I didn't know that, sir. But I don't see how that's relevant?"

"It's *relevant*, Detective Chief Inspector, because I'm going to be making a complaint about how the police have *harassed* me."

"We were just asking some questions about your wife," she said. "That's all. But please do go ahead if you want to complain—you'd be perfectly entitled to say whatever you like. In the meantime, I'd appreciate it if you'd let me know at once if you think of anything that might help us find Alice, and tell us in advance if you're thinking of leaving the city." She smiled sweetly. "Thank you again, Mr. Green. I'm sure I'll be in touch."

He looked as if he was going to say something else, but perhaps thought better of it. His fulmination was obvious as he glared at her, turned on his heel, and made his way across the reception area to the door.

Mack heard footsteps behind her and turned to see Atticus.

"How was that?"

"*Such* fun," she said.

Atticus nodded at the retreating Green. "Difficult?"

Mack watched as Green went out of the front door. "What an awful man."

"He certainly is."

"He was cooperative to start with, but when he realised that he wasn't in the frame, he started to go on about how it was a liberty the way he was being treated and did we know who he was, and did we know who he knew… on and on and on."

Atticus grinned. "I *did* warn you."

"He's that unpleasant with you?"

"From start to finish. He doesn't like it when he can't push people around. What do you think? Would you say he's got anything to do with what happened to his wife?"

She shook her head. "I don't think so."

"I agree."

"No alibi, though," she said.

"Feel free to poke around and make him uncomfortable."

Green stalked off in the direction of the Greencroft at the same time as a young teenage boy made his way inside and went to the desk.

"How did you leave it with him?" Atticus said.

"Just to let us know if he could think of anything that might help us find her."

Nadia got up and hurried across to where they were standing. "Mack," she said.

"What's up?"

She pointed back to the desk where the teenager was standing. "He just came in and said he wanted to speak to an officer. He says he was down by the river on Wednesday when Alice Green went missing. He says he's got information about what happened."

Atticus cocked an eyebrow.

Mack noticed his enthusiasm. "Come with me."

She led the way with Atticus just behind her.

"This is Detective Chief Inspector Jones," Nadia said to the boy. "I didn't get your name."

"Joshua," he said.

"Nice to meet you, Joshua," Mack said. "You have something to tell us about the woman who disappeared at Standlynch?"

He nodded, then swallowed. "I think I'm in trouble."

"I'm sure you're not," Mack said with a gentle smile.

"I've been walking up and down the road since this morning because I've been too scared to come inside."

"Why? What is it?"

"I was down by the river on the day the woman disappeared. Me and two of my friends went after school. We go swimming there."

"And?" Atticus cut in impatiently. "Did you see something?"

The boy looked at Atticus in confusion.

"It's okay," Mack said, glaring at Atticus. "What did you see?"

"There was a camera and something to record sound."

Atticus went ramrod straight. "By the river?"

"On the bank."

"Where are they now? Did you take them?"

The boy looked at Atticus, then back to Mack, and nodded. "See what I mean? I'm in trouble, aren't I?"

81

Atticus listened as Mack questioned the boy, reassuring him that he wasn't in trouble while impressing upon him how important it was that he answer her questions truthfully and with as much detail as he could. Atticus knew she'd want him to stay quiet, so he did, standing to the side and memorising the answers the boy provided while beginning to connect one piece of information with the next.

Josh—he told them he preferred the truncated version of his name—explained that he and his two friends had seen the abandoned car and then found the camera that Alice would've used to record her morning swim. There was another device—he said it looked like something you'd use to record sound—that had also been left on the bank. He explained that he'd wanted to take both items to the police, but that his friends had persuaded him to hold onto them for the night so they could all do it the next day.

Atticus could see Josh was nervous, and with reason; he knew the items didn't belong to him, and that taking them away would have been theft. He could only begin to imagine how frightened the boy must have been when he learned of Alice's disappearance and made the connection between what had happened to her and what they'd taken.

"Where are they now?" Mack asked.

"That's the problem. I wanted to bring them, but now I can't."

"Why not?"

"My stepdad found them in the shed and sold them."

"Why did he do that?"

He looked miserably down at the floor. "To get money for drugs."

"When was this?"

"Yesterday. I hid them, but he saw me doing it. He found them and took them into town."

Atticus couldn't help himself. "Where in town? Cash Converters?"

"I don't know what that is," Josh said.

Mack flicked a glance across at Atticus again. "It's what you'd call a pawnshop," she explained. "They'll buy things—things like the camera—or you can get money if you let them hold onto valuable things. It's on Catherine Street."

"No," Josh said. "I don't think it'd be anything like that."

"What do *you* think it was?"

"Probably the person he buys his drugs from—I had a PS4 last year, and he took that to the man he goes to and swapped it."

"I don't suppose you know who that is?"

He shook his head. "I'm sorry. I don't."

Mack told Josh that she needed to speak to his stepfather and that she'd give him a ride home. She told him to wait and beckoned Atticus over to the desk, where they could speak without the boy overhearing them.

"What do you think?"

"I think we need to move quickly. Something like a camera will be sold on quickly. The longer it's out there, the harder it's going to be to find it—and that's ignoring the fact that it'll get dumped the moment whoever bought it realises that it belonged to Alice."

"I'll speak to the stepdad and get him to say who he sold it to."

"I can think of a couple of people I could ask. Might be quicker."

"Want to split up?"

He nodded. "Wouldn't mind having a photo of the dad I could show around. I don't know about you, but he sounds like the kind of bloke who'll have a record."

82

Atticus went outside, took out his phone and skimmed through his contacts until he found the number he wanted. Finn—he didn't know his surname—was the man Atticus went to for pot whenever he fancied a smoke. He hadn't felt the need for weeks, partly because his happiness had improved since he and Mack had continued their relationship, and partly because Mack disapproved of it. She disapproved of Finn, too, having nicked him for possession on numerous occasions.

He dialled the number and, expecting to be sent to voicemail, was taken by surprise when Finn picked up.

"Hello, stranger."

"Afternoon."

"What's this?" he said. "I haven't seen you for ages."

"Where are you?"

"Having lunch."

Atticus looked at his watch. "Lunch? It's five o'clock."

"And? I got up late. Come over to the house in a couple of hours and I'll sort you out."

"Can I come and see you now?"

"I don't have anything on me."

"It's not about that. I'm not using anymore."

"Disappointing—I hate it when customers try to go clean."

"I need to have a chat about something else. I need a bit of information. It's important."

"It won't be free."

"Didn't for a minute think it would be."

"Boston Tea Party. Top floor, in the window."

"I'll be there in ten minutes. Don't go away."

* * *

Boston Tea Party was a large café on the High Street next to the entrance to the Old George Mall. It occupied two buildings: the entrance was in a brick-clad building on the left, while the timber-framed, double-bayed building to the right sat over the passageway that led into the mall. It had once been a coaching inn and was one of the older buildings in the city, with signs on the wall proclaiming that it had been visited by Shakespeare, Cromwell and Pepys.

Atticus went inside and climbed the stairs to the large dining room on the second floor. A bay window protruded out over the pavement, and Finn was sitting at the table in the bay. He saw Atticus and raised a hand, gesturing him over.

Atticus hadn't seen him for several months, and it seemed to him that his face had become even more weathered in the interim. His features were sharp, with high cheekbones and a pronounced jawline, and his eyes were piercing. The stubble on his cheeks and chin lent him an unkempt appearance, which stood to reason; he'd never been good on grooming and personal hygiene. His shirt was typically eye-catching: a vibrant

Hawaiian pattern with bright colours and bold designs. There was a mug of coffee on the table and a plate with the remains of what looked like eggs Florentine, with half a muffin left and a slick of creamy yolk and bright yellow hollandaise.

"Evening," Atticus said, sitting down.

Finn picked up the muffin between his fingers and used it to mop up the yolk. "How's the mutt?"

"He's very well."

"Still looking after him?"

"No," Atticus said. "I'm feeding him shit like you did."

Finn had been Bandit's owner before Atticus had taken him. The dog had clearly been unhappy in his dingy house, with not nearly enough attention or exercise, and Finn's enthusiasm for him had waned over the months. Atticus had taken him on loan and had been pleased when Finn had said he could have him permanently. It was a little rich for him to ask whether Atticus was caring for him given how unfit the dog had been when he took him, he'd grown fat after scrounging fast food from Finn's regulars, and Atticus had been terrified that he would end up eating something noxious that would be worse for him than the pizza crusts and leftover curry that had been his diet.

"So how come I haven't seen you for ages?"

"Been busy," Atticus said.

"You haven't bought anything for months."

"I told you—I'm not buying today, either."

"You've quit? Seriously?"

"I have."

He spread his hands. "I've got some *really* nice gear at home. Heard of Cookies Gelato?"

"Sounds delicious."

"It is. Stupid on the THC. Really long-lasting high."

"No thanks."

"What about Blue Dream—you always loved that, right?"

"I did," he said, "but—"

"—mixed with Amnesia Lemon Haze and Black Domina." He kissed his fingers. "Beautiful."

Atticus held up his hands. "Enough. I'm taking a break. No more weed."

"Turned over a new leaf?" Finn chuckled. "I remember you telling me that before, and look what happened. Piety never suited you."

"And your sales pitch needs work."

"You know where I am when you see sense."

Finn had always been confounding, and Atticus had even less time for him today than normal. He smiled to hide his impatience. "Like I said—I need some information. And I'll pay if you can help."

"Go on, then."

"I'm looking for a punter, and I wanted to see if he was one of yours."

Finn put up his hands in mock alarm. "Come on, now. You want me to breach my clients' confidentiality?"

"Yes," Atticus said. "Like you've never done that before."

"I'm hurt."

"And yes, before you say, I know it'll be expensive."

Finn finished his coffee and put the cup back in the saucer. "Go on then. Try me."

Atticus took out his phone and navigated to the folder where he had saved the photograph Mack had sent him earlier.

Josh's stepfather was a habitual criminal with several entries on his record, most recently for burglary after breaking into a house in Bodenham and walking out with a television. Mack had pulled his details from the Police National Computer and sent the mugshot; Atticus laid the phone on the table and slid it across so that Finn could look at the screen.

He shook his head. "Not one of mine."

"Never seen him before?"

Finn studied the photograph carefully, sucking on his teeth. "Don't know him. Why do you want him?"

"He swapped a stolen camera and a sound recorder for dope," Atticus said. "Both items are likely to be important in finding the woman who went missing on Wednesday."

Finn nodded sagely. "I heard about that. Fell in the river or something."

"Or something. Thing is, if anyone has either of those things—or knows where they are—and they *don't* come forward, then they're going to get in trouble."

"Come on, now." Finn wagged a finger and pretended to be offended. "You don't need to go and threaten me like that. I'm an upstanding citizen, just like you are."

"Is that right?"

"It *is* right, and you should've said that stuff was what you were looking for. I don't have an earthly who your man is, but I *was* offered a camera for an ounce yesterday."

"By whom?"

Finn put out his hand. Atticus took a roll of notes from his pocket and peeled off two twenties. Finn tutted and held up four fingers. Atticus peeled off another two twenties and handed them over.

Finn pocketed the notes. "You know Fat John?"

"I haven't had the pleasure."

"Used to be a teacher, I think. Lost his job after getting a little too friendly with the kids. He's tubby, hence the name, smells bad most of the time, and he's got problems with boils on his face." He held a finger to his nose. "Had one here yesterday, looked bloody disgusting." Finn mopped up the rest of the sauce with the muffin. "He buys from me now and again, and yesterday he comes in and says he has a DSLR and something they use to record sound, and would I be interested in taking them off his hands? I said no, I don't get involved in hooky gear, and sent him on his way."

"You 'don't get involved in hooky gear'?"

"Not when I don't trust the person selling it to me—no."

"That doesn't help me. Give me the money back."

"Hold on, tiger." Finn held up his hand. "A little bird told me Fat John flogged them to Stinky Pete. You know him?"

"Don't know."

"Smelly bastard," Finn offered.

"I gathered that. What's his name?"

He frowned. "Pete… Weaver."

Atticus nodded. "I've nicked him before. House on Halfpenny Road?"

"That's the one—near Churchfields. I'd wander over there and have a look. That'll be the best place to find them."

83

Atticus knew speed was important, any delay would make it more likely that Stinky Pete would move the camera and the recorder again, and Atticus didn't want to run the risk that the trail might grow cold.

He jogged into the Close, picked up his car and drove across to the industrial estate at Churchfields. He turned right onto Cherry Orchard Road, passed beneath the railway bridge and pulled over. Weaver's house was at the end of the terrace. It was built from red brick with two windows on the upper floor and one on the ground floor. It was in a terrible state of disrepair. The windows had been boarded up, and the panels were covered with graffiti. The front garden was elevated from the pavement and accessible by a set of steps between low brick walls. It was a mess, with overgrown shrubs and bushes. An expanse of out-of-control greenery was to the left, separating the terrace from the embankment and the railway line.

Atticus opened the door as Mack's car pulled up behind him.

"Hold up," she said.

"Funny seeing you here."

"You could've called."

"I was about to," he said.

"Of *course* you were."

"All right, I wasn't. I didn't want to wait."

"I've told you about that—we do things properly, or we don't do them at all."

"Duly noted," Atticus said, knowing that she wouldn't believe him for a minute. "Did you see the stepdad?"

"A very unpleasant man. We've spoken to social services about the boy—I think there's a good chance he goes into temporary care."

"What did he say about the gear?"

"Denied it at first," she said. "But then we explained what'd happen if it turned out he was lying, and he saw sense. He says he sold the kit to a user he knows."

"Fat John," Atticus said.

"Correct. Just been to see him. He said he swapped them for dope here."

"Pete Weaver," Atticus said.

"How'd you work it out?"

"Spoke to someone I know. Fat John tried to sell the gear to him, but he said no. He heard that he went here afterwards."

She cocked an eyebrow disapprovingly. "Did you go to see Finn?"

"In my professional capacity."

"I hope so," she said, then pointed to the house. "Shall we?"

They climbed the steps to the front door. A repossession notice had been nailed into the rotting wood; exposed and dangling wires underlined how poorly the property had been treated.

"Weaver," Mack said. "Do you know him?"

"I nicked him a couple of times."

"Me too," she said. "He only got out six months ago."

"That might only be a temporary reprieve," Atticus offered, nodding at the house. "Looks like he's fallen right back into his old ways."

Mack wrinkled her nose.

"Got a warrant?"

"No." She put her hand to her ear. "But can you hear that?"

Atticus was happy to play along with the charade. "That sounds very much like a disturbance."

"What I thought, too."

The police didn't generally have the power to enter a property without a warrant, but there were exceptions, and dealing with a disturbance was one of them. Atticus had never been detained by any need to do things by the book when he'd been a police detective, Mack had chided him for it, but Atticus knew that she was just as apt to bend the rules if the situation demanded it.

She tried the door, but it was locked.

"Excuse me," Atticus said.

He stepped around her and, before she could complain, took out his lock picks and knelt down so that the keyhole was at eye level. He took out a small wrench and a pick, the lock was old and barely functional, and he had it open in ten seconds.

"I'll pretend I didn't see that," Mack said.

"Probably best."

Atticus opened the door and stepped inside.

The smell hit him straight away: a mix of stale air, rotting food, mould and mildew and the reek of unwashed clothes.

Through all of it was the pungent note of spilled alcohol and the sweetness of dope.

Atticus could guess the layout of the house: kitchen to the right, sitting room at the rear, two bedrooms and a bathroom on the floor above. He stepped through an ankle-deep carpet of litter—discarded food packaging, black bin bags of rotting food waste, clothes—and glanced into the empty kitchen. He dared not look into the small ground-floor WC, save to confirm that it was unoccupied, and continued to the rear of the property.

The sitting room was cluttered with cans, plastic bottles, food wrappers, and pieces of clothing strewn across the floor and furniture. A torn and worn-out sofa was piled high with dishevelled blankets and cushions, while a small coffee table was cluttered with more debris, including burnt foil. There were a couple of incongruous pictures on the walls—a large, framed picture of a beach scene and a heart-shaped wall-hanging with an inspirational message—and in one corner was an old television sitting on a stand amidst a chaotic assortment of electronic devices, books, and more rubbish. A single armchair, upholstered in a floral pattern, was sat alongside, a man asleep on it. A woman sprawled across the floor.

Atticus was about to turn back to check upstairs when he saw movement from the courtyard garden. He went up to the open door and saw a man sitting at a cheap white plastic picnic table. He was facing away, his attention occupied by the spliff he was rolling.

"Excuse me." The man turned, and Atticus recognised him from the last time he had arrested him. "Hello, Pete. Remember me?"

Weaver evidently did. "What do *you* want?"

"A little chat."

"You're not police anymore, though. I heard you got sacked."

"I'm not," he said, stepping to the side. "But she is."

Mack took out her warrant card so that Weaver could see it. "Detective Chief Inspector Jones."

"I remember you, too. Got a warrant to barge in here like that?"

"No."

"So you can't come in then, can you? Piss off."

"We heard a disturbance," she said.

"Sounded nasty," Atticus added. "The DCI didn't really have a choice—had to come in and make sure everything was all right."

"Bollocks," Weaver muttered.

"Of course it is," Mack said, "but we both know it'll do for now."

The air around Weaver was thick with the sour, pungent tang of stale sweat, a cloying odour that clung to his clothes and seemed to radiate from his skin.

Mack pointed down at the joint on the table. "That for personal use?"

"It's just one spliff."

"Would we find any more if we had a look around?"

Weaver knew he was being threatened but bluffed it out. "Do whatever you need to do, but I know my rights. My brief will make mincemeat of you if this ever goes anywhere, and you know it."

"Well," Mack said, "luckily for you we're not here about what you may or may not be up to. We want to know about a couple of items you bought yesterday."

"Didn't buy anything yesterday."

"Really? It was a camera and a sound recorder—have a think."

He shook his head firmly. "Don't know what you're talking about."

"You took them as payment for the two ounces of marijuana you sold to Fat John," Atticus said.

He shrugged. "Don't know anyone called that."

Atticus rolled his eyes. "Come on, Pete. Not playing ball is a really stupid thing to do under the circumstances. Please don't lie."

"I'm not."

Atticus glanced at Mack. "Want to know how I know?"

"His lips are moving?"

"There *is* that. There's also the fact that when he says no, he nods his head yes. It's what a psychologist would call a non-congruent gesture. Big giveaway. Don't ever play poker, Pete. You'd be rubbish."

Weaver laughed. "Am I supposed to be impressed?"

"You want to know how else I know you're lying?"

He shrugged.

"Because the DCI spoke to Fat John before she came over here."

"I did," Mack said. "I told him how important it was that he told me the truth. It'll probably help if you knew why that is, too. The camera and the recorder you bought from him were taken from the scene of a potential crime two days ago. We have reason to believe they might help us work out what happened to a woman who's gone missing. John understood what'd happen to him if he lied."

"Perverting the course of justice," Atticus said.

"And that can be a *very* serious offence."

"Prison?" Atticus said.

"Definitely. For something like this?" Mack pursed her lips in thought. "Four years—minimum."

"And that's apart from the dealing in stolen property."

"Apart from that." Mack pulled out the chair next to Weaver and sat down. "There are two ways for you to do this. The first way is the best—you go and find the camera and the recorder, and we'll leave you to smoke your joint in peace. The other way's much less convenient. I'll get on the phone to the station and have them send over a couple of uniformed officers who'll take this place apart, brick by brick, until we find what we're looking for. Of course, we both know we'll find *other* things that you'd rather we didn't, and I promise I won't be as likely to turn a blind eye to those things as I might if you cooperate now."

Weaver might have been stoned, but he wasn't addled beyond the reach of good sense. "All right," he said. "Maybe I *do* remember."

84

Weaver produced the stolen equipment—a Sony DSLR and a Zoom sound recorder—and Mack put them into evidence bags and sealed them up.

"Thank you," she said.

Weaver tried to look solicitous. "Happy to help."

"I'm sure you are."

"We're good?"

"For now. But I'm going to send someone down here tomorrow morning. You'd better not be selling out of here—you'll be nicked if you are."

"Whatever."

"And, Pete," Atticus said, "have a shower. You *reek*."

Atticus followed Mack outside.

"I need to fumigate my clothes," she said.

Atticus pointed at the bags. "We need to look at them tonight."

"I'd rather send them to Bristol and get the lab to do it."

Mack preferred to follow procedure, and the rules on evidence handling required both items to be couriered to the laboratory for expedited forensic analysis. There was a chance they were dealing with a crime, and the devices might have information on what had happened; that meant the process of securing the evidence was detailed and thorough and couldn't be avoided or abbreviated. The memory cards would be removed and secured before being assessed to ensure they had no physical damage and that they were readable. Then they'd be imaged, with the technician creating a bit-for-bit copy so that original data was secured and to serve as a benchmark against future tampering. The forensic copy of the data would be analysed and viewed, and then a report would be generated with details including timestamps, locations and any individuals present in the recordings. The physical cards would be kept in the evidence room, and the investigation would rely on the copies.

But all of that would take time.

"That's not a good idea," he said. "Alice Green is missing, and there's a chance—a good chance—there's something on those devices that'll help you work out what happened. You can't wait until tomorrow. What if the delay leads to something bad happening to her?"

"Something bad might *already* have happened to her."

"What are you thinking?"

"I'm still not sure."

"The social media stuff must have been upsetting for her. Suicide?"

"I don't see it. I don't see it being an accident, either. I never have."

"So?"

"I think we'll find it's a third party. But don't ask me who or why because I have no idea." He nodded at the bags. "But they might tell us."

Mack sighed. "Maybe I can get a technician to come to us."

"Can I be there?"

"I don't know if that's a—"

"*I* found them," he interrupted. "And you know you could use my help."

She shook her head in helpless surrender. "Let me think about it. Go and get something to eat, and I'll call you when I've got something to report."

85

Atticus went back to the office to feed Bandit and give him a quick walk, then left him to go to sleep and wandered in town in the hope of finding inspiration for his own dinner. He ambled by Hixon, decided a steak was too much, and continued on to Wagamama. It was quiet, and he was able to get a table to himself. He ordered a curry and a bottle of beer and waited for them both to arrive.

He thought about what they'd found. He knew Mack had to be careful, but he was itching to check out the memory cards. He was convinced now that Alice hadn't got into difficulties in the water, and that the alternative—that a third party was involved—made it more urgent that they discover what had happened. There wasn't much to go on beyond what might have been recorded on the cards, and the caution was teeth-grindingly exasperating even if the reasons were good. At least they'd be able to get into them tonight, tomorrow would've been too long to wait, and he doubted he would have been able to sleep.

His phone rang. It was Mack.

"Ready?" he said.

"I've sorted it. The technician's setting up now. Come if you want—I've set you up as a consultant again. I've told the front desk to expect you."

Atticus took out a twenty to cover his meal, put it on the table and got up. The waitress looked over at him in confusion, but he was out of the door and onto the street before she could ask him what was wrong.

"And Atticus?" Mack said.

"Yes?"

"Please behave."

* * *

Atticus hurried to Bourne Hill. Robbie Best was just making his way through the front door.

"Evening," Best said. "Mack said you'd be coming over."

Best signed him in and led the way up to the conference room on the first floor. Mack was waiting, a laptop set up on the desk so that the screen was projected onto the whiteboard. A technician was sitting behind the laptop.

"Good," Mack said. "We're ready. Robbie, Atticus—this is Frances from Southwest Regional Forensic Services in Bristol. Frances—this is Robbie Best, my DI, and Atticus Priest, a private investigator who'll be consulting with us on this case."

The woman's face lit up. "I've seen you on the television, haven't I?"

"Atticus helped us with the case at Hawthorne Manor," Mack explained.

"And helped get Ralph Mallender off," Frances said. "That must've been awkward."

"Water under the bridge," Mack said.

Mack told them both to sit, and they pulled out chairs and arranged themselves so they could see the screen. Frances tapped the keyboard, and the projection mirrored the desktop on the computer. Atticus saw that it had been loaded with two folders: CAMERA and RECORDER.

"Have you looked at anything yet?"

"We were waiting for you," Mack replied.

Frances double-clicked on the folders, revealing that each one held multiple files. "I've imaged both cards," she said, scrolling through them. "There's a lot on them."

Atticus pointed. "Do the camera first."

Frances looked over at Mack and, at her nod, did as he asked. She double-clicked to open it and uncovered the nested files within. They were arranged by date.

"Anything from Wednesday?" Mack said.

Frances scrolled down. "One file."

She double-clicked, and they waited as the player opened and the video began to play. The shot was of a river, the camera angled down to confirm that it had been placed on the bank.

"That's Standlynch," Mack said.

Atticus nodded. "Same place as where the tripod was found."

The footage continued to play. A woman emerged from the right-hand side of the shot, slowly wading out into the water until it was up to her shoulders. She kicked water as she turned back and looked up into the lens.

"Good morning. I'm Alice Green from Real Wild Swimming, and I'm here this morning in my favourite pool near Downton in Wiltshire. It's five thirty, and I'm here alone—it's just me, the sound of the water and the birds in the trees."

The sound was picked up by the camera's microphone, but it was obvious that Alice relied upon the recorder when she edited her videos together. The quality from the camera was adequate, but the dedicated recorder would provide much-improved fidelity.

"I read an article in the Daily Mail *yesterday doubting whether wild swimming and cold-water immersion really is all it's cracked up to be, and I decided I'd spend this morning's video addressing some of the points raised and demonstrating that it was written by a hater who was just looking for clicks."*

She continued, explaining why cold water was such a panacea, and then seamlessly and professionally—if a little cynically—pitching the swimsuit she was wearing. She moved on to encourage viewers to sign up to her mailing list so she could send them an introductory video series on the benefits of wild swimming.

She was halfway through a sentence when the image cut to black.

Mack leaned forward. "What happened?"

"The memory card's full," Frances said. "This file was the last one to be recorded."

Atticus clenched his jaw in frustration. "Play it again."

Frances moused down to the timer at the bottom of the player and scrubbed back to the start. She pressed play, and they watched the video for a second time, with Atticus concentrating on the whole shot—the background and anything that he might be able to hear—rather than just what Alice was saying and doing. There was nothing suspicious.

He pointed a finger at the screen. "She recorded this before she found out about Frank stitching her up."

Mack cocked an eyebrow. "How can you say that for sure?"

"Look at her body language," he said. "Her expression is relaxed and natural. Her voice is steady and clear—I'd expect it to be rapid and high-pitched if she was anxious, and she would definitely have been anxious." He shook his head. "No. She's calm and confident and doesn't have a care in the world. Oblivious to it. No idea at all."

Best frowned. "How does that help us?"

"It helps us build a timeline," he said as Frances minimised the window and returned to the desktop view.

Mack pointed to the second folder. "And that one?"

Frances opened the folder and found the only recording with the same date and time as Wednesday's interrupted video. She pressed play.

"*Good morning. I'm Alice Green from Real Wild Swimming, and I'm here this morning in my favourite pool near Downton in Wiltshire.*"

"Same as the video," Best said.

Frances pressed pause. "She'll stitch them together when she edits."

She tapped the play button again, and the recording continued.

"*It's five thirty, and I'm here alone—it's just me, the sound of the water and the birds in the trees.*"

Alice kept talking, but rather than cutting out where the video had stopped, the recording continued. She kept on all the way to what was evidently the end of what she'd been meaning to say. Atticus held his breath as he heard splashing as she exited the river, and then a muttered curse.

Best gestured at the screen. "Stop it for a moment."

Frances did.

"What was *that* about?"

Mack leaned back. "She's noticed the video didn't record."

Atticus nodded. "Definitely. She finishes what she wants to say, gets out to check it recorded, sees that it didn't and is annoyed with herself." He closed his eyes and tried to picture the scene: Alice, wet and cold; the camera and the recorder; the river; the track leading back to where she'd parked her car next to the old mill. "You want to know what I think happens next? She knows she has to get this recorded today because she's been paid to promote the swimsuit she's wearing and put the promotion out, and, anyway, she's here now, and she doesn't want to have to go home and come back again tomorrow to do it all again and get out of sync with her schedule. She goes back to the car to get another card, but never comes back."

Mack looked uncertain. "Why not just reformat the card in the camera and start again? Why even go back to the car?"

Atticus wrinkled his brow. "Maybe she doesn't think of that. Or maybe there's something on it she doesn't want to lose."

Mack turned to Frances. "You'll catalogue it?"

"I'll go through it and list everything. You'll get a report in the morning."

Atticus gestured for her to continue the playback.

The sound continued. They heard footsteps and then the background noise of the river.

"She doesn't stop the recording," Mack said. "Why not?"

"Because she forgets," Best suggested.

"Agreed," Atticus said. "Put yourself in her shoes. She's annoyed with herself, and maybe it slips her mind. It wouldn't have been a big deal—she just deletes this one and starts another when she's fixed the camera. Or maybe she'll stop it and start a new recording when she's got the camera ready." He glanced down to the timer at the bottom of the player: five minutes had elapsed. He pointed. "How long will it record for?"

Frances moused over to switch from time elapsed to time remaining.

Six hours.

"It records until it runs out of space on the card," she said.

Atticus found that he was holding his breath.

Five more minutes passed.

They heard the grunting of a mute swan, the cheerful song of a skylark, and, as a constant, the hiss and splash of the water as it played over the weir. Atticus strained his ears for the sound of a voice, or anything that would suggest that Alice was not alone but heard nothing.

He closed his eyes and thought back to the scene at Standlynch again: the car had been parked at the mill, and that was at least a hundred metres from the spot where the camera and recorder had been set up.

How long would it take her to walk to the car, get a fresh memory card, and walk back?

The average walking speed for an adult was one and a half metres per second.

Seventy seconds to get to the car.

Another seventy to get back.

How long would it take her to find the memory card?

Surely not long.

She would've been cold, too, and wouldn't that give her a reason to hurry?

Say four minutes from leaving the river to getting back again, maximum.

Ten minutes passed, and still there was no evidence that Alice had returned.

"There's nothing," Best said.

Atticus shook his head.

Mack noticed. "What are you thinking?"

"Pause it," he said, and waited for Frances.

"Atticus?"

"Something like this," he said. "Alice goes back to the car. She takes out her phone. She sees she's had messages from people who've seen what Frank's done. She's still there now"—he pointed at the screen, meaning the recording—"scrolling through it and trying to work out what she's going to do. Trying to work out how much damage has been done. Calling her lawyer, for all we know. She's forgotten about the video. She's distracted."

"That's speculative," Best said.

"Speculating is all we can do until we know more."

"Go on."

"She panics. She knows she's got a crisis on her hands, and she has to get back home or into the office to deal with it. She gets changed, puts the swimsuit in the bag and chucks it on the passenger seat, then tosses the dryrobe and her towel in the back of the car."

"And then?"

Fifteen minutes.

The birds, the water, the wind.

Nothing else.

Best waved a hand in the direction of the screen. "How long are you going to listen for?"

"*All of it*," Atticus mouthed.

Best rolled his eyes and, by pointing to the door, indicated that he'd like to speak to Mack.

The two of them were about to leave the table when they all heard the sound of the scream.

86

It wasn't so clear as to be unmistakeable, but Atticus was in no doubt: the recorder had picked up the sound of a scream.

"*Again.*"

Frances marked the time and scrubbed back ten seconds.

Atticus closed his eyes and concentrated hard.

There it was: a woman's scream, lasting two seconds from start to finish.

Mack lowered her head. "Jesus."

"*Again.*"

Frances scrubbed back and played it for a third time.

"*Not* suicide, then," Best said.

"I knew it wasn't," Atticus said.

"But could be an accident. Maybe she falls?"

"Unlikely."

Best shrugged. "You can't say that."

"Yes, I *can*. She wouldn't scream like that if she tripped and fell into the water."

"You don't *know* that."

"The last time you tripped, did *you* scream? And for two seconds, like she just did? And that wasn't shock or surprise—it was *fear*." Atticus didn't wait for an answer, he knew his forthright manner encouraged argument, but he was as sure as he could be that he'd been right about what had happened, and this had proved it. "She's scared. Someone's frightened her."

Best looked as if he was going to protest, but Mack cut him off. "I agree with Atticus. If that *is* her—"

"It is," Atticus interrupted.

"*If* that's her," Mack insisted, "then I agree—that's someone who's scared."

"All right," Best said, holding up his hands. "Let's say it is. How close would she have had to be to the recorder for it to pick that up?"

Atticus had already started to consider that. He closed his eyes and ran a quick series of calculations. "We'd need to go down and check, but she was probably at the mill, by the car."

"That far?" Mack said. "That's nearly two hundred metres away."

"Just over," Atticus said. "But it'd still be audible."

"How can you be sure?"

"Assume the scream was a hundred decibels."

"*Assume*?" Best said.

"That'd be the average," Atticus said patiently.

"How can you just say you know that?"

"I know *lots* of things."

Mack made a mollifying gesture and indicated that Atticus should go on.

"The distance a noise that loud can be heard—or recorded, in this case—depends on lots of things. The environment, obstacles between the source and the recorder, atmospheric conditions, the sensitivity of the equipment—they'd all be relevant. But sound ought to travel reasonably well down there. Not too much background noise—"

"The sound of the weir?" Best cut in.

"There *is* that, but it's steady, and that's about it. No other obstacles. You use the inverse square law to estimate how the intensity decreases with distance. Sound intensity decreases by six decibels each time the distance from the source is doubled. In other words, it'd be one hundred decibels at the source, ninety-four at two metres, eighty-eight decibels at four metres, all the way down to around fifty decibels at one hundred and fifty metres. Anything below sixty decibels is quieter than usual conversation, but the recorder would pick it up."

"So you're saying she screams near the car?"

"The recording will need to be analysed, but that'd be my guess."

Mack reached both hands to her head and massaged her temples. "I was hoping this might be an accident or something she did to herself after reading those posts, but it's not, is it?"

"No," Atticus said. "I don't think so."

"Shit." She turned to Best. "Round everyone up who can be spared," she said, looking at her watch. "Briefing in here in an hour."

Best said he'd go and make the arrangements and left the room. Frances took the opportunity to do the same, saying that she'd get a cup of coffee and then start work reviewing the rest of the sound files and the other files on the camera.

Mack waited until they had both left the room and then looked over at Atticus with tired eyes. "I need another murder enquiry right now like I need a hole in the head."

"Might not be murder," Atticus said.

She cocked an eyebrow. "But you think it is."

"It's either that or abduction."

"Shit either way."

"Want me to stay?"

"I'm guessing you'd like to?"

"There's a problem to solve. You know how I like solving problems."

"Fine—but you've got to behave yourself. No showboating."

"As if I would."

"Like you just did with Robbie. I don't have time to massage hurt feelings."

"I could sit quietly in the corner."

"That'd be nice. Can you do that?"

"I'll be honest. Probably not."

"But you'll *try* not to piss the others off?"

"I'll do my best," he said.

87

Atticus knew Mack wouldn't have eaten, and, certain that she was going to be busy for the rest of the night as she set up the enquiry team, he made a return trip to Wagamama for supplies. The waitress recognised him from his abbreviated visit earlier and apologised that he was going to have to order—and pay—again. Atticus said that was fine. He worked his way down the menu and picked out a selection of dishes that the team could share: teriyaki beef brisket hotpot, grilled chicken ramen, chicken gochujang rice bowl, and two katsu curries. The food was deposited into two large bags. Atticus paid the bill, thanked the waitress and returned to Bourne Hill. He put the bags in the kitchen and returned to the conference room.

Best had made good progress in putting the enquiry team together. The station operated an out-of-hours on-call system to bring in detectives, forensic officers and other specialists when circumstances demanded, and he'd activated it.

The room had been cleared, with the digital technician decamping into an empty office as she began the onerous task of watching, listening to, and cataloguing every file on the memory cards. The table had been lengthened with a second pushed up against one end, with spare chairs lined up along the wall in the event that they needed more. The smart board at the front was showing a blank screen now that the laptop had been disconnected, and pinboards had been hung from the walls so that evidence and photographs could be posted; a photograph of Alice Green's abandoned car had been pinned to one of the boards, with a screen grab from the video of her in the water pinned to the next one along. Cardboard document trays had been positioned on the table; empty at the moment, they would be used to file incident reports, witness statements, and preliminary forensic results.

Atticus took a seat against the wall where he could listen without making his presence too obvious. He knew the others would notice him, and that some of them wouldn't be pleased that he was involved, but he had made a promise to Mack that he'd irritate them as little as possible, and he was going to try to keep it.

For as long as he could, anyway.

He watched the door as the others came in and took their seats. Best was standing with his phone held to his ear, evidently berating someone—Atticus didn't catch who it was—who was late in answering the call.

DS Mike Lewis and DC Nigel Archer came in together. Lewis was an old lag and Archer a young upstart; Archer followed Lewis in the hope that he might be able to absorb some of the senior man's experience to pair with his whip-smart mind. The two of them had been on the night shift and were already at the station.

DC Stewart Lynas was next, wearing a flashy leather coat and glossy Chelsea boots that suggested he'd been out in town when he received the call. Lynas wouldn't have liked being disturbed. He had an overinflated opinion of his own talent, and Mack had indiscreetly told Atticus about a comment he'd made in his annual report saying that he expected to have taken her place within the next ten years. Atticus—and Mack—found his lack of self-awareness amusing; Lynas had such a *spectacularly* misplaced confidence in his own abilities. He had recently come by an unfortunate nickname after busting a suspected drug dealer and confiscating what he thought were cannabis plants. The plants had been identified as lupins at the station, and the nickname had stuck. Lynas ought to have been pushing for promotion to DS by now, but Mack had picked Francine Patterson for that honour, and Lynas was going to take that very badly when he eventually found out. Atticus wouldn't have been surprised if the snub proved to be enough for him to flounce off to another job entirely.

Atticus's thought of Patterson reminded him that she wasn't here. That was a shame. Out of all of the officers, she was the one with the most potential. She had parlayed her experience as a redcap in the Royal Military Police into a number of impressive results after her transfer into CID. That she had been duped by Thomas Chandler did not affect the high regard with which Atticus viewed her; she was talented and hardworking and obviously destined for a successful career, assuming she wasn't poached away to do something else for much more money than she'd make as a public servant.

Mack came in, shared a quick glance with Atticus and then took her place at the head of the table. She rapped her knuckles against it and waited for the hubbub to die down.

"Thanks for coming in," she said. "Robbie wouldn't have pressed the button apart from the fact that what we thought was a missing person investigation now looks as if it might be something else."

Lynas raised a finger but didn't wait to be asked to speak. "This is about the woman in the river?"

"Alice Green," Mack said, pointing to the screen grab pinned to the board. "That's right. I'll recap for those of you who haven't been involved in that case. Alice has been missing since early Wednesday morning. She's a wild swimmer, and our initial theory was that she went into the river at Standlynch, got into difficulty and drowned. The alternative was that she killed herself after she came under an unpleasant online attack from her ex-husband. Either of those outcomes could *still* be what happened, but we've come into possession of additional information this evening that at least suggests foul play might be involved."

Atticus looked at the officers sat around the table. They were all attentive, even Lynas, notepads open as they took down the details that Mack provided.

"A dog walker found Alice's car by the mill on Thursday morning. We attended on Thursday afternoon and found a tripod on the riverbank when we conducted the initial search. The camera wasn't there, but we had a tip-off from a local schoolboy who said that he and a couple of friends took it and a sound recorder that they found alongside. He came in to see us this afternoon and said that his stepfather had sold both to a dealer to pay for drugs. We found the dealer, and then we found the gear. There are two memory cards to review—they'll be indexed overnight—but our initial assessment is that Alice was in the water that morning, but that her memory card was full, and the camera stopped recording before she finished what she was doing. We've checked the sound recording on the second device, and you can hear a woman's scream after the video stops. On that basis, we have to at least assume there's third-party involvement here—either she's been murdered and the body removed, or she's been abducted."

"You think it was a random attack?" Archer said. "*Please* don't say you think it was random because that'd be a nightmare."

"We have no idea," Mack said. "We don't have any strong leads at the moment."

Archer tapped his pen against his pad. "No suspects at all?"

"No. None."

Lynas leaned back in his chair, his long legs stretched out beneath the table. "Family members?"

"As suspects?" Mack shook her head. "She's been dealing with a messy divorce, and the ex-husband was responsible for the story that ran about her on Wednesday morning. The two of them have been trying to ruin each other, and she grassed him up over a planning scam—we've had him in for bribery. The Fraud Squad are putting that case together, and he's looking at a big fine, maybe even time inside."

"So he's got motive to hurt her," Lynas said.

"Yes, but we don't think it's him. He came over for questioning this afternoon, and I'm happy enough that he's not involved."

"It's Frank Green, isn't it?" Lynas said.

Mack nodded.

"He's minted. Someone like that wouldn't get his own hands dirty, would he? He'd pay someone else to do it."

Atticus cleared his throat. "It's not him."

Lynas turned, his expression changing to one of dismay. "You? What are you doing here?"

"Making sure you don't make a fool of yourself, Lupin."

Lynas looked to Mack and spread his arms in a gesture of helplessness; Mack glared at Atticus and shook her head in an attempt to stop him from saying anything else. "Atticus will be consulting for us again."

"*Really*, boss?"

"He has relevant information, as well as his experience. He was engaged by Frank Green to look into Alice Green before she went missing. He saw her on the Tuesday and was due to see her again on the Wednesday."

"And I've spoken to Frank several times about Alice," Atticus said, "including after she disappeared. And I can tell you that he didn't do this. I'm not saying he wouldn't stoop to it—I think he probably would. I'm saying he's not clever enough, and that he'd be too scared about what'd happen to him if—no, *when*—he was found out. It'd be nice and convenient if you could pin it on him, but I'm afraid it's going to be more difficult than that."

"I interviewed Mr. Green this afternoon," Mack said. "And I agree with Atticus. We're not ruling him out completely, but I don't want us wasting time looking into him when we need to be broadening our scope."

"There's something else to add," Atticus said. "Alice's studio was broken into late Wednesday night or early Thursday morning. I did think that it might have been Frank, but I had a look, and it doesn't make sense that it was him. It's suspicious, though. Not likely to be a coincidence."

"Who attended?" Best said.

"Britten and Carver. I told them they ought to take prints, but they didn't think they'd be able to get a SOCO out to do it."

"I'll have a word with them," Best said.

Mack went through the rest of the administration quickly; it could all be gone over more carefully in the morning. For now, she made Best her deputy as SIO, then picked Archer as office manager and Lynas as exhibits officer, much to his chagrin. Mack left it with Archer to pick the rest of the backroom operation—the action manager, disclosure officer, document reader and registrar, all of them in place in anticipation of a trial or inquest—and to ensure that the HOLMES 2 software was ready.

Best clapped his hands together, eager to get on. "What do you want us to do first, boss?"

"Arrange for a couple of uniforms to go down and seal off the area at Standlynch. All of it—from the mill all the way to the weir. We should've kept a cordon in place after she went missing—let's make sure we keep it nice and tight from now on. I'll arrange for some extra manpower tomorrow for a detailed search. We've only skimmed it so far—we need to make sure there's nothing that's been missed."

"Will do, boss. What about the super? Does he know yet?"

"Not yet. I'll give him a call now."

Atticus knew Mack wouldn't relish that. Chief Superintendent Beckton was difficult to deal with at the best of times, but especially so when it looked as if he was going to have to deal with more outside scrutiny than usual. There'd been a lot of that over the last couple of years, and he'd be nervous about the prospect of another *cause célèbre* coming their way.

Mack stood. "That's all I've got," she said. "Get started. We'll go full speed tomorrow, but we need to start making enquiries now."

PART 6

88

Atticus stayed at the station until after midnight and then, thinking of Bandit, made his excuses and went home.

Sleep had been impossible. He lay in bed and deliberated for an hour over what he was thinking of doing, before acknowledging that even though it was probably stupid, he was always going to do it anyway. He waited until two in the morning before changing into black jeans and a black sweater. He collected his evidence kit and made sure he had a pair of new nitrile gloves.

He checked Bandit was comfortable in his basket, and then went outside.

* * *

Atticus walked to the High Street. He passed by Alice Green's studio on the opposite side, making a pretence of looking in the window of the fudge shop before crossing the road. The front door to the studio had been repaired, as Atticus had expected; he could've easily picked the lock, but going in the same way as the previous intruder felt a little riskier than it needed to be. He had studied Google Maps and, with the benefit of the satellite view, knew there was a large car park behind the studio that served the buildings behind it.

There was a covered passage between the estate agency and the closed hair salon that led to the car park. Atticus went through it and turned to his right, following the rear of the buildings. He was pleased to find what he had expected: the fire door that he'd noticed when he had been inside the studio earlier opened out here.

He took out the gloves and worked them onto his hands, snapping the material around his wrists. He collected his picks and set to work. It was a simple lock, and after setting the teeth and applying just enough torque with his tension wrench, he felt the mechanism open.

He turned the handle, opened the door and slipped inside.

He paused, listening hard for anything that might suggest someone else might be in the building, but heard nothing.

He knew this was a foolish risk and that it might be a wild goose chase. The officers who had attended earlier had done nothing to establish a controlled environment and would have contaminated the scene with additional prints. Alice's assistant would also have been inside, along with any workmen who might have attended to make repairs. But that all being said, he thought it was still worth coming here and risking the consequences of being discovered.

He went to the desk and started there. He pulled the drawer open and saw several pages of paper fastened with treasury tags. He reached down, took them out and put them on the floor. He looked down at the first page: several screen grabs of what looked like WhatsApp messages had been printed out.

The name at the top—denoting the sender—was Frank Green, and what followed were half a dozen messages concerning someone who appeared to be known to both Green and the unnamed recipient. They were derogatory, and, as Atticus turned the page and continued to read, they quickly became both sexist and racist. The final message included the name of the person—Ajit Malik—and concluded with a joke about his ethnicity. Atticus was familiar with the name; Malik was a local councillor who had run to be mayor at the last election. The reason the pages were here was obvious; Alice had either used the screen grabs in her campaign to blacken her husband's name or was intending to. Atticus took photographs of the pages that caught his attention and then put them back.

There was a filing cabinet on the far wall, and Atticus found that it was open when he tried the top drawer. He slid it all the way open and riffled through the papers that were arranged there. It was all about Frank Green: there were emails to and from someone called Beth McTaggart, describing work done on establishing the details of the planning scandals that had caused Frank so much difficulty; there was a long statement from a former Salisbury councillor, the woman admitting that she had accepted Frank's hospitality in return for waving through the planning application for a large house in Bishopstone that Atticus remembered being built; and there was correspondence with the Serious Fraud Office that suggested that Frank wasn't anywhere near the full extent of the legal peril he would face for what he'd done. Atticus opened the next drawer down and then the next; they were both replete with more of the same.

Atticus knew Alice wanted to ruin her husband's business and trash his reputation but had underestimated the fervency of her desire; she wasn't just interested in seeing him brought low, she was *obsessed*.

Something else came into focus for Atticus, too. He'd wondered whether Frank might have been behind the break-in, but that seemed more unlikely now. Alice had plenty of compromising material about her husband but hadn't made any particular effort to hide it. It was difficult to imagine how anyone could have missed it. Wouldn't Frank—or, more likely, whoever he might've paid to break into the studio—have found it and removed it? The vigour with which Alice was prosecuting her campaign certainly gave Frank the motive to wish her ill, but the fact that all of this evidence had just been left here and ignored suggested he had nothing to do with *this* crime, at least.

Atticus took additional photographs, then put everything back where he had found it and closed the drawers.

If it *wasn't* Frank, then who was it?

He went to the desk and saw again that the laptop with the Real Wild Swimming decals was still there. He opened the lid, saw the lock screen and ground his teeth together in frustration; there was a chance the computer might hold something of interest, but it would be difficult to unlock it. Mack could ask the secretary of state for a Technical Capability Notice that would compel the manufacturer to assist with unlocking the device, but that would be time-consuming and didn't even come with a guarantee of success.

Atticus closed the lid and, on a whim, lifted the laptop so he could look at the desk beneath it. There was nothing there, but he noticed a Post-it note had been affixed to the underside of the computer. He peeled it off so that he could read the six-digit number written across it.

374829.

He put the laptop back on the desk, opened it for a second time and typed in the number.

It didn't work.

Atticus swore under his breath.

It certainly *looked* like a password, and, if it was, it might be valuable. He took a photograph of it, then decided he'd outstayed his welcome and it was time to go.

89

Francine Patterson was at the station early to continue looking for Tom Brennan. She had a couple of things on her list that she wanted to cover as soon as possible: his parents had emailed her a list of the old friends they thought he had kept in touch with, and she wanted to canvass them to see whether they had heard from him recently; she'd also emailed his old regiment to see if there was anything in his records that might have indicated why he would disappear like this, and they'd sent over everything they had for her to review. Those tasks ought to be enough to keep her occupied for the rest of the day.

Robbie had texted her late last night to say that the other missing person enquiry at the station—the wild swimmer who'd gone missing at Standlynch—had taken a turn and that it was now being regarded as a possible crime. He'd been rostered for the late shift, so she hadn't expected to see him, but he'd warned her that it was going to be busier than they had expected. Francine was frustrated not to have been called in to work on the enquiry; she doubted it would be that difficult to find Brennan—he'd probably fallen off the wagon and was in the middle of a bender somewhere. She wondered, too, whether Robbie or Mack had avoided involving her on the basis that they both wanted her to stay focussed on the sergeant's exam. She hoped that wasn't true; she'd found the experience of working on the Chandler case exhilarating, and to be kept away from something else that had the potential to be big because her boss and her boyfriend were trying to look out for her—without asking whether she had the capacity to do the work—would have been irritating. Because Francine *would* find the capacity, and she didn't want to miss out because of their misplaced concern.

She was going to speak to Robbie about that, but she'd seen him on the way out as she arrived at the nick; he was with Lynas and had quickly told her he was going out to Standlynch to oversee a search of the area where Alice Green had gone missing. They could have a chat when they went away together on Saturday. Robbie had told her he'd booked the cabin and was looking forward to it. She reminded herself that she needed to get him a present.

She grabbed a cup of coffee from the machine and took it to her desk. The report from the regiment was thorough, and she read it as she sipped the coffee.

Thomas Brennan was born in 1985 and enlisted in the Army right after finishing school in 2003. He completed basic training at Catterick Garrison and then deployed to Iraq as part of Operation Telic. He served with the 1st Battalion, the Parachute Regiment, and was stationed in Basra. The report noted that he was involved in various peacekeeping operations, convoy escorts, and counterinsurgency. His time saw him exposed to intense firefights and IED attacks, including a roadside bomb that turned over his vehicle and led to the death of a comrade.

He returned to England before being deployed to Afghanistan as part of Operation Herrick. He had taken part in a series of high-risk missions, including raids on Taliban strongholds. His patrol was ambushed in Sangin in 2010; three men were killed and another three seriously injured. Tom narrowly escaped with his life; the Army shrink marked this as the beginning of his struggle with PTSD.

He returned to the UK and was assigned to a non-combat role in Colchester. He received counselling, but it didn't improve his mental health, and he was honourably discharged in June 2015.

She turned to the notes she had taken during her conversation with the Brennans. Tom's life post-discharge had clearly been unhappy, with a series of jobs he wasn't equipped to hold down and relationships that went nowhere, everything leading to his problems with booze and, ultimately, his homelessness.

She opened the email that Eliza Brennan had sent last night and reviewed the names of the people from Salisbury—two women and two men—with whom she thought her son still had a relationship.

Samantha Hargreaves.

Nikki Griffiths.

Gaz O'Reilly.

Connor Smith.

Speaking to them would be the first thing that she would do, but it was still too early to be heading out now. She'd have a second cup of coffee first and see if she could find Mack for an update on the new case.

* * *

Francine refilled her plastic cup and drifted over to the conference room that was being set up as the base for the investigation. Nigel Archer was there, removing a sheaf of papers from a printer that had been set up on a table at the side of the room.

"Morning," she said.

He looked up. "Morning, Franny. You okay?"

"I'm good," she said. "You on the enquiry?"

"For my sins," he grumbled. "Was in late last night and early this morning."

Francine pointed to the photograph of Alice Green that had been stuck to one of the pinboards on the wall. "What are we saying—it's suspicious now?"

"We found the gear she was using to record her swim."

"And?"

"The sound recorder picked up a scream. We're not ruling out an innocent explanation, but it looks less likely now."

"No body yet?"

He shook his head. "They've had boats in the river since Thursday and haven't found anything. They're going back up there to search the area now."

"They would've found it by now, surely?"

"Depends. I was speaking to the search team. They've seen bodies pulled miles downstream before they come up again."

"Grim."

"Did you know Atticus is consulting again?"

"I didn't."

He nodded. "He was working for Frank Green—looking for dirt on Alice. He saw her the day before she disappeared."

"What does he think?"

"That it's suspicious."

"The others pleased to see him again?"

Archer chuckled. "Lupin was spitting feathers. He was talking about complaining to the DCS."

That didn't surprise Francine. Lynas was probably her least favourite officer in the team, and she knew that his nose would be out of joint when he learned that she was being put up for promotion before him. She'd worked him out a long time ago: he did his best to appear confident, but she could see that it was all show. He had a brash exterior, but it hid a hollow centre; he was a timeserver who was desperate to hide his laziness and lack of initiative. Francine knew Atticus saw that too, but, where Atticus had no interest in tact or even keeping his views to himself, she was happy to be diplomatic.

"You just missed him and Robbie," Archer said.

Francine forced a neutral smile, paranoid—as always—that any mention of Robbie must mean that their relationship had been exposed. "I saw them going out."

"Down to Standlynch with a dozen uniform. Fingertip search. The full treatment."

Francine gestured down to the papers he had taken from the printer. "What's all this?"

"We had a technician go through the memory cards from her devices last night. The sound recording didn't give us anything we didn't already know, but she found a video on the card with this bloke in it."

He peeled a sheet from the top of the pile and held it up so Francine could see it.

The screen grab showed a picturesque riverside location, with lush greenery and a flowing river. Water cascaded over a small weir, frothing into a deep pool at its foot.

A man was in the river, smiling up into the camera.

She stared at the screen grab and frowned. "*What?*"

"Warleigh Weir in Claverton," Archer said, thinking that she was confused about the location. "You can see it from the Bath train."

Francine picked up the paper and looked at it more carefully.

"What is it? You look like you've seen a ghost."

She pointed to the man. "I know who that is."

"Seriously?"

She stared and was sure.

"That's my missing person. That's Thomas Brennan."

90

Mack came into the incident room to see Nigel Archer and Francine Patterson standing together at the table. Francine was holding a piece of paper in her hand.

"Morning," Mack said.

They both turned. Francine's mouth was agape.

"What is it?"

"Good timing, boss," Archer said. "Franny says she knows our mystery man."

"Franny?"

"You know I've been looking for a missing person?"

"I remember—the ex-soldier. Parents came in yesterday."

"Thomas Brennan," Francine said, turning the paper around so it was facing Mack. "This is him."

Mack raised an eyebrow. "You're sure?"

Francine took out her phone and swiped the screen until she had the photograph she was looking for. She put the phone and the piece of paper on the table and to the side so that Mack could come and examine them. The image on the phone looked to have been taken at a family gathering, with a group of people gathered around a woman who was blowing out the candles on a birthday cake. Mack looked at the man standing behind the birthday girl, looked at the man in the screen grab, then looked back at the photo on the phone. The images looked as if they might have been taken a year or two apart, but it was definitely the same man.

"Thomas Brennan," Francine said. "Thirty-nine years old. His parents came into the nick yesterday to report him missing. He was last seen on Monday leaving his flat at Alabaré. Ex-Army, tours of Iraq and Afghanistan, discharged with PTSD. History of substance abuse and a couple of violent incidents on his record. The last time was just over a week ago—he got into a fight with a friend in town, and we had the two of them in a cell for a night until they calmed down. Apart from that, Tom's been nicked twice for ABH and once for affray."

Mack turned to Archer, pointing at the screen grab. "And Alice Green recorded that?"

"It was on the memory card."

"Have you seen it yet?"

"No. I only just got in."

Mack bit down on her lip. "Give me fifteen minutes to get myself sorted out, and then we'll have a look at the video. Can you get it on a laptop and show it on the screen in here?"

"No problem."

"Good. And call everyone in—briefing in an hour."

Archer nodded.

Mack turned to Francine; she was wide-eyed with enthusiasm. "You'd better stay."

"Happy to, boss."

Mack clapped her hands together. “Let’s hope this is the breakthrough we’ve been waiting for. Well done, Franny. Good spot.”

Mack left them and crossed the floor to her office. She took out her phone and saw that she had a message from Atticus. She opened it.

>> *Have the memory cards been indexed yet?*

She typed out a reply.

>> *Might have found something. Get here ASAP.*

91

The cricket pitch at Harnham was deserted. Atticus and Bandit stood by the river's edge and watched a family of swans as they glided across the water. Atticus was quite happy to lose himself in his thoughts as he continued toward the old mill.

He had just reached the path when his phone buzzed with an incoming text message.

He opened it and saw that it was from Mack.

>> *Might have found something. Get here ASAP.*

* * *

Atticus ran back to the office, a puzzled Bandit loping along behind him, and quickly refilled the dog's bowls with water and biscuits. He spritzed himself with deodorant and set off again, texting Mack on the way and telling her he would be with them in ten minutes and asking them to wait.

He arrived at Bourne Hill, checked in at the desk and hurried upstairs. Mack was waiting for him outside the door to the conference room.

"Sorry," he said. "I was walking the dog."

"We haven't started."

"What is it?"

"Easier if you come in and watch with us."

The space had transformed into an incident room overnight. Francine Patterson and Nigel Archer were sitting at the table; a laptop had been set up in front of Archer, its desktop showing on the wall-mounted screen.

"I wanted Atticus to be here," Mack said to them by way of explanation. "Take a seat, Atticus."

Atticus was too amped up for that. "I'd rather stand."

"The memory cards have been indexed," she said. "There's nothing else on the card from the recorder that we haven't already heard."

"Nothing?"

"No other files at all," Archer said. "It's either a new card, or she formatted it before she used it on Wednesday."

"And the camera?"

"That's where it gets interesting," Mack said. "Franny is investigating a missing person."

She gestured to Francine to continue.

"Tom Brennan," she said "Ex-soldier. His mum and dad came in yesterday to say he hasn't been seen since Monday. I was getting ready to start looking for him when I came in here and saw a screen grab from one of the other videos on the card."

"It was him? The same man?"

She nodded.

Atticus closed his eyes and assessed the new information. Alice Green and this new man, Brennan, were connected—and *both* had disappeared at around the same time.

"Can I see the video?"

Mack gestured. "Press play, Nigel."

They turned to the screen. Archer tabbed across to an open video player, moused up to the play button and clicked it. The video began: Atticus saw another river scene, this one with a small man-made weir to the right of the shot and a pool to the left. A man was treading water, and as the video played, he came closer to the camera.

"Okay," a voice said from out of shot. "Are you ready?"

Atticus recognised the voice: it was Alice Green.

"Ready," the man replied.

"I'm recording. Remember what to say?"

"I've got it," Tom said, smiling. He tapped a finger against the side of his head. "It's all up here."

"Good. Remember—look into the camera, lots of smiles, lots of confidence. And finish with the line."

"I know—I've got it."

"Ready when you are."

He looked away, cleared his throat, looked back at the camera—glancing up at where Atticus presumed Alice was standing behind it—and then started to speak.

"I can't recommend this course highly enough. It completely transformed my perspective on exercise and nature. Alice taught me not only the physical benefits of cold-water immersion—like increased circulation and a boosted immune system—but also the profound mental clarity and stress relief that come with it. As a former soldier dealing with PTSD, I can tell you that wild swimming has been nothing short of a lifeline. It's given me a distraction from the racing thoughts and anxiety that once dominated my life. Cold water is incredibly calming, almost like a reset button for my mind, and has helped with the insomnia I used to struggle with. This course didn't just teach me to swim—it gave me a new coping mechanism and a sense of peace I haven't felt in years." He paused, as if struggling to remember what to say next. "Sorry…" he said with a bashful smile. "Forgot."

Alice prompted him from behind the camera: "'If you're looking to reconnect with nature and discover a new, invigorating way to stay fit and healthy, this course is an absolute must.'"

"Got it."

"Say the line—I can edit it later."

He looked away, then looked back at the camera with a wide smile. "If you want a way to reconnect with nature and discover an invigorating way to stay fit and healthy, this course is an absolute must."

He trod water, smiling into the camera, and then the screen went blank.

92

Mack asked Archer to play the recording for a second time, and they watched it again. Atticus's fingers twitched, and he had to close his fists to keep them still; it felt like they were close to a break in the case.

The recording came to an end with Tom looking up into the camera.

"What do you have on him?" Atticus said.

"Not much beyond what I said."

"Address?"

"He was living at Alabaré."

"Tried his phone?"

"Of course," she said. "I've treated it like any other missing person enquiry. His parents sent me a list of friends in the area they thought he still saw—I was going to start speaking to them today."

Mack looked at him. "What are you thinking?"

"I think the two of them—Alice and Tom—are in a relationship."

"How can you say that?" Archer said. "You didn't even *see* her on camera."

"His body language was clear."

"I didn't see anything."

"You weren't looking, then. Did you see the way his eyes softened when he looked at her? The smile was more genuine when he looked at her than when he was pitching."

"There was no difference."

"It reached his eyes," Atticus said. "You can't fake that. And he blushed when he was asking her to remind him of that final line, too. That's a *classic* sign of nervous excitement."

Archer nodded. "You think he's involved?"

"Do we have anything else?"

"No."

"Then I think it's quite likely."

"But he looks happy," Francine said, gesturing up to the blank screen.

"When was that filmed?"

Archer referred to a printout on the desk. "A month ago."

"A lot of things can happen in a month. Maybe she decided he wasn't the one for her after all. Maybe she cheated on him. Maybe he took whatever it was badly." He turned to Francine. "You said he had form for violence?"

"Yes—but nothing serious."

Atticus shrugged. "So it could be that. The fact he's disappeared too, at the same time, is suggestive. I'm much more worried now than before I saw this. He's key."

Mack knocked her knuckles against the surface of the table. "I agree. We have to treat him as a suspect. At the very least, we have to find him—top priority. Franny—you said you had a list of his friends?"

She nodded. "Four of them—two men, two women." She took out her phone and read out the names that had been sent to her.

"I'll take Samantha and Connor," Mack said. "You and Nigel take Gaz and Nikki. Let's go and speak to them."

93

Sam removed the packaging from the microwave meal, pierced the cellophane sleeve with a fork, put it in the oven and set the timer for three minutes. She took an empty plastic bottle from the recycling bin and filled it with water, and then found an unopened blister pack of Nurofen.

She'd been down in the cellar to see Alice Green before bed last night and had been a little concerned. Alice was lethargic and confused, and after Sam had managed to get her to eat and drink, she'd become lucid enough to complain that her headache was worse. She'd been sick between visits, and the vomit on the floor that had leaked out from between the gag had started to go tacky as it dried; the smell in the confined space was overwhelming, and Sam had gone to fetch a bucket of water and a cloth and had cleaned it all away. Alice had perked up after that and had finished her meal and swallowed another couple of ibuprofen pills to help ease the pain in her head.

Sam stared at the meal as it revolved on the platter and allowed her thoughts to drift. She'd been busy. She'd spent most of yesterday evening going through the finer points of her plan, taking out the notebook that she'd been using for her research and writing headings on the tops of five clean pages:

Preparation.

Leaving.

Money.

Disappearing.

Staying Hidden.

She'd been preparing for weeks, and there wasn't much left to do on the first page. Deciding on where to go had been the most important thing, and she'd put together a shortlist of countries that didn't have extradition treaties with the UK. There were lots to choose from—the Maldives, Vietnam, Nepal, Cambodia—but she'd settled on Morocco. She'd visited Tangiers for a holiday when she was in London and had immediately fallen in love with it. She could buy a place to stay there for a fraction of what she'd saved, and the cost of living was cheap enough that she'd never have to work again. The country offered enough—beyond security—that she'd be able to stay without fear of boredom or frustration. It had a rich culture, varied landscapes—from deserts to mountains to beaches—and vibrant cities. It was perfect.

She turned to the second page. She knew she'd need to avoid all personal devices that could be traced and reminded herself she'd need to get a burner phone before she left. She wanted to set a false trail, too, and was going to book a flight to Florida and pay for a week's accommodation in Orlando. She hoped that her deception would make it more difficult to find out where she'd actually gone, and by the time she arrived, it'd be too late.

The microwave pinged. She opened the door and removed the meal. She peeled the sleeve away, scooped the spaghetti

Bolognese onto a plate, and took it, and the bottle of water, outside. The yard was quiet save for the whinnying of one of the mares who was earmarked for a buyer coming over later. The other horses were out in the field, and the mare was making no effort to hide the fact that she wanted to join them. She'd have to wait. The buyer would want to take her into the manège to see how she rode, and then there would be a thorough vetting.

Samantha caught herself wondering whether the horse might be the last one that she ever sold. Probably.

She was halfway to the stable and the cellar when her phone buzzed.

She took it out and looked at the screen: it was Nikki.

"What's up?"

"I've been calling you for ten minutes," she said.

There was a frantic edge to her voice. "What's happened?"

"The police have been to see us."

"*What?*"

"They came to the house."

Nikki was losing it; Sam did all she could to keep the fear from her own voice. "What did they want?"

"They were asking about Tom. They know about him and the woman—Alice. They *know*."

"What does that mean? *What* do they know?"

"What I just said," she blurted. "About her and Tom."

"Take a deep breath and *think*. What did they say? Tell me *exactly*."

"They said that Tom's gone missing and did we know."

"And *you* said?"

"What you told us to say—that we haven't seen him since the thing at the Haunch."

"Good. Go on."

"They asked how I thought he was doing—they know about the PTSD and the scrap he had with Gaz."

"Of *course* they know about that—they arrested them both."

"I said he's been struggling and that I was worried about him. I told them he was seeing someone, but it wasn't helping. I told them exactly what we said—everything you told us."

"How was Gaz?"

"Fine. I did most of the talking."

"What did they say about Alice?"

"They showed me her picture and asked if we'd ever seen her before. I said I hadn't. I said I had no idea who she was. They asked if Tom had said anything about whether he was seeing anyone, and I said it wasn't the sort of thing we'd talk about, that he was private and kept that kind of thing to himself."

"Okay. Good."

"How've they found out, Sam?"

"I don't know. But it doesn't matter. We're still in control. It might mean we have to have a think about what we're going to do, but it doesn't make us any more vulnerable than we were before. You just need to relax and—"

"'*Relax*'?" she cut across her. "I can't 'relax.' The police came to our house and questioned us."

Sam bit down on her impatience; laying into Nikki now would be counterproductive. Sam would be on her way as soon as she'd sold the cocaine in the cellar, and all of this nonsense—all of this babysitting of grown adults and clearing up the messes they'd made—would be something she never had to even think about again.

"You *can* relax," she said calmly. "They were just looking for background. They'll be going through Tom's contacts and asking if anyone knows anything. That's it. Why would they have any reason to suspect you?"

She didn't answer.

"Nikki?"

"I know," she said at last. "You're right. It's just..."

"It's worrying," she finished for her. "Of course it is. But when you think about it rationally, you know as well as I do that everything is *fine*. Okay?"

She said something in reply, but Sam didn't hear her. She heard the sound of a car turning off the road and bouncing across the rough track beyond the gate. She took a step to her right so she could peer out from behind the horse box and saw a car slowly rolling across the yard.

Sam stepped back behind the box and put the phone back to her ear. "You still there?"

"Yes," she said. "Why?"

"The police," she said. "I think they've just turned up at the yard."

94

Atticus looked around the yard. It was well-maintained, with a dozen wooden stables around a central courtyard that was in turn enclosed by sturdy post-and-rail fencing. Each stable had its own door and window, allowing for light and ventilation. Large agricultural buildings and silos were visible behind the stables. A pallet with twenty or thirty large plastic bottles had been left next to one of the stables.

Mack brought the car to a stop.

"Like horses?" he asked her.

"Long time ago—when I was a girl."

"Pony club?"

"Until my parents realised how expensive it was."

"And you realised boys were more interesting."

"Well," she said, glancing over at him and smiling. "There *was* that."

They both stepped out of the car and made their way into the yard. A woman emerged from one of the stables, closing the door behind her and sliding a bolt home to hold it in place.

"Can I help you?" she called over to them.

Mack stepped up. "Samantha Hargreaves?"

The woman nodded. "Call me Sam."

"I'm Detective Chief Inspector Mackenzie Jones." She gestured behind her. "This is Atticus Priest."

"Hello," she said with the mixture of surprise and concern that Atticus would have expected.

"Nice yard," he said.

"Thanks."

"What do you do here?"

"Mostly buy and sell horses. I get them in, work on them if they need it and then sell them on."

Atticus pointed down at the pallet of plastic bottles. "Kofasil," he said, reading the brand name on the label. "What's that for?"

"It's a silage additive," she said. "We make our own here. You spray it onto the pile, and it helps preserve the nutrients."

Atticus picked up one of the bottles. "Sodium nitrite," he read from the ingredients on the back.

"That's right," she said. "It's pretty standard stuff."

Atticus put the bottle back on the pallet.

Sam watched him. "How can I help you both?"

"We're looking into the disappearance of someone we think is one of your friends," Mack said. "Thomas Brennan?"

Her eyes widened with surprise. "Tom's missing?"

"Since Monday," Mack said. "Would it be all right to ask you a couple of questions?"

"Of course."

"It might be easier if we did it inside."

Sam pointed over to a spot behind the stables. "The house is over there," she said. "I'll put the kettle on."

"Perfect," Mack said.

* * *

Atticus looked around as they followed Sam to a farmhouse at the back of the yard. The house was built from local stone, the walls covered with creeping ivy and the occasional splash of moss. The slate tiled roof was steeply pitched, with dormer windows with white-painted wooden frames and latticed panes. The front door, solid and a little worn, was framed by flower-filled planters. There was a neatly kept garden enclosed by a low stone wall, and gravel paths led to the main outbuildings. It was nice. Homely.

Sam opened the door and stepped into the kitchen. She took the kettle and filled it at the tap, then put it on the hotplate of a large cream-coloured Aga.

"Tea or coffee?"

"Whatever's easiest," Mack said.

Atticus smiled. "Same."

He watched her as she spoke. She had no obvious reason to be nervous, yet he could see that she was: she shifted her weight from foot to foot, and he noticed a gentle tremble as she took the coffee cups down from the dresser. It was possible it was just a reaction to receiving an unexpected visit from the police. Atticus remembered that from his own time as an officer; just showing someone his badge often elicited the standard signs of anxiety, even in people—and sometimes *especially* in people—who'd done nothing wrong.

Atticus glanced around the room. It was pleasant, nicely furnished but not ostentatiously so. He looked back to the Aga and noticed a plug block pushed into a socket with three phones being charged off it. He was going to comment on it, but the kettle boiled, and the moment passed.

"You're here about Tom?"

"Mr. Brennan," Mack said. "Yes, that's right."

"Didn't even know he was missing."

"When was the last time you saw him?"

Sam reached up and held her chin with her hand. "A week ago."

"That was the night Tom and your other friend got into trouble?"

She nodded. "Yes—him and Gaz. But it was a fuss about nothing. They were both drunk." She poured the coffees and took the cups to the table, then went back to the fridge for milk and brought that over. They took their seats and fussed over their coffees for a moment.

"What happened?"

"I gave a statement to an officer when they were arrested."

"Yes, and I read what you said then—I'd just like to hear it from you now."

She spread her hands over the table. "It was like I said. A drunken argument. We ended up in the Haunch of Venison. We'd been knocking them back a bit, and the two of them ended up having a stupid argument. I can't even remember what it was about now."

"Try."

She gazed away. "He's got the worst taste in music. We always used to take the piss out of him about it. There was this one time we found a Britney Spears playlist on his phone. We called him Britney after that. He hated it."

"And that was what the argument was about? Britney Spears?"

"Gaz called him Britney, Tom told him to stop, the rest of us joined in, and it all kicked off. Like I said, it was childish and stupid, and we were all embarrassed that we wasted police time over it."

Mack took her time noting it all down.

Sam shuffled uncomfortably. "When you said he was missing… what do you mean?"

"His parents came to the station on Thursday to say they haven't been able to get in touch with him. He has a problem with drink, doesn't he?"

Sam nodded. "I don't know many soldiers, but from what Tom told me, lots come out with problems like that."

Atticus sipped his coffee and then put it back down on the table. "Do you know if he was seeing anyone?"

"Tom?" She paused, thinking, then shook her head. "He never mentioned anything to me, but that'd be par for the course. He was always a bit of a closed book. Very private."

"Kept things to himself?"

"Things like that," Sam said with a nod. "Women? Definitely. I don't think he's ever told me about a girlfriend."

"Never been married?"

"No. Can I ask why you're asking?"

"Have you seen the news recently?" Mack asked.

"Not really."

Atticus watched her especially carefully.

"Do you know someone called Alice Green?" Mack said.

"No."

"So you wouldn't know if Mr. Brennan knew her?"

Sam shook her head. "Like I said—I don't think I've ever heard the name before. Tom certainly never mentioned her to me."

"We think Mr. Brennan might have been seeing her."

"That'd be news to me."

"The reason I'm asking is because Alice has gone missing. She was swimming in the river near Downton on Wednesday, and no one's seen her since."

"You're not asking because you think *Tom* might be involved, do you?"

"It's very early to be thinking about anything like that."

"Because he's not like that."

"Like what?"

"Like... a danger to anyone else. Tom's a big softie."

"I'm not sure his criminal record backs that up," Mack said. "He's been in trouble before. Before what happened with him and your other friend at the Haunch, I mean."

"I know, but I didn't think any of it was serious."

"You can see why we'd like to find him, can't you?"

Sam shook her head firmly. "There's no way he's involved with that. There just isn't—it's impossible."

Mack got up. "Thank you for seeing us. I appreciate your time. If you do happen to find out where Tom is, please call 999 straight away. My hope is we can quickly remove him from our enquiries, but we'll obviously need to sit down with him before we can do that."

"Of course."

95

Sam watched the officers as they got into the car and drove away from the yard. She thought she'd done a good enough job with their questions, plugging up the fear that they'd inspired, but it bubbled up into panic as they left. They *couldn't* know what had happened, and coming and seeing Tom's friends *must* have been routine, something innocuous and to be expected—*right?* All the same, she could tell herself that until she was blue in the face, but the fear remained, little worms of doubt that wriggled in her gut as they grew and grew and grew.

What if they *did* know more than they were saying?

And what if Nikki and Gaz *had* left something at the river that would give them away, or said something contradictory or suspicious when they were questioned?

What then?

Sam could keep her own house in order, but there was only so much she could do about the others.

The situation felt much more serious than it had an hour earlier, and Sam felt a jolt of urgency. The time had come to put her plan into effect.

No more waiting. It had to be soon.

She went up to her bedroom and pulled out the plain, inconspicuous suitcase from under her bed. She packed the essentials first: a few changes of clothes, sturdy but comfortable shoes, a weatherproof jacket. She moved quickly but methodically, ensuring she had everything she needed.

Next, she turned her attention to the important items she'd gathered over the past months. She slipped a slim leather pouch containing fake identification documents and three passports into the hidden compartment of the suitcase. She added bundles of cash in various currencies—pounds, euros and dinars—and the small, encrypted hardware wallet containing the data she'd need to access her Bitcoin. She took a moment to secure her laptop, ensuring it was fully charged. Finally, she added a few personal mementos: a locket her father had given her, a small notebook of handwritten codes and passwords, and a paperback for the journey ahead.

She glanced around the bedroom one last time, checking for anything that might give her away. She collected her notes and receipts, tossing them into the grate and setting them alight. She zipped up the suitcase and took it downstairs, leaving it in the hall next to the door.

All she needed was to deliver the coke to Freeman. Once that was done, and she had his money, she could go. The thought of the cocaine reminded her: she didn't want him to see the woman in the cellar and freak out.

Easier to move the coke than her. It would take half an hour, but there was no reason to delay.

The microwave meal had gone cold, but she didn't have another, and it would have to do. She grabbed it, the bottle of water and the pills, then put on her shoes and went outside.

96

Mack drove them back into the city. Atticus laced his fingers behind his head and leaned back in the seat. He ran the conversation with Hargreaves back again, trying to pinpoint what she'd said that had left him feeling unsettled.

She looked across the cabin at him. "You're not happy."

"Is it that obvious?"

"I can read you like a book. Did you believe her?"

"There was something that made me uncomfortable, but I can't put my finger on it, and it's annoying me."

"She was nervous."

"No," Atticus said. "Not that. I'd expect *that*. She's just been told we can't find one of her friends and that we think he's connected to a missing persons enquiry. That'd make anyone nervous. There was something else."

"I'll need more to bring her in for formal questioning."

"I know. I think it'll be worth keeping an eye on her, though. Turn up the pressure and see what happens—I'm pretty sure you'll end up speaking to her again."

They reached Harnham Hill, and Mack slowed down from sixty to thirty.

"Finding Tom probably means we find Alice," she said. "I think it's time we go public."

"Agreed."

"I'll speak to Beckton about a press conference. There's already a lot of interest. We had TikTok detectives trying to get down to the river this afternoon."

"Unhelpful."

"Very—they'll get their feelings hurt when we tell them to clear off, and then they'll start posting videos about how we're bungling the investigation, and then Beckton will start shouting at me. And I can do without all of that."

"Then you need to get out in front of it. Don't wait until tomorrow."

She nodded her agreement. "I was thinking of putting out a Facebook post. The *Journal* usually picks them up quickly, so we'll get a little local amplification."

They slowed as they approached the roundabout with the junction that led to the hospital, slowing as an ambulance with its lights flashing turned right and raced into town.

She glanced over at him again. "What about you?"

"What am I going to do?" He shrugged. "The dog needs a walk. I always get my best ideas when I'm out with him. I'll have a think and let you know."

97

Sam was thinking about the practicalities of leaving as she crossed the yard to the stable. The horses would need to be taken care of, but she knew that Heidi—the groom who came in to look after the animals in the morning—wouldn't let anything happen to them. The business wouldn't be worth much, and the yard was mortgaged to the hilt; she wouldn't be leaving all that much behind as she started her new life.

She opened the stable door, cleared the straw away from the hatch and pulled the bolt, then hesitated at the top of the ladder. The familiar faint odour of damp stone from below mixed with something more unsettling, something sour and metallic.

She descended slowly and, as her eyes adjusted to the dim light, saw Green slumped against the far wall.

"I've got your lunch," Sam said. "And pills for your head."

There was no response.

She pulled the cord for the light.

Alice was unmoving. Her skin had taken on a ghastly pallor, her eyes half-open but lifeless. Her head was angled over to the side, and blood had trickled from her ear, drying into a dark stain on the floor.

Shit.

"Alice?"

Sam's heart pounded as she approached, dread pooling in her stomach.

"Alice?"

Sam could see she was dead before she reached her, but a prod of her finger into her cheek confirmed it. Rigor mortis had set in, her limbs were unnaturally stiff, and her skin was pale and waxy like a mannequin's. Dark patches of lividity stained her arms and legs where the blood had settled, lending her a mottled appearance. A faint but unmistakeable odour of decay hung in the air.

Sam put her lunch on the floor and stood back.

She couldn't leave her here, but there was no way she was going to be able to get her out of the cellar on her own.

It would be easier to move the coke and then get the others to help her tomorrow, but that would delay her departure, and she was loathe to do that, even for an hour or two.

Better to deal with her now.

She climbed up and went outside, taking out her phone and trying Gaz. There was no response, and it was the same when she tried Nikki.

Hopeless.

She texted Connor and told him that she needed him to think of an excuse to get to the yard as soon as he could.

98

Tom rested the post rammer against the fence and looked at his hands: they were filthy, with dirt beneath his fingernails and smeared across his skin; blisters had formed across his palms; and the pads of his right hand were stained from where a blister had filled with blood and then burst. His muscles ached—his shoulders, especially, but his biceps and triceps and the muscles all the way down his back—and his right foot throbbed with a dull pain from where he'd dropped the rammer onto it. He was hot, and he stank of sweat, but, in spite of all of it, he was buzzing.

Connor had gone back to the yard to speak to Sam, leaving Tom to get on with the fencing for a couple of hours. He hadn't minded at all. He had beer and music, and he took the temporary solitude as permission to sing along to the radio. He was nicely pissed by the time Connor returned, but not so far gone that he didn't notice the change in mood. Connor had been on edge for most of the week, but Tom had put it down to issues in his relationship with the latest bird he was seeing in his never-ending attempts to find someone he liked better than

Sam. This, though, was different. He was quieter than usual and seemed unwilling or unable to hold Tom's eye.

The radio was resting on one of the new posts. He and Connor had disagreed on what stations to listen to and had, after some negotiation, settled on a compromise: Connor would choose the music in the morning, and Tom would have his pick in the afternoon. They'd listened to Radio Two until lunch and, now Tom was in charge, they were listening to Salisbury Radio. The DJ, Andy Mannion, was someone Tom had met in the pub, and they'd bonded over a love of obscure '80s New Romantic classics. Tom had dared Andy to play something really out there—Strawberry Switchblade or The Mighty Wah! or Furniture—but, so far, it'd all been rather pedestrian. 'Tainted Love' had been as far out as it got, but, as much as Tom liked Soft Cell, it wasn't quite as radical as some of the tunes they'd been talking about. He was going to have to work on him the next time he was in the pub.

They'd worked on the fence all week and had made excellent progress, the southern run was the one that needed the most work, and they'd left it for today. They started in the eastern corner and worked back to the west, replacing the rotten posts with brand-new ones and then nailing the rails to them. Connor had held his own during the morning but had slackened off as the afternoon had drawn into the evening. He'd complained that he'd pulled a muscle in his shoulder, and, after that, it had been left to Tom to use the rammer on his own. He didn't mind; indeed, the day had made him increasingly certain that hard physical work in the outdoors was just what he needed to help with his various conditions. He felt more alive than he had for months, and every twinge and ache just served as a reminder that he had always found this kind of day rewarding.

Connor came over to him.

Tom wiped the sweat from his eyes and looked at the fence. "Three more posts to do, and then we're finished."

"Let's call it quits and do the rest in the morning."

"Don't be daft," Tom said. "We can get it done tonight."

"I'm out on my feet." He pointed up into the purple sky. "It's getting dark, and I need a drink. Let's get pissed and do the rest tomorrow. We can get some burgers on and chill out."

Tom rolled the kinks out of his shoulders. "All right. Get the fire going. I'll finish this one, and then I'll come over."

Tom picked up the rammer and took it over to the first of the remaining posts that needed to be replaced. The wood had rotted away, and it was an easy enough thing to pull and push it back and forward until the post snapped. He went to where they'd left the three remaining new posts, picked one up and balanced it over his shoulder. He grabbed the radio, too, and retraced his steps. Andy Mannion was playing 'Echo Beach,' and the song faded out into adverts for local businesses before the news and weather at the top of the hour.

Connor started off, then stopped. He sat down and worked off his boot, tipping it upside down until a collection of small stones tumbled out.

Tom took the new post and slotted the end into the hole where the previous post had been. An advert for Humphrey and Crockett faded out, and the familiar jingle announced the news.

"*Good evening*," the newsreader said. "*Police in Salisbury are requesting the public's assistance in locating a woman who has been reported missing since Wednesday morning. Alice Green is an enthusiastic wild swimmer, and after her car was found near Standlynch Chapel on the banks of the River Avon, police are concerned that she might have got into trouble in the water. She's described as approximately five feet six and is likely to be wearing a distinctive silver locket. Police are urging anyone with information, no matter how insignificant it may seem, to come forward to help ensure her safe return.*"

Tom glanced over at Connor. The blood had run from his face.

"Change the channel," Connor said. "The football's on Radio Five."

Tom stopped what he was doing, holding the rammer upright by the handles. He frowned: the words seemed odd and didn't make any sense.

"Did he just say Alice Green?"

"Didn't catch it."

He got up, still missing one boot, and took a step toward the post where the radio was sitting.

Tom stepped to the side and held up a hand to stop him.

The newsreader was still speaking. "*…particularly interested in speaking to a man who was believed to be in a relationship with Ms. Green. Thomas Brennan has also gone missing, and police believe he might be able to help them locate Alice.*"

Tom turned to Connor, raised his hand as if to point at the radio, but stopped, his finger upright, his arm frozen by the look on Connor's face. His eyes were closed, and his head was tipped back, as if he was annoyed or frustrated.

"Connor? He's talking about me. What's going on?"

99

The newsreader continued.

"*If you've seen Alice Green or Thomas Brennan, or have any information about their current whereabouts, please contact Salisbury Police. Details of the contact information, and a hotline that has been set up for this matter, are available on the Salisbury Radio website and our social media channels. We'll bring you developments on this story as we have them—but, for now, that's the way it is in Salisbury. Now, the latest on the roads in Salisbury and across South Wiltshire.*"

"Connor?"

"I have no idea what that's all about," Connor said.

"I don't believe you. Tell me what's going on."

"I don't know, Tom. I—"

"The *police* are looking for me." Tom felt panic. "Alice is missing, and they're looking for me." The panic became something else: a blinding anger. "Shit. *Shit*. That's why you had me come up here. You've done something to Alice, haven't you? *Shit*. You've—"

"Don't be daft," Connor said, edging to the right.

"You've done something to her."

Connor took another half step and then set off at a flat run, heading for the tent.

The shotgun.

Tom could've run in the opposite direction, got away from the field and Connor and headed back to the city, but he was consumed by anger and fear and the need to have his questions answered, so he sprinted after Connor. It would have been a close race once, when they were both young and fit, but the years had been kinder to Connor than they had to Tom. The abuse he'd wrought on his body—the booze and the drugs, the bad food and the lack of sleep—had eroded his endurance to the extent that, despite his hard work here in the field of late, he was quickly out of breath. Connor pulled away—five metres and then ten—and Tom knew he'd get to the tent first.

Tom realised he'd made a mistake.

He needed to get away.

He looked left and right, trying to work out which way he should run, and decided to go straight up the hill and into the trees that had grown up around the hill fort. He'd get through there and go down the other side, through the field and the tract of woods to the north until he got to the drove.

The climb was steep, and Tom was quickly panting for breath. The trees were just ahead: oak and ash and beech, all struggling for space on top of the hill. The boundary was marked by a fence, with posts driven into the ground and wire strung from one to the other. The light was fading quickly, and Tom couldn't see anything beyond the first stand of trees.

The ground levelled off, and Tom picked up speed.

There was a boom.

Tom felt a sudden sting on his shoulder.

He stumbled but managed to keep his feet.

Tom heard Connor behind him, his feet pounding the ground and his breath rasping, but Alice needed him, and he was determined not to be beaten. He ignored the pain and reached the fence, sliding between the wires and hurrying into the woods. It was dark, and what feeble light remained was smothered out beneath the canopy of leaves and branches overhead.

"Tom," Connor called from somewhere—not far—behind him.

Tom pushed deeper into the trees, following an animal path through dense thickets of bramble, the thorns snagging against his clothes and scraping across his exposed skin. He pushed through until he reached an old sycamore, working his way around it and resting there, his back up against the thick trunk.

"Tom," Connor called again. "Wait. Let's talk."

Tom took the opportunity to look down at his right shoulder. Pain throbbed from where birdshot had ripped through his flesh. His shoulder and the top of his arm throbbed, but, as he looked at the blood that was pooling into the furrows that had been carved there, he knew he'd been lucky; another few inches to the left and that would've been that. The wounds would need to be treated, but he wasn't going to bleed out in the meantime. They could wait.

"Tom!" Connor called. "Mate—it doesn't have to be like this."

Tom gritted his teeth and clenched his fists to steady himself. He heard the rustle of vegetation from somewhere on the slope of the hill behind him.

"Where's Alice?" he called out.

"What?"

"Do you think I'm stupid? I know what this is about." His mouth was dry. "You're worried I told her about Christopher."

"Did you tell her?"

"No."

Connor was silent for a moment. "Remember what you said at the Haunch?"

Tom held his breath and listened. The rustle was coming from behind him, from the start of the thicket that he'd just passed through.

"You said you couldn't live with yourself," Connor said, much closer now.

The animal track would bring Connor around the trunk to Tom's right.

"You told her what happened, didn't you? You told her what we did."

Tom edged left.

Connor exclaimed and muttered a curse. "I'm getting cut to shit," he called. "Come out, and we can—"

Connor came around the trunk.

Tom launched himself at him.

100

Tom struck Connor with his shoulder, jarring the shotgun to the side and then closing in. Tom wrapped his arms around Connor's torso and pushed, Connor losing his footing and the two of them slamming down onto the hard earth. The shotgun fell free. Tom reached down and pushed it away, the movement giving Connor an opportunity to punch up, his knuckles cracking against Tom's chin. He saw stars, blinked them away, and drove the point of his elbow into the middle of Connor's face.

Connor spat blood.

Tom hit him again, driving down with his elbow, and then, as Connor's head fell to the side, he shuffled up Connor's body so that his right arm and then his left were pinned beneath his knees.

Connor's face was a bloody mess. "Tom," he mumbled between gasps for breath. "Wait."

Tom punched him.

"Where's Alice?"

"Wait," he said again. "I can explain."

Tom punched him again.

"Where's Alice?"

"Who's... Alice?"

Tom hit him. "Do you think I'm stupid?" He hit him again. "I know what this is all about." Tom's mouth was dry; he hit him again. "You're worried I've told her about Christopher. Right?"

Blood ran out of the corner of Connor's mouth and dribbled down his cheek. "Please..."

"What did I say at the Haunch? I know I said something about Christopher, but I can't remember what it was."

"Said you couldn't... live with yourself."

"What about Alice?"

"I don't know... who Alice is."

"*Liar!*"

He punched him again, and then again and again.

"I can see it now," he said. "I said something about telling her, so you bring me out here to get me out of the way so you can get to her."

Connor tried to speak, but the words were mumbled, and Tom wouldn't have been able to understand them even if he had been listening.

"Where is she?"

He saw the shotgun, just off to his right. He leaned over and reached for it.

Connor was woozy, and the words, when they came, blended one into the other. "We're... friends."

"*Where is she?*"

"I'm sorry. I—"

Tom stood, aimed down with the shotgun and squeezed the trigger.

The shotgun boomed.

A brace of pheasants exploded into the air from the woods behind him.

Connor was at point-blank range, and the birdshot struck him in a tight spread, no larger than a hand, starting at his throat and down to the top of his breastbone. The impact tore through flesh and bone. Blood splattered up, and Tom could feel the warm mist on his face.

He stood unmoving, looking through a haze of burnt powder at Connor's lifeless body. His breath raced in and out, and he was aware of the sweet smell of burnt plastic and the otherworldly call of the pheasants, their wings whirring as they fled into the trees.

Alice.

Tom knew he couldn't stay here.

She needed him.

He took the shotgun and went along the top of the ridge and then down to the tent. He found his wallet with his bank cards and the thirty or forty quid he had in notes and looked for his phone; he found Connor's stuff and searched it, emptying the pockets of his spare jeans and then upending his rucksack until everything fell out. Nothing. He went to Connor's sleeping bag and patted it down from top to bottom until he felt something hard, down at the foot, and unzipped it enough so that he could reach down for it. It was his phone. It was switched off. He held the button down to wake it, knowing it'd take a minute for it to power up again, and while it did, he looked up and out of the tent and back across the field.

There was no sign of anyone else.

Tom found the ammunition for the shotgun. He put the box and his phone in his rucksack and then set off at a jog, reached the nearest fence, clambered over it and, without looking back, started running north in the direction of the city.

101

Nikki waited at the table in the covered garden of the Winchester Gate while Gaz went to the bar for another couple of pints. They'd been here since eight, making sure they arrived in time to watch a set from a local musician they sort of knew and sort of liked from coming to the pub for gigs on Saturday nights. It had been a pleasant evening, warm and bright, and there'd been a decent crowd.

Sam had tried to call them both that afternoon, and Nikki had told Gaz they shouldn't answer. It wouldn't be anything good—most likely another job she wanted them to do—and she was worried that they'd say something or give the impression that they were nursing a secret. Better to avoid her until later.

It was coming up to eleven now, and last orders had been called. Nikki had a nice little buzz on, although she'd been careful not to get drunk on account of what they were planning to do later. It was a fine line: drunk enough so they had the courage to do what needed to be done, yet not so drunk that they were sloppy and made mistakes. Nikki felt like she'd nailed it, and she'd made sure Gaz was careful, too. One more drink and a spliff in the car and they'd be good to go.

Gaz came out with a pint in each hand. He stepped around a couple of regulars, saying something as he did, and climbed up to where Nikki was waiting.

"Cheers, babes," he said, holding up his pint.

She touched her glass to his. "Last one—okay?"

"I know. I'm not drunk." He took a long draught of his lager, then eyed Nikki over the top of his glass. "Are you sure you still want to do this?"

"Not getting cold feet, are you?"

"No," he said. "But what we're thinking of doing—it's a big thing."

"It is."

"We won't ever be able to come back."

"We won't."

"And that's okay?"

"Why'd we *want* to come back?" she said. "Look around—Salisbury's nothing special. *Smallsbury*. You want to come here and get pissed every Saturday night for the next twenty years?"

"I *like* it here," he protested.

"So do I—but wouldn't you like to see the world? You don't think it'd be good to broaden your horizons? Just think—this time next week we could be a thousand miles away. We could be in a car on the west coast of America. San Francisco. Los Angeles. They've got those wineries there—we could find somewhere nice, get a bottle of wine and a couple of spliffs and find somewhere to get pissed and stoned while we're looking out over the Pacific. Think about it. You wouldn't want that?"

"Who wouldn't?"

"Exactly." Nikki gestured around her. "There's nothing for us here, is there? Nothing in the city."

"Friends?"

"We haven't got any."

"Sam?" Gaz said.

"*Seriously?* You know what I think about her—wouldn't trust her as far as I could throw her, and that wouldn't be very bloody far. You want my opinion? This *whole* situation is her fault. Everything that's happened this week with Tom and his woman is because she messed up. The thing with Christopher?" She lowered her voice to a tight whisper. "That was the start of it, and it was *all* down to her. You know what I think?"

"I know."

"She's never told us everything about what happened that night."

"You keep saying that," he complained.

"And you're right—I'll never be able to prove any of it, not a word, but they were up to something together, them against the rest of us, and then whatever it was went wrong. That was why he was at the yard. And I don't know, maybe Tom was in on it and what he said about it being an accident wasn't true. Maybe hc *meant* to kill him when he hit him."

"He made a bloody mess of his head."

"He did," Nikki said. "So maybe he and Sam were planning something. It'd explain why he's always felt so guilty about it. Would he be that way if it was an accident like they said?"

"I think he'd feel bad *however* it happened."

"It doesn't matter, though, does it?" Nikki said. "The *reason* Sam can't be trusted… well, it doesn't matter. It's irrelevant. The facts are the facts: she just can't be. End of story."

"And Connor?"

"Takes Sam's side every time. The way he looks at her." She rolled her eyes. "He's been thinking with his dick ever since I've known him. I know the two of you have been friends longer than that—"

"From school."

"I know that, from school, but Connor made his choice, and he's chosen Sam over you. And it's not like we'll be leaving him with nothing. And it's not like *she's* being left with nothing, either, is it? We made good money for a year. We *all* did. But we—you and me—we've made our choice. We don't want to work with them anymore, and we're taking care of ourselves on the way out. Maybe they want to keep doing it after we're gone? Fine. We don't care. They can do it for another year and make another million. But they'll never see us again."

"I still don't know, babes."

She found his hesitancy annoying, but knew she needed to bring him along carefully; she couldn't very easily go and do it herself. "You want another reason? What do you think's going to happen with that bird in the cellar? You think Sam's just going to let her out?" She shook her head firmly. "Come on, babes. She'll say there's a risk she knows too much, that letting her out would be crazy, and she'll say there's nothing else for it. She'll want to get rid of her. And then you know what she'll do? She'll put it on us. You'll see. She'll make sure she has a story lined up so we take the fall for it if the police ever come sniffing around."

"And Tom?"

"Same goes for him. She'll think things can't ever get back to how they were before. We know it, and she knows it—

he's a liability. Maybe it works this time, and we get away with it, but you think he'll keep his mouth shut?" She shook her head again, then tapped a finger to the side of her head. "He's *weak*. He's not like he was when we were kids—whatever happened to him in the Army has given him a screw loose. You want to trust an alcoholic with the secrets we have? With all the things we've done? No. And what if he figures out what's happened to his bird? He's taken out of the way for a week, and when he comes back, she's gone. Even *Tom* is going to smell a rat then, isn't he?"

"Yeah," he said.

"It's simple, babes. *You* can take the risk if you want, but I'm not. *I'm* getting out of here, with the money, and Sam and Connor and Tom and whoever else is left can continue doing what they're doing, or they can do something else. I don't care. It won't be my problem anymore."

"It won't be *our* problem," he corrected.

She rested her hand on top of his. "You're still in, then?"

"Course I am. Together forever—right?"

"Together forever." She looked at her watch. "It's half eleven. Freeman should be there in half an hour."

"We're waiting until he's gone?"

"Do you want someone like that there when we do what we're going to do? You want a head case like him coming after us?"

"No, babes."

"No." She looked at her watch again. "You got those Rizlas?"

He reached into his pocket and brought out the packet of rolling papers.

"Let's go up to Old Sarum and smoke one. We'll give it an hour, and then we'll go and get our money."

102

Tom headed north, staying in the fields rather than taking the drove and using that to bring him into Nunton. His shoulder was bleeding, not enough for him to worry, but not something he could leave forever.

It was just over a mile and half to the village, and it took him thirty minutes before he reached the first houses. The drove bent sharply to the right, and a collection of properties were nestled together with the continuing road forming a boundary to the south and east and a dirt track marking the perimeter to the west. A five-bar gate blocked the track, but Tom hopped over it and continued to the north, looking at the first house on his left and, after seeing that it was occupied, continuing to the next one. This one—a bungalow with a swimming pool and pool house—didn't look as if anyone was home. Tom clambered over the fence, dropped down into the garden and crept up to the house. He peered through the window into the kitchen and saw nothing; he moved around to a window that looked into the lounge and saw that that room was empty, too. He continued along the wall until he reached a wooden door with a glass panel; he looked in and saw that it opened into a boot room. He reversed the shotgun and used the buttstock to stave in the glass, reached inside and unlocked the door.

Tom went inside and waited, holding his breath and listening hard for any sound that might suggest someone else was inside. There was nothing save the crunch of glass underfoot as he took a step ahead. He turned the shotgun around, and with his finger next to the trigger guard, he crossed the room to a door, went into the hall and then to the phone on a small table near the front door.

The whole thing was obvious now: it had been an elaborate set-up to get him out of the way while they worked out how much he'd said to Alice. And what was worse was that Tom knew it was all *his* fault; if he'd kept his mouth shut in the Haunch, if he'd held his tongue rather than blurt out about Alice and what he'd said to her, then none of this would have happened. Tom had already decided that he wanted nothing more to do with any of them. He was going to go to the police and confess; there would be a relief in that, in knowing that whatever happened next would be out of his hands. It wouldn't be good for the others, but that was for them to deal with. He'd ignored his conscience for too long, and trying to keep a lid on his guilt was killing him.

103

Mack had dropped Atticus outside the office and then continued to the station. She had reported back on the extent of the progress that had been made in finding Alice or Tom—nothing—and told him that she'd let him know if anything else came to light. He texted back to ask if Alice's house had been searched, and Mack had replied that it had, two days ago, and that nothing helpful had been found. Atticus told her that the context had changed since then, and that they should go back and conduct a second search with the benefit of the knowledge that Tom Brennan was likely involved in her disappearance. Mack said that she'd speak to the team, but it was with an off-handedness that said she'd put it somewhere toward the end of the list of things that needed to be done.

Atticus knew that was going to nag at him.

He took the dog for a walk and returned via McDonald's, bringing back a Happy Meal for him and a burger for Bandit. After he'd eaten, he paced the office, trying to think of anything that he could do other than to ignore Mack's very firm instructions that he must not—*must not*—do anything that went beyond the bounds of legality.

He'd already broken into her office, though…

He woke his computer and navigated to Facebook. A post from the page for Salisbury Police was at the top of his feed, starting with pictures of Alice Green and Tom Brennan.

Atticus scrolled down and read:

We are appealing for information to help us find two people from Salisbury who have been reported as missing. Alice Green is thirty-five and described as five feet, six inches tall with a slender figure and long brown hair. Tom Brennan is thirty-nine and described as six feet, two inches tall with a large build and short, dark brown hair.

If you know anything about either Alice or Tom, please call us on 101 quoting log 34441061034.

Mack had said she would arrange for a post in lieu of the press conference that would likely happen in the morning. It was *something*, Atticus thought, but the chances of it revealing anything useful were slim, and, even if they did strike lucky, progress would be minimal and slow. Too slow for his tastes, in any event, given that he was of the opinion that there were levers to be pulled that offered a bigger payoff in a shorter amount of time. He was convinced Alice had been abducted, and the longer she was held captive, the greater the chance that something bad might happen to her.

Atticus clicked to close the tab and got up, pacing the room again. He could stay here, wearing out the carpet and staring at his screens in the vain hope that something might present itself to him, or he could be proactive and *do* something. Mack wouldn't be happy with what he had in mind—that was an understatement—but if it didn't produce anything useful, then she didn't need to know. If it *did* help, she'd have to wait to upbraid him, and, by the time she got around to it, it would be churlish of her not to forgive him.

And it wasn't as if she didn't know he'd be frustrated and tempted to push at the boundaries a little.

It wasn't as if what he had in mind wasn't something he'd done before.

He went into his bedroom and changed into the same clothes he'd worn when he broke into Alice's office. He found his bag with his lock picks and box of gloves and slung it over his back.

He went out of the back door, down the steps and out into the street.

104

Tom's shoulder and arm throbbed from the shotgun pellets. He tried Alice's number one more time, but the call went to voicemail again. He went into the kitchen and found a clean tea towel and a bottle of antiseptic in a cabinet. He ripped the towel into strips with his teeth to fashion makeshift bandages, then washed his hands and then his wounds under the cold tap, wincing as the water hit the bloodied flesh. The pain was worse than he expected, and he took a moment to go back to the drinks cabinet. He helped himself to a bottle of vodka, knocked back a large mouthful straight from the bottle and then took it with him back to the sink.

He poured the antiseptic over the wounds. The stinging was severe, and he had to bite down on his lip to stop from shouting out. He held his arm up and to the side so he could look at the damage: the skin was mottled with bruises, and small entry wounds peppered the top of his shoulder and the upper part of his arm, each surrounded by edges of torn skin. Some of the pellets were still visible, lodged just beneath the surface. He would have to deal with those later. The deeper wounds oozed clear fluid, while the shallower ones had already begun to clot. The entire area was swollen and tender.

He grabbed another tea towel, pressed the cleanest part of it against his shoulder, then wrapped the makeshift bandages tightly around his arm, securing them with strips of duct tape he found in a drawer.

He took another slug of vodka and looked at his handiwork. It wasn't perfect, but it'd do.

He took a microwave meal from the fridge and heated it up, demolishing it in double-quick time while finishing half of the vodka. He found a thermal flask, filled it with the rest of the booze and put it in his bag, then took out the boxes of shotgun shells and arranged them on the kitchen table. He opened the boxes and tipped the shells out, counting them—he had thirty—and then putting them into the bag. He was covered in dirt and sweat from his work in the field and was tempted by the prospect of a shower, but quickly decided against it. He didn't want the bandages to get wet, and he didn't have the luxury of time. Connor's absence would be noted at some point, and when that happened, Alice—if she was still alive—would be placed in even more danger.

He had to find her.

He worked out the bones of a plan: he'd visit her house first in the event, however unlikely, that she simply wasn't answering her phone; if that wasn't successful, he'd go back to the others and make them tell him what they'd done.

He'd tried that with Connor.

Connor had chosen not to cooperate, and now Connor was dead.

They'd all get the same choice.

Tom found a cupboard with tools and equipment for small domestic repair jobs. He took out a packet of cable ties and put them in his bag with the ammunition.

There was a little Nissan runaround parked in the drive outside the house. He searched the kitchen for the keys without success, moved into the hallway and found them in a wooden tray next to the telephone. He picked them up, collected the shotgun and went outside. He went to the car, opened the door and put his pack and the shotgun in the back, and lowered himself into the front seat.

He didn't know how long it would take for Connor's body to be found but didn't want to take any unnecessary chances. He could have hidden it, but it was too late to go back and do that now, and there probably wasn't any point. Connor was unlikely to be found now, in the dark, and by the time he was found tomorrow—*if* he was found then—Tom would have done what needed to be done.

He started the car, put it into gear and pulled out.

105

Sam went out into the yard. Alexander Freeman's son Charlie usually made the collection, and he hadn't turned up. It was half eleven, and Charlie was supposed to have been here thirty minutes ago. She went to the end of the track and looked up and down the road, but there was no sign of anything approaching.

She took out her phone, opened the contacts and scrolled down for Freeman's details. He was a frightening man. She knew enough about him to know he was dangerous. He was in his mid-sixties now, and, at least on the surface, charming and urbane. She remembered the first time they'd met. She and Christopher had just started seeing each other, and Freeman's insistence that she call him Alexander rather than the more formal salutation she'd started with had caught her off guard. Christopher had regaled her with stories about the things his father had done as he rose through the underworld in East London during the latter years of the last century, and they'd been enough to give her sleepless nights. Charlie was Christopher's brother, and, although neither son had the edge of their father, he still made Sam nervous.

Christopher had arranged everything and had assuaged her fears by telling her that if things went as well as he expected—and that quickly proved to be the case—everyone would be happy. The relationship had been good for both parties right from the start. Freeman got high-quality product to pass on to his retail buyers in London while Sam and the others were paid handsomely for taking the risk in bringing the cocaine over the border and storing it until Freeman was ready.

Christopher's betrayal had nearly upended everything. If Freeman had found out what happened, they would all have suffered the same fate as his son. They had been lucky. Christopher hadn't told anyone whom he was going to meet, and although Freeman had spoken to Sam about him, she'd been able to lie with enough conviction to be believed.

She touched the number and waited for the call to connect.

"Hello?"

"It's me," she said. "Samantha."

"Samantha," he said.

"I'm sorry to bother you."

"You're wondering where my good-for-nothing son is?"

"I am."

"Just had a message from him. He's been delayed."

"But we're still on?"

"Of course. He says he'll be there around one. I know that's early, and you'd probably rather be in bed, but it's the soonest he can manage tonight. Not a problem, is it?"

"No, no."

"I can rearrange for tomorrow if you'd prefer."

A postponement was the *last* thing she wanted. "No—it's fine."

"Excellent. Sorry again—I'll see if we can't hurry him up a bit."

Sam told him not to worry and ended the call. She was relieved that the deal would still happen tonight, but anxious that business be concluded so she could get away. There really was no point in waiting around. She'd take the money and run. If everything went to plan, she'd be at the airport in time for the first flight in the morning.

106

The gates to the Close were locked between eleven and six, and, although it would still have been possible to make his way to Alice's house that way, Atticus decided that a more discreet approach made more sense. He descended the external steps into the courtyard and went to the wall next to the dentist's premises at the end. He pushed a picnic chair against the wall and climbed up on it, using it to make it easier to clamber over. Sarum College was on the other side of the wall. Atticus stayed close to the buildings, edging around a large car park and then along the side of another building until he was able to follow the driveway that continued down to North Walk. He knew there were cameras here from his investigation into the murder of Clive Mouton, the clerk of works who fell to his death from the tower of the cathedral. The lights that illuminated the spire had been switched off, with just the single red obstruction light at the top of the spire shining out across the city.

He reached the junction with Bishop's Walk and crossed over to the pavement next to the terrace. Everything was quiet: there were lights in some of the windows, but there was no sign of anyone else out and about. Atticus reached Alice's house and saw that the windows were dark. He continued on and then turned back, watching the building for any signs of activity and seeing nothing.

He made his way to the front door, knelt down, pushed the letterbox open and looked through the slot to the hall beyond. He couldn't hear or see anything that suggested that anyone was inside.

He got to his feet again and darted into the covered passageway that led to the rear of the terrace. It looked as if the large house to the north, at the corner of North Walk and Bishop's Walk, owned the garden that ran due south. The lawn stretched back forty metres, with an old brick wall separating it from the playing fields of the school to the east. Alice's property had a fenced yard that had nibbled a small chunk out of the garden. The boundary was composed of a low red-brick wall topped with a wooden fence. Atticus wedged his toes against the lip of the wall and boosted himself up and over the fence, dropping down into the paved yard on the other side.

The façade of the building had large windows and a pair of French doors. Atticus went to the doors, took out his torch and shone it inside. The space beyond looked like it was used for dining. At the centre of the room was a wooden dining table covered with a patterned tablecloth and with six wooden chairs arranged around it. A door on the other side of the room led through to a room at the front of the building that Atticus thought, from his glimpse through the window, was the sitting room. The kitchen was to the right of the French doors, with a single window looking in over the top of the sink.

The rooms all looked empty.

He put on his gloves and tried the door handle; it was locked. He took out his picks, quickly unlocked and opened the door and stepped inside, pausing on the threshold to listen for anything that might suggest Alice—or anyone else—was here.

Nothing.

Atticus crossed the room to the kitchen door and stopped again.

Still nothing.

The floor was laid with large marble slabs, while the compact kitchen had been fitted with black granite countertops and hand-crafted wooden Shaker-style cabinetry. He shone the torch over the counters in the hope of finding something of interest, but it had been kept neat and tidy, and there was nothing of note.

He went back to the dining room and then continued into the sitting room. He was more careful with the torch, the curtains were open, and he didn't want to attract attention to himself. The living area was arranged around an unusual modern metal fireplace that was suspended on one wall, with two small sofas on either side of a low coffee table. There was a side table with a ceramic lamp and a potted plant, and framed art and photographs were hung on the walls. A collection of books and magazines had been left on the coffee table, but, as Atticus quickly flicked through them, he found nothing of interest.

He went to the hall and climbed the stairs to the first floor. He recalled the plan: the principal bedroom, together with an en suite bathroom, was to his right, with another decent-sized bedroom straight ahead and two smaller ones to his left.

He pushed open the door to the principal bedroom, shining his torch across an empty bed. He went to the bed and pulled back the duvet, then lifted both pillows. An iPad was beneath the pillow nearest to him. It looked as if it might have been left there by Alice after she'd used it last thing at night.

He touched the screen, and the device woke. Atticus saw the lock screen and swiped it away until the keypad was displayed.

He tapped in the most obvious possible keycode—123456—but it was rejected.

Atticus wasn't sure how Alice would have set up the device, but it was possible he had only two more guesses before it locked permanently.

He took out his phone and opened his gallery, flicking through the photos until he found the one of the Post-it note with the number written on it that had been stuck underneath her laptop.

374829.

Atticus's stomach was in knots as he tapped the number onto the screen.

The iPad unlocked.

He flicked across the icons, going directly to emails and recent calls. Finding nothing, he swiped to the social media apps, scanning through direct messages and notifications, again seeing nothing that looked relevant or useful. He turned to iMessages and paused, his eyes narrowing as he traced the flow of texts that looked as if they had been mirrored from Alice's phone.

He saw a message from 'Frank' from Wednesday. There was a single message with no words, just the meme from the video for *Thriller* with Michael Jackson eating popcorn and a link to the page on Medium that had broken the story about Alice's disgrace.

There were other messages about that, most of them sympathetic and asking how she was doing; a handful were gloating and celebratory and unkind.

The next thread was a series of messages to and from Sarah, Alice's PA. Atticus swiped up the screen until hc reached the most recent correspondence.

>> *Where are you?*

>> *The studio has been broken into, and the police are asking where you are.*

>> *I'm worried. Please reply.*

Each message went unanswered.

Atticus thought he heard something from outside: it sounded like the creak of an unoiled hinge. A neighbour returning home, most likely; Atticus ignored it and turned his attention back to the screen.

Atticus dropped down to the next thread, this one from a correspondent referred to only as T.

He read:

>> *I can't do it anymore. I keep thinking about Christopher. I can't live with what I did.*

Alice responded:

>> *I told you what I think.*

The conversation continued:

>> *I thought about it, but it's no good. I have to go to the police.*

>> *And they'll charge you with murder.*

>> *I am a murderer.*

>> *You said you were protecting your friend.*

>> *I know. I was.*

>> *Remember what she told you. Why did he go up there?*

>> *To steal from us. She caught him at it. I know all that.*

>> *So he got what he deserved.*

>> *To die?*

>> *You know what I think. But it's up to you.*

He heard the squeak of the hinge again, the noise distracting him for a moment before he put it aside and concentrated on the rest of the conversation.

>> *What would you do if I was arrested?*

>> *What do you mean?*

>> *Would you wait for me?*

>> *You'd be in prison for years. Be realistic—we hardly know each other.*

>> *It's six months tomorrow.*

>> *That's nothing. It's not like we've been together for years, is it?*

>> *So that's a no?*

>> *Be reasonable, Tom.*

>> *Can we at least talk about it?*

>> *We have talked about it. You know what I think. I'm not going to change my mind.*

Atticus stared at the messages, wishing he had his phone to photograph them, then deciding he might as well just take the iPad with him.

He was scrolling up to find earlier conversations between the two when he heard the sound of footsteps from downstairs.

PART 7

107

Atticus froze.

The footsteps were downstairs.

It sounded like someone was in the hall.

The footsteps continued, with whoever it was moving toward the front of the building.

Atticus reached the bedroom door, opened it and held his breath.

Could it be Alice?

The person was making his or her way up the stairs, the treads creaking with each step.

"Hello?"

The voice was male.

Not Alice.

Atticus held his breath.

"I know you're in here. I saw you come in."

Atticus recognised the voice from the video he'd seen at the station.

It was Tom Brennan.

Shit.

"I've got a shotgun."

Atticus looked around, but there was nowhere for him to go. There were two windows on the side of the terrace that faced the cathedral, but he wouldn't be able to get them open in time, and, even if he did, he'd have no choice but to jump to the street below, and he didn't fancy that.

"Did you hear me?" Tom Brennan said. "I've already killed one man today. Shot him. I'll shoot you, too."

"I heard you," Atticus said.

The footsteps reached the top of the stairs and stopped. "Come out where I can see you."

"I'm not armed. I'm here because I'm worried about Alice."

"Come out."

"It's Tom, isn't it? Tom Brennan?"

"Out—*now!*"

Atticus's throat was arid as he reached for the handle and opened the door.

Tom was standing on the landing at the top of the stairs. He was holding a shotgun in both hands: his left supported the barrel while his right held the stock, his index finger curled through the guard with the joint pressed up against the trigger. Atticus recognised him from the video and the images that Francine Patterson had shared, but there was a raggedness to his appearance that he hadn't noticed before. His clothes were dirty, caked with dried mud, and there were streaks of grime across his weather-beaten cheeks. His beard was unkempt, and there was grime in his hair, too.

Tom raised the barrel an inch or two. "Who are you?"

"Atticus Priest."

He frowned. "What?"

"I know," he said. "Weird name. Take it up with my parents."

"What are you doing here?"

Tom was slurring his words a little, and there was an unsteadiness to his gait and the smell of alcohol. He was drunk.

"Answer the question," he said, jabbing the barrel of the shotgun in Atticus's direction.

"I'm a private investigator."

He chuckled. "Bollocks you are."

"It's true. I've got a card." He nodded down to his pocket. "In there. I can get it if you like."

"Keep your hands where I can see them."

Atticus noticed Tom sway a little to the right. How drunk *was* he? He would've been dangerous enough if he was sober, but things would be much more unstable if his judgement was impaired. Atticus had read his file. Tom was a soldier, with a history of mental instability, who'd just admitted that he'd already killed one man tonight… A shiver of fear, as cold as a cube of ice, ran from the back of his neck all the way down to the base of his spine. Mack had always warned him of the consequences of doing something stupid, and he'd always brushed them aside; he didn't feel quite so blasé about that now.

"Private investigator," Tom said, chuckling.

"It's true. I am."

"So who are you working for?"

"I *was* working for Frank Green."

Tom raised the shotgun, and Atticus thought he could see his finger tighten on the trigger. "That right?"

"Was," Atticus said. "*Was*. Past tense. Frank asked me to find dirt on Alice." Tom's finger tightened. "I know about you and her," Atticus added quickly, "and, if it helps, he's one of the worst people I've ever had the misfortune of meeting."

Atticus decided not to mention that he didn't think Alice was all that much better.

"You still haven't told me why you're here."

"Alice went missing on Wednesday. You know that, don't you?"

"Answer the question."

"Frank tricked her into doing something that's ruined her reputation, and I was worried at first that she might have done something to hurt herself."

"What trick?"

"You don't know?"

"I wouldn't have asked if I did," he snapped.

Atticus raised his hands in an effort to placate him. "I'm sorry—of course not. He got her to endorse a product that doesn't exist. It makes her look... bad. Very bad. I thought she might've done something because of that, but I don't think that now."

"She hasn't," Tom said.

"I think someone else has done something to her."

"And you think it's me."

"No," Atticus said. "Actually, I don't."

Tom didn't seem to have heard him. "Because I heard what the police are saying. It was on the radio—I heard it. They want to speak to me about her going missing. They think I've done something to her, don't they?"

"They want to talk to you. That's normal. They know the two of you were in a relationship. And they know you went missing around the same time."

"It wasn't that," he said. "I wasn't missing."

"No?"

"They got me out of the way so they could deal with her."

"They? Who's that?"

Tom tightened his grip on the shotgun. "I ask the questions."

"Easy," Atticus said, raising his hands again, palms out. "Easy. I believe you. Tell me what happened, and maybe I can help."

"You can't," he said. "She's clever—it'll be made to look like whatever they've done to Alice was me."

"*Who's* clever, Tom?"

He ignored the question. "I would've had an alibi, except the man who could have said where I was had been in on it from the start, and it wouldn't matter, not now, not on account of the fact that he's the one I shot." Tom swayed again. "You still haven't said why you're here."

"I'm looking for anything that'd explain what's happened to Alice." Atticus gestured behind him to the bedroom. "I found her iPad. I read the messages you sent to her. That's the crux of it, isn't it? Something happened to you before, and you want to go to the police to confess. Right?"

He didn't answer.

"Who's Christopher?"

He swayed to the left. "Doesn't matter."

"But you killed him?"

"Hit him with a poker," he said. "Back of the head. Whack. Didn't mean to do it—to hit him as hard as that—but there you are. Dead before he hit the floor. She fed him to the pigs."

"Who did?"

"Who else?" He looked at Atticus as if he was stupid. "Sam."

Atticus's mouth fell open. "Samantha Hargreaves?"

"*Bitch*," Tom muttered. "Known her for years. Since school. Thought she was my friend."

Atticus made a startling connection. "When was this? Eighteen months ago?"

"Something like that."

The name and the time slotted neatly into alignment, and more details came back to him. "Christopher Freeman?"

A flicker of pain passed across Tom's face, and the barrel of the shotgun drooped down a degree or two. "She said he went up to the yard to steal from us. She told me he snuck in unannounced, went to where we kept the money and was trying to force the door. He had a knife with him. She found him; they argued; he tried to kill her. I wasn't even supposed to be there that night, but I went to say I didn't want to be involved anymore, I didn't want to be involved with bringing that shit into the country—not after I'd seen what it could do to people—and there they were, rolling around in the front room. He was on top of her, and he had his hands around her throat." His face contorted as his imagination brought him back to whatever had happened, replaying it in his mind. "He was trying to strangle her, and I couldn't get him off, so I picked up the poker and hit him with it."

"What 'shit'?" Atticus said. "What didn't you want to do anymore?"

"It's always the same," he said, shaking his head. "Sam'd laugh if she could see me. 'You always say too much,' she'd say. 'You never know when to keep your mouth shut.'"

"Please, Tom. Let me help you."

"You can't—no one can."

"I can. Let me help you find Alice."

Tom raised the barrel of the shotgun again and stepped to the side so that the stairs were clear. "Down."

"Come on, Tom."

"I killed a man," Tom said, then, with a horribly bitter chuckle, "*Two* men. Christopher first and now Connor. I would've said they were two of my best friends if you'd asked me before. Knew them both for years."

"Go to the police."

Atticus's words weren't reaching him. "Do you know what that *feels* like? Being responsible for something like that? I'm evil. I'm the worst person you've ever met."

"No, you're not."

He kept talking. "You can't help me. I don't even *want* help. I deserve what's coming to me. I'm going to hell for what I've done. I'm just going to make sure they come with me."

"I *can* help. I—"

"Shut up!" He jabbed the barrel at Atticus, then jerked his head at the stairs again. "Downstairs—now."

108

Tom navigated the house with a familiarity that wasn't surprising. He had been in a relationship with Alice and had certainly been here before. He followed closely behind Atticus as he descended the stairs and told him to stop once he reached the hallway on the ground floor. There was a plain door set into the space beneath the stairs with a key in the lock.

"Open it."

Atticus did as he was told and turned the key. He pulled the door back and revealed a set of stairs that led down into the darkness of what must have been a cellar.

"Give me your phone."

Atticus did as he was told.

"Get inside."

Atticus went to the top of the stairs and then paused. "Tom—*please*. I know you think this is bad—and it is bad, what you've done, I'm not going to pretend, there's no saying otherwise—but I promise I can help. I—"

"Will you *please* just shut up!"

Atticus felt a powerful shove between his shoulder blades and stumbled ahead, missing the step at the top of the stairs and toppling over into the darkness.

109

Gaz drove the Discovery out to Odstock and then south on the Nunton Drove until they reached the hairpin bend just before the yard. He dabbed the brakes to bring the Discovery to a halt. The clock on the dashboard showed just after one in the morning; Freeman should have been and gone by now, meaning there was a lot of money at the yard.

Nikki looked over at him. "Ready?"

He nodded. "Ready."

She reached forward and opened the glovebox, but he put a hand on her knee. "Wait—car coming."

Nikki looked in the side mirror and saw the headlights of a car approaching from behind them. It was travelling quickly, slowing for the bend and then continuing in the direction of the yard.

Nikki waited until the glow from the taillights had disappeared, then took out the two handguns that they had bought after Christopher's death. She'd known a day like this might come and wanted them to be ready for it. Gaz had bought them from the Irish, saying he wanted protection from a local criminal who'd been threatening them. They'd sold him two guns—a Smith & Wesson revolver and a Ruger 9mm semi-automatic—and charged a grand apiece for the privilege. Gaz took the revolver—it had the punchiest recoil—and Nikki took the Ruger. She wrapped her hand around the walnut grip and hefted it, getting used to the weight. They'd been out into the woods near Langford Lakes for practice, neither of them was all that accurate, but it didn't matter. Nikki didn't think they'd actually *need* to use them. Waving them around should be enough, but, if it wasn't, they'd be using them up close where it would be harder to miss.

"Love you, babes," she said.

Gaz leaned over and kissed her. "Love you more."

He released the clutch and pushed down on the accelerator, the headlights picking out the sign that announced the yard was just up ahead.

110

Francine looked at her screen and, realising that the characters were beginning to blur into one, reached up and scrubbed her eyes with her knuckles. She'd been racking her brain for a fresh approach that might help her find Tom Brennan, but so far at least, she'd had no luck.

She'd called his parents earlier, apologising for the late hour and asking if they had ever heard him talk about Alice Green, or if he'd said anything that would give her something to go at with regard to confirming that the two of them were in a relationship. Neither his mother nor his father had ever heard him speak her name, but both counselled that wasn't surprising. They reiterated what they'd said at the station: he was a closed book when it came to his female friends, his father going so far as to admit that he'd given up hope that Tom would ever find anyone with whom he could settle down.

Francine pushed away from the table, got up and went for a walk to stretch her legs. She was drifting toward the kitchen and the promise of caffeine when her phone rang. She took it out and saw that Robbie was calling.

"Shit," she said. "I'm so sorry. I totally forgot. I was supposed to be there two hours ago."

"*Three* hours ago, actually," he said, the smile evident in his voice. "Don't worry about it. I know how busy you are."

"It's been nuts," she said. "And we're not getting anywhere."

"Take a break, then. You can't work all night. Come back to it fresh in the morning."

"You're probably right."

"I am right. And you can be here in thirty minutes. Twenty minutes if you switch on the blues and twos."

"I can't do *that*, Robbie. I'd get into trouble."

"But this *is* an emergency. I want to see you."

She looked at her watch. "It's late."

"Doesn't matter."

"Are you there already?"

"We've got to pay for the cabin whether we use it or not," he said. "And it *is* my birthday."

She bit her lip, weighing up the shorter trip to her place on St. Ann's Street or a drive out to Fordingbridge, where Robbie was waiting for her. She knew she ought to get as much sleep as possible, but she'd promised Robbie they could have the night away, and it'd be good to have someone to hear about her day, someone who knew the job and would understand the way she was feeling.

"I suppose so. I've got to be in early tomorrow, though."

"Me too, but not that early—no need to be a martyr. It won't do anyone any good at all if we're knackered."

She put a twinkle in her voice. "You want to *sleep*?"

"Well," he said. "Maybe later."

She glanced up at the incident room and saw Lynas with his head drooping over the table and his eyes closed. Robbie was right: no need to be a martyr.

"Okay," she said. "I'm on my way."

"I'll warm up the bed," he said.

111

Sam heard the sound of the car as it turned off the road and into the yard. She looked at her watch, Charlie Freeman was *seriously* late, and the delay had freaked her out. The plan was as precise as she'd been able to make it, and that included working out a series of timings that would see her on her way to her new life. The first of those timings—leaving the yard and setting off for the airport—had already been missed. Her flight wasn't until seven, and the delay probably didn't matter, but she felt more anxious than usual as she crossed the space between the stables and raised her arm in greeting.

The car pulled up next to the horse box, and Charlie got out.

"Sorry I'm late," he said. "I've been dealing with shit all night."

"No problem," Sam said.

"Spoke to my dad, didn't you?"

"Just wondering where you were."

"I wish you hadn't. He's nuts about punctuality, and he'll end up bollocking me about keeping you waiting."

"Sorry," she said. "Didn't mean to give you any grief."

He waved her apology away. "Forget it. He'll perk up when I bring the gear back. Where is it?"

"Usual place. Got the money?"

He opened the rear door, reached into the car and took out a medium-sized rucksack.

"All present and correct," he said, holding the rucksack up.

Sam nodded. She had been busy. Connor had come back from the field to help her with Alice Green, the two of them pushing and pulling her up the ladder until they had her out of the cellar. They'd draped her across the back of the quad bike and then driven her up to the pigs and dumped her in the pen. The girls had started on her right away, and, if it was the same as it had been with Christopher, they'd be finished in nine or ten hours. She didn't want to think about what she'd find if she went up there now.

They had gone back to the yard and moved the cocaine up from the cellar into her office, stacking the bags neatly on the table. Sam half-turned to lead the way across the yard when she saw the lights of another car approaching on the drove. That was strange, it was a single-lane road that didn't really go anywhere other than Whitsbury, and the chances of anyone using a road like that to get there at this time of night—in preference to coming in via the A338 or A354—were slim.

She paused, watching as the car slowed.

"Who's that?" Charlie said.

"No clue."

The car turned onto the track, the headlights shining between the bars of the gate and painting striped shadows across the stables.

Charlie muttered a curse. "Sure about that?"

"I don't know who it is."

She blinked into the lights, unable to make out who it was. It might make things awkward. She wondered if it could be the police, but surely it was too late for that? If it *was*, though… the pigs would only be halfway finished with the body, and there were bags of cocaine worth hundreds of thousands of pounds just inside the office.

Awkward would be an understatement.

Charlie was agitated. He was halfway between the car and the stable block, the rucksack slung over his back.

Sam held up her hand to shield her eyes and recognised the large, boxy shape of Gaz's Land Rover.

What was he doing here?

The doors opened, and Gaz and then Nikki got out.

Sam took a step in their direction. "What are you doing here?"

"Just wanted to come over for a chat," Nikki said.

"At one in the morning?"

"It's important."

"It'd better be."

Charlie took a step toward Sam. "Who are they?"

"They work with me," she said. "They're fine."

"No, they're not. They've never been here before. It's always been you and no one else. I don't like surprises. I don't like things being changed when I don't know they're going to be changed."

"I get it," she said. "I'm sorry—but it's nothing to worry about."

Charlie turned away from Sam so that he was facing the car. Gaz hadn't switched off the engine, and the lights were still shining out, casting Charlie in silhouette.

"Get back in the car, turn around and piss off," he called over.

Neither responded.

"Didn't you hear me? You're not supposed to be here. Get in the car, back it out and piss off. Don't make me ask a third time."

Charlie wasn't as frightening as his father, but he was still more than frightening enough. Christopher had told Sam a little about his brother, and she knew he'd done time for beating up two men who tried to muscle in on one of the family's legitimate businesses, and that he was suspected—Christopher said he'd done it—of shooting another man to death. He wasn't big, but there was a malignancy to the way he held himself, a promise of violence that would be sudden and brutal.

Nikki and Gaz had never met him or his father, but Sam had told them what the pair of them were like. They should have taken heed of his warning and driven away, yet they stood their ground.

Nikki pointed. "What's in the bag?"

"None of your bloody business," Charlie said.

"Throw it over."

He turned his head so he could look back at Sam. "You need to tell them to go, or we're done."

Nikki held up her hand, and Sam realised—way too late—why they were here.

"The bag," she said. "Throw it over here now."

Nikki straightened her arm and brought it up. Her hand moved through the beam of the headlight, and Sam saw the glitter of something metallic. Gaz did the same, both of them aiming at Charlie.

"*Shooters?*" he said. "Are you serious?" He turned his head and glanced back at Sam. "Are they serious?"

"I really hope not."

"Do they know who I am?" He turned back. "Do you know who I am?"

"Put the guns down," Sam said. "*Please.*"

She knew they couldn't, that they'd both know well enough that if they did, if they let Charlie Freeman walk away, he wasn't the sort who was likely to forgive and forget; he was the sort likely to come back with a couple of brawny mates brandishing crowbars. He was the sort of vindictive bastard who'd take them somewhere into the New Forest where they could batter seven shades of shit out of them before putting them out of their misery with a bullet to the head. Sam knew it, and Gaz and Nikki, for all their drugged-up vapidity, must have known it too: if they pulled guns on someone like Charlie Freeman, they had no choice but to use them.

Yet here they were.

Charlie was consumed with anger, and it didn't look as if he had realised the mortal danger he was in. "I'm going to count to three. If you haven't put those shooters away and crawled back to whatever rock the two of you crawled out from under, I swear to God I'll make the rest of your lives as miserable and painful as I possibly can." He held up his hand. "One."

Nikki and Gaz shared a look.

"Two."

They turned back.

Sam ducked.

Both guns fired at once.

112

The radio buzzed with chatter between Control and the officers working the late shift. Francine's TETRA radio was mounted in a holder that was fixed to the dashboard of her car. There was a separate microphone and speaker system, with the microphone clipped to the centre console, allowing Francine to communicate hands-free.

"All units, this is Control. We have a report of a possible gunshot heard in the countryside south of Nunton. Caller is someone to do with surveying owls. Any available unit, please respond. Over."

Francine was nearby. She reached for the press-to-talk button, her hand stalling as she imagined what Robbie would tell her: she couldn't be expected to answer every call, and she'd be no use to anyone tomorrow if she didn't get at least a few hours' rest.

But she was close, and it was obvious that there wouldn't be anyone who could get over here quickly. It was probably nothing—it wouldn't be unusual to have poachers shooting rabbits—and she doubted it would hold her up for long.

She thumbed the button. "Control, this is DC Patterson. I'm in the area and can respond. I'll handle it. Over."

The operator responded with directions that would bring her to where the birdwatcher would be waiting. "You should see him near a cluster of oak trees by the field on your right. Over."

"Copy that, Control. Taking the right-hand path at the fork and looking for him near the oak trees. Over and out."

113

Charlie Freeman had staggered back to the stable and then slid down the wall. He was on the ground now, his back against the wooden planks, blood running from the holes that had been punched in his chest. He was deathly pale, and he was struggling to find his breath.

Sam stared. "What have you *done*?"

Nikki and Gaz looked stunned at what had just happened, as if they'd been spectators instead of pulling the triggers themselves.

Sam jabbed her finger at him and then at them. "You know who he is—right? Who his dad is?"

Charlie put his hands to his belly in an attempt to staunch the blood, but it made no difference. It ran through his fingers, a dark stain growing against the white of his shirt. His mouth opened and closed, and Sam—incongruously—was put in mind of a goldfish.

Nikki's arm fell to her side as if weighed down by the gun. "Of course we know."

"I wouldn't've have asked, except you can't possibly know on account of the fact that *you just shot him.*"

"You'll find a way to sort it out," Nikki said.

"What? Me?"

"That's what you're always telling us—about how you're always clearing up after us and the messes we make. I doubt it'll be a problem for you, and even if it is, we don't care. You know why?"

"Because we won't be here," Gaz said.

Sam was dumbfounded. "You're *serious*? That's how you want this to end? You steal from the rest of us?"

"Give it a rest," Gaz said. "Pretending *we've* betrayed *you* isn't going to work."

"But that's what you're doing. You *are* betraying us."

"Leave it out," Nikki said. "You can't shit a shitter. You think we don't know what happened with Christopher? That never made sense. What was it—what was it *really*?"

"I told you. He wanted to get rid of us, and I stopped him. I've told you a *hundred* times. He tried to kill me. He would've done, too, if it weren't for Tom."

Nikki shook her head. "Bollocks, Sam. I'm not buying it. I'll tell you what I think happened, shall I? I think you were up to something, and he found out. Or the two of you were ripping us off together, and you decided to get rid of him so you could have it all for yourself." She turned to Gaz. "That's what I've always thought, isn't it? It's what I've always said."

"It is," Gaz said.

"Help me."

Sam swivelled, turning her attention back to Charlie. His breathing came with a whistle every time he inhaled or exhaled. "Help me," he wheezed again. "Hospital."

"Can't," Sam said.

"Please."

Nikki looked at Gaz and then gestured to the rucksack. "Pick it up, babes. Let's go."

Gaz collected the rucksack and slung it over his shoulder.

"That's it?" Sam said.

Nikki shrugged. "What else is there?"

She pointed at Freeman. "Er—him?"

"That's up to you. Finish him off and feed him to the pigs. I don't care."

Sam looked at the two of them, at the guns they held in relaxed and comfortable grips and thought of the disturbing ease with which they had put bullets into Charlie Freeman's gut. She knew there was nothing she could do to stop them from taking the money and leaving. They'd already used the guns once, and Sam was not naïve enough to think that the history they shared would insulate her from the guns being turned on her, too.

She was caught between them and Charlie when she saw movement from the trees to the north of the yard. She might have mistaken it for the wind rustling the branches, but then she heard the crunch of a footstep on the gravel path and then another, and then, silhouetted in the glow from the Land Rover's headlamps, she saw Tom Brennan.

He had a shotgun cradled in his arms, and he turned to point it at Gaz and Nikki.

"Put the guns down," he said.

Gaz turned, too quickly, and Tom shouldered the shotgun and took aim.

"Stop," Nikki said. "Gaz—put it down."

She held up both hands, her gun above her head, and then crouched down and made a show of slowly putting it on the ground.

Gaz did the same.

Tom moved the shotgun through a semi-circle, taking in Charlie and then Nikki and Gaz and, finally, Sam.

"Get in close together," he said to them, jerking the barrel to illustrate what he meant. "We've got lots to talk about."

114

Atticus couldn't tell whether his eyes were open or closed. The darkness was complete, and it made no difference when he raised his hand and waved it across his face. He was lying on his front, his cheekbone pressed up against something hard. He prodded at it with his fingers, and the movement made him wince from a sudden blast of pain that shot down his neck like a bolt of electricity. It was enough to make him gasp, but the pain helped him focus.

He was in Alice Green's house, in the cellar, and Tom Brennan had pushed him down here.

Brennan.

He remembered what he'd said.

He'd killed Christopher Freeman and Connor Smith.

He'd said that he and Samantha Hargreaves had been involved in bringing 'shit into the country.'

What did that mean?

Drugs?

There were more questions than answers, but Atticus knew one thing for sure: he knew where Brennan was going and what he was going to do when he got there.

He had to get up.

He put his palms down and pushed, raising himself an inch, then—with the pain flaring like embers stirred with a poker—lowering himself back down again. He tried to work out where he was hurting and decided—after carefully pressing and poking the fingers of his left hand down his right side—that it was his shoulder. He tried to remember how he had fallen into the cellar. He'd managed to find one or two of the steps on the way down, but then he'd tripped. Not much after that was clear, but it seemed most likely that he'd banged his head and been knocked out. He reached up with his hand again and gently felt the side of his head and up into his scalp; he felt a crust of blood that turned to powder between his fingers and a tenderness across the whole side of his face. He was worried that he might have a concussion and didn't want to think about what he must look like, but both of those concerns could wait.

He had to raise the alarm.

He reached down to his pocket, but his phone wasn't there.

He remembered: Tom had taken it.

He blinked and looked around again, seeing nothing until he thought he noticed a possible lightening of the darkness somewhere ahead of him. It wasn't much—a dark grey line in the otherwise pitch black—but there was nothing else, and, given that it looked as if it was above his head, he wondered whether it might be light leaking into the cellar between the bottom of the door and the floor.

He sat up carefully and slowly, inch by inch, waiting for each fresh escalation of pain to fade before bringing himself closer to a sitting position. He did that, and waiting another moment for a surge of nausea to pass, he moved his weight forward so he could rest on his right knee and then his left. He reached out both arms and swept them around in the darkness, finding nothing until he shuffled over to the right, where his fingers brushed against the abrasive surface of a rough brick wall. His hand scrabbled up and down the wall, eventually finding what he thought was a wooden shelf. He gripped it and, hoping that it would bear his weight, used it to pull himself up. A wave of dizziness buffeted him, and the nausea returned; Atticus waited, holding onto the edge of the shelf until he felt able to take a step toward the grey.

His strength returned bit by bit, but he was still unsteady as he made one step and then another, bracing himself against the wall. He started to take a third step when he swung his shin into something hard and, wincing, lifted his foot and put it down again on a step. The walls were close on both sides now, and he was able to support himself with both arms as he took a second step and then a third. The grey line was more obvious now, and, as he climbed, it moved down from a position above his head until it was at eye level. He leaned forward and put his face to it, trying to see beneath the door. There was some light outside, but it was faint, and he couldn't make anything out no matter how hard he squinted. He climbed another two steps, felt for the door handle and tried it; it turned a quarter, then jammed up against the lock.

Damn.

He wanted to know what the time was, but he wasn't wearing his watch. How many minutes had passed while he had been unconscious? Five minutes? An hour? *Two* hours? It might have been longer. He didn't even know if it was day or night.

Being stuck here was intolerable. Tom had already killed twice on his own admission, and Atticus knew he was likely to kill again unless he could get himself out and warn Mack.

He patted the walls for a light switch but couldn't find one. He ran his fingers across the lock and felt little scabs of rust, suggesting it was old and perhaps, if he was lucky, not as strong as it might have been. He traced the outline of the door, dropping to his knees and knocking on the floorboards, listening for hollow sounds that might indicate a weakness. His fingers found a slight gap, and he pried at it, feeling the board give slightly under pressure.

He carefully descended the steps again and felt his way along the wall to the shelf. He reached up and took down the items that had been stored there—cans of paint, he thought, and empty plastic plant pots—and then dismantled the shelf, yanking the wood from the brackets. He took the shelf up the steps to the door and wedged it into the gap. He used his weight to lever it, hearing both pieces of wood—the shelf and the door—groan in protest. He didn't know what would give way first, but if it was the shelf, he was going to have to think of something else.

The lock began to give way, the metal weakening as the tenon was pushed up into the mortise. Atticus gave it a final determined push, the tenon snapped, and the door swung open.

Atticus emerged into the downstairs hall and looked for a phone. He found one—a hands-free receiver slotted into its cradle—and picked it up. He could have called 999, but he preferred to speak to Mack so nothing was lost in translation.

He dialled her number.

"Hello?" Mack said. "Who's this?"

"It's me."

"What number are you calling from? I don't recognise—"

"Probably best if you don't ask me that," he cut over her.

"The fact you think that suggests the opposite."

"I'll explain everything later. There's no time now—there's something you have to hear. You need to move fast."

She didn't reply.

"Mack? Are you still there?"

"I don't like this at all," she said. "Go on."

"I found Brennan. He says he has nothing to do with Alice going missing, and I'm inclined to believe him."

"How did you find him?"

"Doesn't matter—can we park it for now?"

"Why?"

"Because he just confessed to killing two men. One's historic—he said his name was Christopher, and I think he might have been talking about Christopher Freeman."

"No. We didn't find any evidence of foul play."

"We didn't, but I was never sold on it."

"Shit," she said.

"That's not the main thing. Brennan confessed to a second murder. Tonight."

"Who?"

"Connor Smith."

"One of his friends?"

"Brennan said he shot him, and now it looks very much as if he's going after Samantha Hargreaves. They were in business together—I think they've been importing drugs, probably using the horses and the yard as cover. I got the impression the others were involved as well—Nikki and Gaz. Brennan's had a crisis of conscience about what happened to Freeman, and the others are worried about what he might say. You remember him and O'Reilly were pulled in after the scrap in the Market Square at the weekend. I bet you anything you like it was about this, and it's escalated since."

"Where is he now?"

"Probably at the yard."

"Probably?"

"That's the thing," Atticus said. "I was with him earlier tonight, but he pushed me down a flight of stairs, and I think I might have hit my head."

"Jesus—are you okay?"

He stifled his annoyance, he knew—and was flattered—that she was concerned, but there was no time for that. "I'm fine, but I think I was out for a little bit. Wherever he's gone, he might already be there. He might have been and gone."

"I'll send officers to check on all three of them."

"Be careful," Atticus said. "He's got a shotgun. And he might not think he has anything to lose."

115

Tom pointed the shotgun down at where Charlie Freeman was slumped against the wall.

"Who's that?"

Sam followed his gaze. "That's Alexander Freeman's son. He tried to take the drugs without paying."

Nikki ran with it. "It was lucky we were here."

"That's right." Sam nodded. "Gaz shot him."

Tom smiled, but it was humourless and accompanied by a bitter little chuckle. "You lot… you should hear yourselves sometimes. Do you think I'm *that* stupid?"

"No one thinks you're—"

"Shut up, Sam," Tom snapped. "Just shut up. I've had enough."

Gaz turned to square up to him. "You've had enough? *You?* Put the shotgun down, you pisshead. You drunk, pathetic retard. Do you know how long we've had to put up with your bullshit?"

Sam put up a hand. "That's enough."

"No," Gaz insisted. "He needs to hear this. He's been a dead weight ever since Christopher. We've had to put up with this"—he waved his hand at Tom—"for months. What happened last weekend was the last straw. I'm not pussyfooting anymore."

"Shut *up*, Gaz," Nikki said.

"No, babes, that's just it. We know there's a problem, and we just pretend it's not there. Who's that helping? It's not helping us."

Tom lowered the barrel of the shotgun an inch.

Gaz took a step toward him. "Because you know what's happened here—it's Tom blabbing to some bird he met, giving her the sad eyes and telling her how *bad* his life has been and how everything's so *unfair*. First it was the Army, and now it's this. You've always been a moaner, mate. Moan, moan, *bloody* moan. Ever since school. Whining like a little baby all the time. And now you go to someone outside the circle of trust, and you blab. Is no one else going to be honest and say what needs to be said? That's betrayal, mate. You spoke out of school. You betrayed us."

Tom raised the barrel again and jabbed it into Gaz's chest.

"What?" Gaz said. "You're going to shoot me now? Give me a break. You wet yourself after you topped Christopher. Are you going to wet yourself again—"

The shotgun boomed.

Gaz staggered back.

Nikki shrieked.

Sam clapped a hand over her mouth, and her eyes widened in disbelief. She felt sweat on her skin and closed her eyes in an attempt to hold it together.

It didn't work.

"That's two," Tom said.

Sam opened her eyes and tried to find her breath. "What?"

"Connor and Gaz."

"No," she said. "*No*, Tom. You shot Connor, too?"

He swung the shotgun around, so it was facing her. "You sent me up there with him so I was out of the way. He knew what he was getting himself in for. You wanted him to keep me occupied while you went after Alice."

"Tom," Sam said, pleading. "You're not making any sense."

He stared at her with a steeliness that chilled her. "Where *is* Alice? What did you do with her?"

"I..."

"Didn't catch that, Sam. Say it again."

She couldn't take her eyes away from the shotgun, at the two black holes at the end of the double barrels. "Alice? As in your girlfriend?"

"Like you didn't know. What have you done with her?"

Sam couldn't possibly tell him the truth. "I don't know where she is."

"Try to mess around with me, Sam, and see where it gets you. You're wasting your breath." He swayed a little. "You think you're *so* clever, but you're not. I know what you've done. I *know*." He swayed again, then steadied himself. He turned in the direction of the house. "We're going inside, and I want you to think about how stupid it would be to bullshit me for a moment more than you already have."

"I'm not trying to bullshit you."

He didn't hear her. "Because I'm done, Sam. I'm finished with all of this."

"I know. You told me. Let's talk about that. We've got money here." She nodded down to Freeman. "We've got his money. How much do you want?"

"You don't get it. I'm not like you. I don't want any of that. I'm not just done with *this*—the business, with you—I'm done with *everything*. I can't do it anymore. My life sucks, and I don't want to do it anymore. It hurts too much. So we're going to go inside, and you're going to tell me what happened to Alice, and then I'm going to have a think about whether I take you with me when I top myself. I'm not going to lie—I probably will. Both of you." He glanced over at Nikki and then back at Sam. "We can all go out together." He jabbed the gun in the direction of the house. "You two go first. I'll be right behind."

Sam gestured to where Freeman was still gasping on the ground. "What about him?"

"Bring him," he said. "The two of you ought to be able to manage. I'll think about him while I think about what to do with you."

116

Francine followed the directions that she'd been given, coming off the Downton Road at Bodenham. She drove to Nunton and turned to the south, following the single-track road as it cut deeper into the countryside. It was dark, and as the village receded in the rear-view mirror, the only light was from the moon and stars overhead. She carried on, slowing for a sharp hairpin turn and then squinting into the glow of her lights as a man at the side of the road put out a hand to signal.

She pulled over and got out.

"Police?" he said.

"I'm DC Patterson," she said. "You reported a gunshot?"

"That's right," he said. "Twenty minutes ago. And then there was another one, just now."

"What are you doing out here at this time of night?"

"I'm from the Barn Owl Trust. We're counting nesting pairs."

"You're sure they were gunshots?"

"Definitely," he said.

"Farmer with a shotgun?"

"At this time of night? Doesn't seem likely. First one didn't sound like a shotgun, either. I shoot clay pigeons, and I know what a shotgun sounds like. It was something smaller. The second one, though—*that* was a shotgun."

"Where do you think they were coming from?"

He pointed to the south. "You've got Clearbury Ring to the east. Sounded like it was west of there, but it's hard to be sure."

Francine thanked him, got back in the car and drove on. She kept her speed down so she could look left and right, searching for anything that might give her an idea as to who had been firing a gun. Apart from the eyes of an animal—a fox, she thought—glittering out from the undergrowth, she saw nothing. Thick hawthorn prevented clear views into the fields, and, when there were spaces in the hedges, the fields beyond were thick with darkness.

Francine was about to radio in that she couldn't find anything when she approached a collection of buildings arranged around a yard. She thought she saw movement. She slowed as she approached, she could call it a night and go to Robbie, or she could just check that everything was as it should be here. She came to a full stop, decided that she might as well check, seeing as she was here, and turned off.

She stared ahead, checking out the buildings in the light from the headlamps. It was some sort of equestrian facility, with wooden stables arranged around a manège. There was a farmhouse behind it, and the dark shapes of agricultural buildings looming in the near distance. There were two cars in the yard: a large Land Rover Discovery and a saloon car that was too dark for her to identify.

Her phone rang. She fetched it out of her pocket and saw it was Robbie. She felt like an ungrateful shit as she tapped to accept it.

"Sorry," she said.

"Where are you?"

"I've just made a little diversion. There was a call about a possible gunshot. I was in the area, so I said I'd take it."

She could hear his disappointment. "Franny."

"I know. I'm sorry."

"It'll be poachers."

"Don't think so. The bloke who heard it said it was coming from near what looks like a livery yard on the road south of Nunton. I'm outside it now."

"I'll put the cocktails back in the fridge, then."

"You've got cocktails?"

"Cheap ones in cans. Probably taste disgusting, but it's the thought that counts."

"You're sweet," she said. "I won't be long."

Francine reached for the key to turn off the engine. She squinted through the windscreen at something she'd noticed on the ground. It was dark at the yard, but there was enough light to make out a body.

"Shit," she said.

"Franny?"

"Shit," she repeated. "I think I can see a body on the ground."

It was at the edge of the yard. She squinted at it: male, she thought, face down, one leg bent while the other was straight, one arm reaching out, the other pinned beneath the torso.

"Franny? Speak to me."

"It is," she said. "Male, I think. It's too dark to see anything from here." She opened the glovebox and took out her torch. "I'm going to go and have a look."

"No," he said. "Franny! Drive away and call for help."

It was too late for that; Francine had opened the door and was halfway outside, the phone in her left hand while she held her torch in her right. She swept the beam around the yard, casting the light against the wooden sides of a row of stables.

The body was next to the Land Rover and near to one of the stables.

Francine drew closer and aimed the torch at the body. There was a lot of blood, spreading out in a dark stain across the ground.

Francine had seen dead bodies before, her most vivid memories were from her time in Afghanistan, but those images had been bright, coloured by the burning desert sun, while this was given a sinister cast both by the darkness and the sense of vulnerability that rushed over her now that she knew there *had* been a gunshot, and it didn't have an innocent explanation.

"Franny? Please say you're not still there?"

She fell back on her training and crouched down so she could get closer to the body. "The victim is lying face down on the ground, with a significant amount of blood visible. Due to the position, most identifying features and the exact number of injuries are not visible. The scene appears recent." Providing the information was rote, and now that it was done, she couldn't hold the fear back. "Robbie?"

"Stop talking, Franny. Get away from there."

She stood. "I am. Call it in for me."

"You do it when you're in the car. I'm staying on the line until you tell me you're safe."

Francine thought she saw a shadow pass through the twin beams of her car's headlights. She shone her torch right and then left and, seeing nothing, backed away from the body.

"Franny?"

She stopped. She thought she heard something: the clink of two metal surfaces bumping up against each other.

She shone the torch around her again.

"Franny," Robbie said more urgently, "what's happening?"

"I thought I heard something."

The next sound was unmistakeable: a solid mechanical snap.

She recognised it at once.

The sound of a shotgun's break-action barrel snapping shut.

She swung around, and, this time, the torch picked out the figure of a man walking toward her, a shotgun held in both hands.

She backed away. "He's got a gun. Robbie—I need backup now."

The man aimed the shotgun at her and stepped forward, passing through the glow of the headlights. Half of his face was illuminated, enough for Francine to recognise him.

"It's Brennan. Call it in."

Tom kept coming. He levelled the gun so the muzzle was pointing at her. He was too close to miss. "Who are you?"

"DC Francine Patterson. Salisbury Police. You need to put that down."

Francine still had the phone in her left hand, pressed to her ear. Robbie swore. "Do whatever he says."

Tom was six feet away now. "Put the phone down."

"Okay. I'm putting it down."

Francine crouched down, putting the phone and the torch on the ground. She stood, making sure Tom could see her hands were empty.

The line was still open, and she could still hear Robbie's voice.

"Franny? Are you—"

The sentence was interrupted as Tom brought his boot down on the phone, smashing it underfoot.

117

Mack had raced to Hargreaves's address as quickly as she could, switching on the blue light hidden inside the grille of the car and hitting a hundred on the dual carriageway at Bodenham. She slowed to negotiate the narrow road that led to the yard; it was dark, and the last thing she wanted to do was to drive into a ditch because she took a corner too fast.

She saw the strobes of a patrol car when she was still half a mile away, the blue light pulsing through the trees bunched around the sharp right-left hairpin that was just before the yard. She turned the corner and saw that the road had been blocked, with one car parked across the road to the north of the gate and a second across the road to the south. She pulled over at the side of the road and jogged the last few yards.

Bob Carver was standing next to the car that Mack reached first.

"Boss," he said.

"What's happening?"

"We're still trying to work it out. Franny was out here to check out reports of a gunshot and ended up calling in a dead body."

"And found Tom Brennan."

"Yes, boss."

"Do we know where she is?"

He shook his head. Mack noticed he was pale.

"Who's here from CID?"

"Robbie Best," Carver said. "Just inside the yard."

"And how far out are the ARVs?"

"Coming from HQ. Roads are clear, and they'll be motoring. Five minutes, ten at the outside."

"Good. Send them through when they get here. Everyone else stays back behind the perimeter. If there is a shooter in there, I don't want him taking potshots at us."

"Yes, boss."

She passed through the open gate and saw Francine's car. The lights were still on, and the door was open. She crouched low and moved as fast as she could, hurrying up the track to the nearest building. Robbie Best was standing there, using the corner of the building—a stable—to shield him from the house.

"Robbie," she said, "what happened?"

He pointed to the house. "Franny's in there. It's Brennan. He jumped her." He pointed toward the property. "There's a body on the ground over there—you can just about see it if you look around the corner. Franny called it in—male, face down, couldn't make out much more than that. Brennan must've shot him."

Mack felt sick, but Robbie was panicking, and she needed to keep it together. "We'll figure it out. The ARVs are on their way. Should be here soon."

"They should already be here," he said. "She's in there with a psychopath who's already killed at least once, Mack. What do we do?"

Robbie was an experienced officer, but he was invested. He had confided in Mack about his relationship with Francine, and she'd seen how he'd fallen for her. His objectivity was out of the window, and she should have sent him away, but he wouldn't have accepted that, and Mack didn't have the heart to order him back to the city. She would have to keep a careful eye on him while he was here, though. They all had to stay on script.

It wasn't that long ago that Mack had been called to another remote rural property expecting to find a man with a gun inside. The house in Grovely Woods had not been quite as they had expected, but the procedure was still fresh in her mind. Local officers would secure the perimeter and assist with logistics until armed response officers arrived to take control. There had been no road to block in Grovely, but Carver had already done that here. Mack would be the incident commander and would have to establish a command post where she could oversee the operation and co-ordinate resources. She knew the most important question would be how to proceed: she'd try to contact Brennan and then decide whether it was better to wait him out, or, if Francine and anyone else in the property was at immediate risk, whether the armed officers should storm it.

That was going to be an incredibly difficult decision to take. Beckton would have to be consulted.

"Mack!"

She turned and saw Atticus at the cordon.

"Mack!"

"What's he doing here?" Robbie said.

"He said Brennan was coming here," Mack said.

"What?"

"He found him earlier. Don't ask me how—I haven't spoken to him properly."

"Mack!"

"Stay here," she told Robbie.

She ducked down and scurried back to the road. Carver was blocking Atticus's progress, his arms spread as Atticus tried to get around him.

"It's all right," Mack called out to Carver. "Let him through."

Carver stepped aside, and Atticus ran over.

"What's happening?" he said.

"Reports of a gunshot, and Franny came to check it out. Brennan is here—we think he's taken her into the house."

"Shit."

"I know—there's a body in the yard, too."

"Do you know who?"

"No. We can't get to it safely."

"Armed support?"

"On the way," she said. "Won't be long."

"Has anyone spoken to Brennan?"

"No. We haven't tried yet."

"*I* spoke to him," he said.

She pointed to the bruise on his head. "Went well, then."

"I'm fine."

"You should go and—"

"I'm not going to the hospital," he cut over her. "You need me."

She was cross with him, but knew he was probably right. "We'll talk about this later."

"I was thinking about Christopher Freeman. We never found a body. But I was never happy with the idea that he'd just got up and left. There was nothing to suggest he was depressed. His life was chaotic, but he'd just got engaged to his girlfriend."

"He had a problem with drugs. And he was mixed up with some unpleasant characters."

"I know—he was. And there's his father, too. I always thought foul play was a more likely explanation for what happened, but we couldn't get anything useful out of the Met, and his dad wouldn't talk to us. But Brennan said something to me tonight. He said he'd come here the night Freeman went missing. He said Freeman was attacking Hargreaves. There was a fight, and he hit Freeman with a poker. Killed him."

"Weren't they friends?"

"They all went to school together."

"We spoke to Hargreaves at the time, didn't we?"

"Completely routine. She said she didn't know anything."

"Why would they be fighting?"

"Because they were involved in some kind of scheme, and it went wrong. I think it was drugs. Hargreaves told Brennan that Freeman was ripping them off. He said Hargreaves found Christopher here, at the yard, trying to steal from them. Brennan said Christopher had a knife, and it got nasty. But I remember reading something in the file that makes me think that's not true, or at least there's *something* about it that wasn't the way Brennan was told. Do you remember the Met interviewed all of his friends in London?"

"Vaguely."

"Someone said something about why Christopher came down to Salisbury, but I can't remember what it was."

"So?"

"I want to go through the files."

"How does that help now?"

"Because everything that's happened revolves around Brennan. I think Sam has been manipulating him. I think he's been fed a lie—if we can show him that, maybe we can make him change how he feels about what happened, and maybe we can get him to give up." He looked at her, his eyes wide. "Come on, Mack. It's got to be worth a try."

"Get back to the station. I'll call ahead and have the files delivered."

"It needs to be fast."

"They'll be off-site in the RMU. I'll tell them it's important, but it's late. I'm not sure how long it'll take. I'll do my best."

Atticus turned and ran back to where he'd left his car on the road.

Mack went back to Robbie.

"What did he want?"

"He thinks he might have something helpful. He's gone to find it."

She heard the sound of Atticus starting the engine of his car, a crunch as he drove into the hedge at the side of the road and then a scraping as the thorns scratched the bodywork as he backed out. He ground the gears into first, and the tyres squealed as he sped away in the direction of the city.

Robbie muttered a curse. "That's all we've got?"

"That's what he said. You know what he's like—I learned a long time ago to let him follow his instinct. It's been right more often than not."

Robbie pointed at the house. "Franny is in there. Our plan to get her out is to let him go on a wild goose chase?"

"I trust him," she said. "I know I shouldn't, but I do. If there's something to find, he'll find it."

She heard the sound of engines and looked back to the road as two armed response units rolled up to the gate.

"And here's our Plan B," she said.

118

Tom had put them in the kitchen to start with, but, as they heard the sirens and then saw the blue lights of the two police patrol cars, he moved them to the sitting room on the other side of the house. He stayed at the door and told Sam to close the curtains. The other woman—Francine recognised her from the investigation into Tom's disappearance as Nikki Griffiths—was told to move the man with the gunshot wounds, and, when she'd struggled with the man's weight, Francine had helped too.

She took the opportunity to ask the man who he was, and he muttered through the pain that he was Charlie Freeman. That brought Francine up short: Alexander Freeman was well known and widely feared in the city, and Charlie was the youngest of his three sons. The family had interests in drugs and prostitution, and they'd been involved in the cannabis farm that had been discovered in Grovely Woods during the Mallender investigation. Robbie had told her about them and predicted how the key witnesses would develop amnesia when they realised they would be required to give evidence in court. He'd been right.

Francine looked around the room. The curtains were made of a thick material, and none of the moonlight from outside was able to filter through. The darkness was deeper toward the back of the room, but here, where Francine was, there was enough light from the kitchen for her to be able to see a sofa and two armchairs, and a low bench on the opposite wall that held framed photographs and a television.

"Put him down there," Tom said, pointing to floor next to the kitchen counters.

Francine looped her arms beneath Freeman's shoulders while Nikki picked up his feet. They half-carried and half-dragged him, blood splashing on the carpet, and hauled him so that his back was against one of the cupboards. Francine looked at her hands and saw that they were stained with blood, too; she wiped them on a tea towel draped over the handle of the Aga.

"He needs help," she said to Tom. "He'll die if he doesn't see a doctor."

"Don't care." Tom shrugged. "Not my problem."

He was slurring his words a little, and there were moments when it looked as if he had to work on maintaining his balance. She could smell the alcohol coming off him and realised that he was drunk. That was either good or bad, depending upon your perspective: it might mean his guard would drop, with an opportunity for her to take the shotgun from him; or it might mean he was beyond the point where he would listen to reason.

"Think, Tom," she said. "You shot him."

"No," he said. "I didn't. It was Gaz."

"Gary O'Reilly?"

"That's right."

"The body outside?"

He nodded.

"He wasn't my first—he's not even my first *tonight*—and he won't be my last."

"What does that mean?"

"He shot another of our friends," Sam said. "Connor Smith."

"Shut up, Sam." Tom turned and looked at Francine more closely. "Who'd you say you were?"

"DC Francine Patterson."

"Why were you here?"

"We had reports of a gunshot. *Two* gunshots."

Francine heard a whimper from the other side of the room. She glanced over; Freeman was reaching out a hand.

"Tom," Francine said, "I'm serious. He needs to go to hospital."

Tom looked at Freeman, then back to Francine. "He'll have to wait."

"He'll die."

"You said that, and I still don't care. Ask him what he was here for."

"He's in no condition to tell me that. You tell me—why was he here?"

"To pick up a big shipment of cocaine. We've been bringing it into the country for his dad for the last eighteen months. So I don't have any sympathy for him. He can wait until I've done what I came to do. If he dies, he dies."

"And what *do* you want to do?"

He pointed at Sam. "She's going to tell me where my girlfriend is."

"I told you," Sam protested. "I don't know."

"Liar."

"Who's your girlfriend?" Francine asked. "Alice?"

"That's right—Alice." Tom laughed. "Listen to me. 'Girlfriend.' You want to know the funniest bit of all of this? She dumped me. Before all of this happened, she said we were done. I'm here because I care about a woman who doesn't even want to be with me."

Francine sensed an opening; if she could get him talking, maybe she could distract him. "What happened?"

Tom laughed again. "This is really funny, Sam—right? I told Alice I was going to tell the police and, look—the police are here." The words tripped over one another. "I want to make a confession, Detective Constable. I killed someone. Murdered them. It was here, actually." He pointed to a spot near the big open fireplace. "Right *there*. I came inside, and Christopher was on top of Sam with his hands around her throat. Strangling her. He would've killed her if I hadn't stopped him." He pointed again to a collection of utensils meant to be used with the fire. "See that big old iron poker? I hit him with it. *Whack*. Hard, as hard as I could, right on the back of the head. Killed him stone dead. Didn't mean to, but you're police—that still makes me a murderer, doesn't it?"

Francine decided not to agree with his assessment. "Not necessarily. Like you say—you didn't mean to do it."

"It was self-defence," Sam said. "Tell him it could've been self-defence."

"It *could've* been," Francine said, then turned back to Tom. "You didn't mean it; he was trying to kill your friend… sounds like self-defence to me."

"See?" Sam said. "See? I told you."

"Whatever. Doesn't make a blind bit of difference now, does it? I've got it in me. Fired a rocket into a car full of bad guys in Afghanistan. Gave me nightmares, but I did it. They were my first. Killed Christopher, then I shot Connor and Gaz tonight, and I didn't think twice about it. I'm going to shoot you, too, Sam—and then I'm going to shoot myself."

"That doesn't have to happen," Francine said.

He shrugged. "It does. And I'm sorry. You're just in the wrong place at the wrong time. But I don't have any reason to hurt you—stay out of my way and don't get involved and you can walk out when I'm done."

119

Atticus stamped on the accelerator on the way back into the city, pushing the car as fast as he had ever driven it before. He followed the ring road and came off at Bourne Hill, parking on the gravelled area in front of the registry office. He sprinted to the station, hammering impatiently on the door and waiting for the somnolent night porter to let him in. He went through the rigmarole of signing in and then waited for Nigel Archer to come down and collect him.

Archer was the sergeant on night duty and was evidently concerned about what was happening in the countryside. "What's going on?"

"Franny's inside a house with Brennan," Atticus said. "Brennan's shot at least two people tonight—might be more."

"Mack said you might need help."

"I need to review the file on a misper from a couple of years ago."

"Christopher Freeman—she told me. I've got it ready for you upstairs."

The two of them climbed to the first floor, and Atticus followed Archer to the workspace where he'd arranged access into the Records Management System.

Archer gestured to the screen. "Remember how to get around?"

He said he did, and Archer said he'd leave him to it, taking a seat at the workstation opposite. Atticus knew Archer would stay close to make sure he didn't stray beyond the material that Mack had authorised him to read.

The investigation was all digitised, meaning that the information was easily accessible. Atticus retrieved the related files, including incident reports, evidence logs, and interview transcripts.

The case became more familiar as he started to read. Freeman had moved from Salisbury to London, and the Metropolitan Police had been responsible for the investigation into his disappearance. Salisbury had provided local assistance given he had told his girlfriend he was coming to the city and on account of the connections that he still had here. Mike Lewis had been the junior officer deputed to help.

Atticus had been intrigued enough at the time by the unexplained disappearance to have reviewed all of the material on his own account, and there was something from that quick review that had lodged in his brain. He was about as sure as he could be that it was in a witness statement, but he couldn't remember exactly whose statement it had been.

He was going to have to work through all of them.

120

Mack noticed the lights of two approaching police vans and hurried over to the road to meet them. The vans stopped, and the officers got out. Sergeant Neil Blyford got out first, and the other men in his team—seven in total—hurried out after him. Each man headed to the back of the vehicles to retrieve their weapons from the gun safes.

Blyford approached Mack and shook her hand. "DCI Jones."

"We must stop meeting like this," she said.

Blyford had come out to Grovely Farmhouse when it was thought that Ralph Mallender's brother was still inside with a weapon. Mack had a lot of respect for him. The life of an armed response officer wasn't an easy one, with finely balanced decisions carrying serious professional repercussions for mistakes. She didn't envy him.

"What have we got?" Blyford asked. "Possible shooter inside?"

"Yes," Mack said, "and possibly with one of my officers."

Mack stepped aside as the officers took up their positions. Each man carried a sub-machine gun, together with a pistol or Taser, and they wore ballistic vests and helmets. One officer had a ballistic shield, and another moved a battering ram into a safe position.

"What have you got on the shooter?"

"Ex-military," Mack said.

"Great. Seen action?"

"Yes. We think he might be responsible for his girlfriend going missing, and there's a body in the yard. We haven't been close enough to take a look at it yet, but I think we can assume he's been shot."

"Not auspicious," Blyford said.

"How do you want to play it?"

"Like it was in the woods," Blyford said. "Keep your officers where they are until we confirm we're in position. Tell them to fall back to the road after that, and under no circumstances must they advance without my *direct* orders."

"What are you going to do?"

"Four men outside for containment. I'll take the other three and be ready to go in. Aside from the shooter and your officer, how many inside?"

"I don't know," she said. "We're playing catch-up."

Mack stepped away so Blyford could brief his men. She found a spot behind the trees at the side of the road where she could look into the yard and still see the house. The curtains had all been drawn, and it was impossible to see inside. She was annoyed at herself: she had been meaning to send Francine home earlier and had forgotten. She should never have been in the area to take the call in the first place. She reached for her phone and was about to call Atticus when she decided not to. He wouldn't appreciate his work being interrupted, and there was a very good chance that he was her best hope of getting through this without any more blood being spilled.

121

Tom went to the curtains and opened them just enough so he could look outside. "Good," he said. "The police are here."

He let the curtains fall back into place and went over to the kitchen. He opened the cupboards until he found the one Sam used to store her alcohol, taking down a bottle of vodka.

Francine watched as he unscrewed the bottle and took a long swig. "You sure that's a good idea?"

"I tried being sober," he observed. "Didn't really get on with it. And there's no point worrying about the state of my liver now, is there?"

He chuckled as he walked unsteadily back into the room, slumping into an armchair and raising the bottle in a mock toast. He knocked back another swig, then stood the bottle on the table next to him.

Francine scrambled for a way to keep Tom talking. "Let's talk about Alice. You think she's here?"

"She's here. I don't know *where*, but *she* does." He pointed at Sam. "Don't you, Sam?"

Sam turned her head away.

Tom raised the shotgun and fired one barrel into the ceiling. The sudden explosion was deafening, and birdshot tore through the plaster, sending a cascade of white chunks and powder down to the floor. Francine's heart stopped, and Sam fought to stifle a sob.

"Last chance, Sam. Where is she?"

Sam held her hands up, as if they would protect her were Tom to fire the second barrel at her. "All right, all right. She was here. She was. Nikki and Gaz were supposed to give her a scare, find out what you'd told her and stop her from talking about it, but it went wrong." She jabbed her finger at Nikki. "They messed up, just like they *always* mess up."

"It was an accident," Nikki said. "She fell and hit her head."

Sam waved that away. "They thought she was dead, so they brought her here. She wasn't dead, though. We put her in the cellar until we could work out what we were going to do."

Tom took another mouthful from the bottle. "So go and get her."

"I can't," she said.

"Why not?"

"Because she's dead now, Tom. I'm sorry. She must've done something to her head when she fell—some sort of haemorrhage. She was dazed the first day, and I thought it was a concussion, but then it got worse. She was lethargic and confused the next day, and then she started to be sick. She was disoriented; then she couldn't stay awake. I was bringing her food and drink today, and I couldn't get her to wake up. I checked and…" The sentence drifted away. "I didn't know what to do."

"You 'didn't know'?" Nikki said. "You could've got help for her."

Sam shot up out of the armchair. "Don't you *dare* blame me!" She stabbed out an angry finger. "What happened to her is *your fault*."

"But she's right, Sam," Tom said. "You didn't get help. You would've been found out if you did, so you did nothing. You let her die."

"I'm sorry, Tom. I mean it."

"You're sorry because I've got this," Tom said, hefting the shotgun. "Where is she now?"

Sam shook her head and looked away.

His jaw tightened. "Was it like Christopher?"

Sam couldn't hold his eye.

Francine could feel the tension in the room. "What does that mean? What happened to Christopher?"

"Tell her, Sam."

Sam nodded. "I'm sorry."

Francine knew she ought to keep quiet, but she needed to know. "What happened to Christopher?"

"The pigs," Tom muttered. "She has pigs in the back field."

Francine was about to ask how pigs were relevant when she joined the dots. Her stomach dropped. "Oh, God."

Tom turned to Nikki. "Is what she said true, then? You and Gaz went to scare her, and you hurt her instead?"

"She tripped," Nikki said.

"Just like that?"

"Gaz was trying to frighten her, but she wasn't scared. She went for him. She caught her foot on something on the path and went over. She banged her head on a rock. It was an accident."

"An accident? You can't be serious."

"Want to know the truth, Tom? It's as much your fault as ours."

Tom turned on her. "Say that again."

Francine could see where things were headed. "No," she said. "Stop."

Nikki didn't seem to have noticed the way his finger was tightening around the trigger. "I'm sorry, Tom, but it's true. If you hadn't told her what happened with Christopher, then none of this would've happened."

"Shut up, Nikki."

It was inexplicable. Nikki seemed to have been caught up in her own indignation at what was happening, so much so that she was blinding herself to the threat right in front of her. "If you'd done what we told you to do, if you'd just done as you were asked and kept everything that happened between us, like it should always have been kept, then she'd still be here, still making her stupid videos, still—"

The shotgun boomed again, the report bouncing back at them from the walls of the room.

Tom hadn't aimed at the ceiling this time.

He'd fired into Nikki's chest.

Francine saw her chance.

The shotgun had two barrels.

Two cartridges.

The warning shot.

This shot.

The gun had to be empty.

She threw herself at Tom.

122

An ambulance had just arrived when Mack heard the first shot. Her heart skipped a beat; the muffled report was easily audible even from this far away from the house. She started back to where Blyford was waiting. The plan had been for the team to hold their position outside the house, but that might not be sustainable any longer.

A second shot rang out, this one followed by hurried voices over the radio, too garbled for her to make out clearly. Mack broke into a run.

Blyford was on the radio when she arrived, his face tight with concentration as he tried to work out how the situation had changed.

He looked up as she approached, his expression grave. "All units, hold your positions," he said into the radio. "No one moves until we get a full assessment of the situation."

He was tense. The shots had caught them all off guard.

"Bravo team, what's your status?"

There was a brief silence, filled only with the faint hiss and crackle of static, before a reply came through. "Bravo team, holding position. No visual on threats. Shots came from inside the house, unsure of origin. Curtains are still drawn."

Mack exchanged a look with Blyford. The plan had been to contain and assess and not to engage unless absolutely necessary.

"Hold position," Blyford said. "We don't move until we know exactly what we're dealing with. No one goes in until I give the order."

He clipped the radio back on his vest and turned to Mack. "I'm uncomfortable," he said. "We don't know anything."

"We need to make contact with Brennan," Mack said.

"Do we have a phone number?"

"We tried. It's straight to voicemail."

"We might have to try a megaphone," he said, sucking his teeth.

"Do we have a negotiator?"

"Should be here in fifteen minutes. What about paramedics?"

"Just arrived," Mack said, pointing back to the road.

"Keep them on standby, but they don't move until the scene is secure."

123

Atticus had almost finished his review and had found nothing of use. He was beginning to doubt his recollection and wondered whether he might have confused it with another investigation. He didn't *think* so, but, after spending an hour and finding nothing, it was difficult to escape the conclusion that he was wrong.

The witness statements were arranged alphabetically, and unable to remember anything from the names of the witnesses that might have enabled him to skip straight to the most potentially relevant, he'd started at the beginning and worked through them all.

The investigating officer had interviewed everyone who might have been able to offer information about where Freeman could have gone the night he disappeared. She had spoken to his drinking friends from the Camden scene, the manager of the bar that employed him on an ad hoc basis, and, when she visited Salisbury, his parents and old friends. None of the people to whom she spoke was able to provide anything that might explain where he had gone.

The penultimate statement was from Britt Wikström. The name wasn't familiar to Atticus, but, as he started to scroll down through the statement, he saw she was Freeman's on-off girlfriend in London. He sat up a little straighter, scrolled back up to the start and read it more carefully.

It wasn't a particularly weighty statement. Wikström was a Swedish architecture student who'd lived in Camden, where she had become friends with Freeman after meeting him at a lock-in at the pub where he worked and then going back to a house party with him. She said the two of them had become lovers, although it was obviously not a particularly important relationship for either party.

Freeman had told her he was going to Salisbury for a meeting on the day before he disappeared. She'd tried to contact him afterwards, but on receiving no reply, had assumed he'd ghosted her and put him out of her mind.

There was nothing on the face of it that should have given Atticus pause, but he couldn't shake the feeling that there was something in what she'd said in her interview that hadn't been recorded in the statement. Atticus had spoken to the interviewing officer when she came to Salisbury, and he thought it was possible she'd said something to him in passing that hadn't made it into the final draft.

He didn't know and wouldn't be able to remember; he would have to speak to Wikström.

He found her number in the file and called it.

She picked up after six rings.

Her voice was bleary. "Who is this?"

"Atticus Priest," he said.

"Atticus *what*?"

"Priest. I'm a detective constable with Salisbury Police."

She had no reason to detect the lie and didn't react to it. "Not again. Do you know what time it is?"

"Sorry to disturb you."

"You woke me up. I've got work in"—she paused, probably checking the time—"two hours."

"Very sorry," he repeated. "I would've waited until the morning, but it's very important."

"About Christopher?"

"Yes," he said.

"I spoke to the police about him. I answered all their questions."

"You did."

"I haven't heard from him since then, if that's what you want to know."

"I was involved in the investigation into his disappearance," Atticus said. "I read the transcript of your interview at the time, and things have happened since that have given me a couple of questions. Some things I just wanted to clarify with you."

"And you couldn't have waited until morning?"

"Some things are happening in Salisbury at the moment that have made it very urgent."

"Go on, then. I'm awake now. Ask me."

Atticus clicked back through the witness statement until he was at the second page. "You were asked if Christopher told you why he was going to Salisbury on the weekend he disappeared. Do you remember?"

"Yes," she said.

"And you said he was going on business. What did he tell you about that?"

"I already said," she protested.

"Can we just go through it again?"

"He said he'd been offered a way to get some money. He said it was an 'opportunity.'"

"Did he say what that was?"

"No."

"He was involved in the drug business, wasn't he? Did he ever mention any of that to you?"

The pause before she answered was drawn out enough for Atticus to know she was about to deny it, and that she would be lying. "He didn't. I had no idea."

"Don't worry—you wouldn't be in trouble if he had told you."

"Christopher was into some dodgy shit," she said, edging closer to the truth, "but I never knew the details. He didn't tell me, and I didn't ask. And I was different then. My life was in a mess, and I was hanging out with some people I wouldn't hang out with now."

"Was he one of them?"

"Yes."

"Can I just clarify something else? You said he was coming to Salisbury because he had a way to make money. That's right, isn't it?"

"Yes."

"Was it his choice to go?"

"What do you mean?"

"I mean was he coming to Salisbury on his own account? Or had someone else asked him to come?"

"Oh," she said. "I remember that. He was asked. He got a call the night he drove down."

"You're sure about that?"

"Positive. I was with him when he got the call. He said it was an old friend from home."

"Did he say who it was?"

"No."

"Do you have any idea?"

"No. It was a woman, though. I could hear her voice when she called. I gave him a hard time about it—you know, he's speaking to some woman on the phone, and he won't tell me who she is or what it's about. I asked him if he was cheating on me, and that's when he said it was business and he had the chance to make some money. He went down the same night, and that was it—I never saw him again."

"Thank you," he said.

"Do you know where he is?"

"I'm afraid not."

"If you do see him, you give him a message from me—tell him not to get any ideas about coming back here again. I'm seeing someone else now. We've got a baby on the way, and my life is different. I'm not like I used to be—I'm not interested in any of the shit we used to get up to. Those days are gone now."

"I'll be sure to tell him," Atticus said. "Thank you again. I'm sorry for waking you up. You've been very helpful."

Atticus ended the call and went back to the screen. He'd forgotten about the phone call, but now she'd reminded him: he recalled seeing a call sheet provided by Freeman's mobile provider. He quickly scrolled through the index until he found it, opening it and then going through it line by line. There was a single inbound number listed on the evening that Freeman went away.

Atticus printed out the screen and grabbed the paper from the printer.

Archer looked up. "Anything?"

He started for the door. "Maybe," he said.

"What?"

"Can't talk now," he called back over his shoulder as he started to jog. "Need to get back to the house."

124

Francine never stood much chance against Tom. He was six inches taller than her and several stones heavier, and, as Francine tried to wrestle the gun away from him, he swept her away with a backhanded slap. His knuckles struck her on the cheek with enough force to dim her vision, and the impact forced her to bite down on her tongue so hard that her mouth was quickly full of the coppery taste of blood. Francine fell to the floor, and by the time the dizziness had abated enough for her to get up, ready to go at Tom again, he'd reloaded the shotgun and had backed away so that he was able to cover Francine and Sam.

"Don't do that again," he said.

She dipped her head and opened her mouth so the blood ran out. "You shot her."

"She had it coming."

"Put the gun down, Tom. *Please*. This doesn't need to get any worse."

"I meant what I said. I don't want to hurt you. You can walk out of here when I'm done. I don't have anything against you."

"No one else has to die, Tom. Just stop. Give me the gun, and I promise you'll be treated fairly."

"Walk out of here without getting shot, you mean?"

"I can stop that from happening."

"Don't you *get* it? I want it to happen. I want them to take me out of here in a box."

Sam put her hands together in entreaty. "Please, Tom. Please."

Tom turned the shotgun on her. "You're wasting your breath." He took one hand off the shotgun, reached around with his other hand to his back pocket and pulled out a bunch of zip ties. He tossed them onto the floor in front of Francine. "Do her wrists."

Sam shook her head. "You don't need to—"

"Do it." Tom spoke over her, turning the shotgun on Francine.

"No problem," Francine said. "I'll do it." She picked up the zip ties and went over to Sam. "Just do as he says. Give me your hands."

Sam did as Francine asked, raising her hands in front of her. Francine looped one tie around Sam's left wrist and tightened it. Francine threaded a second tie through the loop of the first, creating a figure-of-eight. Sam put her right wrist in the loop of the second tie, and Francine tightened it.

"Now you," Tom said.

Francine arranged two ties in the same fashion, tightening the second one with her teeth. She held her hands up so Tom could see she hadn't left enough slack to slide her hands out again.

"Good." He pointed to the sofa. "Both of you—go and sit over there."

"What now, Tom?"

"You're going to sit there," he said, holding up the bottle. "I'm going to finish this, and then Samantha and I are going to have a little chat."

125

Mack heard the sound of an engine and turned to see the glow of headlamps through the trees on the side of the road. The car was racing, the sound of the engine changing pitch frequently as the driver changed up and down through the gears. The lights came around the final hairpin on the road from Nunton, and the car picked up speed, slowing just in time to come to a stop before the roadblock. Mack recognised Atticus and made her way down to the road in time to intercept him before he reached Carver.

"That was scary," he said. "I don't think I've ever driven so quickly on a road like that."

"Have you got anything?"

He nodded but didn't answer the question. He set off toward the entrance to the yard, and Mack hurried along beside him. "Has anything happened?"

"Two shots fired."

"Shit. Have you got anything from inside?"

"Nothing. The curtains are closed. We haven't seen anything."

"Any communication at all?"

"No. We tried his phone, but it's going to voicemail. We've called for a negotiator, but he's not here yet."

"That won't matter," Atticus said. "Brennan won't listen to a negotiator, whatever they say. You know what it'll be like. Platitudes. He's beyond that now."

They reached the open gate, and Mack reached for his elbow to stop him. "You didn't answer my question, Atticus. Did you get anything in the file?"

"I did." He turned to her, and she saw his eyes were burning with excitement. "Sam Hargreaves lied to Brennan. He's beaten himself up for what he did to Christopher Freeman, but he doesn't know what really happened. It wasn't the way she told him. She's devious, Mack. She's up to her *neck* in it."

"How? How's she lied?"

Atticus didn't answer and glanced over her shoulder into the yard. "Who's in charge?"

"Blyford," she said. "Atticus—*how* did she lie?"

"I'll explain," he said. He looked down at her, his eyes still shining. "Do you trust me?"

She felt a twist of anxiety. "Depends on the context."

"I need you to trust me now. Franny is in trouble. Brennan was drunk when I saw him, and I don't think he feels like he has anything to lose. We can't leave her in there with him for a moment longer than is necessary."

"I *know* that, Atticus. What do you think we're trying to do?"

"You're just marking time. A negotiator won't be able to fix this, and if Blyford and his boys go in, then it's a toss-up who comes out alive. But *I* can fix this. I can get her out."

"No," she said, but he'd already stepped to the side.

She grabbed for him, but he'd anticipated it and took a wider berth to put himself out of reach.

He set off at a run.

"Atticus!"

Blyford's attention was facing forward, onto the house, and, by the time he heard the sound of Atticus's footsteps and turned to see who it was, he was past him and halfway to the front door.

Mack ran after him.

"Stop!"

Blyford put up an arm to block her way.

"What does he think he's *doing*?"

"He says he's found something out that might make a difference, and he doesn't think it'll wait."

Atticus reached the front door and hammered his fist against it. "Tom," he said, "let me in."

Blyford reached for his radio. "Want me to put a round into his leg?"

Mack turned to see if he was joking; his stern expression suggested he was not. "No," she said. "Of *course* not. He's made his decision."

Blyford pressed the toggle on his radio and instructed his officers to hold position and not to fire.

"Tom!" Atticus banged his fist on the door again. "It's Atticus Priest."

"You'll deal with him afterwards, Mack?"

"I will," she said.

"Tom!" Atticus hammered on the door for a third time. "I've got something you *really* need to hear."

The door opened, just a crack.

Blyford pressed the toggle. "Can anyone see him?"

"Negative," came the reply. "Too dark."

Atticus pushed the door the rest of the way and went inside.

126

Tom backed up, the shotgun aimed at Atticus. "Shut the door."

Atticus stepped over the threshold and, his hands still held out in front of him, closed the door with his heel. He looked up and down the hall. There was a suitcase against the wall that hadn't been there before.

"You again?" Tom said.

"I'm persistent."

"What do you want?"

"To help you."

"You're wasting your time."

"I don't think so. There are some things I need to tell you. Things you need to know."

"Whatever," Tom said. "You're here now."

Tom flicked the muzzle of the shotgun, indicating that Atticus should step around him and go inside.

Atticus looked around, taking everything in. Francine Patterson and Samantha Hargreaves were sitting next to each other on the settee. They were both restrained, and Francine had a bruise on the side of her head. A man Atticus didn't recognise was slumped against the kitchen counter, he was pale, his white shirt was soaked in blood, and blood was pooling around him on the tiled floor. The body of a woman was sprawled out across the tiled floor. Her front was smothered with blood, and she wasn't moving.

"Franny," Atticus said, "are you okay?"

"I'm fine," she said.

"What happened to your head?"

"She tried to take my gun," Tom said.

Atticus pointed to the woman on the floor. "Who's that?"

"Nikki Griffiths," Francine said. "Tom shot her."

Tom went over to the kitchen counter, grabbed the neck of a bottle of vodka and took a slug from it. The blood in the room didn't seem to have an effect on him; the others did not share his insouciance.

"What are you doing here?" Francine said.

"I've come to help." Atticus pointed at the man on the floor. "Who's that?"

"Charlie Freeman."

"The son of Alexander Freeman?"

"And the brother of Christopher Freeman," she said.

The information slotted neatly into the picture Atticus had built. "I think I'm starting to see what's happened here."

"Want to fill me in?"

"I'll do my best." Atticus pointed at Freeman. "He's going to die, Tom."

"I told her—I don't care. You can get help for him once I'm done with Sam."

"Where's Alice?"

Francine gave a little shake of her head, but it was too late. Tom's face darkened. He extended the shotgun so it was inches from Sam's face. "She killed her."

"I'm sorry, Tom," Sam said.

Tom took a half step back, but kept the shotgun aimed at her.

"Atticus," Francine said, "what's going on?"

Atticus had thought about how he would go about explaining, knowing that it was delicate, and that he risked inflaming the situation if he got it wrong. "I thought about what you told me earlier," he said to Tom. "About what happened to Christopher. I went back and looked at the investigation to find him after he went missing, and there are some things you need to know."

"I know what happened," he said. "I was there."

"You don't know everything," he said. "I think you've been tricked."

"How?"

Atticus pointed down at his pocket. "I just want to try something. I'm going to take out a piece of paper. Is that all right?"

Tom nodded, and, with one eye on the shotgun, Atticus slowly reached into his trouser pocket and fished out the printout.

"Can I have my phone, please?"

Tom reached into his pocket, took out Atticus's phone and flipped it over to him. Atticus dialled the number that had called Christopher Freeman on the night of his disappearance. He knew it was a long shot, and, as he waited for it to connect—or not—he closed his eyes to listen.

He turned to the phones charging on the counter that he had noticed when he'd visited with Mack earlier. One of them lit up and started to ring. Atticus went over to the counter and picked up the cheap Samsung handset.

Atticus looked over at Sam and tutted. "Sloppy."

Tom looked over at it. "What does that mean?"

"Someone called Christopher on the night he went missing. The police tried to trace the call, but they didn't get anywhere. They decided the call must've been from a pre-paid phone."

"So?"

"Criminals use them," Francine said. "Burner phones. They're anonymous."

"And usually binned after use," Atticus added. "Samantha took her eye off the ball for a moment."

"So?" she said. "I've got another phone."

"You've got *lots* of phones," Atticus said, pointing at the counter.

"So what? It doesn't prove anything."

Atticus held up the Samsung. "But you called Christopher with this?"

"I called him all the time."

"All from the phone listed in your name. The police would be interested to know why, on the night he disappeared, you decided to use a phone you must've known would have been impossible to trace back to you."

Tom swivelled back to Sam, his finger curling a little more tightly around the trigger. "Sam? Is that true?"

She knew how much danger she was in; how close Tom was to tightening his finger just a little more.

"Okay," she said, her eyes darting between Tom's face and the barrel of the shotgun. "Fine. He's right. It wasn't how I said it was."

"What happened?"

"Christopher came to steal from us," she said. "He was going to take the money for himself."

"No," Atticus said. "That doesn't make sense. You would've told the others that if it were true. You would've been able to deal with it together."

"No more lies," Tom snapped. "Answer him."

She glared at Atticus. "He was trying to rip *me* off."

"You and Christopher had an arrangement outside the arrangement you both had with the others," Atticus suggested. "Right? Maybe the two of you were skimming off the top?" She looked away, biting her lip, and Atticus could see he was on the right track. "And maybe Christopher decided he wanted to renegotiate the arrangement. He told his girlfriend in London he was working on a plan to make more money. Maybe that was it—force you to take less so he could have more. Or take everything for himself."

Tom glared at her. "Sam?"

"He was trying to rinse me. He was always untrustworthy, even when we were at school. You know that's true, Tom. Remember what he was like with you."

She looked over at Tom with raised eyebrows, as if expecting him to back her up.

He didn't. "What happened?"

"It went back to when we got started. The first run we made. He persuaded me we could take off the top and split it, and no one would notice. We did it for the first three months that way, and he was right—I'd tell everyone we were making a hundred every month, but it was a hundred and fifty." She nodded at Freeman. "I was the only one who dealt with his dad, and none of you thought to check the numbers stacked up."

"Because we trusted you."

She shrugged. "Not my fault."

"What happened with Christopher?" Atticus said. "He wanted more?"

"Not just more—*all* of it. He said the deal would never have happened without him, and he deserved more of the money because of it. I told him it wasn't fair, but he wouldn't listen. He said he'd go to his dad and tell him it'd make more sense for them to muscle in and take over the operation and that, if that happened, there'd be no need for us, and he'd have us all shot. I believed him."

"And so you came up with a way out."

She pointed to the phone. "I called him. I said I'd been thinking about it, we needed to talk, and it had to be face to face. I gave him a time when I knew I wouldn't be disturbed, and he drove down."

"And then?" Tom said.

"I poisoned him."

Atticus immediately thought of what she'd told him when he had visited the yard for the first time and the chemicals that he'd seen outside the barn. "The sodium nitrite."

"Yes."

Francine looked confused. "What?"

"She prepares her own feed for the horses," Atticus said. "Sodium nitrite is used to preserve silage." He looked back to Sam. "What did you do? Put it in his drink?"

"He liked gin," she said. "I bought a nice bottle and said we should have a glass while we talked. It doesn't taste of anything, and you don't need to use much. But he started to feel dizzy after twenty minutes and realised what I'd done. He went for me."

Atticus turned to Tom. "And that's when Tom turned up?"

"By chance," she said. "No one else was supposed to be here. I was going to get rid of him, and no one would've known."

"He was on top of you," Tom said. "He had his hands around your throat."

"And he would've killed me," she said.

"But it wasn't like you said. The whole thing—*everything*—was a lie. You lied to me." He looked desolate.

"What else could I have done?" Sam said. "He was dead either way. It didn't make any difference."

"'It didn't make any difference'? Are you serious? I've been torturing myself ever since it happened. You let me suffer."

She didn't answer.

Tom turned to Atticus. "Are you saying he would've died anyway?"

"Probably," Atticus said. "Sodium nitrite is nasty. It creates methemoglobin—stops the blood from carrying oxygen. You get headaches and dizziness, then tachycardia, then fainting, then coma and then death. You can treat it if you get it early enough, but if he was already showing symptoms by the time you arrived..." He shrugged. "He might only have had an hour or two left."

"Shit," Tom muttered to himself.

"See," Atticus said. "All the guilt you've been dealing with—none of it was your fault."

That was Atticus's play. He needed Tom to see that it wasn't all his fault. He knew it was a reach, that Tom was drunk and angry and already committed, but it was all he had.

"I still killed him," Tom said.

"Because you thought he was going to kill Sam—your friend. Thing is, she's not your friend. She might have been, once, but not anymore."

"You don't know what you're talking about," Sam muttered. "I'd never turn on my friends."

"Really? Then you'd better explain what the suitcase in the hall is all about."

Tom looked back at the case.

"She's leaving, Tom," Atticus said. "I'm guessing Freeman was here for the last load of drugs?" Sam didn't answer. "I think she might have thought she could find a way through what you might or might not have said to Alice—that was why she had your friend take you up into the field, to get you out of the way while they tried to scare her—but she lost control of things. She was going to run. What'll we find if we open the case, Samantha? Money? Tickets to somewhere warm where you couldn't be brought back to face justice for what you've done?"

She still didn't answer.

Tom looked as if he was about to cry. "Why, Sam?"

She looked up at him contemptuously. "Why what?"

"Why didn't you tell the truth about Christopher?"

"Because she would've had to tell you and the others that they'd been stealing from you," Atticus said gently. "And by involving you—all of you—she could make sure you all had skin in the game. It was a proper conspiracy then. You were all involved in his death and then covering it up. You'd all be bound together. You'd all be guilty of conspiring in his murder."

"But I couldn't deal with it like the others," he said. "I couldn't live with it."

Francine took over. "That's to your credit. You thought you were stopping him from hurting her. You didn't know anything about what was really happening."

Atticus looked at Tom's face and didn't think they were getting through to him.

"Doesn't matter," he said. "*I* killed him. *I* killed Connor, and *I* killed Nikki and Gaz. My life's over." He turned back to Sam and raised the shotgun again. "But I'm going to take her with me."

Francine stepped between him and Sam. "No, Tom."

"Get out of the way."

"You don't need to do this."

"I do. Move."

127

Atticus's heart was in his mouth. "She's right, Tom. Sam *will* be punished. She'll be charged with murder, and she'll go away for the rest of her life."

Atticus's attention was on Tom, with Francine still standing between him and Sam, so he—and everyone else—didn't notice Freeman until it was too late. He was off to the side, and, the last time Atticus checked, he had been slumped up against the kitchen unit, sitting in a spreading pool of blood. He'd somehow managed to push himself up to a crouch, and with his left hand pressed against the wound in his chest, he reached up with his right until his fingers clasped around the handle of one of the knives in the knife block. Atticus only saw him as he pushed up to his feet, the knife clenched in his fist.

"No!"

Tom and Francine and Sam turned to Atticus, saw what he was looking at, and turned in the same direction.

But too late.

Freeman managed one step, then another, and then a final stumble that brought him close to Sam. He raised the knife as she brought up her arms to protect her head and neck; he drove it down, plunging the point between her ribs. The effort was as much as he could manage, and he collapsed, face down, letting go of the knife with the handle sticking out of Sam's torso.

128

Sam looked as if she was going to be sick.

Francine reached for the knife, her hand hovering over it.

"Leave it," Atticus said.

"She's bleeding."

"She'll bleed even more if you take it out."

Freeman was gasping for breath on the floor.

"Tom," Atticus said, "we've got to get them both outside. They'll die if they don't get help."

Tom backed away. The expression on his face was odd.

"Tom," Atticus said, "did you hear me?"

Tom stepped back again, continuing into the hallway.

Francine saw him, too. "What's he doing?"

Atticus took a step.

Tom jabbed the shotgun in his direction. "Stay."

Atticus froze. "Easy."

"Will you do something for me?" Tom said.

"Put the gun down, and we can talk about it."

Tom was at the door now. He took his left hand from the shotgun and reached around behind him for the door handle. "Tell my parents I'm sorry."

He turned the handle and opened the door.

Atticus knew what he was doing. "No! Tom—don't!"

Tom put both hands on the shotgun, spun around and, with the muzzle pointing out in the direction of the police, stepped out into the yard.

129

The air was thick with tension. The armed officers had taken up positions at the front and back of the house, and the ones Mack could see—in cover behind the vehicles in the yard—had eyes fixed on the front door. She went to where Blyford was standing. He could see the front and the three armed officers who had their weapons trained on the doors and windows. Another group of officers had gone around to the back, meaning that there was no way into or out of the house without being seen.

"Anything?" she asked.

"No," he said. "They must've gone to the back."

"Can anyone see them?"

"Curtains have all been closed. Brennan's a soldier—he'll be careful about things like that. Won't want to give us a shot."

"What do we do?"

"Two choices," he said. "We wait them out, or we go in."

"What do you think?"

He breathed out. "Wait them out."

"How does that change?"

"When we hear shooting."

Mack realised she was biting down hard on her lip. She'd watched Atticus going into the house with a feeling of dread that it would be the last time she saw him. There was anger, too, at his recklessness—at his bravery, perhaps—and frustration at herself for her failure to anticipate he'd do something so foolhardy.

"Have you got everything you need?"

Blyford nodded, but before he could respond, there was a buzz of static from his radio. "Door's opening. Stand by for contact."

Mack knelt down behind the Land Rover and peered around the side. The door opened, and Brennan emerged.

He looked calm. He turned his head and said something to whoever was behind him in the house.

One of the officers called out, "Stay where you are!"

His words echoed, but Brennan didn't listen.

"Armed police!" Blyford yelled. "Stop! Put down your weapon!"

Brennan started to walk with the shotgun clutched in both hands.

Mack looked at the house and saw Atticus in the doorway. "Get back!" she yelled at him.

The officer yelled out, "Stop, or we'll fire!"

Brennan levelled the gun at him.

"Fire!"

The sound of gunshots shattered the stillness as the three officers at the front of the house all opened fire. Brennan stumbled, the force of the impacts taking him down. He crumpled, the shotgun slipping from his hand, clattering against the gravel.

Silence fell again, broken only by the cries of night birds startled by the noise.

EPILOGUE

Mack pulled away from the kerb outside her rented house and drove across town to the station. She hadn't had time for breakfast, and knowing it was going to be a long day—*another* long day—she didn't come off the ring road at Bourne Hill and carried on, going all the way around until she came to Castle Road. She went to Victoria Park, found a space to leave the car and walked to Upshake and Brew, the coffee shop that had set up in the old kiosk near the tennis courts. Robbie Best had recommended it as having particularly good coffee, and after enjoying her first visit, she had decided he'd been right. It was out of the way for the nick, and that was one of the reasons she liked coming; she could grab a pastry and a coffee and sit at one of the outside picnic tables without fear of being disturbed. She hadn't even told Atticus about it; for the moment, at least, it was something for herself and no one else.

The aftermath into the deaths at the yard had been difficult, and there was plenty to suggest that the work was only just getting started. The yard had been secured as a crime scene, with the whole area cordoned off while forensic teams were deployed to collect evidence. They had found the cellar where Alice Green had been kept and, on Francine's instruction, had gone up to the pig pen at the back of the property and found what was left of the woman. Mack had gone up to take a look and had very nearly thrown up her dinner; the sows had only had the body for a few hours and were about halfway through eating it.

The search had also yielded the motivation that had driven the conspiracy: ten kilograms of cocaine with a street value of several hundred thousand pounds and the suggestion that this was just the tip of the iceberg.

The fact that Brennan had been shot by the police added another layer of bureaucracy. The Independent Office for Police Conduct was notified at once, and they'd launched an investigation to determine whether the use of force was justified and in line with police regulations. Mack wasn't concerned about that. She, and the other officers, had seen Tom come out of the house with the shotgun. Atticus had explained that Tom had wanted to be shot—that this was suicide-by-cop, to use the American parlance—but the firearms officers didn't know that, and the order to fire was clearly the right one. She knew it would all be fine, but there would be interviews and statements and hoops to jump through before the conclusion that there was no case to answer was reached.

Samantha Hargreaves had confessed to Francine and Atticus, and the forensics team had uncovered useful evidence that the CPS would use to bolster the case against her: a burner phone that had been used to contact Christopher Freeman on the night of his disappearance and, in a case that looked as it had been packed for a hasty getaway, a one-way ticket to

Marrakech and guidebooks about Tangiers. There was also a black plastic device that Mack had been told was a hardware wallet for cryptocurrency; the device was encrypted and seemed the most likely repository for the funds that Hargreaves had amassed during the time she and the others had been importing cocaine into the country. The money would have been easy to get out of the country in Bitcoin and would make her planned disappearance a little easier to sustain.

Charlie Freeman's role in the conspiracy would take longer to uncover. He had died twice that evening: once in the ambulance and once on the operating table as his wounds were addressed. The doctors had stabilised his condition, and the prognosis was more positive now. His father, Alexander Freeman, had been to the hospital to visit him and had refused to provide an explanation as to why his boy had been at the yard. Mack knew the Freemans would have been up to their eyeballs in whatever Hargreaves and the others had been doing, but proving it might be more difficult. Freeman was a wealthy man, and Mack knew there would be a phalanx of top-shelf lawyers on standby whenever the doctors said that Charlie was fit to be questioned.

Mack hadn't seen Atticus until the day after the shooting. She had handed over responsibility for taking his statement to Nigel Archer and had only called him when she was confident that she would be able to have a conversation with him without jumping down his throat. He had apologised for what he had done, but, surprised by his unusual show of contrition, she'd found that her anger had drained away. There was only relief that he hadn't been hurt. His behaviour had been so typical of him: he'd been presented with a problem, and there had been the usual obsession to solve it, even if getting that solution meant putting himself in harm's way. Mack knew him better than anyone and was annoyed with herself for not anticipating what he might do. Beckton had said that he would want to debrief her on the investigation, but the fact that Francine had walked out of the house with only bumps and bruises—and would say that Atticus had contributed to that—would probably be the insulation that he needed to avoid getting into trouble. It would be difficult for Beckton to complain about him now, especially with his ever-increasing public profile, but that didn't mean that Mack would be similarly immune, and she was going to have to impress on Atticus—again—that there were always other people who could be affected by his impetuousness.

It was still early, but unusually warm. She took off her jacket and laid it over the table just as her phone rang from the inside pocket. She reached inside, half-expecting it to be Atticus but surprised to see it was Kay Adams, her lawyer in the custody case against Andy.

"Hello?"

"Mack," Kay said, "have you got a moment?"

"Yes. But I'm not expecting a call—should I be nervous?"

"No," Kay said. "I've got some unexpected news. Good news."

Mack bit her lip and found her palms were sweating.

"I had an email from Andy's solicitor this morning. I've no idea why, but they've said they're open to discontinuing the custody proceedings."

"Discontinuing?"

"Ending them," Kay said. "And agreeing that the two of you should have joint custody over the kids."

Mack heard the words, but it was as if she'd lost the ability to understand them.

"Mack? Are you still there?"

"I'm here," she said.

"It gets even weirder. They've offered to pay your legal fees."

"What? Why would they do that?"

"I'll read it verbatim: 'My client regrets having brought the proceedings and wants to make it up to your client.' I have to admit—I've been doing this for ten years, and I've never seen anything like that."

"It's…" She couldn't find the words.

"It's remarkable," Kay finished for her.

"I can't believe it."

"The only thing I can think of is he's had a change of heart. Have you spoken to him?"

"No," Mack said. "Not since after the hearing, anyway, and that wasn't what you'd describe as constructive. He was dead set on winning. He was really angry."

"Probably best not to get our hopes up until I've had a chance to speak with the other side, but, assuming they're serious, I don't see why we can't have the agreement drawn up in principle by the end of the day."

"That would be incredible."

"I'll set up a call and get onto it straight away. I just wanted you to hear now."

"Thank you," she said. "That's amazing."

Mack ended the call and put the phone down on the picnic table. She stared at it and, with a thought nagging at the front of her mind, tapped her finger against the screen to wake it and opened Atticus's contact details.

Mack was about to call him, but, after hovering her finger over the icon for twenty seconds, decided against it. She wanted to tell him, but she couldn't shake the feeling that he must have had something to do with Andy's change of heart. She'd made Atticus promise that he wouldn't get involved, but she couldn't think of any other reason why Andy would've done something that was *so* out of character.

Mack didn't know how she felt about that. Atticus might not admit that he'd interfered against her wishes, but even if he did, she was unsure whether she should be angry with him or grateful. The whole thing was hopelessly complicated. Her children were the most important people in her life, and Atticus had been desperate to help. She'd questioned her insistence that she didn't need him to be involved, when, as had been plainly obvious at the hearing, she did.

* * *

Atticus told Hardwicke that they should meet somewhere between Salisbury and Winchester, and he had suggested the Greyhound on the Test at Stockbridge. Atticus hadn't been into the town for several months and was reminded again how pretty it was: the broad High Street recalled its history as a route for the drovers who brought their livestock from Wales, but those days were long gone now. The street hosted tea rooms, a surprisingly grand hotel, pubs, restaurants and a flurry of independent shops. He drove over the little bridge and pulled over next to the pub, painted a mellow yellow with its sign creaking in the gentle breeze. He opened the boot to let Bandit out and went around the side of the building to the garden at the rear.

Hardwicke was waiting at a table overlooking the river.

"Sorry," Atticus said. "Bit late."

"It's fine," he said. "Just admiring the view. I've never been here before."

"I haven't been for a while. I've been meaning to bring my girlfriend."

"The detective chief inspector?"

Atticus nodded.

"Don't worry. I won't pry."

"That's good," he said. "Because I won't talk about it."

"How are you?" he asked. "I mean… what happened sounded pretty intense. I saw it on TV. You were inside when he got shot, weren't you?"

"Yes—but it's OK. I'm fine."

Atticus didn't have any interest in talking about what had happened. He had been inside the doorway when Tom Brennan had rushed the police, but the angle had allowed him to see everything: Tom raising the shotgun, the officers opening fire and the impacts as they studded Tom's body. He'd collapsed onto his back, one leg folded beneath the other and his arms spread wide. Atticus had tried to keep his eyes down when he and Francine had been shepherded outside, but it was impossible not to look. The bullets had struck Brennan in the torso, and blood had already soaked through his dirty T-shirt. Atticus had looked at Tom's face, and in the glow of the lights from the cars and the hallway behind him, he thought he saw a peacefulness in his expression that hadn't been there before.

Atticus tied Bandit's lead to the legs of the table. "Can I get you a drink?"

"That'd be nice. What are you having?"

"Lager shandy."

"Perfect."

Atticus went into the bar and ordered two pints. He had been thinking about what he was going to say to Hardwicke during his drive from Salisbury and hadn't been able to think of a reason why he should change his mind. The bartender handed him the second pint; Atticus paid for both and took them back outside.

"Here," he said, putting the glasses down. "Cheers."

Hardwicke picked up his glass, touched it to Atticus's, and they both drank.

Atticus took another thirsty sip. "I was wondering—what're you going to do with the other stuff you found on Frank?"

"I've emailed it to the papers," he said.

"Any response?"

"A couple of reporters got back to me with some questions."

"They'll run it?"

"I think so."

"Good. I told you he left me a voicemail?"

"No."

"He wanted to know what happened. He pretended to be upset about it, but it was all very transparent. He's worried about what it'll mean for him, not because he's sorry about what happened to her."

"Did you call him back?"

"No, and I'm not going to. He just wants me to reassure him it won't affect him, but I'm not going to do that. As far as I'm concerned, he's awful, and he can suffer."

Hardwicke took another sip. "What about Andy Jones?"

"Thank you," he said. "It was very helpful. He's being *much* more reasonable about things now."

"How are you going to use it?"

"I'm not sure."

"Because it's criminal, isn't it?"

"Bribery? Very criminal."

"Just like Frank."

He nodded. "Just the same." Atticus ran a finger around the rim of the glass. "He won't do it again. And he'll behave as long as I have it to hold over him. I'll probably keep it like that for now."

"None of my business," he said. "Do whatever you need to do."

There was a pause as they both watched a pair of swans go by on the river. The silence was companionable, and Atticus was even more sure that what he had brought Hardwicke here to discuss was the right thing to do.

"I was wondering," he said. "You said business was slow."

"That's one way to describe it. Glacial would be another."

"So I was thinking. How about we work together?"

"Really?"

"Really."

"How would that work—we refer work to one another?"

He shook his head. "I was thinking maybe you'd like to be in charge of a Winchester office for me? I've been busy ever since the Mallender case, and it'll get busier when Sam comes to trial and the media start digging into what happened. I've been too busy to take on all the work that's come in, and I've had to send some away—lots of it potentially interesting and lucrative. I've been thinking about expanding, but I'd have to take someone on to do that, and, I don't know, I thought maybe that'd be something you might like to consider?"

He stuttered a bit, finding it more embarrassing than it ought to have been, but Hardwicke didn't hesitate. "Yes."

"Sure?"

"Yes."

"You don't want to think about it?"

"I don't need to. I'd love to work with you. It's a definite yes."

Atticus was taken aback by his enthusiasm. "Okay," he said. "Good. I mean, we'd have to think about the details. Your salary, to start with, but I suppose we could look at shares in the company—or maybe both—but then that'd need me to be more organised and... and..."

"We can work out the details later," he said, smiling at Atticus's gaucheness. "I doubt it'll be a problem."

Hardwicke raised what was left of his pint. Atticus raised his, and they touched glasses again.

"Well," he said, still a little lost for words. "I suppose this is welcome aboard."

"Yes, boss," he said.

* * *

Francine and Robbie went for a walk at lunch, heading away from the log cabins until they reached Fordingbridge. They walked over the bridge and turned into the George, the pub that overlooked the river. Francine had reserved a table with a view, and she led the way to it.

"This is nice," he said. "Do you know I've never been here?"

"Really?"

"Really. Driven past it plenty of times, but I've never been in."

"My dad used to like it here," she said. "It has nice memories for me. They used to have a resident duck called Karen."

Francine had never told Robbie about her father and what had happened to him. It was intensely personal, and even though she trusted him, she had never felt as if the moment was right to bring something up as heavy as that. She looked at him now, pointing at the ducks on the water and trying to identify Karen, and wondered whether she might be ready to be *that* open and honest with him.

It had been a difficult couple of days. Robbie had insisted that she go to hospital for a check to make sure she hadn't been concussed when Tom had struck her, and when she had demurred and said she was fine and wanted to stay, Robbie had reminded her that she was a DC, and he was a DI, and he was giving her a direct order. The doctors in A&E had checked her over and given her the all-clear, but Robbie had insisted she go home to rest while he went back to the yard. She tried to object, but, once more, Robbie pulled rank and told her she didn't have a choice.

She had reported back to the office for the morning briefing and had sat down to write out her statement of what had happened. Tom and Sam had confessed to what they—and the others—had done, and it was important that she get it down on paper while it was still fresh. Atticus was doing the same, but, as a serving officer, her account would be accorded more weight, and she needed to get it right.

Mack had suggested they postpone the sergeant's exam, but Francine had told her she would be fine. Robbie had surprised her last night by bringing out his copy of Blackstone's Police Q&A and a mock exam, telling her that she could spend the afternoon going through the paper with him checking her answers afterwards.

There was a fizzing noise, and they both turned to see the landlady of the pub coming over to their table with a chocolate cake decorated with a large sparkler candle.

"Happy birthday," Francine said.

The landlady put the cake down on the table and said she'd be back with two plates.

"Sorry I messed up our night away," she said.

The candle spat and hissed as it sputtered out.

"You didn't mess it up," he said.

"No, I think I did."

"You did your job. Next time, though—don't be a hero."

She plucked the candle out of the cake and set it down on the table.

He stared at her. "Promise?"

The landlady came back with the plates and a knife.

"Franny? Promise?"

"Hmm," she said, smiling as she cut the cake in two. "We'll see."

***

Sam reached the gate in the prison yard where she'd started her walk and, for the seventh time, set off on another circuit. The yard was a stark, rectangular space enclosed by high concrete walls topped with coiled razor wire. The ground underfoot was a mix of cracked concrete and patches of worn, trodden grass, with faded white lines marking a small area for informal games.

Sam was trying to get her head around the routine that she was going to have to follow for as long as they held her on remand. The wake-up call was at seven, when she was expected to get up and make her bed. Roll call happened after that to ensure that every prisoner was accounted for, then breakfast in the communal dining area. They had morning activities after that, then lunch, and then time in the yard.

She'd had a visit from her lawyer this morning. The news had been more encouraging than she might have expected. The case against her was based on her confession in the farmhouse and circumstantial evidence, and her lawyer felt there were strategies open to them that would attack both. The confession was the most damaging, but she had given it with a shotgun pointed in her face by a man who had already killed three of her friends that evening, two of them in front of her. They could argue that it was given under the most extreme duress. Alice Green's death was trickier, but they would argue that Gaz and Nikki were responsible for that, and all Sam was guilty of was trying to cover up what had happened. Sam had had plenty of time to work out what she would say and had settled on something that would be difficult to disprove: Connor had been in charge, and she had done everything he told her because she was terrified of what he would do if she didn't.

It was the best they could do, but maybe it would be enough. There would be twelve jurors at her trial; they only had to persuade *one* of them that the Crown's case against her didn't prove her guilt beyond a reasonable doubt.

Sam's lawyer had told her there was a good chance that they would be able to manage that.

She completed the circuit and went around again. Metal benches, bolted to the ground, offered limited seating, all of them occupied now by inmates engaging in conversation or solitary reflection. A few pieces of outdoor exercise equipment, rusted from years of exposure, stood unused in one corner. The atmosphere was tense as the other prisoners paced the perimeter with Sam or huddled in clusters, keeping an eye on each other under the watchful gaze of guards positioned on the catwalks.

Sam reached the gate again but was stopped from continuing by a woman who stepped into her path. Sam hadn't been here long enough to have spoken to many prisoners and had decided to keep herself to herself as much as possible. She knew she hadn't spoken to this woman before. She had fair skin and long, straight brown hair that fell past her shoulders. She had a tattoo of a star on her left cheek, near her eye. Her eyes were grey, and she had a high forehead with her hair parted to the side.

Sam stepped left, and the woman mirrored her.

She stepped right, and the woman did the same.

"Can I help you?"

The woman smiled, but there was no warmth in her expression.

"Get out of my way, please."

"Alexander Freeman says hello."

Sam realised what was about to happen.

She tried to step back, to get away, but someone she hadn't seen grabbed her from behind.

"This is for Christopher."

The woman swung her closed fist at Sam.

She saw—too late—that the woman had something clasped in her fist, something with a pointed end.

Sam felt a sharp pain, followed by pressure and then a feeling of warmth as blood rapidly flowed from the wound. She heard whistles from the guards above and hoots of laughter from the women in the yard. Sam panicked, reaching for her neck, but then there was shock and a difficulty in breathing and dizziness and a sense of unfairness and injustice, the future for which she had worked so hard being ripped away from her, and then a looming end that was impossible to avoid.

* * *

It was a balmy evening in the low twenties, and the swallows were darting to and fro over the surface of the river. Atticus parked the car next to the mill, in the same spot that Alice Green had chosen, and went around to open the boot for Bandit. The dog ducked down, grabbed his lead in his mouth and then jumped out.

Atticus had spent the rest of the day doodling out ideas for what the expansion of his business might look like. He had acted a little impulsively when he offered the job to Hardwicke and hadn't really had much of a plan in place beyond the feeling that he had potential, that it would be nice to have someone else in the business with him, and being brutally commercial, Winchester was another good-sized city and that, if he could pull it off, he'd be able to stake a claim to work between here and there. He didn't regret his impetuosity and was excited about the possibilities; he'd just need to speak to Mack to help him work out exactly what his offer should look like.

It had been hot in the afternoon, and even with the window open, the office had been stuffy. There was a traffic jam on New Street, and the exhaust fumes from the cars drifted up and in through the window, lending a noxious smell that, together with the humidity, was beginning to make Atticus feel light-headed. He'd called Mack to see if she wanted to go for a walk, but she'd replied she was still tied up with the aftermath to the enquiry and would have to pass. Atticus had taken the dog to the car and set off, not really sure where they'd end up but finding himself drifting toward Downton and then along the narrow track to the mill at Standlynch.

He followed the path to the weir and the sloping bank that Alice Green had used to get into the river on the morning she had been abducted by Nikki Griffiths and Gaz O'Reilly. Atticus found a tennis ball in the undergrowth between the path and the river and reached down to collect it. Bandit noticed, sitting obediently and watching as Atticus drew back his arm. Atticus faked a throw, the dog starting in the direction where it looked as if it had been launched and then, realising he'd been duped, turning back to Atticus with what could only be described as an expression of disappointment.

"Busted," Atticus said, drawing back his arm again and launching it into the water.

The dog took a run-up and then rushed forward, leaping from the bank into the river and paddling out after the ball before it could go too far downstream. He secured it in his teeth and then manoeuvred himself around, paddling against the current until he reached the muddy slope. Atticus took the ball from his mouth and, acting spontaneously for the second time that day, took off his shirt and tossed it behind him onto the bank. He took off his shoes and socks and, not worrying about getting his cargo shorts wet, waded out into the water.

The water was icy cold, but, after the breathless shock of it, Atticus felt his skin start to tingle. He felt a buzz of pleasure, and even though he understood the biochemical reasons behind it—the endorphins and adrenaline and dopamine—

it still felt good. He waded out until the water was up to his neck and then lay back, filling his lungs with air and spreading his limbs so that he could just float and look up into the dappled light that was filtering through the canopy of leaves overhead. Bandit, initially confused, swam up to Atticus and started to bark.

He must have been in the water for five minutes before he kicked back to the bank and pulled himself out. He took his T-shirt and put it on, waiting for the warmth in the air to dry him off.

"Mr. Priest?"

He turned. A man was standing on the path behind him. He had angular features and was tall and slender, his frame almost gaunt.

Atticus frowned as he tried to place him. "Do I know you?"

"We've had dealings, but I don't believe we've ever *actually* met." The man smiled. "How's the water?"

"Cold," Atticus said. "I'm sorry—you didn't tell me your name."

He put out a long and slender hand with almost spidery fingers. "I'm Alexander Freeman."

Atticus felt his stomach drop. Freeman's face was pale, nearly bloodless, and accentuated by high cheekbones and a thin nose that gave him an air of aristocratic severity. His eyes were his most striking feature: cold, calculating, piercingly grey and with an intensity that gave Atticus the impression that he saw everything and missed nothing. His dark hair, brown and peppered with streaks of grey, was worn slicked back to reveal a broad forehead. He was wearing a sharply tailored, charcoal-grey suit made from Italian wool and cut slim to his frame, with narrow lapels that accentuated his leanness. He wore a crisp white shirt, buttoned up but without a tie, the open collar lending a touch of nonchalance to an otherwise meticulous appearance. He wore a minimalist black Rolex with a sleek, thin band, subtly yet unmistakably expensive. His shoes were polished black leather Oxfords, and a single silver cufflink, engraved with an intricate pattern, glinted on his left wrist.

"Mr. Freeman," he said, aware that his awkwardness when it came to speaking to people he didn't know might cause him more than social embarrassment this time.

"Please—you can call me Alexander."

The invitation to informality didn't ring true, and somehow made Atticus feel more wary rather than less. "We *have* met," he said. "I was a detective constable. You came in for an interview about drugs that were being sold in the city."

Freeman smiled. "Do you know, I think you're *right*. I'd forgotten all about that."

It was obvious that Freeman *hadn't* forgotten—Atticus was left with the impression that he didn't forget much at all—but that, for whatever reason, he didn't want to worry him with any implied threats.

"I'm not in the police anymore," Atticus said.

"You're not," Freeman said. "I know—you've gone private. I've had an eye on you for a while, if I'm being completely truthful. I think you first came across my radar when you caused me a little trouble with Jimmy Robson and the project he was running for me in Grovely Woods."

Robson had been in charge of a large cannabis farm that had been set up in the gamekeeper's cottage. Atticus had disturbed him, and there had been a scuffle before the police had finally arrived. The farm had been shut down, and Robson had been charged and convicted. Of course, even though Robson had admitted to Atticus that the operation belonged to Freeman, he didn't say that in his interview or at his trial. The police knew the truth, but there was no way that it could be proven. Atticus didn't fool himself though: the intervention would have been disruptive and cost Freeman the chance to make the kind of profit to which he had become accustomed.

"Sorry about that," he said.

"How were you to know? Anyway—it's water under the bridge. I'm not here about that."

"You followed me here."

"I'm afraid so. As I say—I've had an eye on you for a little while."

"This is about your son."

"*Both* sons. I wanted to thank you for what you did—Charlie would be dead if he'd been kept in that house for much longer."

"How is he?"

"It was touch and go for a while. He lost rather a lot of blood. But they've patched him up, and he's a strong boy. I saw the doctor this morning—he said he'll be home at the weekend, all being well. Long recovery after that, but it's much better than it could've been."

"I'm pleased to hear it."

"It's not just Charlie," Freeman said. "It's Christopher, too."

"I'm sorry about what happened to him."

"Were you involved in the investigation when he went missing."

"Not really. It was the Met, mostly. We gave them local backup."

"Did you speak to Miss Sam then?"

"No," he said. "A colleague did that."

"And they suspected nothing."

Atticus nodded. "Nothing."

"She's slippery," Freeman said. "I've always considered myself an excellent judge of character, and I'd *never* have said she had anything to do with what happened to Christopher. I think it was how *brazen* she was—she killed my boy and then kept doing business with me. I spoke to her about him, of course, and she said she hadn't seen him for a week. And I believed her. Not that it would've made any difference—it wouldn't have brought him back—but I would've been able to deal with it earlier, and I wouldn't have been thinking about what might've happened to him for the last I don't know how many months. It would've saved me and his mother a lot of grief. And it would have meant Charlie didn't get shot."

Atticus felt unsettled. Freeman had something about him, and it made Atticus feel uneasy. Freeman's cold, analytical gaze felt like a scalpel, and Atticus was left with the impression that it would be impossible to hide anything from him. The air around him felt as if it was charged with an almost palpable tension; it was as if Freeman was a coiled spring of intellect and malice, ready to snap at any moment. Atticus was on the back foot, he *never* felt second best, but now, as Freeman eyed him, he did. There was the sense that Freeman led the conversation even in silence.

"Can I ask your opinion of her chances at trial?"

"She's hired a very expensive lawyer," Atticus said. "There's no guarantee that the prosecution will be able to prove that she killed Christopher."

"Because all the other witnesses are dead," Freeman said.

"That's right."

"But *you* were there when she confessed. And the female detective."

"Yes, and I'm happy to testify to what I heard, but that might not be enough."

"The burner phone?"

"We can't prove what was said on the call. It's damaging, but it doesn't prove anything on its own. There won't be anything other than circumstantial evidence."

"Not like Alice Green," Freeman offered.

Atticus winced. He hadn't been up to the pig pen, but Mack had, and what she'd told him was enough to make him want to be sick. "That one's different. That one's open and shut. That'll be murder and life."

"Not enough, though, is it? Not for me. I need it on the record that she killed Christopher. For what it's worth, I asked a legal friend for her opinion, and she agreed—*far* from certain that she's convicted. I'm no fan of the legal system, and that's quite without considering the inconvenience it's caused me over the years."

"I'm sorry," Atticus said. "Mr. Freeman—"

"*Alexander*."

"No, Mr. Freeman—I still don't know why you're here."

If he was offended by the snub, he didn't show it. "I have some news, Atticus, and I wanted you to hear it from me. Samantha died this afternoon. There was an altercation in the prison where she's being held, and she was stabbed in the throat with a makeshift knife. A toothbrush handle, I believe, melted in the flame of a candle until it was sharp. Some might argue that it's not justice, but I know you're more *flexible* when it comes to how that term is defined."

It was obvious he was referring to Zöe Chandler, but how could he *possibly* know that Atticus had let her walk away?

Freeman must have sensed his discomfort and looked over at him and winked. "Don't worry. I won't say anything about that, not that it would make a blind bit of difference if I did." He put his finger to his lips. "Your secret is safe with me. I wanted to tell you because I think we might share opinions on certain things—kindred spirits, if you like."

Freeman's calm, almost detached demeanour only heightened Atticus's discomfort, and he felt exposed. It wasn't just fear that Atticus felt, but a deep-seated wariness, as though he were standing on the edge of a precipice with Freeman behind him.

Bandit came back with the ball, blocking the way ahead.

"Lovely boy," Freeman said, reaching down to scratch the dog behind the ears. "What is he? GSP?"

"That's right."

"I have Malinois," he said. "Three of them. Solid muscle and they'd do anything for you. I don't know about you, Atticus, but I can't imagine living in a place like this and not having dogs." He took the ball from Bandit and launched it into the river. "Anyway—I'll leave you to enjoy the rest of the walk. Thanks again. I'm really very grateful. Me and Charlie—both of us."

He turned around and walked back in the direction of the mill.

Atticus watched him go and knew that they would be seeing one another again. The day, still warm, suddenly felt as if a shadow had passed across the face of the sun.

A MESSAGE FROM MARK

Building a relationship with my readers is the very best thing about writing. Join my VIP Reader Club for information on new books and deals, plus correspondence dealing with Atticus's departure from the police. Find out what really happened with this exclusive reader content.

Just visit **www.markdawson.com/AtticusPriest**.

ABOUT MARK DAWSON

Mark Dawson is the author of the John Milton, Beatrix and Isabella Rose and Atticus Priest series. He lives in Salisbury.

For more information:

www.markjdawson.com
mark@markjdawson.com